Acclaim for Jeanette Baker's Wonderful Novels of Scotland and Ireland

IRISH LADY

"It grips the reader from the first page to the last. . . . A wonderful mix of past and present comparing the griefs and tragedies of ancient Ireland with the heart-break and passion of present-day Ireland, and an exploration of divided loyalties and discovered destinies."

—Diana Gabaldon, author of the Outlander series

"A delicious yet poignant read . . . Truly one of the best and most touching books I have read—a true love story complete with a host of emotions."

—Amy Wilson, *The Literary Times*

"The pride of the Irish and their struggle for freedom from the British is brought to life with outstanding skill. Add two amazing heroines, one in the present, the other in the past, but each with a love that outlives time, and the reader is ensured of hours of joy."

—*Rendezvous*

"Inspired writing! Splendid! 4½ BELLS!"

—Bell, Book and Candle

CATRIONA

"Jeanette Baker is rapidly proving herself one of the shining talents of the paranormal genre. *Catriona* is an outstanding blend of past and present that makes for inspiring and irresistible reading!"

—Jill Smith, *Romantic Times*

"Readers of all genres will cherish this prize. . . . *Catriona* . . . comes alive with the paranormal, burning sensuality, and a notable plot of outstanding quality that will have readers eagerly awaiting Ms. Baker's next book."

—*Rendezvous*

"Jeanette Baker has joined the ranks of such award-winning authors as Kristin Hannah, Christina Skye, and Barbara Erskine, who have all striven to create unique stories that blend the reality of history and time so that love will triumph. Baker's *Catriona* and *Legacy* are classics."

—Jody Allen, CompuServe Romance Reviews

"A great read!"   —Waldenbooks *Romantic Interludes*

"An absolutely stunning and unique mixing of several genres (supernatural, historical, and contemporary romances) into a great novel that will delight fans from all three. . . . One of the top novels of the year."

—America Online "On The Shelves"

LEGACY

"[FOUR STARS] . . . A fascinating time-travel yarn. Jeanette Baker has woven history and fantasy into a tale about the Murray clan, and about four women of the clan connected through the centuries by a curse first uttered in 1298."

—Helen Holtzer, *Atlantic Journal*

"Fans of rich and unusual novels are in for a treat and should not miss this truly unique and mesmerizing tale. . . . A marvelous book that is as riveting as it is haunting."

—Jill M. Smith, *Romantic Times*

"Jeanette Baker's love of Scottish history shines forth on every page."

—*Heartland Critiques*

"Tantalizing . . . Ms. Baker is a talented writer. . . . [She kept] me intrigued and enthralled. . . . A thought-provoking novel not to be missed."

—*Rendezvous*

Books by Jeanette Baker

Legacy
Catriona
Irish Lady
Nell

Published by POCKET BOOKS

NELL

JEANETTE BAKER

SONNET BOOKS

New York London Toronto Sydney Tokyo Singapore

This book is a work of fiction. Names, characters, places and incidents are products of the author's imagination or are used fictitiously. Any resemblance to actual events or locales or persons, living or dead, is entirely coincidental.

An *Original* Publication of POCKET BOOKS

 A Sonnet Book published by
POCKET BOOKS, a division of Simon & Schuster Inc.
1230 Avenue of the Americas, New York, NY 10020

ISBN: 0-671-01735-7

First Pocket Books printing February 1999

10 9 8 7 6 5 4 3 2 1

SONNET BOOKS and colophon are trademarks of Simon & Schuster Inc.

Cover art by Peter Fiore

Printed in the U.S.A.

A special thank you to:

Pat Perry and Jean Stewart, as always, for their valuable edits and comments.

Lauren McKenna of Pocket Books for helping me through this novel while Kate Collins, my editor, was busy having twin boys with beautiful Irish names.

Maeve Binchy for never disappointing me.

Loretta Barrett for understanding what I mean to say before I say it.

Angie Ray for playing devil's advocate and bringing a new perspective into the business of writing.

My mother for allowing me to finish this book without interruptions.

My sister for her unconditional support.

The wonderful Irish people on both sides of the fence who open their homes and their hearts and who never give up the struggle for peace in the Six Counties.

The O'Flahertys of Inishmore, a people who pass on to their descendants a love for the sea, a gift for laughter, and an appreciation for a well-told story.

NELL

1

County Down, Northern Ireland, 1972

In Jillian's mind, Francis Maguire would forever be associated with the pungent, woolly smell of wet dog. It never occurred to her that it was the slightest bit unusual for the closed-in world of the Kildare kennel to evoke images of a boy's callused palms and defined calf muscles, of his thin, sun-browned hands and rich, healing voice, of black hair and winter-gray eyes, of warmth and giving and all that she'd ever known of acceptance and compassion and sharing. Considering the privileged circumstance of Jilly's birth and the underprivileged one of Frankie's, the way she felt was beyond unusual. It was extraordinary.

Jilly's mother, Lady Margaret Fitzgerald, had expressed on more than one occasion, to anyone who would listen, that the seed of her daughter's fascination with the son of a Catholic working-class kennel keeper was rooted in nothing more than the unorthodox manner of their introduction. After all, everyone knew that the Fitzgerald children were crazy for animals, especially sleek gold collie dogs with white bibs and soulful brown eyes, the same dogs that rested in the sweet, prickly hay of the Kildare kennels, raced through the long grass of the Kildare boglands, and slept at the feet of generations of Kildare masters.

Others took one look at the archangel beauty of Frankie's features, and another at the bunched muscles of his lean, spare body with its promise of height and breadth of shoulder, and stroked their chins. They watched the way his hands caressed the flanks of a trembling collie, imagined what those hands would be like several years later on another, quite different kind of body, and drew their own conclusions.

The truth behind the children's symbiotic attraction to each other lay somewhere within the core of them, a remote gene that had transferred itself from generation to generation, occasionally hidden but always there, through thousands of years of Maguire and Fitzgerald ancestors, to germinate in the minds and hearts of two children who were the best of those who had gone before.

Jilly, the long-awaited daughter of Pyers and Margaret Fitzgerald, was born with a penchant for fairness and a keen sensitivity entirely missing from most of her class and certainly from her generation of Fitzgeralds. It was only natural that a child like Jilly, craving acceptance and answers and finding none, should be drawn to a boy who had both. That she was rich and he poor meant nothing. The Catholic/Protestant thing meant even less. While Jilly was impetuous, needle-sharp, and completely without prejudice, Frankie was deliberate, compassionate, and tirelessly patient with the small girl whose indefatigable questions nearly pushed him over the edge of tolerance.

Their unusual relationship began in the middle of a rainstorm. It was an unusual wetting for the farm country of middle Ireland, more typical of the drenching sheets that battered the cliffs of Galway, pounded the minerals from the soil, and left the exposed western coast nearly uninhabitable by all but stone-faced fishermen, descendants of Viking raiders who had pillaged and raped and left their height, their love for the sea, and their distinctive ice-flecked blue eyes in every family who hailed from the western isles.

Jilly had wandered down to the creek, nearly a mile from the house, when she felt the first of the raindrops. A mewling sound from the woods stopped her from turning back toward the house. After pushing her way through thick undergrowth, she climbed the bank and found fourteen-year-old Guinevere, her father's favorite collie, caught in a poacher's trap. Jilly could see that the dog was close to death. There was no time to find help.

Using a tree branch as leverage, she worked at the trap, wedging the wood under the metal jaws, pushing and straining and grunting, tears of frustration rolling down her cheeks. Again and again she plied the trap until blood seeped from the torn blisters forming on her palms. "Nell!" she cried, sobbing in earnest now. "Nell, where are you? I need help. Please, find me!"

I'm here, a voice called out, *behind you.*

Jilly turned toward the sound. Walking toward her through the slanting rain was a girl, about fifteen or so, dressed in leather trews and a full-sleeved white blouse. She did not appear at all affected by the weather.

She knelt beside the dog. *What happened?*

Jilly struggled to control her tears. "It's Guinevere. She's caught, and I can't free her."

Nell ran practiced hands over the dog's gaunt ribcage. Then she examined the trap. *This is dreadful. How does it work?*

Jilly looked startled. "Haven't you seen a trap before?"

Not like this.

"There's no way to release it unless you pry the mouth apart. I'm not strong enough by myself. Both of us could manage it, I think."

Let's give it a try, shall we?

Jilly nodded and held out the branch. "If you wedge it open, I can pull Gwenny's paw out."

Choosing a spot near the dog's injured paw, Nell worked the branch between the metal jaws and bore down. The mouth widened enough for Jilly to lift the paw free.

Nell released her hold on the wood, and the trap snapped together again. *There now. We should get the two of you home.*

Rain, cold and sharp as ice-tipped needles, sliced through Jilly's Aran sweater and the dog's matted fur. Miraculously, Nell was not the slightest bit wet. She smiled encouragingly, slid her arms under the injured animal, and effortlessly lifted her from the ground.

Even under the best of conditions, a girl Nell's size would have struggled under the weight of a full-grown collie. Laboring uphill through what was now a barrage of falling water should have rendered it nearly impossible.

Jilly, arms aching and throat burning, led the way, stumbling through the trees and across the meadow, wondering how it was that Nell always appeared at just the right time, somehow managing the impossible. "Please, God, don't let Gwenny die," she whispered. "Please don't let her die."

The words became her refrain, forcing her numbed legs forward against a wind that ripped through fields, flinging boulders, felling trees, and sweeping her back half as many steps as she moved forward. Jilly could never say how long she walked under that icy rain. It could have been minutes or hours. She only knew that somewhere, before she reached Kildare House, Nell had given her Guinevere and that she had stumbled into the kennel, a sodden, wild-eyed girl clutching a half-dead collie against her chest as if it were a child.

Frankie was alone, filling in for his father who had taken the train to Newry. He took one horrified look at the little girl and another at the dog in her arms and decided against voicing the questions forming on his lips. Instantly, he crossed the floor, extricated the animal from Jilly's arms, and carried her to an empty stall. "Call your father," he said tersely, laying the dog on a blanket.

"He's not home."

Frankie swore under his breath, remembered the child, and controlled himself. "Find some milk, eggs, and brandy," he said, automatically moving toward the medicine cabinet, "and tell your mother to get the vet right away."

Jilly gulped and rubbed her cheek with a filthy hand, leaving a peat-colored smear. "She's not home, either. Nell says no one can get across the bridge in this rain, but I'll call anyway."

He barely heard her. After setting the kettle to boil, he pulled out several clean cloths, a roll of gauze, and a tube of ointment. Overhead, the lights flickered twice and went out. This time Frankie made no effort to curb his language. Cursing fluently, he pulled two oil lamps from the cupboard over the stove and lit the wicks from the gas flame. The refrigerator ran on a generator. He opened the door, found a bottle of antibiotic, added it to his supplies, and poured boiling water into a bowl. The dog was still unconscious. Frankie knelt by her side and began cleaning the gnawed and wounded paw. He sensed rather than heard Jilly slip back through the door.

"Did you bring everything?" he asked, his eyes intent on his task.

"Yes."

"Is the vet coming?"

"He said he would try. No one knows if the bridge is out."

Frankie nodded and tied up the bandage. The dog didn't move.

"Will she live?" Jilly whispered.

"I don't know. She's lost a lot of blood." He nodded at the bag in her hand. "I'll take that. You stay here. Touch her if you want. Dogs are like people. They need to be touched. I'll mix up some medicine."

Too miserable to speak, Jilly nodded and reached out hesitantly to stroke the beautiful narrow head of her father's champion breeder.

Frankie moved about the kennel, cracking eggs, pouring milk, mixing in brandy, sugar, and medicine. After dipping his finger into the mixture, he tasted it, poured in more brandy, and carried it to the stall where Jilly waited.

She watched as the boy lifted the collie's head and spooned the liquid into her mouth. The dog's long jaw remained slack, and the medicine drooled out. Again, Frankie tried, and still again.

Tears pooled in Jilly's eyes. "Please," she begged. "Please drink, Gwenny."

Frankie looked at the small girl. The glow from the lanterns rested on her hair. She was dirty and wet and most likely colder than a banshee's curse. But she cared nothing for herself, only for the dog. Frankie's eyes narrowed. It wasn't the expensive prize-winning collie that the child mourned. Guinevere was her pet, an old and beloved family friend.

Setting his jaw, Frankie redoubled his efforts. He wrapped the blanket around the weakened body, handed the bowl to Jilly, and lifted the dog into his lap. Cradling the delicate head in his hands, he rubbed her jowls. "Spoon it into her," he ordered, caressing her throat over and over.

Jilly lifted the bowl and tilted it into the dog's mouth. Frankie stroked and stroked, coaxed and whispered, until at last the tight muscles relaxed and the dog gulped. A low moan came from Jilly's throat. She burst into tears and threw herself at Frankie, wrapping her arms around his chest and shoulders, burying her face in his neck, careful not to disturb the dog in his arms.

Rigid with shock and embarrassment, Frankie forced himself to remain completely still. He was fourteen years old and couldn't remember the last time anyone had hugged him. His mother was dead, and the relationship he had with his father and sister, although loving, did not include displays of physical affection. The boneless feel of the small girl's body, the way she melted against him, warmly damp, needy and terrifyingly intimate, disturbed him. He had never before set eyes on Jillian Fitzgerald, but he knew that tomorrow, when her flood of emotion had run its course, she would regret that the son of her father's collier had seen her cry. He responded in the only way he knew how, by pretending that it wasn't happening.

Moments passed, and Jilly's tears continued to flow. Frankie's self-control was near its breaking point. Something had to be done. Awkwardly, he lifted his hand and rested it against her head. "Easy, lass," he said softly, stroking the silky hair. "Don't take on so. She'll be all right now."

Finally, under the magic of his slow-moving hand, her sobs turned to sniffles and then to hiccups. "You saved her," she said at last. "All by yourself, you saved her."

"I don't know about that. Who was it that brought the eggs and spirits? And who poured it down her throat? Who carried her back here to Kildare House?"

"I brought the eggs and spirits, but Nell carried her all the way to the gate."

Frankie smiled into her hair. "You and Nell saved her. She wouldn't be here without the two of you."

Jilly lifted her head to look at him. If it made him happy to think she'd helped, she wouldn't contradict him. "What's your name?"

"Francis Maguire. Frankie, if you like."

"How do you know so much about sick dogs?"

Frankie shrugged. "My father taught me. Some things I taught myself by treatin' animals that no one thought would survive."

"Will you become a kennel keeper like your father?"

It was an innocent question. Jilly had no idea what she'd done wrong, but she knew instantly that her new friend was offended.

"I'm going to become a veterinarian."

Jilly pressed her hands together reverently. "That's wonderful. Perhaps I'll become one as well, and we can work together."

He stiffened, wondering if she was mocking his aspirations. Staring into the guileless eyes, he decided that she was sincere. "I've never heard of a woman veterinarian," he began cautiously. "You're no bigger than a minute. How could you possibly move large animals around?"

"I'm only ten. I'll grow."

For the first time that day, Frankie grinned. "I expect you will." He held out his hand to clasp hers. "We'll set up practice together."

Jilly beamed. He was really very nice. She admired the lovely lilting way he spoke. "I like you very much, Frankie Maguire. Will you come to the house for tea?"

His face flamed, and suddenly the words that flowed from him so comfortably refused to form. "Nnnuh-nnnuh-nuh tha-tha-thank you," he stammered desperately.

Jilly's forehead wrinkled. Why did he look like that? Everything had been going so well. "I'll go inside, then, and come back later with your tea," she said at last. "You can't go home until the rain stops."

Frankie relaxed. She didn't expect him to go up to the manor house and sit down to tea after all. "Thank you, miss, for thinkin' of me," he said formally.

She stood in the doorway, framed by sheets of slanting rain. "Call me Jilly, and it is we who are in your debt, Francis Maguire."

Frankie stared at the door for a long time. The small girl with the fawn-colored hair had unsettled him. He had never spoken with a woman outside his own class, and he wondered if she was typical of hers. He shivered and pulled the dog closer to his chest. It was cold, and with the bridge out, the night was sure to be a long one.

He was sleeping when she came back with lamb stew and a Thermos of sweet, hot tea. Cook had included a basket of bread and a crock of broth for the dog. Jilly left the food in the oven, lit the pilot, and settled in for however long it would take Frankie to wake up. Not for the world would she have disturbed him. She looked at him, *really* looked at him, for the first time. "He's very nice, isn't he, Nell?"

Very nice, indeed.

"I wish he could see you."

Oh, Jilly. I've explained it all before. No one can see me but you.

"I just wish, that's all."

Frankie lay curled up on his side with one arm thrown protectively around the dog, the other pillowing his head. In the full throes of exhausted sleep, he breathed deeply. Thick black lashes rested on his cheeks, and hair the same color curled over the collar of his threadbare woolen shirt. He was thin and long, and his trousers were too short and badly mended. Soaring eyebrows framed heavy-lidded eyes over a well-shaped nose and a mouth that looked as if it smiled often and spoke with kindness. Jilly sighed with satisfaction. She measured all young men against her brother, and, fortunately, nothing about Peter Maguire's son reminded her of Terrence.

Her eyes moved to his hand resting on the dog's fur. Jilly noticed hands, and this one was especially nice. It was long and brown like the rest of him, with callused tips and chipped nails, a worker's hand, completely different from the soft, pale ones of her older brother. Jilly's mouth curled. Next to this boy, Terrence Fitzgerald was a poor specimen.

Frankie felt her eyes on him. Slowly, fighting a fatigue that never quite left him, he sat up.

"Is she better?" Jilly asked.

He rested his palm on the dog's flank and felt the steady rise and fall of her heart. "Aye. A wee bit better."

Jilly scrambled to her feet. "I brought some food. I'll get it for you."

"Y' needn't wait on me, lass," he said gently, uncomfortable with the child's adoration.

"I don't mind." Already, she had arranged the plates on the table. "I'll sit with Guinevere while you eat."

"There's no need. She'll sleep the night and more." He stood, waiting for her to leave.

Jilly knew he wanted her to go. Somehow, without speaking, he had communicated his need. She hesitated, took another look at the dog, and moved regretfully toward the door. "I'll come back tomorrow," she said. "To see the dog, of course."

"Of course."

Was he mocking her? Jilly didn't think so, but she couldn't be sure. Whether he wanted her there or not, she would come back tomorrow.

Kildare, Ireland, 1537

He came upon her in the gloaming, two leagues from the gates of Maynooth, and knew instantly that she was Eleanor Fitzgerald. It was right, he thought, that they should meet this way without the trappings of wealth, family, and formality, for, in the end, in the sweetly scented darkness hemmed in by ocean and forest and bog, it would be just the two of them, and they must find their way together.

And so, in the space of a moment, after a single startled glance into a girl's light-filled eyes, he made a decision that all the months of negotiation, the subtle bribes, the exchange of gifts, and the pleas of well-meaning relatives could not, until this moment, force him to make.

Donal O'Flaherty was his own man, chosen in the old Celtic tradition for his ability to lead, rather than by accident of birth or lineage. His views on marriage were as definite as his devotion to the Church and his loyalty to his clan. Marriage was a sacrament meant to last a lifetime, never to be entered into lightly. A satisfactory mate was as necessary as nourishment. In Galway, where the winter nights were long, a man and woman spent many hours in each other's company. It would be the height of foolishness to choose a bride merely for the dowry she would bring him.

Donal knew Eleanor would be well favored. He could not imagine himself wedded to a woman who was not. And because she was a Geraldine, he knew she would be small, fair-haired, and versed in many languages. But when she welcomed him in his native tongue, he was not prepared for the low and lovely pitch of her voice, or the heart-shattering purity of her smile, or those eyes, the color of brook hazel, that saw deeply, too deeply, into the depths of his soul and stripped him of all but the truth that lay naked and stretched out between them.

Donal O'Flaherty of Aughnanure had not wanted a Sean Ghall's daughter for his bride, not even a Sean Ghall with the power and presence of Gerald Og Fitzgerald of Maynooth, ninth earl of Kildare. His father, Ruardaigh O'Flaherty, called him a fool. It was the duty of an Irish chieftain to bring gold and powerful allies into his house. Nowhere in Ireland was there a family with the wealth and power of the Geraldines. Some called them the uncrowned kings of Ireland.

Still, Donal hesitated to pledge himself. He was nineteen, young yet for marriage, and his bloodline was pure Celt with a bit of Norse invader to round it out. There was no need to bring a woman of English blood into his house.

The Fitzgeralds had turned Protestant, as English as they were Irish, claiming kinship to Henry Tudor.

Their lands encompassed Desmond, South Munster, and nearly all of the counties of Kildare, Meath, Dublin, and Carlow. Fitzgerald castles stretched beyond Strangford Lough on the coast of Down to Adare, and the Fitzgerald fleet patrolled the Irish seas. Maynooth, the principal seat of Kildare, was one of the richest houses in Ireland. It was no small thing to bring such an ally into one's family. But the taint of England was strong. If he married a Fitzgerald, his sons and daughters would no longer be true Irish. It was a bitter herb to swallow, too much to ask of an O'Flaherty chief, a carrier of the oldest, purest bloodline in all of Ireland.

His reasons for refusing Kildare's daughter were strong. But Donal was more than an O'Flaherty chieftain. He was a man, a man who noticed how the setting sun outlined a woman's figure and turned the thick braid of hair hanging over her shoulder into a rope of pure silver.

When she smiled, the knot of resistance inside his chest dissolved. Donal no longer cared that her father was cousin to Henry Tudor or that her uncles' navy prowled the seas or that the blood of his children would be as English as it was Irish. He saw only Nell, and that was enough. Stepping forward, he held out his hand and smiled. *"Da duit,"* he said, and introduced himself.

At the sound of his voice, Nell's hand clenched the fur of the enormous wolfhound that followed her everywhere. For months, ever since her father told her she must wed, she had thought of little else but Donal O'Flaherty. She had first noticed him four years before at *Emáin Macha* during the celebration of Beltane.

For most of the day, Nell had stayed inside her mother's tent, for only native Irish attended. Nell knew her lineage. She was Sean Ghall, daughter of Maeve O'Conor, an Irish princess, and Gerald Fitzgerald, an Anglo-Irish lord. For a Christian to be seen in the ancient kingdom of Ulster at Beltane would invite the wrath of both the blue-painted druids, who resented the disturbance of their rituals, and the parish priests, who condemned the mystical incantations, the frenzied passions leading up to ancient fertility rites, as devil worship.

But curiosity and muffled laughter from beyond the clearing overcame Nell's fears. When the flames of the sacred fire burned down, after the priestess had danced, evoked the voice of the goddess, and chosen the great horned stag as her mate, Nell wrapped herself in wool and crept through the clearing to the woods. The night was bright with moonlight, and beneath every bush men and women lay together, their bodies joined in various stages of passion.

Nell was eleven years old and unawakened. But her mind was quick, and she was not unaware of what went on between a man and a woman. Before she could fully take in the significance of the scene before her, a hand clamped over her mouth, pulling her back against a hard chest. A thick voice whispered into her ear, "So, I'm not too late after all."

The drug-laced voice and sour breath, the heavy breathing and unnatural stiffness of the masculine body, brought Nell to a fear she had never known before. She began to struggle. The man cursed and released her mouth to cuff her on the side of the head. She fell to the ground only to be jerked back to her feet. "Please," she begged, striving for the dignity befitting a Fitzgerald of Kildare. "Don't hurt me. Take me to my mother. My father will reward you."

Unexpectedly, the man released her. She fell backward into the grass, blinked her eyes, and looked up. Her captor was held at bay by a blade of deadly steel, its handle sparkling with precious jewels. A thin scarlet line of red appeared on the pale skin of his throat.

Nell's eyes widened. Her savior was young, still a boy, and his face was twisted with anger, but still she could see the strength of his features. "She's a wee lass, you drunken son of a whore, and not a willing one," he growled. "You know the law. Rape destroys the magic. 'Tis punishable by death."

The man swallowed and stepped back, away from the menace of the weapon. "Mercy, sir," he whispered, falling to his knees. "Mercy."

The boy lowered his dirk. "Leave here, now."

The man stumbled into the darkness. Nell waited for the boy to speak. When he did, she was too tongue-tied to answer.

Her silence confused him. "Did he hurt you, lass? Can you speak? I am Donal O'Flaherty, and I swear that he will pay."

Nell shook her head. "He had no time." She ducked her head shyly. "I thank you, sir, for rescuing me."

All trace of anger had left him, and Nell, looking him full in the face for the first time, caught her breath. If a boy could be called beautiful, this one would be. Shining dark hair fell past his shoulders, framing a thin, squared-off face. His high-boned cheeks and thin, arrogant nose revealed his bloodline as surely as did the deep-set, rain-colored eyes and soaring black eyebrows. He was pure Celt, of the ancient line of Talesian, marked by the fey black ring around his pupils. Even if he had not offered his name, Nell would have known him instantly.

The O'Flahertys were kings of the isles and bowed to no one. Their courage was legendary on land, and on the sea, where piracy was a way of life, their feats were extolled by the bards around a hundred great hall fires. Those who tried to apprehend them told stories of men and horses disappearing into the mists and melting into the trees.

He sheathed his sword and stepped forward, his hands rough upon her shoulders. "What have you seen this night?"

Nell blushed and looked at the ground. He shook her slightly, absentmindedly fingering the fine wool of her cloak. "Beltane is not for children. Have you a place to go?"

"Yes." Too late, she realized her mistake.

"I'll take you," he said, reaching for her hand.

"No." Nell pulled away.

He frowned. "Come, lass. This is no place for the likes of you."

"You know nothing about me."

He eyed the sable-lined cloak. "I know that you are noble-born."

"They'll think the worst and blame you," she improvised. "You'll have to marry me."

He laughed. "You're an absurd child. I saved you. They'll thank me, and there will be no talk of marriage."

Nell shook her head. "You don't know them." She lowered her voice to a conspiratorial whisper. "My father is English."

He recoiled, distrust and horror mingling with his sense of chivalry. "What are you doing here?"

"My mother is Irish."

"Who are you?"

Nell didn't answer. She took her skirt in her hand and fled. She was thankful he didn't follow her.

Four years later, he stood before her without recognition, an unwilling applicant for her hand. Nell was no longer too young for marriage. She knew the black-

haired boy with the startling gray eyes was Donal
O'Flaherty from the Beltane fires. She also knew that
he didn't want a Fitzgerald for his bride. Nell intended
to change his mind, for it had come to her, suddenly,
like an epiphany, the realization that she would never
want anyone else.

2

Jilly heard his voice long before her legs, pumping at full speed, carried her to the door of the kennel. There she watched in impotent fury as Terrence, her sixteen-year-old brother, tormented Frankie Maguire.

"Speak up, lad. I gave you an order."

Frankie swallowed. "I'm nn-nn-nnnot—"

"What's the matter?" Terrence jeered. "Can't get the words out? Maybe you're demented. That's it." He noticed his sister quivering with anger. "Jilly, look here. We've got a loony in the kennel."

Jillian stepped forward. "Stop it, Terrence."

"It's all right," he said. "The lad needs a lesson in manners." He swung his crop back and forth. "My mount needs saddling. Are you dense, lad? I mean for you to do it."

Frankie neither spoke nor moved, but the crimson ebbed and flowed in his cheeks.

Jilly felt the bile rise in her throat. She watched as

Terrence lifted his crop and brought it down, hard, on the inside of Frankie's wrist. Skin tore. Blood ran into the younger boy's palm and dripped to the ground. Still, he remained silent.

Jilly's eyes burned. She pressed her fist against her mouth. Terrence lifted his crop again, but before he could bring it down, she lunged forward, dragging at his arm with her weight. "Stop it!" she screamed. "Stop it, or I'll tell Mum."

Cursing, Terrence slapped her face and threw her aside as if she weighed no more than a feather pillow. Jilly landed against the fence and slipped to the ground, unable to find her breath. Through the roaring in her ears, she heard a sound like a wolf's howl. Gasping, she struggled to sit up, tears streaming down her cheeks.

The sight of the girl's blue face and racked body mobilized Frankie in a way that his own pain had not. Rage came to him as it comes to all who are slow to anger, with an intensity that grips the mind and sweeps clean everything before it like the path of a hurricane. He threw himself on Terrence, slamming his forehead into the boy's nose and splitting his lip before Terrence gained the advantage and flipped him over, lifting a punishing fist.

Before he could bring it down, Jilly jumped on his back, twined her arms around his neck, found his earlobe, and bit down. The metallic taste of warm blood filled her mouth. Behind her a voice shouted something she couldn't understand. Pain exploded in her head, and then everything went black.

Slowly, through the cobwebs cushioning her brain, words began to take shape and make sense. Jilly turned her head and winced against the pain in her temple. Cool hands moved against her skin.

"There, there, darling," her mother's voice crooned. "Everything will be all right."

Jilly opened her eyes. "I'm hungry."

"You shall have your tea as soon as you can sit up."

"Will you set a place for Nell?"

Margaret Fitzgerald sighed. "Jilly, love, don't you think it's time to put Nell to rest? After all, you're nearly eleven years old."

Jilly turned her face to the wall.

Her mother sighed again. "Very well. I'll have a tray brought up for you and Nell."

"Terrence is a beast," Jilly said.

Her mother's forehead wrinkled. "Whatever possessed you, Jilly?"

"He was hurting Frankie."

"But you're a girl," her mother protested, "and a very small one. Surely, a big boy like Francis doesn't need you to fight his battles."

Jilly shook her head. "He wouldn't fight Terrence. No one fights with Terrence."

Margaret Fitzgerald sighed. "Terrence is"—she searched for the right word to describe her stepson— "difficult. Your father has spoiled him dreadfully, I'm afraid. But it isn't your concern, Jillian. I want you to stay away from Terrence, and from Frankie Maguire."

Jilly tightened her lips.

"You heard me, Jillian," her mother said sternly. "I want you to promise me that you won't go near the kennel when the Maguire boy is there."

Jilly remained silent.

Her mother softened. "Please, Jilly."

Stone-faced, Jilly remained silent.

Margaret recognized the mutinous look on her daughter's face and gave up. Jilly went her own way. She always had. Margaret blamed it on Pyers. Delighted with his miracle daughter after he'd reconciled himself to never having another child, Pyers couldn't bring himself to discipline her. On those occasions when Margaret was completely honest with herself, she admitted to an equal share of the blame. Jilly was such a joy, so spirited and wise, so dear and pretty and full of life, so different from Terrence, that it seemed cruel to curb her. Pyers was flying home tonight. Margaret wondered what he would do about Frankie. It would be a shame to lose an excellent collier like Peter Maguire because of Terrence's cruel streak.

Those were Pyers Fitzgerald's precise comments to his wife after she told him of the incident. Rather than embarrass his son or Peter Maguire, he did what Pyers did best. He ignored the matter entirely, and, because he forgot it, he assumed that everyone else had as well.

He was mistaken. Jilly didn't forget, nor did Frankie or Terrence.

The very next day, Jilly rested her arms on the ledge of the Dutch door and watched Guinevere lap up something that looked like pig slops from her bowl. Frankie was running his hands down every one of her legs but the bandaged one. "What are you doing?" she asked.

"Lookin' for injuries," he said without looking up.

"They said you might not be back."

His hair had fallen over his forehead, and he tossed it back impatiently. "Who said?"

"My father and Mum."

He shrugged. "My da needs the help just now. Besides, I've done nothin' wrong."

Jilly smiled sunnily. "I told Mum that Terrence couldn't chase you away."

Finished with his examination, Frankie sat back on a bale of hay, pulled out a straw, and chewed on it. "You're not much like him, are you?"

She shook her head. "My father was married to someone else before he married Mum. Terrence's mother died. That's why we don't look alike."

Frankie took in the sun-streaked brown hair pulled away from her face in a single braid, the expressive ocean-colored eyes framed in feathery, gold-tipped lashes, and her delicate, heart-shaped face. His mouth twisted in amusement. "It's not yer looks that's different."

"What, then?"

He hadn't planned on telling her what her nearly suicidal leap to his defense meant to him. Clearing his throat, he did the next best thing. "You're a brave one for such a wee lass."

"Nell says I've the Fitzgerald temper," she said solemnly. "It makes me do dreadful things."

He nodded. "I know about that. I've a wee bit of a temper myself."

"Is that why you wouldn't saddle Terrence's horse?"

"It is."

Jilly climbed down from the door and opened it to step inside. "How is Gwenny?"

"She'll be all sorted out in no time. Food and rest is what she needs."

"Why does your father need help just now?"

One black eyebrow quirked. "You're a nosy lass."

Jilly flushed. "You don't have to tell me."

Frankie stared at her burning cheeks for a long moment. "Don't fret it, Jilly. Y' meant no harm. My da's joints act up in the rain. It takes longer for him t' finish up."

"Oh." She thought a moment. "Maybe Nell and I could help him, too."

"Who is Nell?"

"She's my friend."

"That wouldn't be a good idea."

"Why not?"

Frankie nodded in the direction of the house. "Yer mother wouldn't like it."

Jilly laughed. "Mum won't mind. She lets me do anything I want."

Frankie looked incredulous. None of the women he knew shared Lady Fitzgerald's philosophy of mothering. "What about your da and Nell's mother?"

"Nell doesn't have a mother." Jilly sat down on a bale of hay and crossed her legs beneath her. "My father won't care, either. I don't see him much."

Again, Frankie was shocked at her cavalier attitude toward authority. Imagine not seeing your father, not bumping into him around every corner, in the too-small kitchen, on the way to the loo, in the tiny bedroom where they shared a mattress so as to give Kathleen the privacy a girl needed. What kind of life was it where a little girl never saw her da? He looked at her again, racking his brain for another excuse to be rid of her. Not that he wasn't grateful. But it terrified him to think of yesterday's scene. She could have been killed, and he would have been blamed. He knew the fight was his own fault. It wasn't unusual to expect that a collier lend an occasional hand in the stables. Frankie liked horses, especially the way their coats gleamed in the sunlight and the soft, velvety feel of their nostrils against his palm. But he wouldn't lift a finger for Terrence Fitzgerald. Jilly's brother was a braggart and a bully.

Those character flaws in themselves weren't enough to arouse the flame of Frankie's temper. It went deeper than that. He didn't trust Terrence, not since he'd seen him talking with Kathleen out by the henhouse. There wasn't a reason in the world for a girl who scrubbed latrines to be talking with a boy who would inherit half of County Down.

Kathleen said he'd brought a message from the housekeeper, but Frankie doubted if Terrence Fitzgerald even knew he had one. He was an aristocrat, born into old wealth, one of those who assumed his clothing would be automatically pressed, his sheets changed, and his Christmas dinner served hot and on time without once considering the men and women who left their own families to meatless meals while they trudged through bogs and along dirt roads to perform domestic services for the pitiful wages that kept them a hair's breadth on the other side of starvation.

Kathleen was sixteen, with a red-cheeked, full-figured appeal that made grown men turn around for a second look. Terrence wasn't grown, and although Frankie couldn't be sure, he didn't think Terrence was much to look at, either. But he was the Fitzgerald heir, and for Kathleen, who had nothing to look forward to but a husband who would spend half his life on the dole, he was pure gold.

When Frankie hinted that Terrence might want something more than she was prepared to give, Kathleen brushed aside his warning with an evasive shrug, insisting that it wasn't like that. He gave up when his father called him a "meddlesome lad gettin' too big for his breeches." Who was he to put the fear of God into Kathleen when her own father wouldn't? He only hoped they wouldn't all live to regret it. Meanwhile, he continued to regard Terrence with suspicion, which led to the scene yesterday morning.

Jilly was looking at him, her eyes wide on his face, waiting to be told what to do. She was a strange little mite, all eyes and hair and legs, with the patience to sit still for extended periods of time. It was her patience that intrigued Frankie. In his world, the young weren't patient. They were too busy scrubbing and washing and cooking and birthing and scratching to make ends meet. Only old men who'd earned their time in the sun were patient, and young men who spent their Friday dole in the pubs and were loath to go home.

Frankie knew Lady Fitzgerald wouldn't approve, but he saw no way out other than to hurt the tike's feelings, and he didn't want to do that. "You can help me, if you like."

She clapped her hands. "Tell me what to do."

"Come into town with me to the chemist. We're out of gauze and disinfectant."

Her eyes narrowed suspiciously. "You don't need me for that."

"I do," he lied. "Da's not here yet, and the chemist won't give me the supplies without an order."

Jilly tilted her head as if to gauge the validity of his request. Frankie held his breath. All at once, it seemed very important that she come with him.

She nodded. "All right."

He grinned. There was something different about this child. She relaxed him. He couldn't put his finger on it, but for some reason his throat didn't freeze up around Jilly.

She smiled and clapped her hands when he pulled his bicycle away from the shed and lifted her up in front of him. She weighed almost nothing, and after an experimental turn around the yard, Frankie found his balance, and they were off.

Jilly had never ridden sidesaddle on a bicycle before, and Frankie offered no instruction. Reaching behind her back, she gripped the handlebars, braced herself, and held on. Within minutes, she was acclimated to the rhythmic bumping. The wind stung her cheeks and tangled her hair, and when the driver of a huge tractor waved them past, she laughed out loud and unlocked one hand to wave back. Soon she was chattering away as if she'd known Frankie for years, completely undaunted by his silence. She knew he was there behind her, steadily pumping. That was enough.

The tiny town of Kilvara was nearly five kilometers away. As in most Irish villages, there was only one main road through the center with small shops and houses built up to the street. It was market day, and farmers from all over County Down had brought their sheep in for the auction. The street was a river of white wool, and all traffic had come to a complete and frustrating stop. Frankie pulled up his bicycle, and Jilly hopped off, rubbed her backside, and looked around expectantly. She had never been to town on market day. "It's really quite nice, isn't it?" she confided to Frankie. "All the noise and the people and the colors and the lovely smells. Does this happen every Wednesday?"

"Aye." Frankie's head was reeling. He had never met anyone who talked as much without requiring an answer. She'd commented on the wildflowers, the condition of the road, the tractor, the white aprons covering the haystacks in the fields, the weather, the late-model sports car that had passed them on the road, the feel of the sun on her face, and, most unusual of all, she required nothing of him except his presence. It was as if they'd come to a mutual understanding. He would do whatever needed to be done, and she would provide the entertainment.

Frankie grinned. She *was* an entertaining little thing, with her quaint observations, her lack of self-consciousness, and her wide hazel eyes. He felt as if he'd known her forever. "Come on," he said, reaching for her hand. "We'll leave the bike and wade through the sheep to the chemist. Hold on tight, and don't let 'em knock you down."

All of which was more easily said than done. Frankie's hand was a lifeline to which Jilly clung at all costs. At any moment, she felt that her arm would be ripped from its socket as she bumped and shoved her way through the moist, scratchy bodies of mewling sheep. Urea fumes crawled up her nose and stung her watery eyes. Bodies stepped on her toes and knocked against her, throwing her over woolly, wriggling backs. Each time she stumbled, Frankie tightened his grip, lifting her to her feet, pulling her along, until the next time. It seemed a lifetime before she was on the other side of Kilvara's narrow main road. Panting, she swayed slightly and wiped her sweaty forehead. As if he'd done it every day of his life, Frankie's arm curved around her back. She sagged against him, grateful for the support.

"Hey, Frankie, where y' been?" a voice called out over the noise. "Father Quinlan says it's y'r turn at mass on Sunday."

Casually, Frankie dropped his arm from around Jilly and turned to see Sean Peterson leaning in the doorway of O'Malley's Pub. "It's y'r turn, and y' know it," he said. "I altared last week."

Sean grinned and shook his head. "It's Gracie's weddin' in Newry. Y'll have to take my place."

Two more boys walked out from the darkened shadows of the pub. Frankie groaned and muttered something Jilly couldn't hear under his breath.

"Who's the girl, Frankie?" Tommy Dougherty asked, swaggering out to the street to stare at Jilly. "A bit young, isn't she? What's y'r name, lass?"

Frankie scowled. "Leave her alone, Tommy."

"I only want her name."

Jilly hesitated. She didn't like the looks of the boy

with the shocking red hair. Under the enormous brown
freckles, his skin appeared unnaturally white, as if he'd
been ill for a long time. "My name is Jillian Fitzgerald,"
she said quietly.

Tommy Dougherty pushed back his cap and
scratched his head. She was lying. Jillian Fitzgerald
would not ride into Kilvara with the likes of Frankie
Maguire. "And where do y' live, Jillian Fitzgerald, that
we've never seen y' before today?"

"Down the road," she said vaguely. Jilly wanted to
leave. Tommy Dougherty had an insolent mouth and
eyes set very close together. She looked at Frankie, but
he made no move at all.

"Where down the road?" Tommy's voice taunted
her.

"Down the road at Kildare." Jilly tried to walk
around him, but he blocked her path.

"Where at Kildare?"

Jilly felt the familiar churning in her stomach and
knew what it meant. *Easy, Jilly.* Nell's voice soothed her.

Frankie was staring at her oddly. "I live at Kildare
Hall," she announced loudly, "and I want you to get
out of my way."

Tommy Dougherty never knew exactly how he happened to land in the street square on his bum. All he
remembered was that his jaw exploded in pain, and then
he was on the ground surrounded by sheep. Frankie's
face was very close, and when he spoke, his voice was
hard and cold like the knife Tommy's da used for
butchering pigs. "She's Jillian Fitzgerald of Kildare
Hall," he said, "and she's a wee lass who's come with
me to town. That's enough, I think."

Tommy stared up at Frankie's thin brown face, read
the message in his eyes, and nodded. "Sorry, Frankie,"
he mumbled.

"It's not me y' should be apologizin' to."

Nodding miserably, Tommy swallowed. "Sorry, lass. I was just havin' a bit o' fun. No harm meant." He smiled tentatively. "Would y' like a squash from the bar?"

Jillian smiled, all unpleasantness forgotten at the thought of the fizzy orange drink sliding down her parched throat. "Oh, yes, please. Can we, Frankie? Do we have time?"

Frankie hesitated, imagining the scene were any of the Fitzgeralds to learn of Jilly's whereabouts. But then he remembered the uglier scene they'd just come away from and decided it was better to leave Jilly with memories of a free squash from the pub. "Aye," he said, "we have time."

When Frankie went up to the bar to order the drinks, Sean went with him. "What are y' doin' mindin' the earl's daughter?" he asked.

Frankie shrugged. "She's all right."

"She's a baby."

"Aye." Frankie threw forty pence on the counter and picked up two of the bottles.

Sean dug into his pocket for exact change and pulled out half a crown. "Frankie, what're y' doin' wastin' y'r time with the likes o' her?"

Frankie made his way through the tables. "I'm not wastin' time, Sean. Jilly's a wee lass who loves animals, that's all."

"Y' knocked Tommy int' the dirt."

"Tommy's a wanker. Jilly's nothin' to me."

Sean released his breath. "I hope so, Frankie. She's not only a baby, she's a Prod. Don't be forgettin' that."

Frankie handed Jilly her drink and slid into the chair beside her. "I'm not forgettin' a thing, Sean. Don't be worryin' about me. Y' know where my mind is."

Jilly sipped her drink and spoke up. "Frankie's going to be a veterinarian when he grows up, and I am, too. I'm going to help him."

Frankie's cheeks reddened. Deliberately, he avoided the astonished stares of his friends. "Now, don't be goin' around sayin' that, Jilly."

"Why not?"

"Bbb-bbb"—he struggled for the words—"bbb-bbbe—" He gave up, exasperated. Whenever he most needed them, the words failed him. "You don't understand," he managed at last. "Things can change."

Jilly understood all too well. Frankie Maguire was ashamed of her. She stared into her drink, stirring the liquid with her straw, wishing she were home.

Frankie saw her lip tremble and hated himself. She was just a wee lass, and he'd hurt her feelings. But he couldn't have the lads thinking there was anything more to his relationship with Jilly than a trip into town. A rumor like that would cause no end of trouble. Sucking down the last of his squash, he stood up. "Come on, Jilly."

They were nearly home before Frankie remembered the chemist. He was too preoccupied with his own ineptness and her lack of conversation to remember what they'd gone into the village for in the first place. Cursing softly, he pushed back on the pedals to stop the bike. Unprepared for the sudden braking, Jilly tumbled from the handlebars and hit the ground, hard.

Frankie whitened and dropped the bike to kneel beside her in the grass. "Lord, Jilly, I'm sorry. Are y' hurt, lass?"

She shook her head and turned away, hoping he wouldn't see the tears in her eyes. But Frankie wouldn't be dissuaded. Taking her chin in his hand, he gently turned her head. "You are hurt." His gray eyes filled with remorse. "I'm an idiot. I forgot the chemist, that's why. Can y' walk, Jilly?"

Nodding, she stood and limped over to the bike. Frankie groaned. Jilly's silence was worse than a thousand humiliations. "I'm sorry, lass."

"It was an accident," she said woodenly.

"I'm sorry for what I said at the pub."

She turned and looked at him steadily, a small, wraithlike figure with too-long legs and a curtain of silky, brown-gold hair.

"I was afraid they'd make somethin' out of it that wasn't."

Her forehead puckered. "What do you mean?"

Frankie sighed. She wasn't making this easy for him. "Y're not old enough t' understand this, Jilly, but sometimes people my age are more than just friendly with girls. I didn't want anyone to think that about us. Y're too young, and even if y' weren't, it isn't possible." He paused. The puzzled look hadn't left her face. "Do y' understand what I'm sayin', lass?"

She didn't. But Nell would. Nell was smarter and older. "Don't you want to be a veterinarian with me?" she ventured.

His shoulders slumped. She was too innocent for words, and he was disgusted with himself. Jilly was only eleven years old. Of course she wouldn't know what he was hinting at. "Never mind. Let's get y' home and ice that ankle. Maybe if I'm lucky, my da will still have a job in the mornin'."

3

Maynooth, 1537

He was staring at her. Nell could feel his gaze from across the banquet hall. She turned to smile at him, tried to look away, and found that she could not. For the space of their exchange, it seemed that the room narrowed and shortened, the torches dimmed, the crowd silenced until it was just the two of them connected by a power source that neither could explain nor control.

She was the first to break eye contact. The mere act sapped her strength. She swayed and leaned against the man beside her.

Garrett Fitzgerald looked down at his niece and slipped his arm around her waist. "Tired, Nell?"

She shook her head. "Lord Grey came all the way from Dublin to speak with Father. I won't be able to sleep unless I know the reason."

Garrett hesitated. "Go to bed, Nell. We won't know anything until tomorrow."

From the corner of her eye, she could see Donal O'Flaherty slide out from behind his bench and walk toward the door. Where was he going? "How do you know?" she asked her uncle.

Garrett tugged gently on Nell's thick golden braid. "Your father will want to see all of us if he's called to London, and your mother has already gone to her chambers for the night. A banquet is hardly the place to discuss politics."

Nell sighed. More than likely, no one would tell her anything until it was over. An unmarried woman's place was below that of her father's *gallowglass*, mercenaries who sold their services to the highest bidder and made up the bulk of the Fitzgerald army. Margaret, her older sister, had entertained notions beyond those of most women, and her reward was banishment from her family and marriage to Ormond, a man twice her age.

Thoughts of Margaret were rarely pleasant. Nell stifled a yawn. Perhaps it was time to seek her couch. The day had been long and the wine potent. Dipping her fingers into the trencher she shared with Garrett, she found the last piece of honeyed pear and slipped it into her mouth.

Garrett grinned and stood to let her pass. Nell's fondness for sweets had not lessened with maturity. Still standing, he watched as she crossed the room without incident and disappeared behind the enormous carved doors. Only then did he sit down to resume his meal. During the last year, Nell had developed the curves of a woman. She was safe enough at Maynooth while her father and uncles were present, but Garrett had seen the eyes of more than a few of the Irish lords linger on her graceful figure as she moved about the castle. He wanted there to be no doubt that Gerald Og's youngest and loveliest daughter had the full protection of her family.

The hall was dimly lit, and the twisting stair passage had no light at all. Nell paused to find a candle and hold it to the flickering torch flame. The pool of oil in the well was black and evil-smelling. She wrinkled her nose. The wick caught. She lifted the edge of her skirt, twisted the hem around her wrist, and moved toward the stairs.

His voice stopped her. " 'Tis early yet for retiring."

Slowly, she turned. Donal O'Flaherty stood near the open door, his lean height framed by the indigo blue of the darkening sky. "You left early, too, my lord." Her voice was huskier than usual, but he wouldn't know that.

He stepped into the circle of light thrown by the torch. " 'Tis flattering to have a beautiful woman notice my absence, but I am an Irish chieftain, lass. I have no English title. You may call me Donal."

Lord, he was handsome. Nell had been weaned on legends of King Conor and *Emain Macha*. If anyone fit her image of a true Irish warrior, it was this splendid young man with his striking high-boned face and dark gray eyes. She flushed and lowered her candle. "Good night, sir."

Instantly, he was at her side, his hand on her arm. "Don't go yet, Eleanor. Come outside with me and see the stars. The moon is nearly gone, and there are no clouds tonight."

She stared at the lean fingers curving around her wrist and wondered if his flesh burned as hers did. "Call me Nell. There are always stars in Maynooth," she said quietly. "Are there none in Galway?"

"Galway is on the sea. Except for late summer, there is usually heavy fog."

Nell looked up, and her breathing altered. He was very close. "It sounds like a gloomy place, your Galway." she whispered.

He shook his head. "The fog comes at night and before the dawn. Otherwise, 'tis a magical land of blue water and white sand. You will be happy there."

It was the first time either of them had acknowledged their pending betrothal.

She swallowed and looked away.

"Nell?" The sound of her name on his lips was like a soft caress. "Come outside with me and see the stars."

When he spoke in that voice, persuasive and low as if he wanted nothing more in all the world, she would have gone with him anywhere. He took her hand and led her outside, across the courtyard and out the gates, to sit on the hilly bank below the castle. The sky was completely dark now, and the stars were a spangle of glittering silver across the inky blackness.

"I had no idea it would look like this," Donal said in a hushed voice.

Nell's eyes widened. He really had wanted to see the stars. It wasn't just an excuse to be alone with her. "Have you never been here before, my— I mean, sir?"

"I have a name, Nell."

She drew up her knees and clasped her arms around them. "I know."

He waited, but she remained silent. "I have been to Dublin, often," he said at last, "but never by way of Kildare."

"And what do you think of Dublin?"

His mouth tightened into a thin, angry line. " 'Tis an English city ruled by Englishmen. Were I never to see it again, I would not be sorry."

She waited for a full minute before speaking, and when she did, Donal knew that he had offended her.

"Perhaps you think this is an English house as well, sir, and are just as displeased with us?"

He could barely make out her profile, a dark silhouette etched against a darker sky, framed by wings of pale hair. He lifted her hand from the grass and pressed her palm against his lips. He felt her tremble, and it reassured him. "Yours may be an English house, Nell, but nothing about your family offends me. In fact, I am particularly pleased with the company."

"I know you didn't want to marry me," she said bluntly.

He frowned. "Who told you that?"

"You did."

"You are mistaken, lass. I have never seen you before this morning."

She nodded her head. "We met once before at the Beltane fires. It was there that you spoke of your hatred for the English."

The puzzled expression on his face deepened. Surely, he would have remembered a beauty like Nell. "I do not recall such a conversation," he said slowly. "Are you sure it was I?"

Nell laughed. No woman, no matter how young, would forget such a man. "Completely sure."

Donal let go of her hand, leaned back in the grass, and tucked his arms behind his head. "Tell me more of this Beltane and why the daughter of an Englishman would attend such an event."

"My mother is an Irish princess, descended from the house of Munster. Beltane calls out to her Irish blood. Three years ago, she decided I was old enough to accompany her."

"Did you take part in the ritual?" he asked casually, his eyes on the orbs of light above him. Brehon law did not require it, but he preferred that his future wife be a virgin.

"Nearly, until you rescued me."

Suddenly, it came to him, and he whistled long and low. "By the beard of Christ! It was you, the English lass whose father would have forced me into marriage."

"Apparently, it was all for nothing. Despite my warning, you are fairly caught, Donal O'Flaherty."

It was the first time she'd called him by name. It was a good sign. "What of you, Nell? Is this marriage to your liking?"

She looked him full in the face, this man descended from King Conor's warriors of the Red Branch. Could he possibly be serious? No woman in her right mind would refuse him. His hands were open and relaxed, one behind his head, the other resting on the ground at his side. Nell imagined those hands on her skin and shivered. "Yes," she said simply.

Her answer shook him. She was direct and honest and incredibly lovely. He wanted to touch her, to run his hands over the bones of her face, the bridge of her nose, to open his mouth and trace with his tongue the edges of her lips and the column of her throat. His longing was deep and possessive, more profound than sexual. He wanted to mark her as his own so that all other men would know she was promised to him. "Will you come home with me to Aughnanure?" he asked bluntly.

She looked startled. "We must be wed first."

Her hair was liquid silver in the starlight. His hands clenched. "When will that be? Soon, I hope."

Nell smothered a laugh and stood, brushing the grass from her gown. He was not so very different from other men after all. "We have tried to make your visit comfortable, sir. Is your chamber not pleasing?"

He watched the graceful movements of her hands, felt the dark blood of desire fill him, and rose to stand beside her. "My chamber is most pleasing, Nell. I can think of only one thing that it lacks."

Again he was very close. Her hands lost the will to move. She stared up at him, all wide-eyed innocence. "What are you thinking, Donal O'Flaherty?"

"How hard it is not to kiss a Geraldine."

Nell looked at the hard line of his mouth. Embarrassed, she turned away, cheeks burning. She felt his hand on the nape of her neck and something else, something new. The tides within her body announced that she was a woman. The dance had begun.

"Nell," he murmured against her hair. "My beautiful, beautiful Nell."

He smelled of wool and smoke and turf and horse. His voice was pure magic. "Come home with me, Nell. There is a priest there. Come home with me to Aughnanure."

Firm hands settled on her shoulders and turned her around. His face was divided by light and dark, one side shadowed, the other bled pale by starlight. She could no longer think clearly. He was two of her, or nearly so, with wide shoulders, a deep chest, the narrow hips of a horseman.

Neither moving nor speaking, he waited. The choice was hers. Not for others, perhaps, but for him it would always be. *Come home with me to Aughnanure.*

Slowly, tentatively, her hand moved across his squared-off jaw, his mouth, the sharp line of his cheek. "Yes," she said softly, sealing her fate. "I'll come with you to Aughnanure."

His head bent. She had waited a lifetime for the feel of this man's kiss. His lips were firm and pleasant, tasting of rain and wood smoke. One arm circled her waist and drew her to him, while his hand cupped the back of her head, holding her still, his tongue teasing her mouth until she opened for him.

Heat bubbled within her. She pressed against him, her body molding against his, filling his empty spaces. When she could breathe again, she laughed, a low, musical trill in the velvet night.

Reluctantly, his hands moved from the curves of her breasts to settle on her waist. He breathed as if he had been running. "What is it, lass?"

"You didn't want me, not in the beginning. I know you didn't. But you want me now."

Donal looked down at her lovely, laughing face. "Aye," he said softly, "I want you now."

Gerald Og, ninth earl of Kildare, stood in the small hall at Maynooth and looked at the black-haired boy holding his daughter's hand. He had been right to approach Donal O'Flaherty. The O'Flahertys were fierce fighters. "From the fury of the fighting O'Flahertys, may the Lord deliver us" was the motto inscribed on the gates of Galway City. O'Flaherty chieftains were chosen by rites of ancient Brehon law rather than the English practice of primogeniture. Only the fittest, elected by popular vote, became an O'Flaherty chieftain.

Perhaps it was best, mused Gerald Og, his shrewd gaze taking in the young man's muscular legs, his deep chest, wide shoulders, and the hard, uncompromising gray of his eyes. Surely, this man was a fit mate for Nell. Gerald reached out and placed one hand on Donal's shoulder, the other on Nell's. His eyes twinkled. "Your match pleases me. May it please you as well. I leave for London in the morning. The wedding will take place when I return, in four months' time."

He saw Donal's brow darken and continued quickly.

"Henry grows impatient for my report. Unless he is soothed, Ireland will know the taste of English steel. I go to keep the peace. We will all benefit." He waited for the boy to object, but other than a brief tightening of the lips, Donal remained silent. Gerald was more than pleased. The lad knew when to keep his own counsel.

Lifting his daughter's chin, he looked into her eyes. "Take care of your mother, lass. She worries when I am away. Send Thomas to me. You must watch him carefully. I'll not have everything I've worked for destroyed because his patience wears too thin."

Nell smiled. Thomas Fitzgerald was her older brother. His revolutionary tendencies were a source of frustration to his father and uncles, but she adored him. They had spent many happy hours growing up together in the woods and glens of Maynooth. "I'll find him for you, Father." She looked up at her betrothed. "Will you come with me, Donal? I would like for you and Thomas to meet. You have much in common."

Gerald coughed and turned away, holding his hands near the hearth fire. If ever two young men were opposites, they were Donal O'Flaherty and his oldest son.

The O'Flaherty was the elder by two years, and never had two years made more of a difference. Thomas was blond like all the Fitzgeralds and slim as a reed. Every fleeting emotion was revealed on his expressive face, and too often the sulky petulance of an indulged childhood was evident in his manners.

There was no trace of childhood in Donal O'Flaherty's lean, chiseled features, and his true feelings were completely hidden behind the schooled indifference of his expression. At the age of sixteen, he had been unanimously elected chief of his clan, and by nineteen, he'd earned a reputation as a shrewd battle strategist and a courageous fighter. Wise beyond his years, he insisted that the O'Flahertys stay as far away from the Pale as possible, refusing to incur England's wrath by engaging in the common practice of plundering English carracks as they crossed the Irish Sea.

This marriage had been years in the making. With it, Gerald would accomplish what he'd always intended, to ally all of Ireland with the Fitzgeralds, to create a powerful dynasty that would one day lead a successful insurrection against England and form its own royal house.

Four days later, Nell, with the betrothal crest of the O'Flahertys pinned to her bodice, stood in the court-yard of Maynooth, staring up at the man who would be her husband. She felt strangely self-conscious standing there before all of his men, her small hand clasped pos-sessively in his larger one. Her shyness made no sense, not after the hours they had shared alone in each other's company, hours that would have to sustain her until she saw him again.

"Nell," he said softly, the amusement in his voice bringing the heat to her cheeks. "Where are you?"

She blinked. "Why, here with you, of course. Why do you ask?"

He moved closer. The breath caught in her throat.

"Will you think of me, lass?"

"You know I will."

His mouth brushed her lips. "Tell me, with your words."

Nell leaned into him, her forehead resting against the hard line of his jaw. When she spoke, her voice was low and firm and filled with conviction. "I want you for my husband, Donal O'Flaherty. Until then, my heart goes with you. I shall think of you every waking moment."

Donal's heart leaped in his chest. He had only known this girl for a few brief days, but he felt as if he'd waited his entire life for her. Nothing had ever felt so right. She was small and intelligent and incredibly direct. The feel of her mouth under his, her hands on his skin, and the way her smile lit her face to heart-shattering purity left him weak-kneed with an emotion that went far beyond mere desire.

He pressed his mouth against her temple and then whispered fiercely in her ear. "I want you with me, Nell. If Henry keeps your father beyond the harvest, I shall come for you whether he wishes it or not. Our marriage will take place with or without Gerald Og."

She nodded her head and stepped back. "Goodbye, Donal."

His eyes softened. "*Slán leat go fóill*, my heart," he said for all to hear.

She watched as he mounted his stallion and led his men out of the courtyard. When the last horseman rode through the gates, she ran to the battlements and peered through the narrow slits. At the top of the rise, Donal turned, lifted his arm, and then disappeared over the top.

Nell sighed and rubbed her arms. The waiting would be difficult. Why must a woman spend her life waiting? She thought of Margaret and resigned herself. There was no other way.

Six months later

Nell pressed her fist against her mouth and read Leonard Gray's carefully scripted message. Her eyes burned with unshed tears. It couldn't be true. Was it only six months ago that her father had set out for England with such confidence? How would her mother bear it? Her husband most likely dead, her son and all five of his uncles to be executed in one fell swoop. Nell stood near the door of her mother's chamber, where the Flemish tapestry depicting William Strongbow's marriage to the daughter of Red Hugh O'Neill kept out the drafts. Hands shaking, she moved the woven fabric aside and stepped into the chamber.

Maeve O'Conor Fitzgerald was seriously ill. The rumor of her husband's death and the incarceration of her beloved oldest son had taken the life from her pretty features, leaving them sunken and aged. Her mind, never strong, hung on the edge of sanity. Nell feared that the news would push her over the edge.

The huge curtained bed dominated the room. Herbs, cloying and sweet, covered the sickroom floor. Nell motioned the servant away and took her place on the low stool. "Mother," she whispered, "are you awake?"

Maeve reached out to touch her daughter's hand. "Aye, love. What is it?"

Nell swallowed. Her lip trembled as she uttered the unbelievable words. "They are sentenced to death. All of them."

From the bed, there was silence, followed by a low, animal moan. Maeve struggled to sit up, tears streaking her face, red hair falling around her shoulders. "Curse Henry Tudor!" she screamed. "May his soul be damned!" Her voice was raw and ragged with hate. "I curse him and all of his blood. If he takes the son of my body, I swear by almighty God and all who came before Him that Henry shall have no living sons. The name of Tudor, like that of Fitzgerald, shall be forever wiped from the face of the earth."

Nell watched in fascinated horror as her mother lifted

shaking hands to her face and performed the ancient
Irish rite of self-immolation, raking her nails across her
cheeks until the blood ran down her neck, pooling at
the base of her throat, staining the white linen sheets
with streaks that would never come clean.

Beauchamp Tower, London

The ninth earl of Kildare penned his note carefully. His
time was at hand. The message he sent would be the
most important one of his life. He was doomed, as were
his four brothers and his son, Silken Thomas. The corners of his mouth turned down bitterly. *Silken Thomas*,
that absurd name earned by the fringed silk bridle
Thomas favored for his horse, would be the one engraved on his tomb. Rash, misguided boy. From the
day he had called Henry Tudor his enemy and thrown
down the standard in Parliament, his hours had been
numbered.

Henry had planned it, of course. He knew the temperament of Fitzgerald's heir. It was a small matter to
circulate rumors of Gerald's arrest and death in the
Tower. What was a devoted son to do but avenge his
father's honor? If only Gerald could have counseled
him, sent him word, but it wasn't possible. He'd been
snared as tightly as a gull in the talons of a falcon.

For their insurrection against the Crown, the Fitzger-
alds were to die at Tyburn, all of them, James, Oliver,
John, Garrett, and the child born of his passion for
Maeve, his firstborn, Silken Thomas.

Gerald wrote quickly. A black-robed priest who
served the true faith waited in the corner. He would
carry his missive to Nell. Only Nell could save his
younger son. Maeve was—quickly, he pushed away the
uncharitable thought. He had known what Maeve was

when he married her. It was Maeve's temperament that Thomas had inherited, and Maeve could not help what she was. Nell was even-tempered like her father. Upon her slight shoulders would rest the future of his house.

Sprinkling sand over the wet ink, he shook the paper, rolled it, and heated the wax in a small pan over the candle flame. Carefully, he poured it over the scroll and sealed it with his ring before kneeling on the stone floor. "Bless me, Father, for I have sinned," he rasped. "It has been many years since my last confession."

"Continue, my son."

Gerald crossed himself. "For my own gain, I denied Holy Mother Church, and now I must suffer. Forgive me, Father, that I may enter the kingdom of heaven."

The priest made the sign of the cross and rested his hand on the great earl's head. "You will enter the gates of heaven, Gerald Og, but the price will be great. Pray with me."

Gerald groaned and folded his hands. After a moment, he looked up. "May I hope, Father?"

The priest shook his head. "I am sorry, my son. May you rest in peace."

Burying his face in his hands, Gerald waited for the summons that he knew would come all too soon.

"Mallacht De ar a anam dubh," cursed Donal O'Flaherty as he ran down the twisting stairs. It was black as pitch in the entry. The stairs were slippery with wet, and the news he'd just heard sent a chill clear to the base of his spine. The Geraldines were to be killed at Tyburn by order of Henry Tudor.

Hanged from the neck and while still alive, disemboweled and quartered so that no part of their person shall remain intact.

By the beard of Christ, was the man a monster? And

where was Nell? Weeks had passed since her last letter. Donal knew he never should have left Maynooth without her. His sense of foreboding had grown as the months passed and Gerald Og still had not returned from London. Nell's letters, reassuring him that her heart was unchanged, had curbed his impatience. Blaming himself for ignoring the warning signals, he shouted for his men, his mail, and the *ceithearn* that accompanied him everywhere.

Before the walls of Aughnanure had ceased to echo his voice, a small band of soldiers had assembled in the courtyard. They were fully armed, Donal noted with satisfaction, and every one chosen for his ability to ride for twenty hours without rest. Deliberately, without emotion, he spoke. "The Sassanach king has ordered the killing of the Fitzgeralds."

A low murmur passed through the mounted *ceithearn*. "Do we ride for Maynooth, Donal?" a man asked.

"Aye."

Without a word of protest, they swung onto their mounts and urged them forward. Even at a steady gallop, Maynooth was four days away.

The blackened *bothys* dotting the ruins of what was once the richest farmland in all of Ireland deepened the worry lines around Donal's mouth. Silken Thomas was a fool. How could a man like Gerald Og have sired such a son? He pushed the wasteful thought from his mind. The Geraldines were doomed, all but Nell and her youngest brother, a boy of no more than eleven years, Gerald Fitzgerald, the tenth earl of Kildare.

As Donal had suspected, Maynooth was completely gutted. Smoke hung in a black haze over the burned-out walls. He dismounted and walked through the roofless *bawn*, kicking the charred wood, his hand tight on his demilance, his eyes narrowed and hard.

This house, on the edge of the English Pale, had been the grandest estate in all of Ireland. For four hundred years, the Fitzgeralds had ruled as uncrowned kings. Many had envied their power. Even in Ulster, chieftains bearing the royal blood of King Conor, the O'Neills, the O'Donnells, the Desmonds, the Maguires, had fought for the honor of paying homage to the great family of Fitzgerald. They had paid dearly for their allegiance. Gold, land, titles, the faith of their ancestors, even firstborn sons had been delivered into the hands of Englishmen.

Donal shook his head. No one remembered that the Fitzgeralds weren't native Irish. Bards sang of their arrival from Wales with the Anglo-Norman marcher lords. The most powerful family in Ireland, destroyed at the whim of a gout-filled, fat man who could not sire a living male child and whose tenuous claim to the English throne was through the illegitimate line of Margaret Beaufort.

At the Battle of Bosworth, the Geraldines had fought for the Yorkist cause against the first Henry Tudor. The second Henry lived in fear that someone would remember that Fitzgerald blood came from the Plantagenets, a line older and more royal than his own. Gerald Fitzgerald, tenth earl of Kildare, was only eleven years old, but he was still a threat to the Tudor dynasty, as was anyone who tried to protect him.

Fear gripped Donal's throat. It was nearly winter, and Ireland was ravaged by war. Nell was sixteen years old, so beautiful it hurt to look at her, and for the first time in her life, without the protection of her father. Where in the name of heaven was she?

4

Kildare Hall, 1972

Jilly leaned against an enormous yew tree, content just to watch Frankie throw sticks for the frolicking collies to run after and bring back to him. She had an artist's appreciation for beauty, and, while too young to understand why the play of ropy muscles under a boy's sun-browned skin made the breath catch in her throat, she recognized its impact on her senses. He'd taken off his shirt, and she noticed that he wasn't as fair as most Irish boys. The combination of dark hair, bare skin, and fluid motion held her spellbound.

A voice intruded upon her thoughts. *Hello, Jillian.*

Reluctantly, Jilly turned around. "Nell. Where have you been? I haven't seen you for ages."

Nell hesitated. *Things have become rather complicated. I couldn't come any sooner.* She looked across the meadow. *I see that you've found a new friend.*

Jilly shrugged. "He isn't you."

Lowering herself to the ground, Nell folded her legs and looked up expectantly. *Tell me about him.*

"His name is Francis Maguire, and he comes to Kildare twice a week to help his father with the collies." Jilly settled herself on the ground beside Nell. "I wish he'd come more, but Frankie says that with his studies and his work, two days is all he can manage."

Frankie Maguire. Nell held his name on her tongue for the length of time it took her to absorb fully the image of golden dogs, green grass, and the masculine appeal of a boy completely unconscious of the picture he made. *I'd like to paint him,* she murmured out loud.

"Mum said the same thing," Jilly confessed.

Did she? Nell smiled. Margaret Fitzgerald would be horrified that her daughter had overheard and revealed her forbidden, although completely understandable, fantasy. Francis Maguire was only a boy, but soon, very soon, he would be a most attractive man.

Jilly interrupted her thoughts. "How long can you stay?"

For a while.

"Will you come with me to see Frankie?"

Nell shook her head. *You go on. I'll be here when you're finished.*

"You're sure?"

Aye. Run along now.

Jilly started off slowly, gathering speed when Frankie turned, recognized her, and waved.

Nell watched their exchange, and her eyes narrowed. *So, it begins,* she said to herself.

"Hello, Frankie!" Jilly shouted, running through the tall grass to greet him.

He grinned and pulled on his shirt. "Hello, lass. What brings you here?"

"Mum made sugar crisps." She held out a brown paper bag. "I brought you some. Your da told me you were here."

Frankie ruffled her silky hair. "My thanks, Jilly. Will y' share them with me?"

She nodded happily. "I brought enough for two. Nell doesn't want any. She never eats."

Frankie bit down into the buttery biscuit and grunted his appreciation. "Y' better hurry back to the house if Nell is waitin' on you."

"She said she'd be there when I'm finished here."

"Nell sounds like an agreeable lass."

"Very. May I throw?"

"Aye." After handing her the stick, he watched as she positioned her body and used all of her arm to hurl the piece of wood. It landed at the edge of the clearing, close to his own. He whistled. "Not bad. Where did y' learn t' throw like that?"

"Jimmy Brannigan and I toss the ball back and forth."

"Jimmy's a good lad."

Jilly kicked at a tuft of grass on the ground. "He only plays with me when there's no one else, but I don't mind. I know I'm just a girl."

"And what's that supposed t' mean?" Frankie asked around a mouthful of sugar crisp.

She shrugged.

His hand closed around her wrist. "Look at me, Jilly."

He waited until her eyes were fixed on his face. "A lass is a fine companion. Why do y' think that when a lad grows into a man he chooses a woman to marry and not another man?"

She'd never thought of it that way before. "I can't run as fast or carry as much—"

He brushed away her argument. "A man doesn't want a horse, Jilly. He wants someone t' talk with, someone he can trust t' share his burdens, like y'r father does with y'r mother."

Jilly frowned. She had never before considered that her father might have burdens. Suddenly, an idea came to her. "When you're grown, will you choose a woman to marry?"

"Of course. Everyone gets married except for priests."

"Will you be a priest?"

He shook his head. "I haven't the callin'."

Her eyes blazed with light. "Will you marry me, Frankie? You can trust me, and I'll share your burdens. I'll share them better than anyone else ever could. Say you'll marry me, Frankie, please. I don't like anyone half as much as I like you."

Frankie stared at her in shock, the smile frozen on his face. Not in a million years would he have predicted this. He swallowed. How could he explain the impossibility of such a request without hurting her feelings? He could already imagine the look of horror on Lady Fitzgerald's face. Frankie wasn't good with words. He liked to read them and imagine them, even write them down on occasion when there was time. But to speak as Jilly did, quickly and clearly as soon as the thoughts came to her mind, was a skill he didn't have.

He wet his lips. Her face was alive with hope and that fragile vulnerability that made him want to kill anyone who dared to hurt her feelings. "I'm older than you, lass—"

"My father is nine years older than Mum. You're only three years older than me. It won't matter when we're grown."

"We won't be grown for a long time, and y'll be away at school. It wouldn't be fair t' hold you to a promise y' won't want t' keep later on."

"I will want to keep it," she insisted. "I know I will."

"We're not the same religion."

Jilly frowned. "What religion are you?"

"Catholic."

"Is being Catholic important to you?"

Ruffling the head of the collie puppy that lay panting at his feet, Frankie tried to speak casually. "I think it is, Jilly."

"Then I'll be a Catholic, too."

Her words melted something hard and tight inside his chest. He laughed. "I believe y' would, lass. I really believe y' would."

She slipped her hand inside his. "It's settled, then?"

Her palm was small and warm. His hand tightened around her fingers, and he swung her arm slightly as they walked to the edge of the thick growth of trees. "I'll tell you what, Jilly. I won't marry anyone else unless you do. That way, you can decide if y'r still of the same mind after y'r grown."

Jilly frowned. It wasn't the promise she wanted, but she suspected it was the best she would get from him. "All right."

Tilting back his head, Frankie squinted into the sun. "There's one more thing y' have to promise me, lass."

"What's that?"

"Don't mention a word of this t' anyone else. It will have t' be our secret."

She stopped, withdrew her hand, and planted herself firmly in front of him. "Why?" she asked bluntly.

"Y'r mother won't like it."

"I've already told you. My mother won't mind. She never minds anything I do."

"Christ, Jilly." Frankie shook his head. "This is different. She will mind, and so will y'r da. We're not the same, don't y' see?"

"Of course we're not the same. That's why I like you."

"Y' don't understand." He rested his hands on her shoulders. "Y'r Jillian Fitzgerald of Kildare Hall. Y'll have men lined up the length of the county when y'r old enough. They'll be rich and titled with pedigrees that go back a thousand years just as yours does. I'm not like that, Jilly. My grandda could barely read, and my da left school when he was younger than me. My sister, Kathleen, works as a maid, and she'll never be anythin' more. Y've a great bedroom all to y'rself in a house with sixty other rooms. I've nothin' like that, nor will I ever have. The most I can hope for is to educate myself out of Kilvara. I'll have a flat somewhere in the city and later maybe a house." He drew a deep breath and pushed aside the hair that had fallen over his forehead. "Don't y' see? Y'r family would think I'd forgotten my place if y' said we were plannin' to marry. They might tell me to stay away from here altogether, and then I couldn't help my da."

Jilly couldn't take her eyes off his face. Passion blazed within him as if it were a living thing. She didn't understand what any of it had to do with the two of them, but she knew that it mattered desperately to him. "I won't tell anyone," she whispered. "I promise I won't tell anyone until you want me to."

Frankie sighed and dropped his arms to his sides. Suddenly, he felt exhausted. She brought out emotions in him that he didn't know existed. Truthfully, he didn't know how he felt about Jillian Fitzgerald. He enjoyed her conversation. She made him smile with her constant barrage of questions. The first day he met her when she'd carried the dying collie into the kennel, and the next when she threw herself at her own brother in an attempt to defend him, Frankie knew she was out of the ordinary. But none of that accounted for the sick feeling in his stomach when she struggled against tears or the fierce anger that pooled in his chest that day in the village when Tommy Dougherty made fun of her.

"Thank you for the biscuits," he said slowly. "I've got t' get back. If y'r lucky, Nell might still be there."

"She said she would wait," Jilly said confidently. "Nell always does what she says."

"She must be a very loyal friend."

Jilly nodded. "I wish you could see her, Frankie."

He whistled for the dogs. "I'll be at the kennel if she can spare a minute."

"She can come to the kennel, but you won't be able to see her," Jilly explained as they walked side by side. "No one has ever seen her but me."

Startled, Frankie glanced at her. She stared straight ahead, refusing him all but her stoic profile. Poor little lass, he thought. She was so starved for friendship that she'd created an imaginary person. Reaching across the space that divided them, he took her hand in his own and kept it all the way to Kildare Hall.

"Jillian, this is ridiculous," said her mother. "I can't possibly allow it. Francis Maguire wouldn't be at all comfortable at your birthday party."

Jilly thrust out her lower lip. "If I can't have who I want, then I won't have a party at all."

"Pyers," his wife appealed to him, "explain to your daughter why this just won't do."

"She's my daughter now, is she?"

"Pyers, please."

"Mum's right, Jilly. Frankie's too big to come to your party. The chaps in the village will never let him live it down."

"If he doesn't want to come, I won't make him. But he's my friend, and it isn't polite not to ask him."

Pyers Fitzgerald stretched out his legs and leaned

back in the comfortable recliner that had been delivered that morning. "She's got a point, Margaret. Manners and all. Wouldn't do to offend anyone."

"Good gracious, Pyers." Margaret walked to the tea tray and poured herself another cup with a shaking hand. "He's a servant, or as good as one. How would it look to invite the kennel keeper's son and not the children of everyone else in service to us?"

Pyers looked across the room at his daughter. "What have you got to say to that, love?"

"Frankie is my friend. Although we should probably ask Jimmy Brannigan. He's my friend, too, even though I don't care for him as much as Frankie."

"Jimmy Brannigan?" Margaret's teacup was suspended halfway to her mouth. "Who on earth is Jimmy Brannigan?"

"Mr. Brannigan cuts our turf and brings it around to the kitchen on Mondays," Jilly replied. "Jimmy throws the ball with me."

Margaret's cheeks were very pink. "This is what comes from keeping us isolated in the country all year long, Pyers. How can the child possibly meet anyone?"

"She's young yet, Maggie. Not to worry. In a few years, we'll pension off the governess, and Jilly will be off to school. Plenty of connections at Kylemore Abbey."

Tears rose in Margaret's cornflower-blue eyes. "How can you be so cruel as to bring that up? Besides, it's a Catholic school. Why does Jillian have to go there?"

"Maggie." Pyers's laugh hovered on the edge of exasperation. "Since when have you objected to Catholics? You know it's the finest girls' school in all of Ireland. Fitzgeralds have always enrolled at Kylemore. Is there anything I can say that will please you?"

Margaret flushed. "If you will be so good as to give

Jillian an answer regarding the Francis Maguire issue, I
will see to the invitations."

"Very well, Jilly," her father said agreeably. "Invite
whom you please. After all, it is your party."

Pleased with the decision she knew was inevitable,
Jilly could afford to be magnanimous. She slipped her
hand inside her mother's. "I won't invite Jimmy, Mum.
It's just that Frankie is such a good friend, you see."

Margaret stared down into her daughter's face and
knew a sudden stabbing fear. Streaks of brown-gold hair
framed a face that was rapidly changing. Cheeks were
hollowing, roundness disappearing. Bones were prominent. Eyebrows arched, winglike, over eyes the color of
ocean foam, rising from the sea and touched with gold,
and that mouth—Margaret caught her breath. Jilly
would have to be very careful with a mouth like that.
Immediately, Margaret thought of Frankie Maguire and
groaned. She felt as if she were on a train hurtling
forward in a direction over which she had no control.

She knelt down and looked straight into her daughter's eyes. "You must promise me that you'll be kind
to everyone at your party, Jilly, not just Frankie. Please,
promise me that."

"Of course, Mum."

"And what of Nell? Shall we invite her as well?"

"Nell?" For a moment, Jilly's eyes went blank. She
recovered quickly. "I don't think so, Mum. Nell doesn't
visit me so much anymore. I have Frankie now."

With a low sound that was almost a moan, Margaret
Fitzgerald left the room.

He didn't come to the party, after all, begging off
with the excuse that he would be in Newry for the day.
Margaret breathed a sigh of relief. Apparently, Peter
Maguire had raised his boy correctly. She must remem-

ber to put a bit of something extra into the kennel keeper's Christmas envelope.

Nothing would have induced Frankie to come to a party hosted by Margaret Fitzgerald. But neither had he wanted to disappoint Jilly. He promised he would bring her present later that evening, after her guests had gone.

Lit up with anticipation, Jilly balanced a plate with two pieces of cake in one hand and a Thermos of lemonade in the other and headed toward the kennel.

He came shortly after she did, holding out a box wrapped in brown paper and tied with string. "Happy birthday, Jilly," he said softly.

Eagerly, she reached for the box and tore off the wrapper. Her eyes widened with pleasure. "It's lovely, Frankie. Whatever is it?"

"I'll show you." He took the glass dome, turned it upside down, and righted it again. Instantly, the water was alive with miniature dolphins swimming around a silvery castle. "It's supposed t' be the lost continent of Atlantis."

"Oh." She breathed reverently. "It's the most beautiful thing I've ever seen. You shouldn't have, Frankie. It must have been very dear."

He shrugged. "It's not every day that Jillian Fitzgerald has a birthday."

"Would you like some cake and lemonade?"

Frankie grinned and sat down at the small table. "Thank you, lass. I'd like that very much."

The cake was rich, and Jilly, who had her pudding every day, soon put her plate aside. She watched with interest as Frankie relished his last crumb. "What were you doing in Newry?" she asked.

Frankie washed down the last of his cake with a swig of lemonade. "Findin' y'r birthday present."

"What else?"

Frankie pushed aside the plate and considered his answer. How much could an eleven-year-old understand? "There was trouble in Belfast. Kilvara is too small t' hear all the news. I wanted t' know what happened."

"What kind of trouble?"

"The RUC fired into a group of protesters. Two men died."

"What were they protesting?"

He looked at her steadily. "There are some who want the North of Ireland to be united with the Republic. Others don't. Do y' know what the marchin' season is, Jilly?"

"Of course. It's when the Orangemen march through the streets to celebrate William of Orange's victory over King James."

"Not everyone believes we should be celebratin' such an event, and when the Orangemen march through those neighborhoods, fightin' breaks out and the RUC are called in."

"Who died?"

A thin white line appeared around Frankie's lips. "Two nationalists. The RUC don't kill loyalists. They only kill Catholics."

Deep in thought, Jilly leaned her chin on her hand. "Why?" she asked at last.

"Because the RUC are Protestant Orangemen themselves."

"Why don't the Catholics have their own RUC?"

Frankie laughed harshly. "They do, Jilly. They're called the Irish Republican Army. But they're an illegal force. When they're caught, they go to prison."

"It doesn't sound very fair to me," Jilly decided.

"Nor to me."

The expression on his face frightened her. "Are you angry, Frankie?"

"Not at you, lass."

"Did you know the men who died?"

"No."

Wisely, she remained silent and let him talk.

"They were only boys, Jilly, not much older than I am. Now they're dead, and all because they wanted the same things everyone does."

"You said they wanted us to be united with Ireland. Everyone doesn't want that."

His eyes were dark with anger. "More do than y' think, but that's not what I meant. Did y' know that it's nearly impossible for a Catholic to find work in the city just because he's a Catholic? Our votes don't count as much as Protestant votes, and housing is almost impossible to find in Catholic neighborhoods because no one wants t' build there. Do y' know why no one will build there, Jilly?"

She shook her head.

"Because every twelfth of July, bands of loyalists drink too much and burn down Catholic neighborhoods. It's enough to make a man join the IRA."

Clammy fear crawled up Jilly's spine. "But you won't, will you, Frankie? You won't join the IRA."

Her words brought him to his senses, and he smiled sheepishly. "What am I thinkin'? 'Tis a poor guest I am to be bringin' up the subject on y'r birthday."

Jilly sighed with relief. She had heard of the IRA. Her father cursed them regularly every time he had to wait at road blocks for British soldiers to search the cars ahead of him. The Fitzgerald Volvo was inevitably waved through, but the indignity of having one's neighbors harassed was annoying.

Frankie stood. "I should be leavin' now, Jilly. Thank you for the cake."

"Thank you for my present. It's the nicest one of all."

He moved toward the door. "I'll see y' tomorrow."

"Frankie." She caught up with him and touched his arm.

He turned around and smiled. Jilly stood on her toes and kissed his cheek. "Thank you for coming."

Frankie reached out to tug on a sausage-shaped curl. "It was my pleasure, lass."

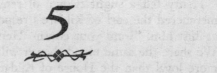

Whitehall Palace, London, 1537

Henry Tudor rubbed his aching leg. The pain was sharp, piercing. Spirits brought relief, but it was only temporary, and he hated the groggy feeling that dulled his senses and brought the pounding to his head. Everything was more difficult since Wolsey had acquired principles. For years, the cardinal had padded his coffers with gold from the royal treasury, mounted mistresses, bestowed land and favors on his bastards, only to refuse stubbornly to renounce his Catholicism. His reward was the executioner's blade. The good cardinal fought until the end, but he was no match for a Tudor.

Light from the casement window illuminated the room and the sinister figure of Henry's chief secretary. Thomas Cromwell pored over the rolls of parchment on the massive desk. Despite the pain in his leg, Henry managed a smirk. Cromwell was invaluable to him. Hated by gentry and common folk alike, with his sly rat's face, he was the current scapegoat for Henry's often ill-received strategies. The burning monasteries, the boarded-up churches, and the Geraldine executions could be laid directly at the feet of the priest-hater, Thomas Cromwell.

Henry felt a slight twinge of remorse when he remembered the earl of Kildare's response to the charge against him. "I am your cousin, Henry. We are Celts. We share the same blood. Never will you find a house more loyal than the House of Kildare." But the blood they shared was Plantagenet blood. Geraldine and Plantagenet, a dangerous combination when the Tudor succession was still not established.

Again, he rubbed his leg. The child that Jane Seymour carried in her belly would be his last. Henry could feel the ardor of his youth growing dimmer, replaced by pain and an ulcerated wound that refused to heal. It was a miracle that he had gotten Jane with child. She was young and fertile but very small. Daily he prayed that the child would be born alive. This time, it must be a boy. If not—

Henry refused to consider such a possibility. England could not be ruled by a woman. Tudor enemies surrounded her. Catholic Spain to the south. Catholic France to the east. Catholic Ireland and Scotland to the north. Without a king on her throne, England would succumb to the papist scourge. He clenched his fists and shouted even though his secretary was only feet away. "Cromwell, bring me the boy. Bring the last of the Geraldines. My heir will not be safe until every Fitzgerald is dead."

Thomas Cromwell crossed the room and knelt at the king's feet. Not by the slightest flicker of an expression did he reveal that such an order had been sent out the day before and was at this moment being executed. "It shall be done, Your Grace. Robert Montgomery was ever your faithful servant. Shall I give him your message?"

Robert Montgomery. Henry concentrated. Robert Montgomery. Robert— Then it came to him. The Welshman. "Yes. Send Robert to Ireland. He will find the boy."

Cromwell backed away toward the door. "It is already done, Your Grace."

Donore Castle

Nell wrung out the linen cloth and wiped her brother's feverish brow. His face was marked by the oozing boils of the dreaded pox, and his fever burned dangerously high. Fearing for their lives, the physician had left Donore Castle the day before with the *gallowglass* and the last of the servants. He had warned Nell that the fever would rise before it fell. The boy's tenuous hold on life would grow slim. Nell brushed away tears as she bathed the face of the only member of her family still living. There was Margaret, of course. But since her marriage to the earl of Ormond, Margaret had ceased to be a Fitzgerald.

"Please, Gerald," Nell pleaded. "Don't die." Her eyes blurred, and she lowered her head into her hands. It was a miracle that after so many sleepless nights, she wasn't ill herself. After her mother's death, Nell's mind had gone numb as if it recognized that she could bear no more and still keep her fragile hold on sanity. It was enough that she grub for food, that she search the grounds for kindling, that she bathe the emaciated body of her brother, that she wake and sleep and wake again. There was only today, only this moment and the next and the next after that. She dare not think of tomorrow. For with thoughts of tomorrow would come other thoughts, dangerous thoughts.

For weeks, she had struggled to keep her focus. But now, on the edge of sleep, her mind wandered. What would happen to them now, to the last of the mighty Fitzgeralds of Kildare, whose roots were embedded in the ashes of Troy, in Latium and Etruria, in the glory of ancient Florence, in Normandy with the Conqueror? From Wales, they had invaded Ireland, ruling within and beyond the Pale for four centuries, only to be snuffed out by a man, an English king, a cousin who feared his own mortality and searched beyond the borders of the Pale for an eleven-year-old boy and his sister.

Nell had exhausted her options long ago. Her first inclination had been to seek refuge with the O'Flahertys at Aughnanure. The king would not risk his gold or his army to find her in the wilds of Galway. But there was Donal to consider. For the O'Flahertys, who had no stake in the future of the House of Kildare, it would mean war with England. She would not ask Donal to risk his birthright for her brother. Nor could she tell him where she was. The Fitzgerald standard had fallen. If her letter were to fall into the wrong hands, Henry would find them. She shivered. Her only hope lay with her cousin, the earl of Desmond, head of the Munster Geraldines.

Unlike her own, this branch of Geraldines harbored a deep mistrust of the English. They had cut themselves off from England completely, becoming more Irish than the Irish themselves, taking on their customs, their clothing, their language, refusing to attend court or the council in Dublin. Every native chief owed them fealty. For that reason, she must take Gerald to Desmond at Askeaton Castle.

She must have slept. When she opened her eyes, the light from the narrow recessed window had completely disappeared, and the chamber was shrouded in darkness. Shivering, she left the room and returned with a torch, touching it to the mound of stacked kindling in the hearth. She pulled her cape around her shoulders and waited for the chill to leave her bones. Gerald stirred. Outside, there was a sound on the cobbles. Nell froze. Horses with riders waited at the gates.

Fear spurred her forward. Securing the door against the chill, she left Gerald asleep in the warmth of the heated room and moved swiftly down the spiral stairs into the courtyard and the ground level of the barbican. Keeping out of sight, she peeked through the portcullis, and her eyes widened. There were twenty men, all with the stirrupless saddles, long mantles, and fringed collars of the native Irish.

With a fluid, effortless motion, a single rider separated himself from his horse and walked toward the portcullis gate. Nell's throat closed with relief. She knew of only one man who walked with that light, athletic gait. Even now, she could see the fall of his hair, black as a crow's wing beneath the moonlight. Donal. Thanks be to God! Her prayers had been answered. It was Donal O'Flaherty.

She whispered his name into the hushed darkness. "Donal."

He stopped and turned toward the sound of her voice. "Nell?" he said incredulously. "Nell, is that you?"

"I'm here, Donal, in the barbican."

He moved toward the loop. "Let me in."

"I cannot. 'Tis the pox."

He stretched his arm through the aperture. "Are you affected?"

"Not I. 'Tis Gerald." She stepped backward. "Come no closer, Donal. You dare not risk it."

"By the sword of Conor, Nell. I've searched the length of Ireland for you. Do you think I would leave you? Open the gates. You're coming with me to Aughnanure."

He still wanted her. It was more than she'd hoped for. But it couldn't be. Not yet. Summoning the last of her reserves, she refused him. "You've not had the fever. Come back in a se'enight. If Gerald lives, we shall accept your escort to the earl of Desmond at Askeaton Castle. If he dies—" Her voice broke. "If he dies, I'll come with you to Aughnanure."

Donal understood her worry, but he did not share it. He was pure Irish from a lineage that was already old three thousand years ago when his ancestors built the great rath of *Emain Macha* near Armagh. He carried the title of chieftain, the most ancient, most prestigious title in all of Ireland. Donal O'Flaherty feared no one, most especially not this Welsh upstart on the English throne. As far as the O'Flahertys were concerned, there was only one law in all of Ireland, and that was Brehon law. "Come closer, Nell," he said softly.

She hesitated.

"I only want to see your face. I won't touch you."

Nell moved toward him and lifted her chin, swallowing bravely. She was dreadfully thin, and weeks had gone by since she'd bathed properly and washed her hair. It was not an auspicious way to meet one's future husband after nearly a year.

Donal stared down into the gaunt beauty of Nell's tear-smudged face, and his heart broke. Forgetting his promise, he reached through the aperture and cupped her chin. "Don't cry, *a stor*," he murmured softly. "I won't leave you. We shall camp in the glen, and at the end of the week, you will leave this place and never come back."

His tenderness weakened her. She leaned against him briefly, caught up his hand and pressed her mouth to his palm. His skin tasted of salt and leather. Quickly, she thrust his arm away, afraid that the price for so much pleasure would be more than she could pay. "*Dia duit*, Donal," she said softly.

"*Dia es muir duit*, Nell."

Unable to watch him ride away, she walked quickly across the courtyard and up the stone stairs into the chamber she shared with Gerald.

The Tower of London

Silken Thomas sat on the wooden bench and stared at the two initials he'd carved in the stone wall. The lettering was crude, almost infantile, but it couldn't be helped. His chisel had been a spoon. Not that it mattered. No one would pass judgment. No one cared. All who mattered to him in the world were here with him, sentenced to die before him so that he might watch what he had caused. Damn Leonard Gray. He'd assured the Geraldines they would be released after Henry had secured promises of fealty. Now, Silken Thomas wondered if it had ever been true or if Gray had lied from the beginning.

Alone in his tower room, Thomas had time for reflection. It was his own rash temper that had brought down his house, beginning with the scene in St. Mary's Abbey before the King's Council. Throwing down his sword and pledging himself enemy to the king had been the act of a hot-tempered child. There was no room for child's play in the world of English politics. For his immaturity, he would pay with his life, and for their loyalty to him, his uncles would die with him, hanged, then drawn and quartered at Tyburn.

He lowered his head into his hands and was surprised to feel the wet of tears against his face. Nell and his mother would blame him. He would have liked to see his mother again.

Voices on the stairs disturbed his reverie. It was time. They had come for him, before he was ready. He almost smiled at the absurdity of his own mind. Was a man ever ready to die?

In the courtyard, his eyes burned from the sun's glare, and he lifted his hand to shade himself. His uncles stood in a line between two rows of guards. Averting his eyes, Silken Thomas embraced them quickly. His guilt was nearly a physical thing.

They were forced to lie spreadeagled and bound tightly on top of the horse-pulled hurdles. The portcullis was raised. Across the evil-smelling waters of the moat into the city of London, by way of Tower Street and into the Shambles, they came.

Crowds gathered to watch. The spectacle was not an unusual one. Since King Henry's break with the Church, the citizens of London and the surrounding countryside had witnessed many a noble's execution, although one family had never before been so unfairly represented.

The hurdles rolled through Newgate and Snow Hill. At Tyburn, the crowd had swelled to more than a hundred. It was February. A cold wind had risen from the Thames. Five ropes swung against a pewter-colored sky, and a butcher's block stood atop a high platform.

Silken Thomas looked at the ropes, and a curious trembling took hold of his body. Garrett, the uncle closest to his own age, laid a hand on his shoulder and squeezed. "Dear Jesus, forgive me," Thomas whispered.

Garrett nodded and looked toward the ropes. "It will be over soon."

John was the first to be hanged. The executioner climbed the stairs of the platform and lifted two knives and a cleaver above his head. A collective murmur rose from the spectators, as if it came from one throat. John was dragged up the stairs. The rope was placed around his neck. Slowly, he was hoisted until his feet left the ground. Silken Thomas saw his uncle's body jerk and closed his eyes.

He missed the lowering of John's nearly unconscious body to the block, missed the first cut of the knife. He did not miss John's inhuman shriek of pain, the crowd's roar, the smack of limbs as they were tossed into the wooden bin. He did not miss the scent of fresh blood.

Five times the procedure was repeated. Five times Geraldine limbs were cut off, heads severed. When it was his turn, Silken Thomas had entered that state of mind where pain did not go. He welcomed the executioner's blade, welcomed his passing into a place where there was no sight, no sound, no smell.

While his entrails still lay on the wet boards of the block, the executioner held up the golden head of Thomas Fitzgerald. Silently, the crowd looked on. A woman bowed her head and wept.

To the north, in the cold dampness of Donore Castle, Gerald Fitzgerald, tenth earl of Kildare, awoke without the fever. Rubbing his eyes, he looked around the dim chamber. "I'm hungry, Nell," he said, "where are we?"

For the first time in weeks, Nell laughed. "We are at Donore, love. Lie still, and I'll bring you food."

Gerald managed most of the weak gruel that Nell spooned down his reluctant throat before he fell back upon his pillow and slept again. Relieved and hopeful that her brother might live after all, Nell stirred the

fire, added kindling, and considered the possibility of a
bath. It would not be a satisfying one. She was not
strong enough to lift the many buckets it would take to
fill the wooden tub in the corner of the room. But at
least she would be clean.

More than an hour had passed, and the first bucket
of snow she'd lugged up the twisting stairs and heated
to boiling was now stale and tepid, but it would be
comfortably warm when she added the one that had
just now begun to steam. Working quickly, Nell untied
the soft leather coil from around her hips, lifted her
gown over her head, and dropped them both on the
floor. She glanced over at Gerald. He hadn't moved.
Shivering, she pulled off her shift, stepped into the tub,
and sat down. Disappointingly, the water only came up
to her belly, but the feel of its delicious warmth against
her skin was an unexpected shock of pure pleasure. She
moaned and leaned back. Gerald would sleep for hours.
There was no need to hurry.

A rider with only five *gallowglass* pushed his mount
through the February snow, toward the men camped in
the clearing outside Donore Castle. The man's short
cape, velvet doublet, and low flat hat proclaimed him
an Englishman.

Donal O'Flaherty sat on his haunches before a smoldering fire. Only the tightening of his jaw and the casual
movement of his hand toward the dirk at his waist gave
away his prejudice. He rose as Leonard Gray approached. The man was out of breath, and his face was
very red. Silently, Donal waited, offering no welcome,
until the king's deputy dismounted.

"My God, O'Flaherty, 'tis sad news I bring."

"Speak, Lord Gray."

Sweat ran down his florid cheeks. "Three weeks past,

the Geraldines came under the executioner's knife by order of the king."

Donal nodded. "It was expected. We heard the news of their sentencing nearly a month ago." He left unsaid the words that burned in his brain. *But for your interference, they might still be alive.*

Leonard Gray shook his head. " 'Tis not for old news that I risked this journey. Henry demands the boy. Gerald is heir to castles and land. The king will not rest unless he is dead. 'Tis an old Tudor story, to murder the rightful heir and steal what is his."

"Your sentiment does not sit well on the lips of the king's deputy," Donal said contemptuously. "Why are you here, my lord?"

Gray whitened. "I swear by all that is holy that I believed the king when he offered clemency. I am not the enemy, O'Flaherty. Gerald is my kinsman. Do you think I relish thoughts of dead schoolboys? I came only to warn them."

"There is pox at Donore," said Donal. "The boy may not live."

"If he does, will you take him?"

Donal met Leonard Gray's pale gaze steadily. "No," he said at last, offering nothing more.

Gray backed away. "Keep him far from the Pale, O'Flaherty. Trust no one, especially the countess of Ormond. The king's eyes are everywhere."

Donal waited until Gray and his entourage were no more than dark specks against the snow. Ormond's countess was Margaret Fitzgerald, Nell's sister and a most powerful adversary. He needed answers, quickly. Swinging himself up on his horse, he ordered his men to their saddles before heading for the gates of Donore.

Nell stared out the small slitted window of her chamber at the men camped in the snow. It was something she did every day, as much to alleviate her boredom as to reassure herself that they were still there. Donore was the most spartan of her father's estates, and she'd brought nothing with her but a change of clothing, her brushes, and a small jeweled dirk that she kept tucked inside her girdle.

Today there had been more activity than usual in the O'Flaherty camp. Several riders had approached, stayed only a moment, and departed again. Now a single rider was making his way toward the gates. He was too far away for her to see his features, but Nell was sure he was Donal. Color rose in her cheeks. She was clean, her gown was fresh, and Gerald's fever was gone.

Pulling on her cloak, she moved swiftly down the stairs and across the courtyard to throw back the bolt on the heavy gates. Then she hurried into the small hall and lit the fire. By the time he arrived, the worst of the chill was gone. Candles flickered on the mantel, reflecting the jewel-bright colors of the stained-glass windows lining the room. On a small table, twin goblets bearing the crest of the Fitzgeralds were filled with mulled wine.

Donal stepped into the room, stripped off his gloves, and rubbed his arms against the cold. He looked around appreciatively. Even a remote Fitzgerald outpost like Donore was appointed with more luxury than Aughna-nure. Lured by the warmth, he walked to the hearth and held out his hands to the licking flames. Where was Nell?

As if in answer to his silent question, she stepped out of the shadows. "Welcome, Donal," she said softly, and smiled.

He turned quickly, all thoughts of comfort forgotten. His mouth dropped, and the cool implacability for which he was known disappeared entirely from his face.

It had been nearly a year since he had really seen her, and now he looked his fill.

Her face was thinner than he remembered, the bones sharp and clean under her skin. Her mouth was wide, her teeth even and white. Winged brows slightly darker than her hair framed hazel eyes that carried equal amounts of green and brown and gold, harvest colors, the same gold as her hair that hung loose, thick, and straight to her knees. He had never seen her hair loose. He imagined it wrapped around his hand, and his fingers curled. She was small, but no man alive would find fault with her figure. Donal could see the pulse moving at the base of her throat. Christ. Had celibacy affected his brain, or was she truly the most beautiful thing he'd ever seen?

"Nell," he whispered hoarsely.

"Gerald lives," she said, not moving from her place.

She would not be coming with him to Aughnanure. Donal willed his expression into smooth lines of pleasure. "Thank God."

"You will take us to Desmond?"

"Aye."

Why were they discussing this? She was his betrothed. They hadn't seen each other in a year, and they were alone in a warm, comfortable room.

Nell frowned. "Donal, are you pleased to see me?"

He looked startled. "Of course. Why would you ask such a question?"

Her eyes widened innocently. "Are your legs made of wood that they can no longer move?"

He turned his back to her and stared into the fire. A smiled played at the corners of his mouth. She was very good with words. He'd forgotten that. But he'd driven his men through the thick of winter to protect her, and still she insisted on taking Gerald to Desmond. If the great earl of Desmond cared so much for his cousin, where was he? Donal had every intention of keeping his promise, but first Nell must come to him.

"Donal?" She sounded worried.

"I can hear, Nell." He turned around. "Perhaps 'tis I who should ask the questions."

She frowned. "I don't understand."

"Are you pleased to see me?"

The color left her cheeks. She nearly ran across the room to where he stood and clutched his arm. "I've thought of nothing but you for months. Our marriage is fated, Donal. There is no one else for me."

He lifted her chin and stared steadily into her eyes. "Why, then, will you not bring the boy and come home with me?"

She answered honestly. "You are not Geraldine. Henry has no quarrel with you. I would not risk your house for mine."

His hand tightened on her chin. "Leave Gerald with Desmond and come with me. He is of an age to be fostered."

Her hand rested on his chest. All at once, Donal found it difficult to breathe. "I will," she said, "as soon as he is well."

He released his breath. "Leonard Gray came to me this morning. Henry demands Gerald's surrender." He squeezed her hand. "Your father and Silken Thomas are dead, Nell."

She nodded. "I have already mourned. 'Tis Gerald I must think of now."

"We must leave immediately."

Nell rested both hands on his chest and looked up at him through her eyelashes. "Surely not immediately, Donal," she said softly. "I have wine, the room is warm, and it has been such an endless length of time since I have seen you."

The ball of warmth that had begun in Donal's chest when she agreed to come with him radiated into every part of his body. He blazed with heat. Taking care not to frighten her, he slipped one arm around her waist and drew her to him. His free hand slid up her throat and around the back of her neck. Slowly, he bent his head and kissed her. Her mouth, inexperienced at first, found its place and then opened. She pressed against him, filling the places only a woman could fill.

Donal forgot that the king's men were nearly upon them. He forgot that an eleven-year-old boy slept upstairs, that Gray had warned him of the countess of Ormond, and that his men waited impatiently in the snow for his return. All he knew was that silver-gold hair smelled of sunlight, that a woman's lips and hands were all that he wanted of heaven, and that the fires in his body, long dormant since his betrothal to Nell, had leaped to life with an intensity that would not be quenched.

6

Kildare Hall, 1974

"Trout aren't stupid, Jillian," Frankie said gently. "Y've got to keep quiet."

Stung by the rebuke, Jilly climbed over the rocks and headed upstream to find her own spot. She hadn't mastered the art of fly-fishing yet, but she could cast as well as anyone. Stepping into the current, she found her balance and with a quick flick of her wrist sent the line far out into the water. She didn't need Frankie Maguire, thank you very much. He could just keep his comments to himself.

Two hours later, he found her barefoot, asleep in the sun, her catch staked nearby in the running water. Deciding not to wake her just yet, he spread the blanket and laid out the lunch Mrs. Barbour had prepared for them. He was nearly finished when she opened her eyes.

"I hope y'r hungry," he said. "There's enough food here for a banquet."

Keeping her mouth shut, Jilly nodded and reached for a deviled egg.

"Are y' not speakin' t' me, Jilly?"

"You said I talk too much." There was no mistaking the frosty note in her voice.

"You were scarin' the fish."

"I wasn't. They're underwater. No one can hear anything underwater."

Frankie struggled to keep a straight face. "I'm sorry, Jilly. I didn't mean t' upset you."

She ate her egg without speaking, wiped her fingers, and poured lemonade into her cup.

Frankie bit into a sandwich. "Y'll be glad t' hear that I'll be away for a while. I'm goin' int' Belfast with Willie McLeish for my A levels."

"When are you coming back?" Her vow to remain silent disappeared.

Hiding a grin in his cup of lemonade, Frankie shrugged his shoulders. "A week, maybe two. My auntie lives there. I'll be stayin' with her."

Jilly bit her lip. It was summer, and this would be her last before she left for boarding school. She had expected to have Frankie to herself. "There's trouble in Belfast," she said.

"I know."

"Why are you going?"

Frankie turned to her eagerly, their quarrel forgotten. "The British are settin' up a government where power is shared between the Protestants and Catholics. I want t' be where it's happenin', and the place is Belfast."

Leaving her lemonade untouched, Jilly turned to stare out over the stream, showing him only her profile. "Do you think our lives will be any different, Frankie?"

Struck by the maturity of her question, he stared at her, noticing for the first time the way the morning light outlined the delicate edge of her cheek and chin, the shape of her nose, and the pure clean line of her throat. He remembered that she was only thirteen, and a wave of color swept across his face.

Turning away, he considered her question. "Maybe not so different, but at least we'll have hope for somethin' better. That's more than we have now."

Slowly, she turned to look at him with that new maturity he had never noticed before. "What could be better than this?" She waved her arm to encompass their surroundings.

"For me, this is the exception," he said, keeping his gaze averted. "You wouldn't know about that."

"It's not always like this for me, either, Frankie. Would you care to change places and see?"

"Don't be ridiculous."

"Answer the question. Would you want to go home to my family, to Terrence, my mother and my father?"

"Perhaps not Terrence," he said, attempting a note of levity.

"I didn't think so."

She stood and walked toward the stream to dip her feet. Frankie couldn't take his eyes off the slender curves of her bare legs under the rolled-up overalls or the way her body dipped in at the waist and flared slightly at her hips. Christ, what was the matter with him? This was Jilly. She was a schoolgirl, and he was nearly seventeen. There were plenty of girls in the village for what he had in mind, even more in Belfast. His spirits lifted.

Tomorrow, Monday, was the day he would leave. By Wednesday, his examinations would be over, and he would have seven days to himself, seven days of freedom, of pubs and films, of Guinness and music, seven days of museums and theater, of shops and *craic* and women. Sheer heaven to one who measured the success of his entertainment by the size of the crowds in Kilvara on market day. Tomorrow, he would have forgotten all about his sudden fascination with a tomboy with too many freckles, a girl who thought fishing for trout was the best life had to offer, a girl he had no business noticing in the first place.

The streets of Belfast were dirtier and more crowded than Frankie expected. But they weren't a disappointment. *Disappointment* would be too strong a word. A Catholic from a town like Kilvara was born into disappointment. Like original sin, he was weaned on it, raised on it. Disappointment was trudging to the privy in February, thirty frozen meters from the house. Disappointment was oats for breakfast, oat cakes for tea, and potatoes for dinner. Disappointment was going so long without meat that the smell of it cooking raised the saliva in a boy's mouth. Disappointment was working until bones ached and muscles burned and eyes were too tired to do more than stare blankly at school books, their black print blurring across the pages.

Catholic Belfast was dirty and busy and exciting. Divided from the Protestant Shankill by the winding Springfield Road, the Clonard was a mix of row houses, pubs, shops, grade schools, churches, vendors, and news agents. Nuns walked freely down streets with odd-sounding names like Kashmir and Bombay. At Mackie's, the foundry bordering the Shankill, Protestants on their breaks traded insults with unemployed Catholics loitering on the corner. Men cursed and drank and sang with a reckless abandon not found in small towns like Newry and Kilvara. Priests from the Redemptorist Monastery frequented the streets Monday through Friday, calling out greetings to their cursing, spatting parishioners. They drank in the tea shops, read in the reading rooms, and on Saturday, cloaked in the dark anonymity of confessionals, wiped sins clean for the celebration of the eucharist on Sunday morning.

Frankie loved it. Never had he felt such energy. His body throbbed with the rhythm of the city. He measured his days by the pealing of church bells, the bellow of fog horns, the whistle of factories, the screech of delivery trucks, the monotone shouts of paperboys hawking *The Telegram* in Donegall Square and the Shankill and *The Irish Times* in the Falls, Portadown, and Andersonstown.

Stormont Castle, the center of British occupation, hummed with a life of its own. Everyone, from Belfast's member of Parliament to the lowliest drunk who collected his dole on Friday afternoon and drank it away the same night, knew that the future of loyalist supremacy was toppling. Even David Temple, one of Belfast's most educated and eloquent Protestant politicians, advocated the sharing of power with Catholics. Only radical extremists like the Ulster Defense Alliance and the Ulster Volunteer Force, paramilitary organizations that boasted of murdering Catholics, railed against the compromise.

Catholic Belfast was drunk with anticipation. The tricolor fluttered from every row house. Curbs were painted green, white, and orange. Sinn Fein posters the size of billboards sprang up overnight. Frankie and the fifteen thousand unsuspecting residents of the Clonard were delirious with excitement. At last, Catholics would be represented in the North.

Because he kept country hours, Frankie was one of the first to learn that it was not to be. His morning ritual began with a stop at O'Brian's café on the Falls Road for his tea and a paper. Immersing himself for nearly two hours, he would read the entire newspaper before the town woke.

The morning headlines announced the strike first. The Reverend Ian Paisley, a staunch proponent of "Northern Ireland for Protestants," called for a government recall. All electric lines had been cut, and petrol would no longer be sold in the stations.

Frankie folded the newspaper carefully, stood, and walked out the door into the empty street. The knot in his stomach that began when he read the headlines had intensified to a dull ache. The elections that had brought such hope to the hearts of nearly half the population of Ulster were a farce. There would be no democratic process in Northern Ireland. Catholics would never sit in Parliament. Gerry McLeish said it all along. The loyalists would never share power unless they were forced into it, and the only force they recognized was the Irish Republican Army.

Frankie had no idea how he ended up in front of the Sinn Fein office. He certainly hadn't intended it. But now that he was here, the tricolor draped across the inside of the window was oddly comforting. It was just past eight o'clock, but already he heard voices inside. He stepped up to the door and knocked.

A long minute passed before Frankie heard the sound of footsteps moving in his direction. A tall, thin young man with a full beard, a head of curly dark hair, and piercing black eyes opened the door. "Aye, lad. How can I help you?"

"I want to join the Irish Republican Army," Frankie blurted out.

"Jaysus, lad." The man grabbed his arm, pulled him inside, and slammed the door. "What on earth are y' thinkin' t' be tellin' a stranger somethin' like that?"

"Is this the place?" Frankie demanded. "Is this the place t' join?"

The dark eyes narrowed. "Slow down, lad. What's y'r name?"

"Frankie Maguire."

"Who told you t' come here?"

Frankie shrugged. "Everyone knows this is the Sinn Fein office."

"Is it Sinn Fein y'r wantin' to join or the IRA?"

"Aren't they the same?"

The man held out his hand, and Frankie took it. "I'm Robbie Wilson, lad, and they are not the same. Sinn Fein is legal, the IRA isn't."

"Is that the only difference?"

"Just about." He waved Frankie into a straight-backed chair. "Have a seat. I'll be back."

Frankie watched as he disappeared down the hall. Then he looked around. The room was sparse, with freshly painted white walls and no pictures. A desk, completely bare except for a notepad and pen, faced the front door. Beside it sat a small nightstand with a hot plate and an electric kettle. Tea bags were neatly stacked in containers beside a bowl of sugar, and two half-filled cups shared their saucers with empty biscuit wrappers crumbled into tiny balls. Frankie no longer heard voices from another room.

Less than five minutes later, Wilson returned, pulled another chair opposite Frankie, and sat down. "Tell me about y'rself, lad. Y'r not from Belfast, are you?"

"No. I was born in Kilvara."

"Any IRA activity in Kilvara?"

"None that I've seen."

"It's in the middle of sheep country, isn't it?"

"Aye."

Wilson leaned back in his chair. "Mostly Catholic, if I recall, except for the land around it."

Frankie's face lost all expression. "The Fitzgeralds own the land."

"Tough landlord, is he?"

"No, sir."

Wilson looked steadily at the tall boy with the startling gray eyes and noted that he desperately needed a new jacket. "Why are y' itchin' to join the IRA?"

Frankie's fists clenched. "They're not going to let us in, not ever," he said hotly. "The only way is t' fight 'em."

Robbie Wilson stretched out his long legs. "Are you alone in this, Frankie, or does y'r family share your politics?"

"No one knows anythin' about me. The only person I ever talk to is—" He stopped. "She knows nothin' about this, either."

"You've got a girl back home?" Wilson asked casually.

"No, sir. Jilly's not a girl." He frowned. "I mean, she's a girl, but she's not for me. She's Pyers Fitzgerald's daughter, and she's Protestant."

Wilson stared long and hard at the boy seated before him, wondering if the lad had any idea how much he'd divulged with such a confession. There was more here than met the eye. How did a Catholic laborer with shabby clothes and an unschooled accent capture the interest of the daughter of one of the richest men in Northern Ireland? Quickly, he made his decision. Leaning forward, elbows on his knees, he said, "Let me tell you a bit about the provisional IRA."

Burning lorries, manned by masked Protestants blocking the entrance to the Falls, cemented Frankie's decision. He squeezed through a hole in the fence that separated Springfield Road from the Shankill. Along the barrier, bonfires flared, illuminating the faces of teenagers, smoking and drinking beer and gesturing angrily at masked men arming the barricades. Men dressed in the official uniforms of Ulster's police force, the RUC, stood by laughing and chatting with the masked men. A wave of fury rose in Frankie's chest, and he turned away.

Rows of dark, silent houses stretched out before him. Not a single electric light relieved the blackness. His aunt greeted him. "Thank God y'r home, Frankie." She shooed him inside and locked the door. "I imagined the worst. First the lights went, and now we're barricaded into the neighborhood. There's soup on the stove. The Lord was on my side when I decided on wood instead of gas. At least we've hot food in the house."

A single candle flickered on the table. Frankie lowered himself into a chair and waited to be served. Mary Boyle was his mother's sister, and by his standards, her two-bedroom house was a palace. It even had its own toilet. Since the death of her husband, she lived alone. Having Frankie in the house brought the bounce back to her step.

She set a plate of wheaten bread with a single pat of butter before him, walked back to the stove for the soup, and brought two bowls to the table. Frankie sniffed appreciatively. Aunt Mary believed in eating well. The broth was rich with meat. She watched while he ate nearly half the bowl before she picked up her spoon.

"This is delicious, Aunt Mary," he said sincerely. "Thank you for waitin' on me."

"Will y' be leavin' now, Frankie?" she asked anxiously.

He thought of his conversation with Robbie Wilson

and shook his head. "Not just yet. The whole thing may blow over."

She set down her spoon, leaving her soup untouched. "They're threatenin' t' close the water and sewer plants. I don't know how we'll manage. Think of the disease."

He smiled reassuringly across the table. "I think we've seen the worst of it."

But the worst was something not even Frankie could have foreseen. Fourteen days later, every moderate unionist who'd expressed an interest in sharing power with nationalists pulled out of the Stormant talks and resigned, but not until three bombs had been detonated in the Republic, killing thirty-three people, not until masked gunmen closed shops, took over factories, and ordered everyone out, not until all water and sewage relief had been cut off to everyone in the county, not until the hum of industry in the entire six counties had been effectively put to a stop, and not until every Catholic was convinced he would be slaughtered at the hands of Protestant death squads. At the end of those fourteen days, Ulster was as staunchly and firmly a part of the British Empire as it had ever been.

Frankie Maguire had left Kilvara with the youthful exuberance of a lad who believed in miracles. His original two-week stay had become two months. When he returned to the small town where he was born, he was a harder, more cynical version of himself.

It wasn't an obvious difference. Jilly couldn't put her finger on it. He went about his business as usual, working the dogs, performing odd jobs for his father. But he spoke only when he had to, and he smiled less often than he had before. The strangest change of all, and one that no one else seemed to notice, was that he no longer stuttered. Not that he ever had with her, but now, for some inexplicable reason, the speech impediment had disappeared entirely. When he spoke, it was with the cold, clear purpose of delivering a message or answering a question. Gone was their cheerful conversation amidst the fading, sepia-toned light of afternoons in the kennel. No longer did they share the witty banter of a comfortable friendship or the unexpected revelation of a sudden epiphany. Frankie had gone away from her completely.

If only he hadn't gone to Belfast. With the simple logic of childhood, Jilly rationalized that the city had changed him. Somewhere in the streets of Northern Ireland's capital, Frankie Maguire's soul wandered without its body. When or even if it would come back, she had no idea. There was nothing to do but wait.

Jilly sat on the knoll above Lough Neath absorbing the unusual heat that lay heavy and shimmering over the water. It was late summer. Soon she would leave for Kylemore Abbey. Normally, she would have lamented the end of her holiday, the loss of freedom, the structure of living her life by the ringing of bells and the hands of the clock. But this year was different. Frankie was different. She could only hope that the sooner she left Kildare Hall, the sooner she could return and everything would be the same again. She sighed, leaned back on her elbows, and closed her eyes. The drugging warmth of the sun worked its magic, and she dozed off.

Frankie released the stone and watched it skip across the lake, breaking the glassy stillness and sending concentric ripples to the shoreline. At least his aim never failed him. Neither did the dogs. He reached down to caress the bib of the collie beside him. The Fitzgerald champions were trained from birth to behave predictably, exhibiting the manners of true show dogs. Only the best came from the Kildare kennels. No incessant barking, nipping, or growling was tolerated. No bib could be muddy, no coat too dark, no ear less than perfect. All noses must be within the correct dimensions, all paws must be white, all gums a deep pink, all eyes a deep, dark brown. The Kildare collies always bred true, which was why the breeding and the puppies that resulted commanded ludicrous fees. Frankie's mouth twisted bitterly. If only his own life could be so easily arranged.

Peter Maguire could no longer perform the services required of the Fitzgerald's kennel keeper without his help, yet he had no intention of retiring. Neither did Pyers Fitzgerald, as far as Frankie knew, intend to pension his father off. It was a problem without a solution. Frankie chafed at the delay of his own plans. With every passing day, he ached to leave Kilvara and begin his life. Instinctively, he began withdrawing from everyone he cared about.

The Maguires had never been a communicative family. Peter was up before dawn, bicycling the five miles to and from Kildare, working long hours and nodding off shortly after tea. He had little time for his children. Kathleen had moved out of the Maguires' tiny cottage in the village to a room in Kildare Hall's servants' quarters. Occasionally, Frankie met his sister for an afternoon meal. But Kathleen, infatuated with Terrence Fitzgerald, knew that Frankie disapproved and was only too happy when he made his excuses.

It was Jilly whose life had changed. To Frankie's credit, he understood that she was the one who would suffer the most by his absence and deliberately began the separation process that could have only one conclusion.

That he would suffer as well did not yet occur to

him. That would come later, when his world was measured by four bare walls and a barbed-wire fence, when
the scent of feminine perfume drove him over the edge,
when the memory of sun-streaked hair and freckled
cheeks woke him in the night, his sheets drenched with
sweat, shaking and terrified that he would never see the
face behind them again.

But Frankie was not born fey, nor did he believe in
the sight. So he went on his way, ruthlessly exorcising
from his life everyone he loved, everyone he felt was
even slightly dependent upon him. His father and Kathleen were surprisingly easy. It was Jilly who held his
heart, Jilly who'd defended him, Jilly who believed they
would spend their lives together, Jilly who trusted him
with the secrets of her soul, Jilly whose shining, ocean-
colored eyes shifted between need and devotion. How
could he ever say goodbye to Jilly?

7

Ireland, 1537

Through a causeway bordered by boglands and forests of primeval black oak, their branches laden with fresh snow, Donal O'Flaherty led Nell, his men, and the cart upon which Gerald Fitzgerald slept away his fever. Donal had seen immediately that the boy, frail and mottled with illness, could never sit astride a horse. He ordered a covered wicker basket to be filled with hay and blankets. There Gerald slept the untroubled sleep of a child while those entrusted with his life cursed at every snapping twig, every crack of thin ice, every twisted rut that threw the unwieldy cart off balance.

The journey seemed endless. Donal, who'd crossed the entirety of Ireland in four days, chafed at the delay. The countess of Ormond had eyes in the back of her head, and if she were truly Gerald's enemy, she would know of their halting progress. In a fair fight, Donal knew his men to be superior to Irish forces, but he had only a small company, and the countess of Ormond had the might of England behind her.

He frowned, turned back to look at Nell, and felt his heart contract. She had done nothing more than lift her arm to brush a loose strand of hair away from her forehead. Everything she did, the slightest movement, the way she arranged her cloak, the tilt of her head, the low, soft laughter that bubbled freely within her, filled him with wonder. Where had a woman raised amidst the splendor of Maynooth learned to accept such hardship uncomplainingly?

It was for her that he relinquished his comfort. In winter, Aughnanure was sinful in its welcome and accommodation. Fires, taller than a man, roared in every room, and wine and ale flowed. Visitors spent the season sated with drink, curled up in warm furs, their daze interrupted by an occasional hunt or wager of the dice. Were it not for Nell, Donal would be home, his head filled with nothing more than the tales of his bard relaying the past glories of his ancestors.

Geraldine or Tudor, it was all the same to him as long as neither insinuated its way into the western isles. He smiled ruefully, wondering if ever an O'Flaherty had gone to such lengths for a woman.

The sun lay low in the sky, staining the snow-covered hills and glens with shades of pink and gold. Nell watched as Donal reined in his horse and spoke to the man beside him. The man nodded, said something in return, and Donal threw back his head and laughed. Nell swallowed and looked away. She wanted Donal O'Flaherty for her husband more than she wanted anything in her life, and the depth of her wanting frightened her. Nothing was certain, not even the betrothal contracts signed by her father's hand. The last year had proven how tenuous the plans of men really were. And yet Donal had the look of one who meant what he said. Hadn't he come all the way from Galway to find her?

A wave of color rose in her cheeks. He wanted her. She knew that for certain. He'd made sure she knew exactly how much before they left Donore. Lord, she'd been wanton. But when he'd taken her wrist and kissed her where the blue veins met, again and again, she couldn't help the cry that rose in her throat. And when he'd covered her mouth to swallow the sound, his kiss had been sweet and slow and gentle. But later it was none of those things. It was rough and seeking, giving her a taste of what her mother had once told her about, the secret pleasure that men and women shared.

Nell wanted that kiss to go on and on, even when his mouth left her lips and moved to her throat and down to the rise of her breast. Through his clothing, she could feel the bunched muscles of his chest, the hard planes of his legs. Her gown was unlaced, and his tongue was tasting skin that no man had ever seen before.

Nell was sure she would never be cold again. With her face pressed against his neck and her arms wrapped around him, she begged him to take her. But he would not. Putting her gently away from him, he closed his eyes and breathed rapidly for several minutes. When he opened them, he was in control once again. His eyes were very bright and his smile assured, but his voice was not at all steady. "You do not fear the marriage bed, do you, Nell?"

She shook her head.

"Have you done this before?"

"No." She turned away. "Does it matter?"

He took her chin in his hand and turned her face so that she looked at him. "I think so. I would have it that you have known no other man."

She sighed with relief and watched as his cheeks darkened.

"Have you no questions for me, lass?"

She thought for a moment and then shook her head. "I will take you as you are, Donal O'Flaherty. It matters not that you have had other women before me, as long as you have none after."

This time, it was his turn to be relieved. He could speak honestly. "There has been no one since we plighted our troth."

She had not expected that, but it pleased her immensely, as had the care he'd taken to keep Gerald comfortable in his basket of hay.

Now Donal was riding toward her on a black stallion that few men would attempt to ride. He pulled his *morion* off and sat bareheaded before her. "Are you tired, Nell?"

The note in his voice and his admiring glance brought fresh color to her cheeks. "No. It is too good to be riding again. I feel as if I could go on forever."

"We may after all. The cart delays us."

"I'm sorry."

He grinned. "I've never seen such a lass for blaming herself. Gerald's illness could not be helped. The boy wouldn't last the journey without the cart."

"You've been very kind to us, Donal. I don't know how to thank you."

His eyes, intent on her face, were the gray of blanketing mist and cool rain, of smoking peat fires and deep, ice-stilled lakes. She couldn't look away. Emotions, raw and powerful, swallowed her words. Nell could no longer think. She closed her eyes and felt his hands against her throat. Slowly, his fingers caressed her skin. "I will take my thanks, Nell," he said, "in more ways than you can imagine."

She opened her eyes. The beautiful, chiseled lips were very close to her own. This man, this Irish chieftain, held her happiness in his long brown fingers. God help her if she should lose him.

To avoid attention, Donal led his party through the thick forests of Kilmore and Clonish, past giant yew trees, ash, birch, oak, and alder. The inconvenience of traveling through the frigid terrain of Ireland in January with a woman and an ailing child was no small thing, and Donal wondered, more than once, if he shouldn't take them out into the open to make better time. What was the point of security if his charges died of the elements? Once he looked up into the leaden sky and sent two men ahead to find the source of the smoke that circled above their heads. The men returned with news of an army of five hundred *gallowglass* camping in the bog bearing the standard of Ormond.

"Why does your sister hate you so?" he asked Nell one evening as she warmed her shivering limbs by the fire.

Nell stared into the flames for a long time without answering. Finally, she spoke, but the words came haltingly, as if she had no wish to say them. "Margaret is the oldest. She was ever my father's favorite, keeping his books, representing the Fitzgeralds in council, joining his guests at the table when no other woman was welcomed. She was so clever, our Margaret. She should have been a man." Nell's mouth turned down. "But she wasn't, and when Garrett came back from fostering, she learned what it was to be a woman. Father took it all away from her, all the duties she once had, shaming her mercilessly when she protested. Finally, he betrothed her to Ormond, our inherited enemy, a man whose house we were taught to loathe."

Donal squatted down beside her, resting easily on his haunches. "I've heard the marriage is a satisfactory one."

Nell shrugged. "Margaret is very lovely and very shrewd. Ormond has need of both."

Donal twisted a strand of Nell's loose hair around his finger. "Traits her younger sister shares."

"I thank you, sir," she said smoothly. "But you should know that few can compare with Margaret."

"Yet she wishes to wipe the Fitzgeralds from the face of Ireland. Why is that, I wonder?"

"Ormond ambushed the Fitzgeralds on their way to Kilbartin. Garrett killed Margaret's only son. She still grieves."

"And seeks her vengeance," he finished for her.

"Aye. Margaret is twisted. She does not see Gerald as an innocent child. He is our father's son and Garrett's brother."

Donal took her hand in his, feeling the fragile bones. "What does she think of you, Nell?"

Nell tilted her head and pressed her finger to her lips, something she did when formulating an answer. "I know not," she said at last. "More than likely, she does not remember having a sister. I was a mere babe when she left Maynooth to be wed."

Turning her palm face up on his knee, Donal traced the lines with his forefinger. "For generations, the O'Flahertys have been Christian, but many in the west still cling to the old religions. Do you know what the druids tell us, Nell?"

She shook her head. It was only her hand that he touched so intimately, but still it was difficult to concentrate. She noticed that Donal O'Flaherty was a man for touching. It was the way he gave of himself and the way he held back. The very thought of what that meant sucked the air from her lungs.

"They tell us that we are all equal in importance," he said in his beautiful, reverent voice. "Trees, rocks, the grain that grows in our fields, the cattle, dogs, sheep, and humans. No one is more important than the other, because all things come from the earth, who is mother to us all. It is the female from whom all things come, and for that she is to be worshipped. Do you know what it is that I am telling you, Nell?"

"No."

"Margaret was foolish to wish herself a man. We men wage our battles, steal our neighbors' cattle, and increase our holdings for our sons. What is that compared to what a woman can do? Only a woman can bring forth life, and that is the greatest of all feats."

She looked up at him, her hazel eyes filled with light and awe. "Are you a druid, Donal?"

"I'm an O'Flaherty, descended from pirates and mermaids. All of us have a bit of the druid in us." He grinned, and once again Nell wondered how a man, strong and hard as tempered steel, could be called beautiful. Donal O'Flaherty, with his fey, mist-drowned eyes and scooped-out cheeks, was the most beautiful creature she'd ever seen. It wasn't right that a man should look like that.

Nell tried to speak and couldn't get past the lump in her throat. Something was wrong. For some time now, her dreams had been troubled. The Irish part of her, the part she'd inherited from her mother's people, told her to beware. This man, this life she craved to the point of desperation, was not to be.

She wanted nothing more than to cling to Donal, to go with him, to bind him to her in the most primitive of ways. Everything she knew of men told her that he desired her. But he would not be seduced. Donal wanted her for his wife, and he was more traditional than even he knew. They would wed first in his church and then at Aughnanure in the old Brehon way of the Irish.

Nell rubbed her arms and shivered. What if her destiny and her desire took separate paths? What if she never knew what it was to have Donal O'Flaherty for her husband? A darker thought consumed her. What if the man who took her maidenhood was other than the man who sat beside her? Would Donal still want her? His words came back to her. *I would have it that you have known no other man.* Women had little control over their lives or the men who shared their beds.

But they were together now. She could tell him what was in her heart.

Nell wet her lips. "I want to come with you," she whispered. "Desmond may be my kinsman, but he was not my father's friend. What if he refuses to honor the betrothal contract?"

She had voiced the very thought that occupied Donal's mind. Nell was beautiful, and a beautiful woman was a strategic weapon in the hands of the wrong man. Donal knew enough of the Munster Fitzgeralds to worry. The earl of Desmond was an ambitious man. Now that the House of Kildare was destroyed, Desmond's position in the world of Irish politics had improved. There were rumors that he saw himself as the future king of Ireland.

Donal frowned and looked at the basket where Gerald slept. Hadn't the first Henry Tudor done the very same thing? By murdering the Plantagenet princes in the tower and marrying their sister, he had joined the houses of Lancaster and York, ended the Hundred Years War, and secured his position as king of England. Suddenly, Donal's chest felt very tight. In bringing Gerald and Nell to Askeaton Castle, he was playing right into the earl's hands.

"We are two days from the borders of Desmond," he said slowly. " 'Tis risky, and our food supply is low, but we can make our way back through the forest and across the ridges of the Paps. If we do not tarry, we might make O'Flaherty land in four days." He looked away. "The boy will suffer, Nell, but he may survive. With Desmond, his chances are no better."

"My father sent us to him. Surely he knew his cousin better than you."

Donal shrugged. "Perhaps. But the great earl is dead. Those who once swore oaths of loyalty have sought other protectors. Such is the nature of Irish politics."

"Gerald must go to Desmond," she insisted.

A puzzled frown marked Donal's brow. "You said you wanted to come with me. Did I mistake your meaning?"

This conversation was not going the way she'd intended. Shaking her head, she stared into the fire. No power on earth would make her look at him.

"Nell." His voice, smooth as silk, raised the goose-bumps on her arms. This was a man who knew something of women. She felt him lean in to her. His breath was warm against her cheek. "Nell, look at me."

Against her will, she turned her head. His eyes were the color of clouds and bright with held-in laughter. Quickly, she turned away. "Talk to me, Nell," she heard him say. "I would hear your thoughts."

"They are worth very little."

He lifted her hand to his mouth. "Not to me," he said, his lips moving against her skin. "Never to me."

She was trembling now, and if he stopped touching her, she would die right here before this very fire, less than two days' ride from the gates of Askeaton. She would die of an excess of passion, because the man she wanted was too slow in the taking of her.

Suddenly, her shyness seemed absurd. They might be

dead tomorrow, or worse, she could be given to another, a toothless lord three times her age, and Donal would forget he ever wanted a Geraldine for his bride. She pulled her hand away. "Gerald must go to Desmond," she repeated. "My father wished it as he would wish that I stay with Gerald until his future is secure." Her voice lowered. "He also wished for us to be wed, as I do. But I want something else, Donal."

"What is that, Nell?"

She faced him directly and said the words she had carried in her heart since the day he'd crossed the snow and called her name before the gates of Donore. "I want us to lie together, tonight, in my tent, before we reach Desmond land."

Not by the twitch of a muscle did Donal reveal the effect her words had on him. He wanted her so much that the wanting did strange things to his mind. His only recourse was to stay away from her, something he could not bring himself to do. She pulled at him in ways he'd never imagined. He knew he held her heart. The look on her face when he'd come to Donore told him more than words ever could, and it shook him thoroughly. Loving was new to him. Knowing she loved him changed everything. His senses were filled with her, what it would be like to claim her, taste her, fill her, mark her, watch her belly swell with his seed. A man looked at a woman with new eyes when he knew that she loved him. And now she wanted him to lie with her, before they were wed.

Donal rested his hands on his thighs and allowed the rush of desire to fill him. His heart felt loose and unsteady inside his chest. "Why?" he made himself ask. "Why now?"

She had pulled the plaits from her hair, and it framed her face, pale as moonlight. He wanted to smooth it

over her bare skin and bury his face in it. With every
play of light her face grew lovelier.

"Brehon law allows us to handfast, to claim each
other as husband and wife for one year and a day. If at
the end of that time we choose to part, it is as if the
marriage had never been, and the child, if there is one,
is recognized as legitimate."

"Is it me you are unsure of, Nell, or yourself?"

A smile hovered on the edges of her mouth. She
reached out to trace his lips with her finger. "Neither,"
she said. "But I am Geraldine and have learned that the
fortunes of fate do not always go as planned. I have
never been with a man, and I want very much for you
to be the first."

His face stilled, and try as she might, Nell could read
nothing behind the blankness in his eyes. "I will be
your husband," he said slowly. "If you wed with me,
there will be no one else for you."

Nell rested her hands on his chest and searched his
face for the slightest sign of emotion. *So this is what he
is like when his anger has gone beyond words.* "We are not
all masters of our fate, my love," she whispered. "I
know not what plans my cousin has made. But he is
Sean Ghall, more Irish than English, and a handfasted
marriage according to Brehon law will weigh with him."

He had been right after all. Nell was shrewd as well
as beautiful, and if they did not seek her tent immediately, he would take her here in the snow. Rising, Donal
held out his hand. She placed her own in it and followed
him into the darkness of her flimsy lodging. He drew
her into his arms and stood for a moment without moving, his lips pressed to her forehead. His words were
raw, as if he'd ripped them from his throat. "Are you
sure, Nell?"

"Aye. Very sure, Donal. What do we do now?"

His mouth moved from her forehead to the curve of her throat and down. "I'll show you, *a stor*," he murmured, finding the spot where he knew she was most sensitive, the meeting place of her neck and shoulder.

With every touch of his mouth on her skin, the boneless feeling in her limbs intensified. A low mewling sound escaped her lips. Muffling it against his shoulder, she melted against him, welcoming the removal of her clothing and his, the movement of his hands, and the ache that grew more urgent within her as his mouth followed the places his hands touched.

Pressing her down into the fur-lined blankets, he covered her body with his, searched for her lips, and found them. He kissed her gently, and when she gasped for breath, he put all gentleness aside and filled her mouth with his tongue, coaxing and pleasuring until she knew the way of it. Beneath him, her body trembled with the ebb and flow of the tides within her.

Donal had intended to take her slowly, to make the sweet rise of her desire peak, but he wanted her too much. She cried out when he entered her. He covered her mouth, kissing away the sound, filled her completely, his seed mixing with her virgin blood where the ground was at its most fertile, waiting and ready for the union of two royal Irish houses.

"I knew it would be like this," she murmured much later, her lips moving against the bulging muscle of his arm.

"Hmm." He opened one eye, lifted his head to see her face, and smoothed back her hair. "What would be like this?"

"Loving you."

Donal was humbled. He had been rough and clumsy, and yet she had not complained. Pressing a kiss on her temple, he pulled her protectively against him. "I promise you it will be better next time."

"When will that be?"

He grinned in the darkness. "You're a lusty wench for one so new to the game."

His skin tasted like salt against her tongue. "Do I please you, sir?"

"More than—" Donal stopped without finishing his thought. There were voices outside the tent, strange voices. Motioning for Nell to be silent, he pulled on his clothing and slipped the dirk from his boot. He shook his head at the question in Nell's eyes and stepped out into the darkness.

Two *gallowglass* held flaming torches on either side of a small, elderly man sitting astride an enormous gelding. His brown hair, worn Irish fashion, long over the shoulders, was streaked with gray. Wrapped around his slight frame was a cloak, and Donal could see that his saddle had no stirrups.

An amused smile lit the man's crafty features. "I see that we are too late to offer assistance. The O'Flaherty has the advantage."

Donal stepped forward. "You know my name. Now tell me yours."

The man looked beyond Donal to the lovely girl who followed him out of the tent. "Tell him who I am, lass."

It had been years since he had come to Maynooth, but no one would mistake him. " 'Tis my cousin, Desmond Fitzgerald," Nell said.

Donal nodded. He'd guessed as much. "Welcome, my lord. We bring you Gerald Fitzgerald, earl of Kildare."

The earl smiled through his beard. "And his sister?"

Donal's hand tightened on his dirk. "Nell is promised to me by the betrothal contracts signed by her father."

Again, Desmond smiled. "How fortunate for you. But now we will relieve you of your charge and save you a lengthy journey. The Lady Eleanor will come with us to see that the boy is settled. When the time is right, she will come to you."

It wasn't what he wanted, but Donal had no right to question his logic. Nell had planned to stay with her brother until he was completely recovered. Why, then, although he tossed and turned through the night, did morning come too quickly, and why had the sight of the wicker cart as it disappeared through the woods with the girl who sat so bravely on her white mare smote his heart?

8

Kildare Hall, 1974

By the time Kathleen Maguire was ten years old, she made up her mind to leave Kilvara permanently. But it never occurred to her that she could be the instrument of her own desires. Young girls in Kilvara weren't raised to think they could be anything more than their mothers before them. Kathleen wasn't what anyone would call a student, but she could count to nine, and when she looked in the family Bible and saw the date of her parents' wedding and that her own birthday fell short of that date by six months, she stored it away in her mind. And when the time came, she did what her mother had done.

Kathleen never really believed Terrence Fitzgerald would marry her, but she thought he might part with a considerable amount of money if she turned up pregnant and had to go away. After all, the future earl of Kildare Hall couldn't have his by-blow living in Kilvara, no more than a minute's ride from his legitimately born children.

She had other options. There wasn't a man in Kilvara who didn't entertain lustful thoughts when Kathleen dressed up in her miniskirt on a Saturday evening. But she wasn't interested in a village man. In Kathleen's mind, Terrence was a gentleman, better educated, more well spoken, more sophisticated, and cleaner than any slouch-hatted bloke in Kilvara. Once she'd met him on the road to Newry, and he'd given her a ride to the gates of Kildare in his car. That had been terribly risky. She'd stepped out and closed the door just before the earl and his lady came rambling down the lane in their new Volvo.

Most of the time, they met in the old hunting lodge. No one ever used it. In the dim light of the peat fire, it was almost as elegant as Kildare Hall.

After Kathleen left home to move into her room in the servants' quarters, she managed to sneak out nearly every night that Terrence was home from university. He didn't love her, but that was all right because she didn't love him, either. Kathleen wasn't looking for love. She wanted out, and the child she carried was her ticket. Not once did she consider keeping it. There wasn't a maternal bone in her body. Besides, brand-new babies were always put into the best situations, much better than any she could ever offer. Terrence's money would get her through the pregnancy and set her up in London. After that, who could tell? She might even end up in New York or Boston.

Because Kathleen saw nothing wrong with blackmailing a young man who had more money than he could ever spend, she didn't anticipate Terrence's rage when she told him of her plan. Nor did she anticipate his financial circumstance. He had no money of his own until his twenty-fifth birthday. Every purchase over one hundred pounds was approved by his father, and Kathleen wanted a great deal more than a hundred pounds.

They were at the lodge when she told him. After the first rush of anger, he calmed down and explained that he had some money left from last quarter's allowance, but it was far short of what she wanted. She was welcome to it, but three hundred pounds was all he could give. He promised to send more later if she left Kilvara immediately.

It wasn't nearly enough. She followed him out of the lodge and clung to his arm. He pushed her away. Kathleen lost her temper and threw herself on him. He stumbled on a stone, slippery from the afternoon rain, and fell heavily. She waited for him to get up, but he never did.

"Terrence, are you all right?" Kathleen squatted on the ground beside him and jostled his shoulder. "Terrence, get up and stop y'r jokin'." Still nothing.

With all her strength, she rolled him over, and her eyes widened with shock. A deep gash marked his forehead, as if an ice cream scoop had dipped into his head. There was very little blood. Kathleen bent down and rested her ear against his chest.

Sweet Jesus. Terrence was dead. Wild with fear, she ran away from the lodge, through the forest of black oak and pine, down the road toward Kilvara.

Peter Maguire was still at the pub, and Frankie had just turned out his light when Kathleen burst into the room sobbing, her hands rusty with dried blood, her words incoherent.

Frankie gripped her shoulders and shook her. He had been wanting to shake her senseless for a long time. "Christ, Kathleen, whatever's come over you?"

Neither his words nor the bite of his fingers had any effect. Her breathing quickened. Her eyes rolled back, and a painful wheezing sound came from her chest. Frankie knew what that meant. Kathleen was asthmatic. Unless he acted quickly, she wouldn't be able to pull the air into her lungs. Raising his hand, he slapped her cheeks, first one and then the other.

She gasped, coughed, and breathed deeply, taking in gulps of air for several minutes. Then she sagged against his chest. "God, Frankie," she rasped. "I've gone and killed him. Y've got t' help me. I've killed Terrence Fitzgerald."

Frankie's heart felt as if a giant fist had taken hold of it and squeezed. "What happened?" he asked in a voice that couldn't possibly be his.

She told him, leaving nothing out—the clandestine meetings, her pregnancy, her request for money, Terrence's answer, and the way he looked when she last saw him, with his head split open and his chest still.

Frankie's head spun with the horror of it. What to do. What could he do? "Wash y'r hands," he ordered in a voice that demanded obedience. "Go back to the Hall, and stay in your room until I send word."

"What are y' going t' do?" she whispered.

Frankie pulled on his trousers. "I'm goin' to the lodge to be sure he's dead."

"Don't go, Frankie," she begged him. "He's gone. I know he is. No good will come of y'r goin' back there."

He found his shoes and stepped into them. "Never mind, Kathleen. Just do as I say."

She turned toward the door, but his voice stopped her. "Y'll have t' go away from here. Don't tell Da. Father Quinlan will help you."

Kathleen flushed and nodded. "I'm sorry, Frankie. You were right. I'm so sorry."

He nodded and searched for his shoes. "Go along now. I'll see y' soon."

Frankie's first stop when he reached the Hall was Jillian's bedroom. She was reading a forbidden novel and at first paid no attention to the rain of pebbles on her window, but when the sound persisted, she pushed open the sash and leaned out over the ledge. Her mouth dropped open. Frankie never came to Kildare Hall at night. "What is it?" she whispered loudly.

He held his finger against his lips and motioned for her to come down. Jilly pulled a jumper over her night-gown, stepped into her slippers, and hurried down the wide staircase. The door to the library was slightly ajar. She could hear the drone of her father's voice. He must have been reading something to her mum because it went on without interruption. Jilly glanced at the clock. It was only ten. They wouldn't check on her for at least an hour. She considered going out the front door but decided against it. The pantry would be better. After sliding back the bolt, she slipped out the door and ran to the garden at the back of the house. Frankie sat by the gate leading to the pasture. She knew at once that something was terribly wrong.

He gripped her shoulders. She winced at the pain. "What is it, Frankie?"

"I need y'r help, Jillian."

He used her full name, something he rarely did. "I'll do anything for you, Frankie," she said, and meant it.

"I need you t' lie for me."

"All right."

The fierceness in his expression dissolved. "Bless you, lass, for not asking why."

She stood completely still, staring up at him, bearing the weight of his hands, all of her heart in her eyes.

He couldn't stand to look at her. A harsh moan rose from somewhere in his throat. He dropped his hands and turned away.

"Frankie," she whispered, "are you in trouble?"

His voice sounded like the rustle of dry paper. "Aye. Terrible trouble."

Jilly's lower lip trembled. She reached out to touch him and stopped midway. "It can't be that bad. Together we can sort it out."

"Not this time, lass."

Her heart ached for him, and fear, more profound than any she had ever known, rose within her. "What can I do?"

He turned, and she stepped back, dismayed at the bloodless color of his skin.

"I need you t' go to Kathleen and bring her back to y'r room. Keep her there with you until someone sees the two of you together. Be sure they know she was with you the entire night." She opened her mouth, but he held up his hand, allowing no interruptions. "Make up a reason for her being there, any reason, and stick t' it no matter who questions you. Do y' understand?" His eyes, silver in the moonlight, held her spellbound. She nodded.

He let out his breath in a long sigh as if he'd been holding it for a long time. "Sweet lass. I knew y' wouldn't fail me. Go now, and do as I say."

He watched her climb the terraced steps, watched her turn and wave before she disappeared around the corner of the house. Then he sprinted through the meadow to the line of trees separating the woods from the pasture. He slowed to a walk. Frankie wasn't familiar with the wooded areas of the Kildare estate. Carefully, he made his way through the inky darkness toward the lodge. In the distance he could see a glow from the window. Kathleen must have forgotten to turn out the lights.

Then it hit him. At any moment now, he would stumble upon Terrence Fitzgerald's corpse. The burning began in his chest and spread throughout his body.

By the time he knelt on the stone steps of the lodge and pressed his hand against Terrence's throat to feel for a pulse, he was almost incapacitated with the pain of it. Light from the wood-paneled sitting room spilled out over the slabs falling on the lifeless form of Jilly's half-brother.

Frankie sat back and rested his hands on his knees, careful not to touch anything. Terrence looked far less formidable in death than he had in life. His eyes were open, and his face seemed younger, more vulnerable, his expression almost appealing, much as he must have looked as a child before wealth and dissipation had changed him into the spoiled, sullen young man Frankie remembered. Despite Terrence's faults, Frankie had never wished him dead. It was bad luck to wish someone dead. The thought of Jilly's face when she learned of her brother's fate made his heart ache.

A thought occurred to him. Kathleen was carrying Terrence Fitzgerald's child. She would be a mother, and Frankie would be an uncle. The idea appealed to him. The baby wouldn't be born under the best of circumstances, but then who was? With Da's help, they would raise it. Maybe the Fitzgeralds would help. Or maybe it would be better if they never knew. They might even try to take the child away from Kathleen. With their money and their lawyers, they could probably manage it.

He should leave immediately. Frankie glanced down at Terrence. Giving in to a compassionate impulse, he leaned over the body to close his eyes.

A voice, colder than mountain runoff, froze his hand in midair. "Hold it right there, lad. Don't move another inch."

Frankie couldn't have moved if he tried. A hand on his shoulder pressed him down into the ground and held him there. Dirt worked its way into his mouth, and still the man's iron grip kept him in place. Out of the corner of his eye, Frankie could see the flannel brogues and worn boots of the Kildare *ghillie* as he knelt to examine Terrence's body. A low whistle came from his pursed lips.

"You've done it this time, Frankie," Kevin Feeney said. "What did he do t' you, lad?"

Anything he might say would incriminate Kathleen, and there was the baby to think of. Frankie remained silent.

Feeney's grip tightened around his arm, and he hoisted Frankie to his feet. "Come along, now. You've some questions to answer. I expect they'll want to see you up at the Hall."

All the way through the silent forest and across the meadow, Kevin Feeney kept up a light, calming flow of conversation. He also kept a tight grip on Frankie's arm.

With each step that he took, the magnitude of the responsibility he'd taken on himself weighed on Frankie, slowing his steps. The words, never ready when he wanted them, failed him once again. Struggling, he tried to make Feeney understand. "I didn't do it, Mr. Feeney."

"I hope not, lad. The truth will out. It always does."

Frankie heard the doubt in his voice and despaired. If Kevin Feeney, one of his own, didn't believe him, what chance did he have? Cursing his own stupidity, he thought quickly. What reason could he possibly make up to explain his presence at the lodge? His mind was blank. He would be accused of murder. If he claimed he was innocent, there would be an investigation, and Kathleen would be questioned. He wasn't the only one who had noticed her preoccupation with Terrence. Frankie knew what he had to do. He hoped the law would take his age into consideration and go easy on him. But then it was a Protestant law, never easy on those not of their own persuasion.

Light that should have been welcoming blazed from the windows of the second- and third-floor rooms in Kildare Hall. The *ghillie* told Frankie to sit on the stoop. He pounded loudly on the door. A servant answered. The *ghillie* whispered something to her, and she ushered them both inside.

Frankie's legs could no longer stand his weight. He half sat, half slid into a wooden chair, resting his elbows on his knees. Minutes later, a frowning Pyers Fitzgerald, resplendent in a gray smoking jacket, walked down the stairs. The *ghillie* cleared his throat and led him away from Frankie.

Frankie knew the exact moment that the *ghillie* told Fitzgerald that his son was dead. The man gasped, swayed, and braced himself against the wall. Again the *ghillie* spoke, but the words were too low for Frankie to hear. Fitzgerald nodded, and Feeney reached for the phone. Frankie's brain could process no longer. He blocked out everything, concentrating on the throbbing ache in his chest.

The police came immediately. Frankie heard the sing-song whine of the sirens long before they turned into the gates of the Hall, and he knew that they came for him.

Upstairs in her garden bedroom, Jilly also heard the sirens. She glanced over at Kathleen, who hadn't said more than two words in the entire hour they'd been together. Jilly frowned. "What is happening, Kathleen? Tell me now."

The older girl's face crumbled. Jilly, who had never considered her pretty, noticed for the first time the striking bones of her face and was reminded of Frankie.

"I never meant for this to happen," Kathleen sobbed.

Jilly unfolded her legs, slid off the bed, and crossed the room to the chair where Kathleen sat wringing a sodden handkerchief. Inside her chest she felt the weight of her own heart. "What have you done, Kathleen? Tell me now, or I'll tell them the truth about you. Whatever it is, I'll tell them it was all you."

Kathleen gasped and stared at the girl she had once dismissed as too young to notice anything. Jilly, dressed in her white nightgown with her hair curling around her face, looked like an avenging angel sent down to earth for the purpose of punishing Kathleen. "I'm in trouble, Miss Fitzgerald," she burst out, "and the baby is your brother's."

"You've been running after Terrence for years. That news won't surprise anyone except my mother," said Jillian baldly. "The police are downstairs, Kathleen. As far as I know, getting a girl pregnant isn't illegal."

Kathleen swallowed. "I told Terrence that I needed money t' go away. He wouldn't give me any." Her hands shook as she pleated and smoothed the handkerchief in her lap. "He started t' walk away. I grabbed his arm. He slipped and hit his head on a rock." Her eyes filled up again. "He's dead, Miss Fitzgerald. I never meant for anythin' to happen, but he's dead."

Jillian hadn't blinked in a long time. Her eyes ached with the effort it took to keep them open. The magnitude of what she had just heard was slow to wash over her. Terrence was dead. Good God, Terrence was dead, and Kathleen was responsible. The horror of it seeped through her. "Frankie," she whispered. "What has Frankie to do with it?"

"He was goin' back to the lodge to be sure Terrence was really dead," Kathleen said. "I told him not to go. I told him Terrence wasn't breathin'."

Jilly raced for the door and pulled it open. Her heart slammed in her chest as she ran down the stairs, through the long hallway to the front parlor. She barely registered the five policemen, the *ghillie*, and her father. Jilly had eyes only for Frankie. He sat in a chair, his head in his hands. With no thought but to offer comfort, she crossed the room, sat down at his feet, and curled her arms around his legs.

"Go away, Jilly," he whispered fiercely. "I can't do this with you here."

She only tightened her grip and rested her head on his knees.

"Jillian." Her father's anguished voice pierced the low hum of conversation. "Stay away from him. Go find your mother."

Jilly ignored him and buried her head between Frankie's knees.

Pyers's voice was very high. "For God's sake, Jillian—"

Just then, two more policemen walked through the door, bearing Terrence's lifeless body on a stretcher. Pyers forgot Jilly and leaned over his boy. Tears streamed down his face. "Yes," he said brokenly. "He's my son. There's no mistake."

Jillian refused to look up. Something was terribly wrong. They thought Frankie had killed Terrence. She must tell them it was an accident. If anyone was to blame, it was Kathleen. She lifted her head to meet Frankie's gaze. Gray eyes met hazel and locked. His message was unmistakable. *You promised*, he said without once moving his lips.

She shook her head and mouthed the words. "They'll put you in jail. It was an accident, Frankie. Kathleen told me what happened."

His eyes blazed, and his hand tightened on her arm.

"Do this, Jillian. Do this for me. I've never asked you for anythin' before. Do this one thing, love. If y' care for me at all, do this."

She shrank from the agony in his expression. Every instinct told her this was wrong. Why couldn't he see it? Frankie, always so wise, so dependable, was making a terrible mistake.

Her father's strong hands slid under her arms and lifted her across the floor away from Frankie to where Margaret Fitzgerald stood in her bathrobe and slippers. Jilly looked up at her mother. Mum had never liked Terrence much. Surely she would defend Frankie. But Margaret stood there without speaking, her face white as bleached bone, her eyes wide and strange and colorless in the artificial lamplight.

A yellow-vested police officer reached out to grab Frankie's arm. "Y'r comin' with us, lad. I'll send a man around to get a message to y'r father."

Frankie stood, his face ashen, his mouth silent.

"No," Jilly said into the silence. "Frankie didn't do anything. You can't take him away. Frankie," she appealed to the stone-faced boy, "say something. Tell them it wasn't you. Please tell them." Her mother reached for her hand.

"That's enough, Jillian." Her father had never spoken to her in that tone of voice before.

"But Da," she sobbed, pulling at her mother's hand. "They're taking Frankie away."

Frankie cleared his throat. "I'll be all right, lass. Don't take on so."

"No!" she screamed, on the verge of hysteria. "No. I love you. I won't let them take you!" Rage gave her strength. With a mighty tug, she pulled away from her mother and threw herself against Frankie's chest.

He buried his face in her hair, and his free arm came

around her shoulders, hugging her fiercely. Reluctantly, the policeman released him.

"Don't cry, Jilly," Frankie muttered under his breath. "It will be all right. I'll come back t' you, lass. I promise I will. Wait for me, Jilly. Let me go now, and I'll come back."

She lifted her head. "Truly, Frankie?"

"I promise."

"Swear it," she said.

"Jilly." His voice had an edge to it as if he were living on nerves alone. "What will I do with you, lass?"

"Swear it on this." Her fingers slipped inside his collar to find the chain that held a tiny gold cross against his heart. The metal was warm against his neck. She held it to his lips. "Swear that you'll come back to me, Frankie. Kiss it and swear."

For a single, piercing moment, Frankie looked into the eyes of the girl who loved him. Awareness dawned, and he realized what he had lost. His words came harshly on the jagged edge of his pain. "I love you, too, Jilly," he said, dropping a quick kiss on the cross.

Then he reached out and gripped her shoulders, kissing her full and fiercely on the lips. "Y'r just a wee lass now," he said in a voice that was strong with purpose, "but when y'r grown, I'll come back here one day t' remind you of another promise I made. If y' still want me, I'll take y' away from here and be damned t' all of 'em."

Margaret Fitzgerald gave a low moan and stretched out her hand to her daughter. But Jilly paid no attention. Her eyes were riveted on Frankie's back as he walked freely out the door, down the wide stone stairs of Kildare Hall and out of her life.

9

❧❧❧

Kylemore Abbey, Connemara, Ireland, 1978

Kylemore Abbey, located in the heart of remote and breathtakingly beautiful Connemara, was home to fifty-two Benedictine nuns and one hundred twenty female boarders between the ages of twelve and eighteen. Kylemore, whose focus was academics and character building, attracted girls from all over the world. Although students were instructed in Catholicism, the nuns did not discriminate, and Irish Catholics found themselves in the minority at the Abbey.

At first, Jillian was too overcome with grief over leaving home to notice the spectacular landscape on the N59, better known as the Clifden-Westport Road. But when she did, she understood why her parents had chosen it. The fairy-tale appeal of a glass lake and haunted forests framing a gothic palace complete with a mini-cathedral, tree-lined walkways, and the purest air in Ireland made it the perfect sanctuary for a young girl who believed in magic and ached for home with every beat of her broken heart.

It was at Kylemore that Jilly's resolve was formed. Amidst the stern discipline of the Irish Benedictines, her ideals materialized, were challenged, sharpened, and set in stone. In the mahogany-appointed library surrounded by ancient manuscripts, written by the finest minds in Anglo-Irish history, she came to an understanding of her country and the role of her family in its struggle.

Slowly, painstakingly, like the unfolding of a moth from its chrysalis, she understood why Frankie had been so reticent about publicizing their relationship. Jillian's cheeks burned when she remembered how she had forced herself on him, demanding his attention, his acceptance, his loyalty, his undivided allegiance, even his love.

It did not surprise her that she never heard from him again. All requests made to her parents to know his whereabouts were met with stony silence. She would have appealed to Kathleen, but the girl was no longer employed at Kildare, and Peter Maguire had been pensioned off shortly after the night Terrence was found with his head split apart. Once, after her sixteenth birthday, when she was of an age to have earned some unsupervised time, she'd used her quarterly holiday money to ride the train to Belfast and consult a prominent barrister, the father of one of her school chums. His efforts turned up the astonishing news that Frankie Maguire had escaped from Long Kesh prison along with a number of other inmates. No word of him had ever been heard. He was believed to have left Ireland permanently.

And so, realizing that a poor Catholic boy from Kilvara could no more claim the daughter of Pyers Fitzgerald than he could become king of England, she forced herself to put that part of her life behind her and fo-

cused her efforts on something she believed Frankie
would approve of: finding his sister and her child.
Somewhere there was someone who had attended Kathleen Maguire when she gave birth. It was only a matter
of time.

For Jillian, the road from freedom-loving, adored only
daughter of Pyers and Margaret Fitzgerald to a female
boarder at Kylemore Abbey, where every waking moment was shared with schoolmates and every sleeping
one with three roommates, was not as difficult as she
had anticipated. She adapted well, and by her second
year at Kylemore, it was clear to the reverend mother
and to most of the nuns at the abbey that Jillian Fitzgerald, their most despondent and prickly first-year student, had been transformed into an unqualified
success.

Jillian was happy at Kylemore. The nearby village of
Letterfrack, less than five kilometers to the west, provided the girls with an occasional movie, a chemist, a
café, a grocery store, and several dress shops. It also
provided male attention, if not companionship. Local
lads frequenting the village pubs fell over themselves
for glimpses of the Kylemore girls dressed in navy
sweaters and pleated skirts going about their business
on the streets.

Not that they would have entertained the notion of
doing anything more than looking. Kylemore was the
local Catholic school, and girls from Kylemore and Letterfrack were able to attend at no charge, but few did.
Ireland's rigid class system was even more rigid in the
Republic, and the Kylemore girls were as untouchable
as if they'd been a different species.

Jillian had just passed her sixteenth birthday. It was
near the end of the term, and she had earned some
precious time alone. Walking paths cutting through the

hills surrounding the abbey, forested with oak, pine, ash, and one of the few natural yew trees left in Ireland, gave her the few moments of rare privacy that she craved. One day, she changed into slim-fitting blue jeans and set out on her walk. The day after, she would take her exams and then return to Kildare Hall for the summer. If all went well, she would attend Trinity in the fall, her father's alma mater.

Her mother had campaigned for a come-out in London, but Jillian had been adamant. It was college she wanted, not a husband, and her father had agreed with her. Jillian knew that his acquiescence had to do with Terrence. If her brother had lived, or if there had been other children, Pyers would not have considered her education to be important. Some good had come out of Terrence's death, after all.

At the foot of a rise, a patch of deep gray that Jillian had dismissed as a boulder moved unexpectedly, disturbing her reverie. Her eyes followed the patch as it changed shape, sat up, and scratched. Her eyes widened. Then she laughed and held out her hand, calling softly. "Here, girl. Come here, love. Whatever are you doing here? Are you lost?"

The huge wolfhound whimpered deep in her throat and crawled forward in supplication, burying her nose in the girl's palm before lying quietly at her feet. Jillian frowned, knelt down, and ran her hands over the animal's flanks. The dog's hair was matted and not terribly clean, but she looked well fed, and her manners were exquisite. The hound, a rare breed in Connemara and obviously alone, had been carefully trained. But why was she here? Except for thick foliage around the abbey, the terrain of the Irish Gaeltacht was rocky and barren of trees, similar to the remote harshness of the Scottish

Highlands, sheep country. Wolfhounds were territorial and did not do well with sheep.

A soft breeze from the lake brought the dog's pungent odor to Jillian's nose. The corners of her mouth turned up in a bittersweet smile. Dogs always reminded her of Frankie. Everything warm and sweet and male and smelling of sweat reminded her of Frankie. Would she ever be through with him? Would she ever want to be?

The dog was restless now, her long legs unfolding from beneath her. Jillian gasped at the sheer height of her. Her head was nearly at the height of a man's shoulder. Just now, she was fixed on something beyond the rise, in the thickest part of the trees. Jillian rested her hand on the dog's head. "What do you see out there, girl?"

The hound moved forward, ears perked, eyes focused on an unknown spot beyond Jillian's vision. Suddenly, she turned, grabbed Jillian's sweater in her mouth, and pulled.

"My goodness." Jillian laughed, allowing herself to be pulled along by the dog's gentle mouth. "Why didn't you say so in the first place?"

Another whine came from deep in the wolfhound's throat.

"I'm coming," Jillian reassured her. "I only hope this isn't a wild goose chase. I'm ruining my shoes." Regretfully, she looked down at the dull film coating the loafers she had polished only that morning. Parting the branches, she followed the dog deeper and deeper into the undergrowth, until the misgivings she felt when she first left the path became full-scale doubts. "This is it, girl," she called out, leaning heavily against a moss-covered tree trunk. "I'm not going any farther."

There's no need to go any farther, Jillian, a voice spoke softly from the undergrowth.

Tiny hairs lifted on the back of Jillian's neck. She'd heard that voice before, a long time ago. Hesitating, she moved forward and stepped into the darkest part of the growth. But it wasn't dark at all. She could see quite clearly. The dog was gone, and a woman stood before her, a young woman in a green gown with exaggerated sleeves, slashed and foaming with lace, trimmed in fur. Above the molded busk, her breasts swelled, forming a hollow from which an emerald pendant reflected the green flecks in her eyes. Moon-gold hair was pulled away from her face by a satin headpiece. It fell thick and straight across her shoulders and past her waist.

But it wasn't the woman's clothing, more suited to the sixteenth century than the twentieth, or her hair, thicker, longer, and lighter than hair could possibly grow, that bleached the color from Jillian's cheeks and sucked the breath from her chest. It was her face. She had despaired of ever seeing that face again. "Hello, Nell," she said softly. "It has been a very long time."

Nell smiled. *You've grown up. We are finally of an age. You're very lovely, Jillian.*

"I've missed you."

And I you.

Jillian sank to the ground, where she wrapped her arms around her legs and rocked. "Why did you leave?"

Nell leaned against a tree trunk. *There were pressing matters that needed my attention. My father, the ninth earl of Kildare, was killed.*

Jillian nodded. "I know. So was his son, Silken Thomas, and all the Geraldines of his line except for Gerald." She smiled. "But you know that. It's your history, isn't it?"

Nell's eyes had brightened, and twin spots of color

burned her cheeks. *Aye, 'tis my history, and yours. But much of it lies ahead of me.* She knelt down and leaned forward until her face was level with Jillian's. *I need your help, Jillian. Too much is at stake to wait for time to show me the way.*

"I don't understand."

Don't you see? You will tell me if Gerald is to live or die. Tell me, Jillian, whether the house of Fitzgerald dies with Silken Thomas. If so, there is little reason to sacrifice my own happiness.

Jillian shook her head. She had never seen Nell in such a state. "You're asking the impossible," she said slowly. "I'm surprised you don't see it. You want to know the future so that you can arrange the past, but it doesn't work that way. If you change the past, the future is already affected. If you decide differently from what fate originally intended, entire generations may be harmed." A horrifying thought occurred to her. "I might never even be born."

How long have you known who I am?

Jillian thought for a moment. Had there ever been a time when she didn't know Nell's identity? "I'm not sure," she said slowly. "Maybe I always knew. I remembered things you said. Every time I looked into the mirror, I was reminded of you. Then there were the portraits lining the dining hall at Kildare. We are both definitely Fitzgeralds. The resemblance is unmistakable."

Nell's lower lip trembled. She caught it between her teeth. *Please, Jillian. I'm in love, and I carry his child. What is the harm in knowing if I may go to him?*

Jillian's forehead creased in thought. "You should decide on your own. Whatever you do will be right, for you and your child, and for all the children to come."

You're exaggerating.

"I don't think so." Jillian rested her hand on Nell's stomach. "What if the future of the Fitzgeralds lies right here? Or what if your baby dies before it's even born and the next child you carry is the one from which my family is descended? How would you ever know if you'd done the right thing? If you tamper with fate, the entire world might be a different place."

Nell straightened and looked down at Jillian's bent head. *You've changed. I thought you would help me.*

"I am helping you."

What if I did something for you?

"Oh, Nell." Jilly's laugh hovered on the cusp of exasperation and amusement. "You've already done a great deal. No one was closer to me than you were. I couldn't have managed without you."

There was someone else you loved even more than me.

Jillian's heart gave a great thump in her chest.

What if I show you what happened to Francis Maguire?

Jillian thought she had shouted the words, but they came out in the merest whisper. "How can you show me that when you can't see your own future?"

Nell shrugged. *I can see everything after my own lifetime but nothing within it.*

Jillian stood. "I'm going now. I don't care to see Frankie. It wouldn't do either of us any good."

You were never a coward, Jillian.

"I'm still not."

Aren't you?

Jillian parted the bushes and began climbing through the thick foliage to the path. "I know what you're doing, Nell, but I'm not a child any longer. You won't get what you want that way."

Tell me how I can get what I want.

A branch slapped Jillian in the face, leaving a red welt across her cheek. "You won't this time, but in the future you might try convincing me that it might be of some importance to others beside yourself."

Effortlessly, Nell floated behind her, as if thick roots and tangled branches did not block her path. *So that's the way of it. Have the Benedictines converted you to their level of holiness? Will you be taking the orders now that there's no hope for a future with your own love?*

Reluctantly, Nell laughed and turned around to face her nemesis. "Wouldn't that be the scandal of the century?"

Which? Taking up with Frankie Maguire or becoming a nun?

Jillian gave her a withering look. "Becoming a nun, of course."

It would have been much more so in my world. It would have meant your head.

"Was he really as dreadful as he seems?"

Nell knew immediately whom she meant. *Henry was much worse. He beheaded two of his own wives, not to mention thousands of others who would not convert.*

Jillian shook her head. "I can't imagine it."

Nell smiled tentatively. *Please help me, Jilly. I don't want to be another of his victims.*

"There's no danger of that," Jillian protested. "What has Henry Tudor to do with you?"

Nell's eyes widened, and once again Jillian was struck by the richness of her beauty.

You really don't know, do you?

"No."

I thought you had become expert in Geraldine history.

"Not expert, Nell, just better informed than when I last saw you."

Robert Montgomery, a Norman lord commissioned by the king, is on his way to bring Gerald back to London. I am to accompany my brother to Henry's court.

"Is that so terrible?"

Nell stamped her foot. *Never before has a Geraldine been so dimwitted. I wish to go to Aughnanure and wed Donal O'Flaherty. 'Tis his child I carry. Tell me what you know of Gerald's future and mine.*

Jillian was very aware of the silence stretching out between them. Not a breath of air stirred the leaves. The stillness of the woods was deafening in its absoluteness. She knew very little, really. What harm could it do? Slowly, she shook her head. "I know nothing at all about you, Nell. I've never seen your name in the history of the Geraldines. But I can tell you that Gerald will live to his majority and win back a portion of the land that was taken from your father. The Geraldines never regained the power they once had."

A frown marred Nell's forehead. *Do you recall if the O'Flahertys were involved in a conflict with England?*

"Not during Henry's time. There was something between Grace O'Malley who married an O'Flaherty, but it was nearly fifty years later, during Elizabeth's reign."

A woman ruling England? Doubt edged her words.

Jillian laughed. "For a very long time. It was considered to be England's golden age."

A Tudor dynasty. Henry won after all.

"You must have lived to be very old if you know nothing of Elizabeth." A thought occurred to her. "She must be part of your future. Otherwise you would have known about her."

Nell's voice was very low. *I care nothing for Elizabeth.*

"I'm sorry, Nell, but I really don't know anything else."

I cannot believe history has no record of me. Perhaps there's something you've missed, something I've neglected to tell you. She hesitated. *I wonder—*

Jillian watched Nell's mind work. She knew desperation when she saw it, and her uneasiness grew. "Will you be all right, Nell?" she asked anxiously. "If I don't start back now, I'll be missed."

Nell smiled. *You've brought me hope, but 'tis not enough. I need more, Jillian. I need to know if Gerald's survival depends on me. Will you help me?*

"What can I do?"

Come with me to Askeaton Castle.

Nell gasped. "You're not serious."

Yes, I am.

"I can't." Jillian could hardly get the words out. "It isn't possible. What purpose would it serve?"

You would help me to see what I cannot. You're a woman now. We can truly be friends. I was there when you needed me. Now I need you.

"You're not being fair, Nell." Jillian's voice hovered on the edge of panic. Deliberately, she willed herself to remain calm. "My exams are tomorrow, and then I'm going home. I can't just disappear from the face of the earth. Besides, it isn't possible."

You're wondering whether I'm really here, aren't you? You think I'm a figment of your imagination.

Jillian's face blanched. It was exactly what she was thinking. Of course, if Nell really was an apparition, she would know her thoughts, and nothing Nell said should be a surprise.

Haven't you ever wondered why someone you've never seen before appears so familiar?

Jillian shook her head.

Of course you have. You're just being difficult. There are fissures in time, Jillian, channels by which those from one world may enter another.

"This is absurd." Jillian climbed up to the path and began walking briskly back toward the Abbey. "I'm going mad," she muttered to herself. "Six years. I haven't seen you in six years, and you want me to travel through time with you. I won't do it."

Just for a little while.

Jillian clapped her hands over her ears. "No."

I would do it for you.

Jillian began to run, but Nell's voice kept up with her. *Be reasonable, Jillian. No one will even know you are gone.*

Her breath came in deep, uneven gasps, drowning out Nell's words. The Abbey was in sight now. Jillian ran gratefully up the stone steps of the small chapel, knelt down in front of the altar, and closed her eyes. Surely hallucinations wouldn't follow her into this house of sanctuary.

Slowly, her heartbeat normalized, and serenity replaced the terror in her heart. She opened her eyes and stared at the image of St. Christopher, the patron saint of travelers, over the altar. Was it a trick of the light, or was there something different about the eyes and the way they glittered? She shifted slightly to move out of the statue's direct gaze. It wasn't far enough. She moved again. A tiny bubble of fear grew in her chest. Was it her imagination, or was the saint's obsidian-dark gaze following her?

Jillian couldn't look away. She stared into the shining blackness of the cut glass. Her lids wouldn't blink, and a burning sensation crept from the outer edges of her eyes to the centers. Deeper and deeper she was drawn into the icy darkness until it engulfed her. A single word hovered on the edge of her memory. Why couldn't she remember it? Her tongue touched the back of her teeth. "Nell." That was it. "Nnnneeellll." The sound, foreign in its harshness, erupted from the back of her throat. "Nnnneeellll, heeeelp meeeeee!" she screamed.

10

Askeaton Castle, 1537

It was the first time Robert Montgomery had crossed the sea to Ireland, but it did not seem unfamiliar. The mist-shrouded bogs rough with marsh grass and sucking mud, the thick forests and haunting glens, the rugged cliffs stained white with bird droppings, reminded him of his native Wales. Even the castles were similar. The Irish were a proud people and eschewed everything English, but, like it or not, Norman invaders had built their stone fortresses in Ireland as they had in Wales.

Robert was the descendant of a Norman marcher lord, but he had no quarrel with the Irish or with any other race for that matter. His own bloodline boasted a strain from Owain of Gwynned, the last Celtic king of Wales who fought English occupation. This mission was not of his choosing. He had no taste for the blood of schoolboys, but Henry had promised him a title and castles. For a second son with no hope of succession, the offer was a godsend.

It was late in the year for fresh snow, but an off-season dusting fell from the sky, blanketing the rocks and trees, freezing the breath of both men and horses as they rode toward an uncertain welcome. Desmond Fitzgerald was Sean Ghall, but reports told of a man who hated all things English. It would be the height of foolishness to ambush an emissary of the king, but the Irish were unpredictable. Robert kept a sharp eye on the rise ahead.

Suddenly, out of nowhere, the forest was alive with men on horseback bearing steel-tipped lances and the odd, cone-shaped helmets preferred by the Irish. There appeared to be hundreds of them.

Instinctively, Robert reined in his horse, and his hand moved to where his sword rested in its scabbard. A man, older than the others, bare-headed, with a sly, weathered face and an air of command, rode to the swell of the rise and looked down. He smiled through his beard and urged his mount down the hill until he was less than two meters from where Robert waited.

"Trespassing is illegal in Ireland," the man said in the cultured accent of an English gentleman.

"We mean no disrespect," replied Robert.

"You are on Desmond land. What is your purpose here?"

Robert could see the color of his eyes. They were the cold gray of hammered flint. His soldiers were outnumbered ten to one. Who would know or care if a party of Englishmen disappeared on a mission far from the Pale? He swallowed. "Henry wishes to have the Geraldine at Whitehall. I am sent to find him and bring him back."

"Indeed."

The mocking arrogance reflected in the earl's expression sent warning signals ringing through Montgomery's brain. "We mean no harm, my lord. Henry wants the Geraldine. He is afraid of a rebellion. You would do the same."

"The boy is my kinsman. What assurances do I have that he will not meet the fate of his father?"

Robert stiffened. It was the same question he had asked of Henry before departing on this misguided mission. "You have the king's word."

Desmond laughed, a loud, raucous cackle that sent the first squirrels of the season dashing into the tree branches. "The king's word. That's rich. Your king has no honor, Welshman. His word is worthless here in Ireland. We have six dead Geraldines to prove it."

Robert refused to be drawn into an argument. "Henry has no quarrel with you, Desmond. Give up the boy, and you will be rewarded."

"No."

"There was no love lost between you and the Kildare Geraldines."

Desmond Fitzgerald's jaw hardened. "They were of my blood, Sassanach. Take your men and leave my land, or prepare to meet your God."

Robert swore under his breath. "Do not cut your own throat, Desmond. Henry's sweep is wide. He will not soon forget your treachery."

"Tell my cousin that here in Ireland, I am the law."

Raising his left hand, Robert signaled his men to turn back. It would have been much easier, but his expectations had not included acquiescence from Desmond. He would wait at the lip of the cliff, beyond the borders of Desmond land. The boy could not stay within the gates forever. When the Fitzgeralds least expected it, Robert would strike.

Nell stepped out of the damp gloom of the castle and lifted her face to a milky spring sun. It was early morn-

ing and very cold, but after weeks of rain, the meager
sunlight lifted her spirits. Gerald was completely recovered. She watched as he walked toward her, laughing
and talking with the tutor Desmond had appointed.

Thomas Leverous was an Englishman fostered to the
Desmond Fitzgeralds years ago. He had become so fond
of life in Ireland that he had remained at the castle,
acquiring the skills of the clergy. He had thought to
enter the holy orders but found himself with a penchant
for women and no true vocation. Gerald was the answer
to his prayers. He would teach the Fitzgerald heir, remain at Askeaton Castle, and fantasize of a future with
Gerald's sister. Thomas was nearly thirty years old, but
the sight of Nell Fitzgerald coming toward him, a smile
of welcome on her face, brought the blood to his cheeks
and a hollow feeling to his stomach. He bowed slightly.
"Good morning, my lady."

"Good morning, Thomas. How fares my brother?"

"The lad has a fine mind and many questions."

Gerald broke in. "I've worked hard all morning, Nell.
You said I might ride out of the gates if I finished my
letters early."

Nell smiled, completely oblivious to everything but
her brother's pleasure. "So I did. Shall we allow him
his ride, Thomas?" She lifted light-filled eyes to the
tutor's face.

"Aye, my lady," Leverous stuttered. "I'll see to the
saddling."

Less than twenty minutes passed before Gerald
stepped into the groom's locked fingers and was hoisted
onto his mare's back. Nell reined in her mount to wait
for Thomas and her brother. It was good to feel a horse
beneath her again, good to look back at the heavy turrets of Askeaton Castle, at the flags flying and the turf
smoke from the chimneys spreading across the sky,

comforting signs of Fitzgerald prosperity. Only a small
worry nagged at the back of her mind. Although she
was healthy as a horse and her appetite never failed her,
she had missed her courses twice. Soon she would have
to confess to Desmond that she was handfasted to
Donal O'Flaherty.

Gerald had cantered ahead. Nell dug her heels into
the sides of her mare to catch up with him. "Take care,
Gerald," she warned. " 'Tis foolish to ride at such
speeds when the ground is unfamiliar to us."

"Look, Nell." The boy pointed into the woods where
twin fawns shivered near a motionless doe. The doe's
dark eyes were fixed on something deep in the shadows.
Suddenly, she leaped into the air, and the three of them,
doe and fawns, melted into the trees.

So quickly had they become one with the mist that
Nell was tempted to rub her eyes. She blinked twice,
quickly, and gasped. Horsemen carrying spears, dressed
in the light mesh of the English, materialized out of
nowhere and surrounded them. A man on a brown gelding with a nosepiece that distorted his face and made
the dark brown of his eyes glitter strangely through the
slits uttered a harsh command. In unison, the horsemen
closed in.

Thomas Leverous spoke first. "This is Desmond
land, sir. You are trespassing. The lady and her brother
are Fitz—"

"Hush, Thomas," Nell hissed. "Say no more."

Robert Montgomery smiled beneath his mail. Eleanor Fitzgerald was no fool. Still, her caution would avail
her nothing. Henry had spoken, and there were lands
and castles at stake. Robert lifted his reins. Automatically, his horse, trained to respond to the slightest pressure of his knees, moved forward and stopped in front

of Nell. Pushing back the nosepiece of his helmet, he stared into angry green-gold eyes.

"Christ," he muttered under his breath. Wetting his cracked lips, he spoke. "I regret the circumstances that force you to leave Ireland without a proper farewell, my lady."

Nell met his eyes without flinching. "Who are you?"

"Robert Montgomery, sent to escort you to London."

"Are we under arrest?"

She was direct, intelligent, and incredibly lovely. Looking into those cool, discerning eyes, he could not dissemble. "Aye."

"Will we be executed?"

He flinched and mentally damned Henry Tudor to the fires of hell. A girl like this should not be forced to ask such a question. The ferocity of his resolve sent words he had no intention of uttering past his lips. "You will not be harmed."

"Do you swear?"

Robert nodded. He could not look away from her eyes. "I swear."

Later that night, far from Desmond land, Robert held out his hands to warm them at the fire. He couldn't sleep, and apparently neither could Eleanor Fitzgerald. Wrapped in her cloak, she sat motionless, staring into the dwindling flames. "Why did you attempt to hide from Henry?" he asked.

She threw him a withering look. "We had nothing to lose."

"You've done nothing. Henry would not dare harm you."

She curled her lip, and to Robert, who was close to becoming besotted, even that gesture of contempt was lovely.

"How reassuring you are, Sir Robert, and how naive," she said. "Henry needs no excuse for murder. Two of his wives face eternity without their heads, the evidence for their crimes nothing more than the pathetic ramblings of torture victims. You will pardon me if I am unconvinced of Henry's compassion."

"Your father stirred up rebellion in Ireland."

Nell shook her head. " 'Twas my brother Thomas who incited the uprising, but only after my father was unjustly imprisoned and killed in the Tower." Her voice lowered, and she turned back to the fire. "Gerald had nothing to do with it. He is only a boy."

"A boy all Ireland would follow."

Nell's mouth turned up at the corners, and Robert wondered what it would be like to run his finger across her lips, to feel them soften and open beneath his. Cursing his distraction, he caught the tail end of her words.

"You know little of Ireland, Welshman," she said. "We are a fragmented people with mixed loyalties. Even my cousin Desmond Fitzgerald has English blood. The only true Irish are to the north and the west, the O'Donnells, branches of the O'Neills and the O'Flah—" She stopped, aghast at how loose her tongue had become. There was something unusual about this man, this English soldier, something in the uncompromising set of his mouth and the steady brown gaze that inspired trust.

"You were saying?" he asked politely.

She shrugged, laughing self-consciously. "Never mind. I am not myself tonight. Tell me how you came to be the king's knight."

Robert grinned and knelt to throw more wood on the fire. The light illuminated his face, and her eyes widened. He was younger than she thought, possibly no more than thirty. His serious expression and the deep grooves in his cheeks made him appear older at first than he really was.

"I am a second son whose older brother has four healthy boys," he said ruefully. "With no hope of inheriting and no vocation for the church, I must make my way in the world."

"You do not seem displeased with your fortune."

"The life suits me." He looked at Nell, her face touched with firelight, and the breath caught in his throat. He swallowed. "In truth, I am fond of children. I would have what my brother has."

"And that is?"

"A home and family enough to fill it."

The intensity of his gaze made her uncomfortable. She looked away, pulling her cloak tightly around her.

"And what of you, Eleanor?" It was the first time that he had used her name. "How would you arrange your life?"

Heat rose in her cheeks, and she was grateful for the concealing darkness. "My father arranged my life. I am betrothed to Donal O'Flaherty of Aughnanure, and I am satisfied with his decision."

Robert stood and looked down upon the silvery head of the girl he had searched the length of Ireland to find. "May you achieve everything that you desire, lass," he said gruffly. "I bid you good night."

"Good night, Robert," she said, using his Christian name.

The Royal Palace, London

"Your grace." The boy bowed his head and kept his eyes on the floor, but Henry ignored him. It was the girl who held his attention. The Fitzgeralds were known to be a well-favored family, but this young woman was like no one he had ever seen before. She was dressed in gold brocade with a deep, squared-off neckline that revealed delicate bones and full, round breasts. Silvery hair, brushed smooth and held away from her forehead by a simple headpiece, framed a face that cried out for an artist's canvas. When she lifted her hazel eyes to meet his gaze, Henry, a man known for surrounding himself with beautiful women, drew a deep restorative breath. Suddenly, his wife, who only a short year ago inspired him to sonnets praising her beauty, seemed insipid and rather common.

"Welcome to Whitehall, dear cousins," he said unsteadily. "Finding you has put me to great inconvenience and expense. However, you are here now, and I bear you no ill will. This is your home." He stood and motioned to his steward. "Thomas, take the boy and find him a tutor. His sister and I shall walk in the conservatory." He held out his arm. "Lady Eleanor."

Nell rose and rested her hand on the king's outstretched arm. She hoped that the conservatory was close by. Henry Tudor was enormous, and his ulcerated leg was twice the size of his normal one. It would not do for him to take a fall or have a seizure while in her presence.

He kept his eyes on her profile. "Do you fear me, cousin?"

"Yes, your grace."

"Because of your father?"

Nell sucked in her bottom lip between her teeth. What game did he play? She knew his reputation. What could she say that would keep her away from the executioner's block? Frantically, she discarded one response after another. It was past time for answering. "Because of my father," she answered defiantly, "and my uncles and my brother."

"They were traitors, Eleanor," he said gently. "Look at me, and tell me that your father did not wish to rule all of Ireland in my place."

So he had. The answer came to her as clearly as the bells of Westminster. Her father had wished to rule all of Ireland. Admitting the truth would keep her alive and convince Henry of her integrity. "Aye. That was his dream, albeit a distant one."

Henry chuckled. "Good girl. I'd not expected that." He stopped and took her chin in his hand, turning her head so that she was forced to look at him. "We shall get on well together, Eleanor. You are clever. I enjoy clever women, although I prefer not to marry them."

"I am indeed fortunate that your grace is well and truly married and that soon you will be a father again."

His eyes glittered strangely as they moved over her face. Deliberately, he rubbed her jaw with his thumb. "All in good time, Eleanor. All in good time. The child does not sit well with Jane, but she is England's queen, and so she shall be honored."

Henry's thumb was at the corner of her mouth. Nell prayed that she wouldn't gag. Affecting a sneeze, she stepped back out of his reach. "Your sentiments do you credit, cousin," she said. "I look forward to meeting your wife. Great care must be taken to keep her calm. After all, the succession is at stake."

They were at the entrance to the conservatory, and no one else was in the hall. He held open the door and followed her inside. Nell looked around, and her heart sank. The room was a riot of blooming color and completely empty of anyone but the two of them. She could feel the king behind her, so close that the repulsive, unmistakable odor of rotting flesh reached her nose.

She willed herself not to flinch when his hands came down on her shoulders. His breath was hot against her ear. "We shall deal well together, Nell," he said hoarsely.

"Of course, your grace," she replied in a cool voice.

"You are so lovely." His lips seared the nape of her neck.

Nell's back teeth locked. "Your queen would not approve."

"We must be very discreet so as not to alarm Jane and bring on the babe. You do understand how important a son is to me, don't you, Nell?"

She suffered his hands as they slid down her arms and settled on her waist. "It must be your sole concern, your grace."

"Call me Henry. I would hear my name on your lips."

"Henry."

He turned her around and pulled her against him. Feverishly, he ran his hands across the exposed skin above her neckline. "Holy God, how I want you. You are driving me mad with wanting." Bending his head, he covered her mouth with his own.

When she could stand no more of his probing tongue, Nell pushed him away and fought the urge to scrub her mouth. "This is madness," she gasped. "They will look for us and gossip. Word will spread throughout the court and reach the queen." She locked her fingers together and left her future to fate. "I have no wish to become a royal mistress, your grace. Surely there are others who can satisfy you until Jane is recovered."

Henry adjusted his corset and stretched his aching leg. He needed whiskey quickly. The exertion pained him more than he would admit to anyone. He frowned. The Fitzgerald chit needed reminding that his power was absolute. He would rather she be willing, but he would take her whether or not she wished it. "I can do much for you, Nell."

"My needs are few."

He took her hand. "There is young Gerald to think of. Is his life less than your maidenhood?"

She would make him say it. "You would spare Gerald if I agree to share your bed?"

"I would. And when we finish with each other, I will settle gold upon you. You will be a rich woman."

She sent up a silent prayer of thanksgiving that Donal's child would soon be in evidence. Henry would not want her then. "Shall we bargain, your grace? My body for as long as you want it in exchange for gold and my brother's life."

He stroked her cheek. "Not so quickly, lass. We must arrange this carefully. Jane must never hear of it."

The warm air was making her head ache. "She will not hear of it from me, Henry."

His fleshy face broke into a wide grin. "Good girl. You may wait on me tonight in my chambers."

Bowing her head, she allowed him to place his arm around her waist and lead her out of the room.

Nell gritted her teeth and paced back and forth from one end of her small chamber to the other. Forward three strides and back three, forward and back, back and forth, kicking the confining skirts from between her legs. The man was thrice her age and gross enough to make her skin crawl. She imagined the oozing sore on his leg, and the mere thought of it made the nausea rise in her stomach. Her mouth twisted humorlessly. Hadn't she predicted that she would be given to just such a man? If only she had gone with Donal to Aughnanure.

She heard a hissing sound. The flames rose and spit

as if a gust of rain had blown down into the hearth. Her eyes widened, and the hairs on the back of her neck lifted. She felt something, a presence in the room that had not been there before. There could be no mistaking it. Her mother had brought her to an awareness of the netherworld after her first Beltane.

Nell blinked and rubbed her eyes. A form, oddly familiar in its strangeness, stepped forward out of the licking flames and into the room. Nell gasped. It was a girl dressed like a man. She stared at the apparition for several seconds before finding her voice. "Who are you?"

The girl brushed the soot from her sleeves. *You know perfectly well who I am, Nell. I told you I wouldn't come. Now send me back immediately.*

Nell lifted her chin. "Identify yourself, or I'll call a guard."

That's rich. I wonder if anyone will be able to see me here, in your time. After all, no one can see you in mine. Why don't we try it? Call the guard.

Nell inched toward the door. "I've never seen you before. Tell me who you are."

Jillian frowned. *I'm Jillian Fitzgerald,* she said slowly. *Please say that you know me. You've visited me all of my life until a few years ago. For some reason, you decided that I should come back here with you.*

Nell's mouth dropped open. She would have spoken, but a soft scratching noise at the door stopped her. She looked at Jillian, a question in her eyes.

Jillian shrugged.

"Come in," Nell called out.

A servant stood at the door. "Did you wish for a bath, my lady?"

"Yes." She looked from the serving girl to Jillian and

back again. "Anne, was anyone in my room this afternoon?"

"No one but me, my lady." She looked around. "Was anything out of place?"

"No, not at all. A bath will be lovely. But not until later." Quickly, she closed the door on the confused servant and spun around to where Jillian stood in the center of the room. "She didn't see you."

Apparently not.

"But why?"

I've already told you. I'm not of this time. I haven't been born yet. I don't exist.

Nell sat down weakly on the bed. "From what time period do you come?"

The twentieth century, nineteen hundred seventy-eight, to be exact.

"In your century, can people move freely back and forth across time as you do?"

No. At least, I've never heard of anyone doing it.

"And you expect me to believe you?"

Jillian flushed and balled her fists. *I don't expect anything but to be sent home immediately. You brought me here, now send me back. I didn't want to come in the first place.*

The fire crackled and a log snapped, sending a shower of sparks onto the brick hearth. "I do believe you, Jillian Fitzgerald," Nell said softly, "and I'm very sorry, but I have no idea how to send you anywhere."

Jillian's face lost its color, and she sank down onto Nell's feather mattress. *How can this be? Why don't you know me?*

Nell tilted her head and thought. "Tell me what it is that I should know about you."

Pressing her fingers against her temples, Jillian shook her head. *Most of it was a long time ago. But there was something strange that happened recently.*

"Go on."

After six years, you came back and told me you were carrying a child. You asked me to tell you everything historians had written about you because you had to make a decision. I wasn't much help, I'm afraid. There is no record of a Nell Fitzgerald in anything I've researched. It's as if you never existed at all.

Nell's forehead wrinkled. She stared at the stranger with her shoulder-length hair, her slim curves revealed by the odd clothing she wore. "How strange. Perhaps there is something you've overlooked."

You've come to me all of my life, Nell. It isn't likely I'd miss your name.

"Eleanor is a family name," Nell explained. "There is one of us in every generation. Perhaps you've confused me with someone else."

Jillian's mouth dropped. *I'm stupid,* she whispered. *Totally, completely stupid, an idiot, a blind idiot.* She jumped up and rewalked the path that Nell had recently worn into the floorboards.

"I'm sure you'll enlighten me when you've finished maligning yourself," Nell said, allowing the faintest tinge of mockery to color her voice.

Don't you see, Nell? Jillian had come to a complete stop in front of her. *I didn't know your name was Eleanor. All this time I've been looking for* Nell.

"Good Lord."

Exactly.

Nell's eyes gleamed. "Then you *can* tell me what lies ahead."

Not a great deal of it, said Jillian reluctantly. *If I remember correctly, Eleanor Fitzgerald was married briefly to Robert Montgomery. Later, she was kidnapped by an Irish chieftain, and all traces of her were lost.*

"That's impossible. Robert Montgomery has no wish to marry me, nor I him."

Jillian leaned back on the bed and crossed her arms under her head. *Do you know him?*

"We've met." Nell blushed, remembering a conversation late one night by the fire and the way the knight's eyes had lingered on her face. "Jillian, I must ask you one final question. Do not spare me, for I would know the worst. Does history tell of Henry Tudor's women?"

It has a great deal to say about his wives.

Nell wet her lips and looked away from Jillian's expressive sea-colored eyes. "What of the women he bedded who were not his wives?"

Jillian stared at Nell and, for the first time, realized the disadvantages of beauty. When she spoke, her voice was very gentle. *I'm sorry, Nell. I've never really given it much attention. Perhaps if I went back, I could find out.*

Nell's laugh was bitter. "I haven't time for that. Henry expects me tonight."

Jillian thought for a minute. *When you came to me, you said that you carried a child. You told me the father's name, but I can't remember it. Whose child is it, Nell?*

Nell shook her head. "I will not say. The less you know, the better."

No one can see or hear me. I don't exist. It doesn't matter what I know.

"Why do you need to know anything?"

To help you and to get back to where I belong. My life is just beginning. I want to live it.

"How can you help me?"

I'm a Fitzgerald. My family can trace its ancestry back a thousand years. If you tell me who the father of your child is, I may be able to tell you where he fits on our family tree and who his descendants are. Her own innate honesty forced her to admit another possibility. *There is the chance that I may find nothing at all.*

"You're forgetting that I have no idea how to send you back."

A voice through the door interrupted them. "Your bath water has arrived, my lady."

Jillian and Nell exchanged identical looks of dismay. "I've run out of time, Jillian," whispered Nell. "There is nothing more to do except pray."

Ordinarily, that would reassure me, said Jillian dryly, *except that is exactly what I was doing before I ended up here.* She thought a moment. *I may be able to help you, temporarily, if you do exactly as I say.*

Nell looked puzzled. "I don't understand."

History has a great deal to report on Henry Tudor and the kind of man he was, Jillian explained. *One thing historians agree on unanimously is that he was a man with a tremendous ego.*

"What is that?"

Jillian slipped her shoe off and relieved the itch on her heel with her big toe. *It means that he thinks very highly of himself and wants others to feel the same way.*

"I don't see why that would help me."

Have you ever heard of psychology?

Nell shook her head.

Jillian shrugged impatiently. *Never mind. All you need to know is that there are men and women who study the reasons people behave the way they do. By understanding behavior, we can change it.*

"Are you saying that I can change the king's mind, that he won't want me for his mistress?"

Jillian nodded. *It's possible. Just listen . . .*

11

Despite the chants she'd recited for the purpose of bringing on a sense of detachment, Nell was desperately afraid. Her hands were blocks of ice, and her glass reflected a face completely leached of color. The intimacies she'd experienced with Donal O'Flaherty had been an awakening, a bonding of body and spirit, a union of the kind she'd always imagined. Sharing Henry Tudor's bed would be something entirely different. She would be fortunate if she made it through the night without losing her dinner.

If it were Thomas instead of Gerald whose life was at stake, or if Gerald were a grown man—but he was not. He was a boy, a boy with a hint of childish sweetness lingering in the bones of his face and in the curve of his smile. She could not stand by and see Gerald harmed.

The king's amused voice interrupted her thoughts. "Are you a virgin, Nell?"

"No."

Henry chuckled, and the entire bed vibrated. "I am glad of it. Deflowering a virgin is more work than a man of my age desires. 'Tis far more pleasurable to sleep with a woman of experience."

Nell could hardly manage the words. "I am not so very experienced, Henry, but I shall try to please you."

He patted the empty space beside him. "Come, Nell. Lie beside me, and we shall know each other better."

She crossed the room and sat down on the bed. Again, the odor of decaying flesh assailed her nostrils. Her stomach churned. Perhaps she would faint, he would have his way with her and she would feel nothing at all. "Shall I dim the candles, your grace?"

He pulled her down into his shoulder where a hollow should have been. "Henry," he muttered. "Call me Henry." Pawing at the laces of her gown, he managed to untie them.

"Henry," she gasped, closing her eyes against the sight of his passion-flushed face and the feel of his hands heavy against her skin.

"I would see you, Nell."

The voice came from above her. Through her lashes, she could see him looming over her. Dear God, let it be over soon. What was it that Jillian had told her?

Laugh, Nell. Jillian's voice penetrated the haze fogging her brain. *Henry's pride is easily hurt. Do as I say and laugh.*

Summoning her last reserves, Nell opened her eyes, forced herself to glance at the massive shoulders and sagging belly hovering over her, and laughed contemptuously.

Immediately, his hands stopped their movement. Nell laughed again, and he sat up and frowned. "You are amused, my lady?"

Again, the voice assailed her. *Tell him that he is working so very hard. Ask him if he is enjoying himself.*

Nell swallowed. She couldn't possibly use those words. He would have her head. " 'Tis just that you seem so very urgent, Henry," she stammered. "Are you enjoying yourself?"

"Quite," he said sarcastically. "Shall we return to it?"

"Of course."

His hand slid up her bare leg. He groaned deep in his throat and lowered his head to her breast.

Laugh again.

Desperation gave her courage. Nell laughed.

Annoyed, Henry lifted his head. "What is it now, Nell?"

Tell him that you've never had so desperate a lover. Ask him how long he's been celibate.

Nell's eyes danced. That she could say. "I've never had quite so desperate a lover," she repeated. "Has it been a long time since a woman has shared your bed?"

She felt him wither against her leg. He shifted away from her and crossed his arms behind his head. Her spirits lifted.

"Have you entertained many men, Nell?" he asked casually.

This time, she needed no prompting to play her part. "A few, although none in your—" She swallowed and searched for the words that would suggest without offending. "None in the prime of his life, as you are, Henry."

"I see." He was silent for a long time. Then he threw back the covers and pulled on his dressing gown. "It appears that I am tired after all," he said coldly. "We shall have to postpone our coupling."

"Of course, your grace." She sat up and retied the laces of her gown. "Your reputation for virility is unparalleled. Every woman who has shared your bed considers herself most fortunate. I am honored that you chose me. Still"—she looked puzzled—"is it something I've done that has put you off? Perhaps I should ask the Lady Anne if she knows why you couldn't—" She hesitated, apparently searching for a delicate way to describe what had not happened between them.

Arrested, Henry stared at her. Lady Anne Thomlin had been his latest interest. She was also a notorious gossip. He had no desire to have rumors of his impotence spread throughout the court. He tested the waters. "You have learned a great deal in the short time you've spent in my court, Nell."

She hid a smile. "Women are fond of gossip."

"Are you prone to gossip, Nell?"

She shook her head. "I am a solitary person. I prefer my own company and have little discourse with other women."

He sighed. She really was too young for him, little more than a child. "I'm glad to hear it, cousin."

"May I retire, your majesty?"

Henry nodded and waved her away. She forced herself to walk slowly to the door, closing it softly behind her.

The fire had gone out in her chamber. Nell shivered and bolted the door. Jillian was sitting on the bed, awake. "It's cold," Nell admonished her. "Why didn't you add more wood to the fire?"

I didn't notice. I haven't been cold or hot, hungry or tired since I got here.

Nell's warm heart ached. "I'm so sorry, Jilly," she said softly, walking to the bed to sit beside her. "I wish I could help you."

What did you call me? Jillian's eyes were enormous in her freckled face.

The intensity of her expression puzzled Nell. She frowned. "I believe I called your name."

You said Jilly. No one uses that name anymore. It was my childhood name. Only people who knew me then call me Jilly.

"I don't understand."

Jillian sat up on her knees on the bed, trembling with excitement. *You do remember, Nell, not all of it yet. But it's there, and someday you'll remember.*

Nell's eyes softened. "I hope so. But Jilly isn't such a far cry from Jillian. It might have been a natural shortening of your name, a gesture of affection."

Are you feeling affectionate?

"Yes." Nell smiled. "You were right. Henry Tudor is a man with an ego."

Jillian slid off the bed to stretch her legs. *I'm pleased for you, Nell,* she said after taking a turn around the room. *What will happen now?*

Nell looked surprised. "I don't know."

Is your brother out of danger?

"For the moment, until Henry's child is born. He won't risk upsetting the queen with another execution. Apparently she has grown fond of Gerald. After that, I don't know."

Leaning against the mantel, Jillian crossed her arms against her chest. *Would you care for some advice?*

Nell looked thoughtfully at the leggy girl standing there in her man's breeks and a shirt the color of her eyes. The material was something Nell had never seen or felt before. It was thin and warm and wonderfully soft. Jillian was very attractive despite her shorn head and mannish ways. Thick brown-gold hair curled against her shoulders, framing a high-boned, striking face. Although she was tall for a Geraldine, her lines were slender, almost delicate, and her small waist and full breasts would catch the attention of any man with eyes in his head. Her skin was darker than most women preferred, and dotted with freckles, a testament to long hours spent in the sun. But it was her eyes that revealed her lineage. They were Fitzgerald eyes. Thickly lashed and large, with prominent lids, they shone sage green, sometimes smoky blue, with striking gold lights running through the centers. She looked quite familiar, but then the Fitzgerald bloodline always bred strong. "Your advice has been helpful, Jilly. Tell me what you think I should do."

You need protection for yourself and your child. Find someone who can give it to you.

"Do you have someone in mind?"

History is fact, Nell. Robert Montgomery will be your husband. Why not accept the inevitable and make the best of it?

Nell's hand moved protectively to her stomach. It was an O'Flaherty that she carried. Donal would not thank her for raising his child a Montgomery. "Have you ever been in love, Jilly?"

The moment passed when Jillian could have denied it. Now she would have to explain. *I don't think so.* Her hands twisted in her lap. *No. Not really.*

Nell laughed. "Tell me about him."

There was never a him. *I was thirteen years old. He was seventeen, the son of my father's kennel keeper. He—* Jillian bit her lip. *He was accused and most likely convicted of a crime he didn't commit. I don't really know what happened to him. No one would tell me.*

"I'm sorry."

Jillian looked away. *It doesn't matter anymore. It was impossible.*

Nell sighed. "Aye. A servant lad and the daughter of a noble would be an impossible match."

Frankie wasn't a servant, Jillian said quickly. *He was going to be a veterinarian.*

Nell looked puzzled.

It's an animal doctor, she explained, *and it isn't impossible for men and women of different stations to marry.*

"If that's so, then why wouldn't they tell you what happened to him?"

Because of what they thought he did. Jillian rubbed her arms and walked to the window. The world, shrouded in fog without streetlights, was a deep, unrelieved black where the hills and sky blended together. *There's more. My mother was worried about him for a long time. Frankie was Catholic and the Fitzgeralds Protestant. It's a long story, Nell, but between my time and yours, the battle between the two has been one long bloodbath. Ireland is divided now. The North belongs to England and the South, the Republic, is an independent nation. In the North, the majority is Protestant. We own the land and take the jobs. The Catholics are poor and unemployed. It's dreadful, and I'm very ashamed, but those are the facts. Frankie was one of the poor and unemployed. My family never looked beyond that to see his potential. When my brother was killed and Frankie was accused, they never spoke of him again.*

Nell nodded. "I see." She really didn't. She was Protestant, and Donal was Catholic. Her mother had been Catholic, her father turned Protestant by order of the king. As far as Nell could see, the two religions were identical. Everyone did not agree, of course. Many remained loyal to the Church and lost their heads when Henry split with Rome. The Fitzgeralds were God-fearing, but the Church never held great influence over them. Nell wondered what her father, the great Gerald Og, would have made of the strange world to which his descendant belonged. "Religion can be difficult at times."

Jillian brushed aside her comment. *Religion no longer has anything at all to do with it. The conflict comes from people like the Fitzgeralds who wish to keep what they have at the expense of people who have nothing at all.*

"You sound very bitter."

I have nothing to be bitter about. I'm one of those who have more of everything than they can possibly need.

"Except Frankie Maguire."

At first the slip didn't register, but when it did, Jillian's eyes blazed with light. *How did you know his name?*

"You told me."

Only his first name, only Frankie, not Maguire.

Nell thought. "I'm sure—"

No, said Jillian, shaking her head emphatically. *You knew his name. It came from you. Somewhere inside you are memories from when you came to me.*

"What good are they if I can't remember?"

You will, said Jillian. *The more we talk, the more you'll remember.*

Nell hung her head. "I'm sorry for bringing you here, Jillian."

If I hadn't come, I may never have figured out that you were really Eleanor.

They were silent after that, lost in their own thoughts until Jillian brought up what Nell knew but would not admit. *You should cultivate Robert Montgomery's friendship. Anyone would make a better mate than Henry Tudor.*

Nell recalled Henry's fleshy lips and pawing hands and shuddered. Robert Montgomery was not a man to be cuckolded by anyone, not even a king. He was strong and not ill favored for a man of his years. But he was not Donal. "I am handfasted to Donal O'Flaherty," she explained. "The child I carry is his. Even were I willing, no man would take a woman to wife knowing she carries another's babe in her belly."

Have you told anyone?

"No."

Why not tell Robert the child is his?

" 'Tis too late for that, and even if it weren't, the immorality of such a deception troubles me."

Then tell him, and let him decide. You've nothing to lose.

Nell wondered at this strange new world to which Jillian belonged. Had men changed so much that they no longer cared if their women took others to their beds? She took another searching look at this self-possessed young woman from the future. "Perhaps I shall tell him. If only you could take my place and tell him for me. I'm very sure you would know what to say."

We aren't enough alike for that, said Jillian practically.

Nell wrinkled her forehead and stared at Jillian for a long moment. "I wonder if we are so very different, after all."

I'm much taller, and our coloring is completely different. Besides, no one can see me.

"I'm not suggesting that you pretend to be me, Jillian. You won't be me, but you'll be with me, the way I've been with you. Without you, I would be sharing the king's bed this very minute, and without me, your Guinevere would have died. Two minds are better than one. Perhaps that's the reason you are here."

Jillian felt a trembling deep within her, and for a single thunderous second her heart stopped. Nell remembered Guinevere. *You may be right,* she said slowly. *I'll do what I can to help you.*

Nell stared solemnly from the window at the rain-wet coffin borne by Lord Seymour, his two sons, and a nephew. Jane had not lasted beyond the christening of her newborn son. For three dreadful days, her body battled to expel the infant she carried. Finally, when it seemed the child would die in the birthing, the physician ordered away the midwife, produced a knife, wiped it clean on his doublet, and opened her stomach.

The babe was blue. Fearing for his life, the physician blew into the tiny mouth. His reward was a gasp followed by a mewling cry. Henry's son would live, but his mother, torn and burning with fever, would not.

Ten days after the birth of her son, Jane Seymour, queen of England, drew her last bubbling breath, turned her face to the wall, and died. Two days after that, Henry called for Thomas Cromwell to discuss the future of Gerald Fitzgerald, tenth earl of Kildare.

Robert Montgomery looked down at the parchment still wet from the king's signature. "I don't understand, your majesty. The boy was to be spared."

Henry stroked his graying beard. "I have a son. His succession will not be troubled by Geraldine ambitions."

"How can a child who resides here at Whitehall threaten your majesty's power?"

"Stranger things have happened."

Robert's jaw tightened. He would not be the one to confirm Gerald's execution. "The queen favored the boy," he said.

"Jane was ever a fool. She is dead, and I will not speak of her."

Robert tried again. "A Fitzgerald ally would be to your advantage. Gerald is a warm-hearted lad. With the proper guidance, he will bring you great loyalty. Others will follow."

Henry paused. "Does a mentor come to mind?"

"I will be his guardian, your grace. Give me his sister to wed, and I will see that the boy serves you well."

Henry paused, arrested, and stared at Robert. Was there actually color in the man's cheeks? "How long have you aspired in this direction, Robert?"

"Never until this moment, your majesty. I know the match is an unequal one, but Lady Eleanor is fond of her brother. She will not dismiss me."

"By God, she will not," roared Henry. "Else I shall have *her* head. Bring her to me. Bring her at once."

Robert was sweating beneath the fine linen of his shirtsleeves. "Please, your grace. Allow me to speak to Nell first."

Henry glared at him. "She shall not be allowed to refuse, Robert. Tell her it is my desire that she wed at once. I shall give you Cilcerrig Castle. Take the boy, and raise him well."

"It shall be as you wish, sire."

"Go, Robert. Go and tell her at once."

Nell, locked in the throes of a drugging sleep, heard the scratching at her door long before she recognized it for what it was. At first, she burrowed her head into her pillow, hoping it would go away. But the sound persisted, and finally she sat up, pushed her hair back, and slid off the bed to open the door. Her eyes met the solid wall of a masculine chest and widened.

Robert Montgomery smiled down at her. "Good evening, my lady."

"Good evening, sir."

"There is something I wish to discuss with you."

Nell swallowed and stepped back. "Now?"

"Only if it pleases you, Nell. Later will do just as well." She lifted her hand to her throat. "Perhaps you'll allow me a few moments. I was sleeping."

He took her hand and lifted it to his lips. "I shall wait in the retiring room. Take as long as you like."

Nell bolted the door and looked around the room. It was empty. "Jillian," she whispered loudly. "Are you here?" There was no answer. She expected none. She must have fallen into a very deep sleep to have dreamed so vividly. *Jillian Fitzgerald*. She had seemed so real. Nell could still see the freckles across the bridge of her nose, the clear sharp bones of her cheeks, and that mouth. Jillian Fitzgerald had the mouth of a courtesan, the lips full and pouting, slightly chapped, filled with perfectly straight teeth, not unlike her own.

She sat down at the dressing table and stared dispassionately at her reflection. The glass was badly scarred, and the curved contours distorted her image, but even so, she knew that she was beautiful. Robert Montgomery, a landless knight of thirty years, might very well decide that a pregnant bride was a small price to pay for youth, beauty, and the Fitzgerald strain flowing through the blood of his grandchildren. She would tell him about the child. Something told her that no matter what he decided, Robert Montgomery would be a kinder gaoler than Henry Tudor.

He rose the moment she opened the door to the small room where he waited. Nell knew that his patience had worn thin. She came directly to the point. "You have news for me, sir?"

"It is not good news, my lady."

She blanched. "Is it Gerald?"

"Aye. Now that Henry has a true heir, he is more afraid than ever of your brother's influence in Ireland."

"But Gerald has no ambitions in Ireland."

He heard her speak, but he had no idea what she said. Entranced by the play of shadow and light across her face, he stared down at her. She was smaller than he remembered, fine-boned and slender. He wondered if she would breed well and then surprised himself when he realized that he no longer cared. He wanted her whether or not she gave him children.

"What shall I do?" Her anguished question brought him back.

Robert's hands clenched. He knew she would accept his offer. Her brother would die if she refused, but he had a perverse wish to make her want him without the condition. "You ask nothing for yourself, Nell. Have you no thoughts for your own future?"

"I am no threat to Henry. 'Tis not my life the king threatens."

"If it could be arranged, would you leave Whitehall?"

She lifted her chin, a small woman with a spine like steel. "Not without Gerald."

"Nell." His voice cracked, and he reached out to grip her shoulders. "Marry me, and Henry will spare Gerald. I will take you to Wales. The boy will live if you become my wife."

Her eyes blazed an angry gold. "You bargain with my brother's life and expect me to marry you?"

He saw his error at once. "I will not lie to you, lass. The notion was mine. I have wanted you for my own since the first moment I saw you. But 'tis Henry who threatens Gerald's life, not I. He was planning the lad's execution until I convinced him otherwise." He tightened his grip on her shoulders. "You have no choice, Nell. Marry me, and Gerald will live."

She stared at him, a thousand thoughts twisting inside her mind. He shook her slightly. "I'll be good to you. There is nothing left for you in Ireland. You will find happiness in Wales."

Nell wet her lips. "I cannot marry you, Robert. I cannot marry anyone."

"Why not?"

She took a deep breath. "I am handfasted to Donal O'Flaherty. I carry his child."

"Why did you leave him?"

"Gerald needed me."

The tightness eased around Robert's heart. "You left O'Flaherty for Gerald. For Gerald's sake, come with me."

Her voice was the merest whisper of sand across paper. "What of my babe?"

"The child will be raised as my own."

Nell smiled faintly. "Perhaps, if the child is a girl, but a boy—" She shook her head. "You cannot possibly accept another man's son as your heir."

He grinned. "Without you, I would have no heirs at all."

His smile was infectious. She returned it with one of her own. "Surely you would marry someone."

Robert looked down at the bewitching loveliness of her face and wondered if he would ever spare another woman a second glance. "Unless you have me, lass, I will not be anyone's husband for a goodly length of time."

"Why not?"

"I told you before, I am a second son. My brother has healthy heirs. I must make my way in the world with service to my king. I depend upon his appreciation."

Gently, she extricated herself from his grip. "Will he extend his appreciation if I marry you, Robert?"

"Aye, lass."

"What of Donal and the Brehon law under which we handfasted? 'Tis my law, Robert. I am a Fitzgerald."

"Nell," he said desperately, "there is no law in Ireland but Tudor law. Marry me. Your brother will live, and your child will have a name and a father. You have no choice." The words stuck hot and choking in his throat. He was not a man for begging. "Please, Nell," he managed. "I'll not touch you unless you invite me."

She bit down on her lip. Something wasn't right. She felt very unlike herself. "Is the land so important to you, Robert?"

He knelt down and lifted her hand to his lips. "My dearest love, the land no longer has anything to do with it."

12

Donal O'Flaherty crushed the parchment in his hand and threw it into the roaring flames that heated the third-floor living quarters of Aughnanure castle. Damn Desmond Fitzgerald! The mighty Geraldine who wished to rule all of Ireland could not even protect his own.

"What will you do, Donal?"

For a long time, the O'Flaherty looked deep into the leaping light of the fire and pondered his kinsman's question. The young man waited patiently. Finally, Donal turned to speak, and Sean O'Flaherty, related to Donal through the blood of his father, stood rooted to the floor rushes. The O'Flaherty's anger was not the raging fury of heated words and closed fists, easily lit and quickly spent. It was a physical thing, slow to catch and rise, but when it peaked, it became so fearsome that the younger man shuddered to think it might one day be directed at him.

Donal was neither loud nor blustering nor profane. His was a quiet, ice-filled rage, colder and far more deadly than those who had led before him. Young as he was, the O'Flaherty chief did not bend easily, nor was he known for his mercy. He was slow to lift his standard in battle, but when he did, those who invaded his lands and stole his cattle paid the ultimate penalty. Sean wondered what price the O'Flaherty would exact from the man who had stolen his woman.

The frozen fury in his chief's eyes lifted the young man's spirits. Surely, now, there would be a fight. Months had passed since the O'Flahertys had taken up arms. The men chafed under the burdensome yoke of inactivity. A steady sword arm required a turn now and then with a true enemy. Sean's smile brightened as he waited for his chief's answer.

"We shall host a party," the O'Flaherty said slowly. "Every Irish lord and chief will be invited."

Sean's disappointment was almost comical. The O'Flaherty laughed and clapped his young cousin on the shoulder. "Come now, Sean, a good *cruinniú* will please everyone, even those anxious for war."

"Will there be women?"

"Not this time, lad."

A sigh escaped Sean's lips. "When will the gathering take place?"

Donal paused to think. A week to send the missives. Another to prepare and yet another to travel. "Thirty days," he said slowly. "We shall arrange the gathering to take place in thirty days."

One month later, the cooks of Aughnanure swore and fretted as they stumbled over castle dogs gnawing on the slippery entrails and discarded bones of wild fowl, spring lamb, and game. Fish wrapped in bark lay smoking on banked coals, while soot-blackened kitchen maids turned giant haunches of venison on carefully sharpened spits. Loaves of oat cakes browned in open hearths, and in the cellars below, casks of wine, *uisce beatha*, and honeyed mead were rolled out and poured into goblets and flasks lining the trestle tables of the great banquet hall.

Outside, it was still light with that fey glow that illuminates the western isles long after the rest of Ireland has put aside the day. Inside the hall, stewards heavy with the keys of their hereditary professions ushered guests across the rush-strewn floors to their places at the tables. The vaulted corbel-beamed ceiling of solid oak was bright with the standards of visiting chieftains, the boar of Desmond, the O'Brien lions, the O'Neills' red oak of Ulster, the stag of the MacCarthys, and, above them all on a giant stave, the golden dragons of the O'Flahertys bidding hospitality to one and all.

Not by the merest flicker of an eyelash did Donal reveal the intense emotion he felt as he watched his guests assemble in the banquet hall. Chieftains in quilted coats and leather trews, lords of the Pale, brilliant in their colorful doublets, all had come without exception. Even the great O'Neill had stirred himself, as had his hated enemy, Magnus O'Donnell, lord of Tirconnaill. Blood ties and marriage united them all, but most looked upon each other with suspicion, and few called each other friend. Yet they had come, united in their love of independence and their hatred for Henry Tudor. Only once during the height of their power had the Fitzgeralds managed to unite Gaels and Sean Ghalls under one roof.

Donal stared at the empty benches still to be filled. For two days he had worked to forge an agreement between the men who would fill those seats, if they would indeed fill them. He held his breath, waiting.

Moments passed. It would all come to naught if they decided against him. He drew in a slow, controlled breath.

As if on cue, a tall man in his mid-thirties with long hair curling past his shoulders strode into the room. A murmur rose from the chiefs of the western isles as they recognized Felim O'Connor, descendant of the last high king of Ireland. He was followed by Conor O'Brien of the line of Brian Boru, kings of Munster, and Conn Bachach O'Neill, descendant of the kings of Ulster and the legends of *Emáin Macha*. A hush fell over the crowd as they waited expectantly for the last seat to be filled.

Myles MacMurrough of Kavanagh, scion of the House of Leicester, walked to his seat, head held high, deliberately ignoring the hisses and taunts alluding to the unforgiven treachery of his royal ancestor, whose invitation to the Norman-Anglo lords led to the invasion of Ireland in the twelfth century.

Donal released his breath and crossed the room to take his seat under two hundred curious eyes. A wild cheer erupted in the hall. He smiled and lifted his goblet to signify the beginning of the feast.

Wooden trenchers of boiled meat and fowl were carried to the tables. Goblets were filled and filled again with foaming ale and spiced wine. Huge chunks of bread were torn from steaming loaves, a sop for fragrant meat juices rich with the fat so necessary for survival through frozen Irish winters. Later, after the trenchers were removed, potent *uisce beatha* was passed around, and eyes glazed over as the fiery brew burned its path to sated stomachs.

Donal ate sparingly and drank even less. His eyes moved over the assembled chieftains, waiting and watching as the alcohol-induced voices grew ever louder and higher. Finally, he waved his hand, and the chief steward pounded on the wooden dais three times with his *bata*. Donal stood, and a hush filled the room.

In the leaping shadows, the torches threw arcs of light against the lime-washed walls, picking out the high bones of the young chief's face, shadowing the hollows, emphasizing dark and light, hair and eyes, skin and bones, angles and planes. He stood above them, well over normal height, muscles flame-lit and defined, hair like night, sculpted cheeks, eyes the strange glittering orbs bearing their Talesian mark. When he spoke, his words held them spellbound as he spun around them the magic of his lineage, the lineage of Merlin and his lady of the lake.

"Gaels and Sean Ghalls, Irish men, I bid you welcome." He looked around the room, pulling them with the hypnotic, rain-swept power of his gaze. "You have come together for a mighty cause. Geraldine blood has washed the streets of London, and still the Tudor king is not satisfied. He holds Gerald Fitzgerald, tenth earl of Kildare, son and heir of Gerald Og, and his sister, the Lady Eleanor, hostage at Whitehall. The boy will not be allowed to live."

His eyes shone silver in the torchlight. He fixed his glance on the chieftain of each house, plying them with the beauty of his voice. "Today the House of Kildare will be wiped from the face of Ireland. Tomorrow the O'Donnells may fall, or the O'Malleys or the McCarthys. Before another season passes, I leave for England. When I return, it will be with the Geraldines."

At last he came to it, the reason for which he'd summoned these men over hundreds of miles of forest and bogland. "Henry's army will follow me. What say you, my lords? Do you stand with me? Will you fight the English scourge and keep Ireland for the Irish?"

His words reminded the Gaelic chieftains of the bitter taste of Irish subservience, a position they had assumed three hundred years before with the Anglo-Norman invasions. To the lords of the Pale whose allegiance to the English Crown was as ingrained as that of the Irish to their high kings, it was a clear case of treason. But they were no match for the fire that burned like a heavenly flame within the young messiah who appealed so earnestly to them. Every eye was upon him, every heart stirred by his outrageous request. He asked them to forsake their security, to lift up their swords, to defy the king of England for a boy's right to live.

Unbelievably, O'Neill of Tyrone stood and deliberately placed his hand on the hilt of his sword. "I stand with you, O'Flaherty," he said loudly.

Magnus O'Donnell, O'Neill's hereditary enemy, rose. "I, too, stand beside you," he said.

A collective gasp swept over the room. Not since the betrayal of the O'Donnells by the O'Neills three hundred years before had the two clans ever sided with each other on matters of politics.

One by one, like wooden ninepins, the chieftains stood and raised their goblets in salute to the silent figure on the dais. The lords gazed at one another furtively. The proposal was a radical one. To break ties with England meant war to the death. Only the Kildares had been strong enough to organize such a feat. Finally, William Burke, lord of Galway, stood and pledged his sword. He was followed by Lords Dunsany, Carlisle, Fielding, and Gray. MacWilliam of Mayo spoke reasonably. In the thick speech of the western isles, he asked the question on everyone's mind. "Under whose banner will we fight?"

A smile so brief it was the merest flicker of muscle appeared on Donal O'Flaherty's lips. "Kildare's."

It was the answer they waited for. Every man still seated rose in unison. The habits of a lifetime were strong and loyalty to their ruling house overcame the last lingering remnants of doubt. Passion replaced caution, and *"Crom aboo!"* the ancient war cry of the Kildares, erupted from every throat. The Geraldine League was born.

Donal pulled his cloak over his face and walked close beside a donkey cart filled with hay. The guard at the city gates allowed him to pass through without question. Inside the walls, he made his way through the twisting streets to the front of the royal palace, where the poor begged for alms.

It was customary for the ladies at court to offer the leavings from their banquet tables at noon and again in the evening. Huddled beneath his cloak, Donal waited for three days before he heard the gossip he'd crossed an ocean to hear. Gerald was in Wales, the ward of Robert Montgomery of Cilcerrig and his wife, Eleanor Fitzgerald of Kildare.

There was something different about her. Robert couldn't put his finger on it. It was more than a natural preoccupation with the child she carried within her. She appeared unusually interested in the most ordinary of matters, the making of perfume, the fermenting of grain, the weaving of rushes, as if she were seeing everything with new eyes. Sometimes she was as he remembered her, a lord's daughter, filled with the grace and dignity of her position. And then there were moments when she was something else entirely, a combination of fire and ice, irreverence and compassion, sharp-tongued, blistering, combining an astute intelligence with a witty sense of the absurd. He had never met a woman like her.

Nell settled into the well-appointed castle as if she were born to it, supervising the servants, planning the meals, embroidering linens, arranging entertainment, caring for Gerald, and gracing Robert's table. She was everywhere at once, in the kitchens, the banquet halls, the library, her sitting room, the laundry, the smoke-house, everywhere except his bedchamber.

Robert had exhausted his list of duties. Under his guidance, walls were built, stores replenished, and guards trained, fields were tilled and crops planted. He had supervised the purchasing of horseflesh for the sta-bles and ridden the boundaries of the estate, meeting for the first time those tenants who depended upon him for their survival. For the past week he had done noth-ing more promising than dicing and drinking in the great hall with his men, chafing at his inactivity.

Nell's changing moods unsettled him, as did the tight-ness in his belly and the empty space in his bed. He had given his word not to touch her, and he would keep to it unless she gave him reason to believe that she wanted what he did. Robert prided himself on his pa-tience. Perhaps after the child was born, she would be more receptive. Meanwhile, there was the evening meal ahead, and Nell had promised to dine with him.

She came to the table dressed in a flowing white gar-ment that concealed the bulk of her pregnancy. Her hair was loose and hung to her knees, heavy and gleam-ing like a sheaf of wheat after a spring rain. She said little as she stabbed an oyster with her knife and lifted it to her mouth, but she smiled as sweetly as any ador-ing bride when her eyes inadvertently met his. His throat locked, and immediately he choked. Reaching for his wine goblet, he drained it dry, clearing the obstruction and breathed deeply.

The frown between Nell's brows disappeared. "Have a care, Robert. You are very dear to us."

His hand clenched around his bread knife. "Am I, Nell?"

"Of course." Her eyes were wide and innocent and filled with concern. "How could you think otherwise?"

He tore at the bread until it was a mess of crumbs in his trencher. To speak from his heart would ruin the ease between them. But if he did not, he doomed himself to a lifetime of frustration. "I know that you are fond of me," he mumbled, refusing to meet her eyes.

"You saved Gerald's life, Robert. I am more than fond of you."

Hope filled his heart. He looked up. "Truly, Nell. Have you come to care for me?"

She smiled, and he felt as if she'd touched him.

"You are a dear man, Robert Montgomery. I will always care for you."

He searched her face, lovely and gold-touched in the firelight. Her lips were smiling and parted in invitation. Throwing caution to the winds, he stood and walked to where she sat. Then he leaned over and touched his mouth to hers. She did not respond, but neither did she draw away. Encouraged, he rubbed her jaw with his thumb. His voice was hoarse, his emotions raw. "You are so lovely, Nell, and I have waited for so long."

"I, too, Robert. But soon the child will be born, and it will be over."

His breath caught. He could barely form the words. "Then will you be my wife, Nell?"

She looked confused. "I am your wife."

"In name only."

"I don't understand."

Could a woman great with child truly be so innocent? "You gave yourself to the O'Flaherty, did you not?" he asked gently.

Nell was not cowardly. She lifted her chin and looked directly at him. "I did."

"Were you willing?"

She bit her lip. "I was."

"Then you know what I want."

He knew the exact moment she understood. "What if I told you that I cannot lie with you because I still love Donal O'Flaherty?"

His mouth hardened. "Love that is not returned eventually dies."

She waited, listening to the pounding of her heart and the hiss of rain on the fire.

Robert continued. "A corpse cannot love you, Nell. You are my wife. If he comes for you, I must kill him. Any man would do the same. Then I will wait until you are ready to love again."

Something flickered and disappeared behind her eyes. When she spoke, her voice was clear and calm and completely devoid of expression. "May I have until the child is born?"

"I love you, Nell. I would never force you."

She nodded and pushed her chair away from the table. "Pardon me, my lord. I am very tired."

Robert nodded. She had never before asked permission to retire. "As you wish, Nell. Good night."

Hours later, unable to sleep, Nell rolled over, pulled the blankets up to her chin, and stared through the darkness at the outline of her window. She rubbed her lower back and groaned. It was past time for the child to be born, and until he was, sleep, comfortable sleep, where a body could fold effortlessly into a number of preferred positions, was a longed-for luxury. Nell looked at her left wrist, frowned, and rubbed it. She'd done that before, always in the dark for no particular reason, eyes squinting at the space between her hand and her arm as if she expected to find something.

She sat up, pushed the covers away, and walked to the fireplace. It was cold but not so cold as Ireland. With the poker, she stirred the embers into a small but steady flame and pulled up a chair to its meager warmth. Tucking her legs beneath the weight of her stomach, she thought. The moment she dreaded had finally come. Robert was her husband, and he wanted what any husband would have demanded long before. For months, he had been most patient, sharing everything that was his, asking nothing in return, until tonight. Even then, he had played the gentleman, asking, not demanding. She could do much worse. It was not so very hard a thing to do, to lie with a man. She had done so before, even though the details of her coupling with Donal were hazy, as if they had happened years instead of months ago.

"Am I foolish to dream of a man who never comes?" she whispered.

Shadows gathered on the wall, took on female shape, and became three-dimensional. A voice followed. *A better man than Robert Montgomery would be hard to find. But you are wise to wait, Nell.*

Surprise faded into pleasure. "Jilly, you're back."

For a bit.

"Why?"

A slight fluid shrugging of her shoulders settled Jillian on the fur rug at Nell's feet. *I never left you, Nell. I'm always here.*

"In spirit, perhaps, but not like this."

No, Jillian agreed. *I don't understand it, either. All I*

*know is that you see me when you are faced with a particular
dilemma. Most of the time, you do fairly well alone.*

Nell sighed. "It isn't really a dilemma. I have no
choice."

If you really believe that, why did you ask Robert to wait?

Nell spread her hands across her stomach. "Look at
me. Who would want me like this?"

I thought the idea was to make him not want you.

" 'Tis true. I want only Donal."

You haven't heard from him in months, Jillian finished
for her.

Nell nodded. "Our year of handfast is almost over,
and still he has not come."

You told him to wait because of Gerald, Jillian said
reasonably.

Nell hung her head. "He should have found a way.
But if he has forgotten me, I should make a life with
Robert. As you say, a better man would be hard to
find."

Wait a bit longer, Nell. Your child will be born soon.
Jillian's voice was very low, and the outline of her body
began to blur.

Nell panicked and reached out, finding nothing but
air. "Don't leave yet, Jilly," she begged. "Please, don't
leave."

Jillian's voice, barely intelligible, drifted back to her.
Wait, Nell. You are right to wait.

13

O'Flaherty held up his hand, and the small company of men behind him reined in their mounts. They had ridden hard for most of the day, and it was past time to camp for the night. Mountains, jagged and intimidating, broke the straight line of the horizon, and a thick, soupy mist settled around them like smoke. This was Wales, land of spirits and magic, King Arthur and Merlin, the druid from whose bloodline the O'Flahertys had descended.

Donal frowned into the mist and narrowed his eyes. It was madness to continue with so little visibility, but, so far, he had found no auspicious place to bed down for the night. His men were Irish. Superstition ran thick through their blood. He could not ask them to sleep in this fog-drenched land of swirling mists with inhuman sounds calling to them from hidden places behind every tree.

It was a testimony to their loyalty that they continued

behind him with no thought of mutiny. But they would not camp on this ground, wrapped in their blankets, alone in their thoughts, with no activity other than sleep to occupy their minds. Still, it was several hours to Cilcerrig, and the horses needed watering. A respite, however short, was necessary.

He pitched his voice so that even the last of the men would hear. "Halt," he called back. Instantly, every man stopped. Donal did not miss the tight mouths and anxious eyes as they looked around the fairy-steeped darkness. "We rest here," he said firmly. "Refresh yourselves. Tonight we camp within sight of the towers of Cilcerrig."

The lessening of their tension was a visible thing. Donal dismounted and reached into his bag for an oat cake, a morsel of dried beef, and his sheep's bladder. Through the trees he heard the sound of water. Draining the last of the liquid from the bag, he made his way down an embankment to a narrow stream. He knelt on a flat stone, cupped his hand under the falls, and drank deeply before refilling the bag and tying it off. Then he splashed the icy water over his face and squatted on the stone, resting easily on the balls of his feet.

The fog was thinner here. Something bright moved just outside his line of vision. He tensed and turned toward the flickering light. Instinctively, his hand moved to the dirk at his belt, and he readied himself to spring. Then his eyes widened. His hand dropped to his side, and he whistled long and low. "Sweet Mary," he muttered as the light came closer, revealing a figure that could only be female despite her breeks and the odd cut of her shirt. She carried no candle, but her body was surrounded by a yellow glow. Donal waited for her to speak.

I'm looking for Donal O'Flaherty, she said when she

reached him. Her voice was somehow both Irish and foreign.

Donal stood and replaced his dirk in his belt. "What do you want with him?"

I bring him a message.

"From whom?"

She hesitated. *I need to speak with the O'Flaherty.*

"Who are you, lass, and what brings you here?"

Jillian could see him clearly now, and her breath caught. It was him. There could be no doubt. Nell had described him often enough, but even if she hadn't, Jillian would have known him. He had the look of a man born to command. Young as he was, the still planes of his face and the bunched muscles of his arms and chest revealed both strength and wisdom. He was beyond handsome, and those eyes—she drew a deep, shaky breath. Those eyes were a powerful weapon. If Donal O'Flaherty ever looked at her with more than a curious interest, she would follow him anywhere. No wonder Nell had no interest in her husband. This was a man of whom legends were made. She swallowed. *I bring a message concerning Nell Fitzgerald.*

Before she could blink, he had crossed the distance between them. "What do you know of Nell Fitzgerald?" he demanded.

Jillian's eyes flashed. Not since she was a child had anyone spoken to her in anger. *Lower your voice, please,* she said, keeping her back teeth locked.

Donal frowned. There was something different about this girl. She wasn't dressed as a lady, and yet she was no servant. He stepped back. "Who are you?"

Jillian ignored him. *You've taken a long time to claim your betrothed,* she said instead. *Nell has given up on you.*

His intentions regarding Nell were no one's business.

Donal's beautifully cut mouth tightened. "She is married," he said shortly.

Jillian fixed the power of her gaze upon him, and Donal felt his will dissolve. Her eyes were the color of the North Sea with the full strength of the sun upon it. There was something about this woman that transcended beauty.

Nell is handfasted to you, Jillian explained. *What she did was done to save Gerald.*

Donal forced himself to look away. "Always Gerald," he muttered under his breath. "For all the trouble he has caused me, I could wish the lad on Henry."

Nell will appreciate your sentiments, I'm sure, Jillian said sweetly.

Donal grinned. He was sure he'd never seen her before, but she reminded him of someone. He felt a connection to her. There was something about her that drew him despite her shorn head and mannish clothes. Her hair glowed like rare silk, and it smelled delicious. He had the strangest desire to run his hands through the smooth and shining length of it. "You are too well favored to sport such a shrewish tongue, lass," he said softly. "Who are you that you know Nell's thoughts and yet appear before me, hours from Cilcerrig, with no mount or escort?"

Jillian's mouth was very dry. His voice was spellbinding. She had never been this close to a man before, but she knew instinctively that this was no ordinary man. He was Donal O'Flaherty and most likely her direct ancestor.

Through the mist, she heard a masculine shout, and sanity returned. She pulled away. How far away was a sixteenth-century Irish chieftain from his Talesian roots? How much would he accept? *My name is Jillian,* she began softly, *and I came here to be sure of your inten-*

*tions regarding Nell. It's important that you take her away
from here.*

In the space of a heartbeat, something alive and sympathetic traveled between them. Jillian was close to
tears, and when Donal spoke, there was something different in his voice, a note of wonder that had not been
there before. "Are you an angel sent from God?"

Good Lord, no, she blurted out. *I'm—* She searched
for the right words. *I'm more like a spirit or a ghost, and
no one sent me, at least I don't think so,* she added
honestly.

Donal shook his head and watched his image reflected in the seafoam green of her eyes. "You are no
ghost, Jillian. I can see you, touch you." He reached
for her.

She stepped back. *You may see me as Nell does, but
others can't.*

He frowned and dropped his hands to his sides. "Nell
and I are fortunate to have so concerned a *ghost.*"

You're making fun of me.

Tiny lights flickered in the black of his eyes. "Nay,
lass. I would like the truth, but if you are unwilling to
give it, I'll not pester you." He stepped down from
the rock and held out his hand. "Come. We'll ride to
Cilcerrig together."

She backed away from him. *No, thank you. I'll manage
on my own.*

He moved toward her. "Don't be absurd." Something
was happening to his vision. Donal blinked and rubbed
his eyes. It had suddenly gone dark. "It's freezing!" he
shouted after her, "And there are wolves in the woods."
He started forward, pushing aside the tree branches to
follow her. "Jillian!" he called out. But she was gone,
and somehow he knew that he would not find her.

Giving up, he retraced his footsteps back to the

stream and climbed the bank where his men waited. It wasn't until much later, when the torches on the battlements of Cilcerrig Castle flared in the distance, that he realized the only footsteps in the damp earth had been his own.

The men he chose to help him play out his charade spoke English without the telltale lilt of western Ireland. Even so, his story of duty in Dublin would serve him even better. After pulling out a doublet and hose from his saddle pack, he changed quickly, mounted his horse, and arranged the short English cloak so that it fell in folds around his shoulders. Then he surveyed his men, nodded with satisfaction, and approached the gates of Cilcerrig.

The guard took an interminably long time in returning, and when he did, it was with his lordship himself, Sir Robert Montgomery. "By whose orders are you sent?" Montgomery asked.

"Lord Leonard Gray wishes to learn of the circumstances of his kinsmen," Donal answered.

"Who are you?"

"David Carlisle, heir to the earldom of Dunsany," said Donal.

Robert squinted into the darkness. So much for his evening alone with Nell. The torches revealed three men mounted on English saddles wearing English clothing. He nodded to the guard, and the gate was pulled up.

Donal urged his mount across the bridge, through the portcullis, and into the courtyard. The linkboy who waited at the entrance to the hall was waved aside, and Donal watched his men lead the horses to the stable. They would dice and sup with Montgomery's guards, making sure the whiskey flowed freely.

Robert stood by the fire, pouring a dark wine into a glass of Venetian crystal. "You will join us at our table, Carlisle."

Donal bowed and moved into the light. "I shall be honored, my lord."

Robert Montgomery was the son of a Welsh hill woman and knew a fellow Celt when he saw him. He took one look at the young man walking toward him and knew that not one drop of English blood flowed through his veins. The lad was pure Celt from the V on his forehead dividing his face, preventing perfection, to the mist-gray of his eyes circled by rings of black, as black as the hair that fell in a primitive tangle to shoulders that had never spent a day in the mincing splendor of King Henry's court.

David Carlisle, or whoever he was, was a warrior. Only the frequent use of a claymore could have produced a chest and arms of such size. Robert kept himself fit by light eating and daily sparring, but he found himself puffing out his own chest and wishing that it was not too late to ask Nell to sup in her chambers and leave him alone with his guest. He would not measure up in comparison to this splendid young man who was very near to her own age.

The door opened, and Nell stood on the threshold. "Good evening, my lords," she said in her lovely voice.

"Good evening, my love." Robert, walking forward to lead her into the room, missed the sudden blanching of Donal's face as his eyes moved over Nell's figure. "You must welcome our guest, Lord David Carlisle, from Dublin. Your uncle has commissioned him to bring you a message."

Nell had known David Carlisle for most of her life, and even though she saw only the man's back when she first entered the room, she knew at once who it must be. She kept her expression blandly pleasant and did not once betray the hurt in her heart at the wintry look in Donal's ice-gray eyes. "Welcome to Cilcerrig, my lord," she said calmly. "I trust your journey was not difficult."

"Not at all, Lady Montgomery." He did not sound at all like the man she remembered. "Lord Gray is concerned for your welfare. To hear that you have settled in so well will bring him great joy."

There could be no answer to such a comment, not when Robert was standing between them. "I am very hungry, my lord," was all she said.

Nell could barely manage her soup. Taking no part in the conversation, she declined the fish and said very little when the roasted venison and onion gravy were placed before her. Pushing it around on her plate, she managed the appearance of a hearty appetite. Refusing the jellies, she stood. "Please excuse me, gentlemen."

"My wife tires easily of late," Robert explained to Donal. "The birth of our firstborn is imminent."

Without waiting for Donal's reply, Nell left the hall and hurried up the stairs to her bedchamber.

She did not change into her night robe. Donal was there, and despite his foul mood, he must have come for her. Pulling her cloak around her, she climbed onto the bed and waited. The minutes passed slowly. Nell yawned, climbed off the bed, replenished the meager fire, and sat down in the rocker. Why would he not come?

She was wrong to have left him all those months ago. She knew that now. It was too much for a man, to ask him to wait, to put his needs behind that of a child not his own. At the time, it seemed to be the only decision she could have made. But it was the wrong one. She had accomplished nothing except to stir Henry's lust

and involve herself in a marriage that would only serve
to break the heart of the kindest of men. Better to have
stayed with Donal and taken her chances on his ability
to keep Gerald safe.

Nell shivered. The fire was low again, and her back
felt stiff. Where was he? Perhaps he would not mind if
she waited for him in the comfort of her bed. She
crawled under the woolen blankets and pulled them up
to her chin. Within minutes, her eyes closed, and she
slept.

The cock crowed, and the pale light of dawn filtered
through her window. Nell did not open her eyes. She
knew something was wrong. The dull pain in her chest
had become very familiar to her in the last two years,
but she was in that state between waking and sleeping
and couldn't remember the reason for it.

Then it came to her. Donal had not come. She threw
back the covers and slid off the bed. Her gown was
wrinkled, and her eyelids drooped from lack of sleep.
Opening the clothes press, she pulled out a simple
woolen tunic cut to conceal her stomach and threw it on
the bed. She would bathe and join the men at breakfast.

Nell picked up the glass and hummed nervously as
the girl divided her hair into three sections and plaited
it with golden thread to bring out its silvery lights. The
gown not only hid her bulk, it brought out the green
in her eyes. She was pleased with her choice. "Thank
you, Susan," she said as the serving girl twisted the
thread several times around the end of the braid. "That
will be all."

When she was alone, Nell opened a bottle of scented
oil and rubbed it behind her ears and over the pulse
points on the insides of her wrists. Her heart beat
quickly. Soon Donal would take her away from here,

and the life her father had intended her to have would begin.

The narrow stairs, unevenly hewn for the sole purpose of slowing down an enemy, were tricky for a woman in her condition. By balancing herself against the walls, she managed the dangerous spiral.

Breakfast was served in a small dining room off the hall. A smile parted her lips as she pushed open the door. The room was empty. Surely it was too early for Robert to have eaten already. Nell walked back through the hall to the outside kitchens. The servants were in the middle of food preparation. She sighed with relief. It was not too late after all.

Robert called to her from the courtyard. "Nell. Come out and bid our guests farewell. His lordship must return to Dublin immediately and cannot stay even for breakfast."

Nell felt as if a giant boot had kicked her in the stomach. Her heart stopped and she fought for breath. He was leaving without her.

"Nell?" Robert's concerned voice, closer now, broke through her wave of nausea. "Are you ill? Is it the child?"

She shook her head and forced herself to smile brilliantly. "No, my lord. 'Tis nothing. I shall be there directly." Slowly, slowly, she managed the distance from the kitchen to the castle gates. She looked past Robert to where Donal waited with his men. He was mounted on the enormous stallion she remembered, and his eyes, reflecting the leaden sky above him, looked right through her.

Nell willed herself not to cry. "God speed, my lord," she said, lifting her chin.

He nodded briefly. "My lady." Without the hint of

a smile, he turned and rode across the drawbridge into the forest.

Robert stroked his chin. "I wonder who his mother is?"

Nell's brow puckered. "My lord?"

"The lad is pure Celt," Robert replied. "I'm surprised you did not see it, Nell. No race but the Irish can manage a horse like that. Carlisle is either a changeling or an impostor."

She spoke carefully. "If that is true, why did you not keep him from leaving?"

"His manners are those of a gentleman. I saw no harm in him. He came with only two men, and whatever his motive, he is gone now. Let him tell his source that you and Gerald are well and happy."

Nell watched the gate drop into place, securing her behind the walls of her husband's castle. *Well and happy*, he said. She would soon break down in tears. Robert would understand. A woman near her time occasionally lost control of her emotions. He was a most considerate man. She reached out to touch his arm. "If you will excuse me, my lord, I did not sleep well last night. Forgive me, but I must leave you to breakfast alone."

He was all concern. "Allow me to escort you, Nell."

She shook her head. In another moment, she would be completely undone. "Susan will take me. Please, Robert."

He watched her turn away, his eyes troubled. Nell was not given to fits of temper. Even in her most uncomfortable moments, she was good-natured and pleasant in mood. It was one of the things he most valued in her. It must be the child. Poor darling. It would come soon, and then she would be herself again.

Robert's spirits lifted. He had not forgotten Nell's promise. After she had recovered from the child, she would truly become his wife. No more castle whores. No more unsatisfactory couplings, withdrawing prematurely to avoid an unwanted bastard. No more empty beds. Nell would be his wife. He would get his heirs on her. If his luck ran true, the child she carried would be a girl. If not, children born in summer and weaned in winter did not always survive the first year. One way or another, Robert would see to it that a Montgomery inherited Cilcerrig Castle.

14

It was nearly midnight. Donal pulled himself up and over the portcullis gate. It was not so difficult for a man who had spent his youth scaling the guano-stained cliffs of Dun Aengus to maneuver his way across a mere bridge and over a wall. Finding Nell's chambers would be more difficult. To maintain warmth, sleeping quarters were usually on the top floor. He would start there. After locating the stairs, he climbed quickly to the top. No one was about.

Resigning himself to a lengthy search, he placed his hand on his dirk and moved stealthily to the first door in the long hall. He leaned against it at the same time as a familiar voice whispered in his ear. *Not this one. Follow me.*

He froze and then slowly turned and looked into eyes that had seen things he had never imagined. Donal felt his heart give a mighty thump before it settled into its normal rhythm. Questions would only delay them. Jillian was not of this world. There could be no other explanation for her presence.

She held a finger to her lips. He followed her to a heavily engraved door at the end of the hall. It wasn't bolted. Silently, he slipped into the room. Nell was awake. She stood before an inadequate fire, wrapped in a blanket, rubbing the ache in her back.

Donal felt as if a giant fist were squeezing his heart. This was Nell, his Nell. How could he ever have looked at another woman with the stirrings of desire?

Feeling his eyes upon her, Nell turned, and her mouth dropped open. With a low cry, she dropped the blanket, ran across the room, and threw herself into his arms. They closed around the bulk of her stomach, and she buried her face in his shoulder.

Donal couldn't think. Neither could he move or speak. Thoughts, angry and confusing, crowded his brain. Nell was with child. He'd counted back the months and wondered if the babe could be his own, but Montgomery's words put an end to his hope. No castle lord would claim another man's child as his own.

Nell was married, and yet she'd flung herself into his arms as if nothing had changed between them. "I'm taking you back to Ireland," he said gruffly.

She lifted her head. "I must wake Gerald." Her hand tightened on his arm. "When my absence is discovered, he will be killed."

Donal extricated himself from Nell's embrace. "I have no intention of leaving the lad behind. You must go to him yourself. Do not trust a servant."

Nell touched her tongue to her lips. "I shall send Jillian. Gerald won't be able to see her, of course. But she has a convincing way about her. He'll not refuse if I send her."

All at once, he found it difficult to breathe. "Who is Jillian?" he managed.

"She is a friend." Nell busied herself at her dressing table.

He decided to leave it. "Why would the lad refuse?"

"Gerald is happy here. You must understand, Donal. He cares deeply for Robert and knows nothing of Henry's threats against his life."

"I see." Donal understood only too well. "Fetch the boy any way you please, but hurry. The hour grows late, and we've a great distance to ride before sunrise."

Nell frowned and turned to study his face. There was something different about Donal, something cold and terrifyingly distant. Without looking away, she reached for the woolen gown hanging over the bed rail and pulled it on over her shift. "I'll go myself," she said, and left the room.

Donal judged that a full hour had passed before he set out to look for them. Somehow he knew not to bother with the remaining bedchambers lining the hall. Instinctively, as if he were following someone who walked the floors of Cilcerrig every day, he climbed down the stairs to the second landing and the row of rooms Gerald and his tutor occupied. He found Nell in the smallest chamber, in earnest dialogue with a man who had the look of a scholar. They were so engrossed in their words that neither noticed when he stepped into the room.

"We cannot take you with us, Thomas," he heard her say. "Robert is a fair man. You will not be held responsible for Gerald's disappearance."

"Do not ask this of me, my lady," Thomas Leverous pleaded with her. "I am fond of the boy. There is nothing for me here without him. I shall lose my position."

Nell sagged against the bedpost and looked up at the

crucifix on the wall. "Holy Mother, give me strength," she moaned, rubbing the ache in her back that intensified with every passing moment.

Donal deemed it time to announce his presence. He stepped into the light. "It appears that I intrude," he said, withdrawing his *scian* and testing the blade with his thumb, "but it grows late, and my men expect us."

Leverous flushed. "I ask your pardon, my lord, but I am Gerald's tutor and would travel with you."

He almost felt sorry for the man. "We are unable to accommodate another rider, lad," he said regretfully. "I am truly sorry."

Thomas moved in the direction of the door. "I shall ask you once again, O'Flaherty. Will you take me with you?"

Donal shook his head, mindful of the tutor's furtive movements. He was ready when the man bolted for the door. Quick as a cat, Donal was ahead of him, circling his neck with a restraining arm. Nell pushed the door shut and leaned against it.

"You won't get far," Leverous gasped.

Pressing his *scian* against the man's throat, Donal swore. "*Mallacht go deo air*. Give me reason not to kill you."

Leverous strained to look at Nell and winced as the movement brought the knife blade in direct contact with his skin. "You would allow him to kill me?" he rasped.

"You leave us no choice," replied Nell.

"I would be of great use to you," begged Leverous. "Tell him, Nell."

"We cannot take you with us, Thomas," she said softly, "and now it appears that we cannot leave you behind."

Donal's arm tightened, and Leverous choked. "Do it quickly, then."

Across the room, Nell's eyes met Donal's, and something flashed between them. "Fetch the boy," Donal said into the stillness, and Nell obeyed him.

It did not suit him to skewer a man of letters, especially one who couldn't tell one end of a sword from another. Donal lost no time. He pulled a chair into the corner and forced the tutor into it. After tearing the bed linens into strips, he fashioned them into ropes and tied Leverous to the chair. Then he tied his hands and feet and stuffed his mouth with cloth before following Nell into the adjoining room.

Gerald was still groggy from sleep and mercifully asked no questions. Nell led them through the silent castle to a small retiring room near the great hall. Flickering torches lit the room. The walls were lined with sturdy oak, and on each panel was engraved a Lancastrian rose. She pressed against one of the panels, and a door, well concealed by the intricate carving, opened inward. "The passage leads to a clearing outside the walls," she explained. "I found it only weeks ago."

Donal caught up an evil-smelling torch from a wall sconce and motioned for Nell and Gerald to precede him. Then he stepped inside and closed the door behind him. "Pray that no one else has discovered it," he muttered, and lifted the torch above his head. The flames threw arcs of light against the roughly hewn walls, but he could see that it was definitely a passage. "Stay close beside me," he said, and led the way through the silent tunnel.

Nell had used the passageway once before, but Jillian had been with her. They'd left the door ajar and carried both a candle and a flaring torch. Even though no sunlight had ever found its way into the dark cavern, the knowledge that day would greet them at the end of their trek had brought Nell comfort. There was no comfort at all to be found on this journey.

Her back ached severely now. It was bone-chillingly cold, and moisture dripped from the walls. Every whisper took on an eerie cadence, and, once, she brushed against something scurrying, furry and alive. She had recoiled in horror, but Donal continued his inhuman pace, and, because she was more terrified of being left behind than she was of rats, she continued to pull Gerald along behind her.

At first, the passage had descended. Nell could feel the way the packed earth had fallen away and the way the pressure built on the balls of her feet. But now, just as surely as she had known they were traveling downward, she knew they were on their way up. Fresh air and the concealing forest were only steps away. Eagerly, she hurried forward, released Gerald's hand to grasp Donal's, and clambered up the slippery stone steps to the clearing.

The night, with its half-moon and stars blanketing the sky, appeared bright as day. She breathed deeply and pressed her hand against her pain as she watched Donal pull Gerald out of the blackness. The lad, too spent for questions, leaned against her, and she placed her arm protectively around his shoulders and waited.

Nell, watching the play of muscles under Donal's shirt as he pulled back a boulder to conceal the passage, marveled at his confidence. What other man would walk boldly into a fortified castle and steal the wife and ward of a newly made earl? She saw him turn back toward the castle turrets, scanning them to judge his location. Deep in thought, she jumped when he laughed out loud.

"The saints are with us, Nell," he said. "We've come

out less than a league from where my men are camped. If they've the sense for which I chose them, we should come upon a scouting party very soon."

Sure enough, five minutes had not passed before two riders materialized behind the trees and called out a warning.

Donal's voice rang crisply in the night air. " 'Tis the O'Flaherty," he announced. "I have the Geraldines."

Nell breathed a sigh of relief as one of the men dismounted to lift her into the saddle. Immediately, the pain receded. Donal climbed up behind her and settled Gerald between them, signaling the two men on the remaining horse to follow.

She did not miss the relief on the faces of the O'Flaherty men when Donal rode into their camp unharmed. They were past ready to leave this land of haunted glens.

Donal gave Gerald his own mount, but after one look at Nell's pain-ravaged face, he decided to keep her with him. They rode through the night and reached the harbor town of Pembroke, where an O'Flaherty carrack, the *Banshee*, lay anchored in a hidden harbor.

Riding with his arms around her, Donal felt the tightening and relaxing of Nell's belly throughout the long night and believed he knew the reason for the agony reflected in her face. There was nothing to be done, no midwife to be found, no time for delay. He knew that Nell would keep her pain from him for as long as possible. He counted on the enormous pride she carried before her like a banner and did not acknowledge the labor that was most definitely upon her. Saying nothing, he pushed forward, ignoring the comments of his men, stubbornly refusing to stop for food or rest, until they reached the ship.

Dismounting, he reached for her. She fell into his

arms and attempted to stand. The blanket he'd wrapped around her parted, and he stared at the front of her gown. It was stained with fresh blood.

She swayed and would have fallen, but he caught her in his arms and ran for the ship. Clumsy with the weight of her, he managed the climb onto the deck and disappeared into the companionway. The door to his cabin was shut. He kicked it open and placed her on the bed, shouting for his cabin boy. "Fetch the cook," he said when the boy appeared. "Bring hot water and soap, twine and linen. Be quick."

The boy took one look at the moaning, bloodstained woman on the bed, and his face whitened. "Aye, sir, right away, sir."

Donal frowned. Conflicting emotions warred in his mind. To find Nell about to give birth had shaken him beyond words. He wanted no part of Robert Montgomery's child. But he was a fair man, and he knew that women often had little choice in the hand fate dealt them. Nell had welcomed him with sincere pleasure, and not for a moment had she exhibited the slightest reluctance in leaving Montgomery. Even though she spoke highly of her treatment by her Welsh husband, nothing in her manner revealed that she had fallen in love with the man.

The cook appeared in the hatchway with a bowl of hot water and a pile of clean linen. "I'm no midwife, sir," he said immediately, "and y' know how me hands shake without the rum."

"I wouldn't trust you to touch her, Liam," replied Donal tersely as he dipped the linen into the water and pushed Nell's gown up to her waist. "Just see that the knife is sharp and the water is kept clean and hot."

"I'll do that, sir. A few more pillows t' lift her would ease the pain a mite."

Donal sponged down Nell's legs and reached for the soap. "What would you know about it?"

"At last count, I've eight of me own," the cook confessed, "although six of 'em were born whilst I was at sea."

"Fetch more pillows, then," Donal ordered. He had washed between Nell's legs and cut away the soiled part of her gown. She lay on the bed staring up at him as unashamed as if he saw her spreadeagled and naked every day. "I'm sorry, Nell." His voice was low and humble. The deck rolled beneath his feet. "It was too dangerous to stop before now."

She reached for his hand, clutched it, and smiled. "I'm glad he waited."

Was she rambling? "Who, lass?"

"The babe. I wanted him to be born on Irish soil."

Donal shook his head and tried to smile. "Montgomery may not be so pleased."

Suddenly, Nell understood the reason for his coldness. She released his hand. Her eyes widened, and a look of pure outrage shone in their golden lights. "Robert has nothing to do with this, Donal." She spoke carefully so there would be no misunderstanding. "The child is an O'Flaherty, and his life should begin as his parents' did, in Ireland."

The incredible words swept over him, and his face stilled. Nell's child was his, not Montgomery's. She had conceived that very night, the only night, they'd lain together. And yet she'd married Montgomery. He stared down at her. She was so sure the child was his. How could she be so very sure, unless—

Realization dawned, followed by relief and a shattering happiness that turned his legs to jelly. Weakly, he leaned against the wall.

Nell felt the pain coming, sharper and deeper and

longer than any that had come before, and she gathered her resources to bear it. "Never mind," she said, hearing the words he'd left unsaid. "We know little of each other, after all." The pain mounted, surging, inevitable. "Help me, Donal," she gasped. "Help me."

Instinctively, Donal leaned over the bed and spread his hands over her stomach. It was tight as the skin of a drum, and it leaped and bucked beneath his touch like a thing alive. Nell's lips were bitten raw, and her gown was soaked with blood and sweat. The cook hovered anxiously at the entrance to the cabin.

"What is happening?" Donal asked him.

" 'Tis the child straining to be born."

"Why must it take so long?"

"The first is always so. 'Twill be hours yet."

"No!" Nell tensed for the next round of pain and lifted tortured eyes to Donal's face. "Please, Donal. Give me your hands, and speak no more."

Her grip was bone-crushing. Time passed. Donal lost count of the hours. Her legs were slick with sweat, and her hair hung close to her head, wet and lank on the pillow. Birthing blood drenched the sheets, and the primitive smell of it filled the cabin.

By the time her daughter's head made its appearance, Nell had nearly given up the fight. Her face was bloodless, and the bones were very prominent under her tightly drawn skin. Beneath her closed lids, her eyes looked twice their normal size.

The cook pointed to the place between her legs that began to separate. " 'Tis the head," he exclaimed excitedly. "She must push now. The wee 'un is nearly born."

"Did you hear, Nell?" Donal leaned close to her lips and spoke against them. "You must push now, love. The babe is nearly born."

Her eyelashes fluttered against her cheeks and then parted. "I don't want to."

He had never felt so frustrated, so helpless. "You must."

Her head moved to one side and then the other. "No."

Donal's forehead puckered. "Nell," he said anxiously, "you have no choice. The babe will be born. Unless you help, it will take longer."

She formed the words through cracked lips. "I have no strength left."

He leaned forward. "I think—" Then he felt it, the violent spasm that lifted her body from the bed and shaped it into a clumsy arc.

Panting heavily, with renewed strength, she sat up, gripped the headboard behind her, and bore down, every muscle heaving with her effort. Donal watched first in horror, then in awe, as the entirety of a tiny head was expelled into his hands, then the shoulders, and finally the legs. "'Tis a girl," he whispered hoarsely. "A girl no bigger than a minute."

Nell laughed raggedly and fell back on the pillows, her breathing slowed. The baby gasped, choked, sucked in her first breath of air, and wailed. "Give her to me," she said. "I would see my daughter."

Gently, Donal placed the babe, all redness and wrinkles and softness, on her chest. Nell's hand came up and caressed a mucus-soaked, blue-veined head that felt too tiny to be alive. "Oh, my," she breathed. "Oh, my."

The cook handed Donal a clean towel and a knife. "There's the afterbirth to come. Lean on her belly. Then cut the birth cord and tie it off."

Years later, Donal would never recall how he'd managed to bathe Nell and dress her in one of his saffron-dyed shirts, how he'd washed his daughter and changed the bed linens, how he'd dismissed the cabin boy and scrubbed the blood and stench from the floor. Somehow it all happened, and in less time than it took to down two flagons of ale, Nell and the babe were clean, the cabin was fresh, and they were alone.

He stood by the bed and stared down at his woman and child. His woman, his child. A curious trembling started in his legs. When he could no longer control the boneless feel of his knees, he fell to the floor and buried his face in her side. "Nell. Holy God, Nell."

She rested her hand on his head and smiled tenderly. He had such beautiful hair, so clean, black and shiny as a crow's wing, the same color that grew in wisps along the top of his daughter's tiny head. From a source deep within her, she voiced the wisdom that passes unspoken from mother to daughter. " 'Tis always the way, Donal. I suffered no more than those who have borne children before me."

Donal wondered why it was assumed that women were fragile creatures with little conviction and no tolerance for pain. What Nell had experienced this night would have unmanned many a battle-seasoned warrior. He was to marvel more than once on the journey home at the inconsistency of a world in which women were sheltered from the terrors of war only to be subjected regularly to the horrors of childbirth, fertility a virtue deemed more necessary than beauty or brilliance or courage or character.

The sun was low on the horizon, and the wind blew west from the Irish Sea when Donal sailed the *Banshee* into Galway Bay. The message inscribed above the city gates of the harbor town never failed to bring a grin to his lips: "From the fury of the O'Flahertys, deliver us, O Lord."

Lord William Burke, the Norman governor and protector of the king's rights in the west of Ireland, stood on the ramparts of his fortress and groaned. The swift return of the *Banshee* could mean only one thing. The O'Flaherty had been successful. The king's hostages were on board, and even now, Henry was preparing an army to sweep through Ireland.

In a moment of passion, when the hot blood of his Irish ancestors rose within him, Burke had pledged his standard to the Geraldine cause. A thousand times since, he had castigated himself for the pride that proved him a fool. To break his word to the O'Flaherty would banish him from the world in which he moved. To betray Henry Tudor meant certain poverty and eventual death. Those minor nobles who hung on the fringes of the great lords already had reported the names of the men who took the oath in the great hall of Aughnanure. It went against the grain of common sense, but there was nothing left for Burke than to align himself with the Gaels and Sean Ghalls of the north and west.

With a sense of inevitable doom, he gave the order for the city gates to be opened for the crew and passengers of the *Banshee*.

15

Aughnanure was a fortress and far more stark a place than Nell had ever seen before. It was built in the old Norman style of round turrets connected by long passageways and tiny windows designed to repel intruders. What beauty there was lay in the remoteness of its location.

Set amidst a forest of oak and ash at the end of a freshwater stream running with trout and teak-colored water, the castle gates rose violently out of the greenery. Only the guardhouse roof was visible from the ground. Visitors saw nothing but huge wooden gates linked with iron and an impregnable roof. Defenders peering out through the slats had an enormous advantage. The entire east side of the castle was built over a seawater gorge that filled at high tide.

It was here, on a deck that some besotted O'Flaherty ancestor had built for his lady, that Nell regained her strength. Weeks before she should have left her bed, she walked the deck, lifting her face to the saltwater spray. The midwife shook her head and grumbled, predicting fever and illness if Nell did not immediately seek her couch. But contrary to the woman's predictions, her legs grew strong again, her stomach flat and smooth, and her skin the gold-kissed color of winter light.

The child was six weeks old and flourishing, but Nell worried. She was still nameless and not yet baptized. For centuries, O'Flaherty children were carried to the Royal Abbey of Cong to be christened by the lord abbott. But Donal would not speak of it. Indeed, he came daily to hold his daughter and speak of insignificant matters, but that was all.

Inside Nell, a fierce determination was born. She loved Donal O'Flaherty and had borne him a daughter. Even more, she had been faithful to their pledge, possibly more faithful than he had been, given the nature of men. This land of thick forest and wind-hammered beaches had worked its way into her heart. She had nowhere else to go. Nothing short of death would tear her away. If waiting was what he wanted, she would wait, but she was Irish-born, and the stirrings of something she did not understand simmered within her. For nine long months she'd carried a daughter, spurned a king's bed, and thrown away an English earl, all for love of a stubborn Irish chieftain who'd claimed her heart when she was a girl.

She watched him below her now, standing on the edge of the tide, reaching for a stick of driftwood to throw to the wolfhound that sat by his side like a shadow. He wore only a linen shirt over his breeks, and the play of muscle under the cloth made her throat close and brought the sting of tears beneath her lids.

The movement of man and dog against the backdrop of churning sea and setting sun was magic. Inside her chest, her heart flapped like a sail on the *Banshee*. She recognized the source of the tension that made her heart feel too tight for her chest. Leaving her cloak in the press, she ran out of the room and down the stairs to the damp, bird-tracked sand of the shoreline.

Wind tore at her gown and pulled her hair from its tidy plait. She called his name, but the crash of the waves was strong. Battling the wind, she reached his side. He looked at her, accepted her presence, and said nothing. Adam himself could not have been more beautiful than the man who stood beside her.

"Curse you, Donal O'Flaherty!" she shouted across the inches that separated them. "I love you, and our daughter needs a name."

"She shall have one."

"When?"

His words crossed between them and slapped her in the face. "When you are no longer Robert Montgomery's wife."

She stepped backward. "You blame me." She'd whispered, but he read her lips.

Donal shook his head and accepted the wood from the dog's mouth. "Not you, and not for the marriage."

"Who, then, and for what?"

He lifted his arm and let the stick fly effortlessly into the wind. "I blame myself for leaving you with Desmond."

"You had little choice in the matter," she argued. "He found us."

Donal turned toward her and took her chin in his hand to tilt her face up. "I left you, Nell. Knowing the dangers, I left you and the lad. What purpose did it serve? Listen well, my heart, and understand. You were forced to wed another man. By law, both English and

Brehon, our daughter belongs to him and should bear his name."

The trembling started in her legs. "It isn't possible. The babe is yours."

Donal gripped her shoulders, and through his fingers she felt the depth of his emotions. "We know the truth. But to the rest of the world, the child is Montgomery's."

"My marriage to him was never consummated."

He was gratified to hear it, but that wasn't the subject at hand. "He must have agreed to raise the child as his own."

She nodded, and Donal continued. "I've spoken to a priest, Nell. Your marriage is legitimate. Because you and Montgomery are both Protestant, the rites stand. You must annul the marriage and marry me. Only then can we declare the wee lass our own."

"Our marriage was not a true one," she repeated. "Surely that is reason enough for an annulment."

"I've heard that Montgomery swears you were kidnapped and that the child is his. He disputes your claim of an unconsummated marriage."

Nell pulled away and pressed her fingers against her mouth. "He lies."

" 'Tis your word against an Englishman's."

Her eyes were huge and turbulent in her face. "What shall we do?"

"He leaves me no choice, *a stor*. I must kill him."

Nell dug her nails into her palms. "And if he kills you?"

He turned to face the sea. "You must go to him. Tell him you were forced. Tell him the babe died."

Nell gasped. "I will never leave my daughter."

"She is my daughter and an O'Flaherty. I will not have her made into an English lady."

"Is that why you keep yourself away, because you have so little faith in me?"

The ghost of a smile touched his lips. "Ah, Nell. I would give my last drop of blood to lie with you, lass. But if my time is at hand, I want no more babes to bear Montgomery's name."

Nell hesitated. "What would you call our daughter, if we could name her today?"

His eyes searched her face, remembering the first time he'd seen her, wondering if it was possible for a woman to be more lovely. "Maeve," he said, "after your mother. It was she who brought us together on your first Beltane."

Not a touch of the gratitude she felt lightened the seriousness of her face. "Mother would be pleased." She wiped a drop of moisture from her eye. "When will you leave?"

"Word has it that Montgomery has landed in Dublin. He has the king's support. It is fitting that I meet him near the ruins of Maynooth. I leave at first light."

She would have walked away, but his words, earnest and humble, stopped her. "There can be no harm in holding you, Nell."

With a guttural sob, she threw herself into his arms. They closed around her, and she clung to him, filling his empty spaces just as she had the first time.

He wondered if she had any idea how much he wanted her or how long he'd been without a woman. It was as if she'd bewitched him on that long-ago night at Maynooth when he'd come upon her in the gloaming and she sat with him under the stars. Her hair was the texture of silk against his mouth, and her ear, pink with cold, was pressed against his nose. The pounding surf matched the beating of his heart and brought the fever to his blood. His resistance, built up over long months

of abstinence, melted away. This was Nell, the mother
of his daughter, the woman he'd handfasted with and
for whom he'd broken faith with a king. She was his.
Robert Montgomery had no claim on her.

Nell lifted her head to look at him. Her face was
streaked with tears. He wiped them away with his
thumb. Mirrored in her eyes, he saw his own desire.
Slowly, he bent his head to find her mouth. She met
him eagerly, her lips parting, accepting the thrust of his
tongue, holding it inside her. The kiss was rough and
searching, hot and hungry. And when it was finished,
there were more kisses and still more, until all that was
left of his resistance melted away. He scooped her up
and staggered across the sand and up the stairs to the
room where Nell had spent too many nights alone.

They were drenched and shivering from the sea
spray. But someone had replenished the fire, and the
room was warm and lovely with light. Tenderly, he
pushed back her hair, unlaced her gown, and pulled it
down from her shoulders. It slipped to the floor. She
stood before him, backlit by the fire. Tentatively, he
reached out to trace the slopes of her breasts, the dip
of her waist, the curve of her hips, all temptingly visible
beneath the finely woven cloth of her shift. Her gasp,
slight as it was, undid him, as did the fluid, effortless
way she drew the shift over her head, moved to the
bed, and climbed between the sheets. He was drowning
in desire. Cursing his clumsiness, he managed to unlace
his shirt and kick off his breeks.

Nell leaned back on her elbows and watched him
walk toward her. He was the first man she had seen
completely naked. Somewhere in her chest, her breath
stopped, and she stared at him, waiting. He knelt over
her. The width of his shoulders blocked out the light.
Moisture ran in rivulets down the planes of his chest.

She felt his eyes, then his hands, and finally his mouth on her lips, her mouth, her breasts. Wallowing in pure sensation, Nell closed her eyes and gave herself up to the heat of his lovemaking, his mark on her throat, his arms gathering her close, his leg nudging hers apart, and the splendid length of him entering her, thrusting deeper and harder until his release was imminent. Pushing back with his arms, he tried to withdraw.

Nell, on the verge of something she had not yet begun to understand but had no wish to lose, deliberately tightened the muscles of her thighs. Her fingers gripped his bare buttocks and held on.

"Holy God, Nell." He breathed raggedly. "Don't do this."

She pulled his head down and moaned against his mouth. "Stay with me. Please, Donal. I will never go back to Robert. No matter what happens, I will never go back."

"Nell." His laugh had more air than substance. Brushing her cheeks with his fingertips, he kissed her mouth and fought the urges of his body. "I cannot leave you with child. You've Maeve to consider."

She shifted beneath him. Her fingers relaxed, flattened, and began kneading his backside. It was exquisite torture, and he was rapidly losing control. In a final attempt at reason, he whispered against her ear. "I will fight until my last breath to keep you, Nell, but battles are not won by the cautious. The future is uncertain for us."

Nell arched her body, taking him more deeply inside her. Pressing her face against his shoulder, she spoke softly. "My father spoke of you long before I knew he wanted a match between us. There is nothing of caution in the heart of an O'Flaherty chieftain. There should be none in the heart of the woman who stands by his

side. I ask nothing of you, Donal, nothing but this
night, for all the nights we should have had and for
those that may never be."

After that, there were no more words. Under her
hands, she felt the ripple of muscle and the slow, sweet
slide of him as he entered her and withdrew, over and
over until the edges of her reason blurred and the heat
between them rose and flamed and died and rose again.

Nell woke from her doze just as the first streaks of
dawn touched the eastern sky. Beside her, Donal stirred
and opened his eyes. She was intensely aware of him,
of the rise and fall of his chest, the darker hue of his
skin against the sheets, his scent mingling with hers.
Rolling over, she pressed her backside into the cradle
of his hips and felt him harden. She released her breath.
He wanted her still.

"Don't, Nell," he whispered into her hair. "There is
no more time left."

"Tell me you aren't sorry."

"Sweet Jesus, lass." He rolled her over on her back
and frowned down at her. " 'Tis a gift you've given me.
I could never be sorry."

She kissed him briefly, resolving to send him on his
way without tears.

Hollow-eyed and tousled from lovemaking and lack
of sleep, Nell was still beautiful. Donal could not get
enough of her. He touched her cheeks, her lips, and
the line of her jaw. Once, before he knew her, he believed that her Fitzgerald blood was tainted, that the
Irish in her was not enough to make her a fit mate for
an O'Flaherty chieftain. Now he knew better. Nell was
no political prize to be bartered for the alliances she
brought to her father. Gael or Sean Ghall, she was a
woman who gave her heart only once, and he, Donal
O'Flaherty of Galway, was her chosen.

A strange burning began in his chest and beneath his eyelids. The feeling was not completely unfamiliar. It stayed with him while he dressed, ransacked the larder, checked the hooves of his stallion, and swung up on his back, rallying his men with the ancient war cry of the O'Flahertys. It intensified when he looked back, after the drawbridge had been drawn, and saw Nell standing on the battlements, holding the tiny lass they had made together. The feeling moved to his throat when she lifted the child in her arms the better to see his departure. Lifting his arm in a final salute, Donal vowed on the souls of his ancestors that he would not leave Nell to mourn another loss.

Robert Montgomery's rage increased as he paced the length of his well-appointed tent. Margaret Fitzgerald, the countess of Ormond, her dark blue eyes glinting with malicious amusement, sat at a small table off to one side and tapped her fingers. "Come, Montgomery," she said at last. "You will wear the rugs thin. Tomorrow will not come any sooner whether or not you walk to it."

He clenched his fists and turned on the woman who claimed to be Nell's sister. "You have no natural sentiments, my lady. How can you sit there so calmly when the very life of your sister is in danger?"

Margaret's lips thinned. "Nell does not inspire the same passions in me that she does in you. Let me remind you, dear brother-in-law, that 'tis most unlikely that Nell was abducted unwillingly. Cilcerrig is a large castle with many rooms and servants. The O'Flaherty could not possibly drag a trussed and struggling woman down the halls, out the door, and through locked gates. Think, Robert. Nell was betrothed to Donal O'Flaherty. She believed herself to be in love with him."

"She is my wife," Montgomery said through his teeth. "Whatever promises were made before we wed no longer apply."

Margaret picked up a sweetmeat and nibbled it daintily. "I was merely suggesting that Nell is still infatuated with her former betrothed." She selected a shiny red apple and pretended to study it. " 'Tis an odd thing for a new mother, is it not, to keep a man's firstborn from him?"

Robert's feet stilled. Margaret of Ormond had a reputation for cleverness. But could any woman, or man for that matter, be clever enough to know the truth about the babe? Someone from Cilcerrig must have revealed that he and Nell did not live together as husband and wife. His jaw locked. He would lash the skin from the backs of every servant on his estate.

Margaret threw back her head and laughed like a man. In truth, even though she was lovely to look at, with deep blue eyes and hair the same silvery color as Nell's, the countess was not the least bit feminine. Her stride was masculine, and there was a hardness to her expression and a calculating twist to her lips that reminded Robert of a predatory wolf.

"Fear not, Robert," she said as if she could read his very mind. "Your servants are true. 'Tis merely my knowledge of Nell that brings on my suspicions. She was never one to give her heart lightly, and you, my dear Robert, are very much the gentleman. I imagine my younger sister has persuaded you to postpone your wedding night. Am I correct?"

"No," Robert lied. "The child is mine."

Her voice hardened and grew cold. "Look at me, Robert Montgomery."

He turned and gazed into her eyes. It was rumored

that she carried the sight of her Celtic mother and the curse of *Emáin Macha* in her blood.

"I have destroyed more important houses and men than yours. Do not lie to me."

Robert swallowed. "Why do you hate her so much?"

"Who?"

"Nell, of course."

Margaret shook her head. "I have no feelings at all for Nell. She is too insignificant to hate. 'Tis Gerald, the runt of the Kildares, who must be destroyed."

"He is your flesh and blood, your only living brother."

She looked amused. "Who do you think began the destruction of the Kildares?"

"You?" He managed to form the word.

"Very good, Robert. A word here, an innuendo in the ear of the king. First my father fell, and then my uncles, and finally Silken Thomas. Gerald is the only one left. Then my revenge will be complete. Nell is only a woman. She is unimportant."

"As are you, my lady."

Margaret stared somewhere over his shoulder. "You know nothing of it, Robert Montgomery. I was not raised a woman. For that, my family shall pay dearly."

He remembered that her son had been killed five years before by a Geraldine dart, and that she had been given as a young girl to Piers Butler, earl of Ormond, hereditary enemy of the Fitzgeralds. It could not have been an easy thing for a mere lass to wed a man whose treachery was renowned throughout Kildare. Somewhere in the distant past, before the conquest, the Ormonds and Kildares had vied for power in Ireland, and their enmity had continued through the centuries. What cruel twist of fate had convinced Gerald Og, the great Kildare, to sacrifice his oldest daughter?

In Margaret Fitzgerald an acute intelligence had combined with a twisted and sensitive mind. Robert could see that her nature was not an affectionate one. Nell had told him as much when she revealed the tragic story of Margaret's displacement by her brother and her subsequent marriage to Ormond. What Nell had not known was Margaret's role in the destruction of the Geraldines.

Robert stared at the coldly beautiful face of Nell's sister and resolved, when this was over, to keep his family safely in Wales.

16

Donal O'Flaherty looked down from the knoll where his army was camped on what had once been the lordship of Kildare, the most fertile farmland in all of Ireland. No cattle grazed on the grassland. No villagers or farmers toiled in the fields. There was only blackened wasteland where Henry's troops had torched the plains. He felt a strange melancholy for this land that wasn't his. Yesterday seared by fire, tomorrow stained with blood.

Conn Bachach O'Neill, chief of Tyrone, stamped his feet as he approached the young chief. Even among allies, it was wise to announce one's presence. Although their armies had joined at Castlerea, the two men had found no time to converse privately until this moment. "I wonder if the countess of Ormond derives satisfaction from such a sight?" Tyrone said around the stem of his pipe.

Shrugging, Donal hooked his fingers through his belt. " 'Tis said she finds little satisfaction in anything at all."

"Aye, 'tis the way with Margaret." They were silent for long, comfortable moments. "How are my cousins?"

"They are well."

O'Neill hesitated. " 'Tis rumored that Nell bore Montgomery a child."

"The rumors are false."

" 'Tis relieved I am to hear it." O'Neill did not miss the clenching of the younger man's hands. "As you well know," he observed, "Brehon law allows a woman to divorce her husband if he does not please her, but children are another matter."

Donal's eyes glittered with a strange, unholy light, and for the first time in many years, Conn Bachach was afraid of a man's anger. "The child is mine," said Donal. "Nell and I handfasted before Montgomery abducted her from Desmond. She married him to save Gerald's life. The marriage was never consummated. He lies if he says otherwise."

O'Neill nodded. He was more than ready to believe this splendid young man with the powerful shoulders and archangel beauty. Personal matters were uncomfortable for the O'Neill. He was pleased to turn the subject. "Tomorrow, O'Brien and O'Donnell will make up the left flank of the formation. MacMurrough and I have agreed to the right. Your army is the largest. 'Tis seemly that you should lead us into battle."

"MacWilliam joins with me in the center," Donal said, agreeing with O'Neill's strategy. "The earl of Ormond's *gallowglass* and *ceithearn* have joined with Montgomery."

"Is there word of Henry's army?"

Donal's lip curled contemptuously. "His royal highness is busy preparing for yet another bridal. Word has it that he has complete confidence in Montgomery and Ormond."

The O'Neill's teeth showed white between the gray-brown of his beard. "So much the better for us."

"Aye." Donal did not look pleased. "Our numbers are even and our men canny fighters, but the countess is driven by hate, and Montgomery will not be easily defeated."

"No battle is easily won."

"This will be a bloodbath," replied Donal bitterly, "and when 'tis over, we will have won nothing. Gerald will still be in danger, and there will be those who believe I hold a man's wife and child hostage at Aughnanure."

Conn Bachach O'Neill frowned and looked down at his feet. The young O'Flaherty chieftain was in need of encouragement, and O'Neill was not known for his facility with language. He would have repeated the words of his concubine after he told her that Nell had been abducted by young O'Flaherty, but outside the bedchamber such bluntness embarrassed him. Brianne had laughed. Her eyes had softened in the way a woman's did when she was ready to receive a man, and she told him only a fool would believe the O'Flaherty chief must resort to abducting women. More likely he would be fending them off with his *bata*. O'Neill cleared his throat, determined to put his oratory skills to the test. "Why is an Irish chieftain concerned with gossip at the English court?"

" 'Tis not the English court that concerns me."

"If that is so," said the O'Neill slowly, "you need have no fear. Look around you, lad. All of Ireland is here. Would your army be the size it is if their leaders had no confidence in you? As for Gerald, he will be taken to France. I have been in communication with the old earl's friend, Robert Walshe, confidant of King Francois. He will keep the lad safe. From there we will appeal the restoration of his lands and title." He shrugged his shoulders. "There is little hope, of course, now that Henry has an heir, but who knows what journey fate has marked for young Gerald?"

Donal was still not convinced. "What of Montgomery? He will never give Nell up, not so long as he is alive."

O'Neill puffed on his pipe. "There can be only one answer to that, lad," he said softly. "There are few things for which a man deserves to die. Montgomery stole your woman. He has made his choice."

The O'Flaherty watched the English army ride toward them. The red crosses of Saint George emblazoned across white pennants fluttered in the morning breeze. Every English mercenary was covered with metal and carried a bill hook and sword. Hard-eyed, they stared out from behind iron *morions* worn low over their foreheads. Their clipped beards ran with rain.

Donal waited with the center guard under cover of the trees until the English archers had released their first volley of arrows. Then, shouting *"Crom aboo!"* the battle cry of the Geraldines, he led his foot soldiers forward.

Up the knoll and into the trees, the English infantry met the Irish, first discharging their spears and then pulling swords from their scabbards. Metal clanged against metal, and within minutes the black grassland was red and slippery with blood. Later, when the initial fighting slowed, the center cavalry of both armies charged forward, and the cries of wounded men and horses rang out above the heavy breathing, the hollow clanging, the thud of claymore against targe.

Donal's opponent, his face distorted behind his metal

morion, was losing ground. He lunged forward, missed, and buried himself to the hilt on the O'Flaherty's sword. Pushing the lifeless body away, Donal pulled out his blade, wiped it on his trews, and turned to meet his next attacker. The man was already wounded. Feinting to the left, Donal severed an arm and watched dispassionately as the man slipped to the ground, his body crushed under his horse's hooves.

Once again, he wiped his sword clean, threw back his rain-wet hair, and looked around, quickly assessing the situation. No one was unengaged. Already O'Donnell and O'Neill had closed in on the right and left flanks. Ahead, less than ten men away, under the Ormond standard, Donal recognized Robert Montgomery in heated combat with an Irish foot soldier.

Climbing over bodies, dodging men in the throes of battle and death, he made his way to where Montgomery fended off his attacker. Gripping the hilt of his sword with both hands, Donal came up from below, knocking apart the blades. "Leave us!" he shouted to the Irishman. "This man is mine."

"You!" Montgomery stepped back, his face streaming with rain, his eyes red-rimmed with fatigue and fury. He lifted his sword. "By God, I'll kill you where you stand!"

For Donal, this was the battle. This was the reason he'd gathered an army and defied a king. Here, at last, was the man who presumed to claim his woman, to lay his hands on her, to give her his name. Donal lifted his sword. "Come for me, Welshman," he taunted him softly, "you who dare lift your sights to a Geraldine."

Robert lunged, but his sword was effortlessly blocked. He parried and aimed straight for Donal's heart. Again, his sword was easily turned away. Rage lent him courage and speed but not caution. A careless thrust nearly sliced his arm in two. By rights, Donal should have stepped back and allowed him to tie it. But this was not England, and their match was not one between gentlemen. Both men knew this fight would be to the finish.

Donal was no longer aware of the battle waged around him. The cries, the stench of blood, the pounding rain all disappeared. He heard nothing but the sound of his own breath, felt nothing but the pain in his laboring chest, saw nothing but Robert's distorted face and the blood running down his arm, staining his sleeve, welling up into his hand, dripping off the sword metal. Another minute, and it would be finished. Donal knew himself to be the superior swordsman. Montgomery was skilled, but his reach was too short, and his tendency to thrust and then draw back was both predictable and dangerous.

With a lightning-swift riposte, Donal slid his sword into Robert's shoulder muscle, knocking the weapon from his hand. Pressing the point of the blade against the downed man's throat, he spoke. "Make your peace, Welshman. Your God awaits."

Robert struggled to breathe. "She is my wife," he panted.

Donal increased his pressure and watched two drops of blood appear on the tip of his sword. "Nell is mine," he said savagely. "We were handfasted on the journey to Desmond. Against her will, you stole her from me. She married you only to save the life of her brother. 'Tis my child she bore. I know the truth, Welshman. You insult Nell with your lie."

"I love her," Robert gasped.

" 'Tis a poor sort of love that destroys a woman's honor."

Montgomery was bleeding heavily now. "Tell her,"

he gasped, "tell her I had no such intention. I meant only to save her life."

Donal knew it was true. He had learned from Nell's own lips how Montgomery had saved her life and Gerald's. Until now, the Welshman's reputation had done him only credit. Perhaps, if he gave up his claim on her, Donal would allow him his life. "And now," he asked, "if I choose to spare you? Will you renounce your claim?"

"Have mercy, O'Flaherty. Kill me and be done with it. I would rather die here in battle than at the end of the executioner's block." He choked, and blood bubbles formed at his mouth.

Removing his sword, Donal knelt by his side and pressed his hand against the pulse still beating in the Welshman's throat. It fluttered erratically for a moment and then stopped completely. The man was dead. Crossing himself, Donal lifted his face to the rain and uttered two brief prayers, one for the repose of Montgomery's soul, the other for his own absolution.

Nell watched the fog settle like giant spider webs on bare tree branches, where it hung suspended, muffling the sounds of water, the crackling of twigs, and the panting of Donal's wolfhound stepping carefully beside her. She shivered and pulled her sable-lined cloak tightly about her body. Her months in the south of Wales had spoiled her for Irish weather. Winter would soon be upon them, but despite the bone-chilling cold, Nell eagerly anticipated the isolation and freedom it would bring. She could rest easily. Only the hardiest of Irish *gallowglass* would attempt to march during winter. No Englishman would dare. Mercenaries, often unpaid for months at a time, were forced to pillage the countryside for food and shelter. They would find none among the Gaels and Sean Ghalls of Ulster.

The dog pushed a woolly head under Nell's palm. Absentmindedly, she rubbed the animal's velvety nose. Her thoughts led her in strange directions, back to Maynooth when the Fitzgeralds ruled in Kildare and Munster. Her eyes watered. Shocked at her unexpected emotionalism, she wiped the tears away with two quick swipes and looked around as if she were being observed. Laughing self-consciously, she caught the dog's head in both her hands and caressed it. The wolfhound wagged her tail and whimpered with appreciation. Then she pulled away, ran back, butted Nell's hand, and loped into the trees. "Come back, Triane," Nell called out.

The dog barked, and Nell followed the sound. Soupy and thick, the mist swirled, making it impossible to see more than a foot in any direction, but the hound's deep bark was clear and close. Nell followed the sound, arms outstretched, carefully positioning one foot in front of the other. "Triane!" she shouted. "Come back."

This time, the bark was very near. Missing her step, Nell fell forward, rolling down an incline, soft and springy with decaying leaves. When she stopped, staggered to her feet, and brushed herself clean, the fog and the hound had disappeared. Standing before her was a girl with sun in her hair and eyes the color of light on water. Nell's eyes widened, and a smile of pure pleasure lit her face. "Jillian."

Delighted, Jillian laughed. *You know me.*

"Of course."

But you didn't before.

"Everything is quite clear now."

I'd like to go home, Nell.

"I should imagine so."

Jillian pushed the hair off her forehead. It fell back again. *Can you do it this time?*

"Aye."

Why not before?

"I don't know," Nell replied honestly.

It's been such a long time. Will everything be different, I wonder?

Nell took a deep breath. "I suspect that your life has gone on exactly as before in that future place from where you came. I know that you aren't real, Jilly. I'm not sure what you are, a spirit perhaps, or a ghost. Whichever it is, you've been a great help to me. I had no one else, you see."

And now?

"Now I am a mother and must learn to stand on my own."

You won't be alone, Nell.

Nell held up her hand. "Say nothing more. I no longer have a need to anticipate fate." She stepped forward and clasped Jillian's hands. "There is something I must say to you, Jilly. My circumstances were forced upon me suddenly, and my losses over the past two years have been great. I think my heart and mind must have frozen with grief. Without you, it may have gone differently for Gerald and me. I needed you to survive. That is no longer true. Now I know that I will manage whether or not Donal returns."

Will I see you again?

Nell's laugh was nearly a sob. "Once more, you ask me a question for which I have no answer."

Goodbye, Nell.

She watched as the mist rose from the ground once again, closing in, swallowing first Jillian's body, then her face, and finally her voice.

"Farewell, Jilly," Nell whispered into the encroaching grayness.

Donal found her in the small sitting room attached to her bedchamber. She was nursing Maeve and humming a ballad of Ulster. The babe pulled greedily at her breast. He could hear his daughter's delicate sucking sounds from across the room, and his heart leaped in his chest. Finally, it was all here, within his reach, everything he'd dreamed of.

Feeling his gaze, Nell looked up, saw him, and a light flared within her.

He crossed the room and knelt by her chair, resting his hand on the tiny dark head at Nell's breast. She hardly dared ask the question. "Is it all right, Donal?"

His face changed, became still and unreadable. "Robert Montgomery is dead, Nell."

She swallowed and nodded.

"There was no other way."

"I know."

"I'm sorry."

She leaned forward and rested her forehead against his. "I am truly sorry for Robert. He was a good man. But he knew from the beginning how it was with me. I never deceived him. Perhaps he believed that I would come to love him." Her smile was soft and tremulous. "But I am a Geraldine. We love only once."

With her words, Donal felt the ache he carried in his heart dissolve. Lifting her chin, he covered her mouth with his own. "Nell." He laughed shakily and pulled away. "I brought someone with me. I hope you will approve."

She shifted the now sleeping baby to her shoulder. "I will always welcome your guests to our home."

"He is not a guest. 'Tis a priest. I brought Father Michael."

Hope and a queer breathless feeling made her chest tight.

"I brought him to marry us, Nell, and later to accompany us to the Royal Abbey where Maeve will be christened." Suddenly, he felt unsure of himself, as if he'd never made the journey to Maynooth two long years ago, never sat with her under the stars or felt the softness of her body beneath him on the furs.

Pressing his lips against her forehead, he murmured against her skin the words he'd held in his heart. "When I was but a lad, my father told me of the mighty Geraldines who ruled all of Ireland outside the Pale. He told me of a palace called Maynooth and a princess who lived there. If I was a wise lad, he said, I would travel to Maynooth and wed the princess, for the blood of a Geraldine would strengthen the O'Flaherty line."

Nell waited, spellbound, for him to continue.

"I wanted none of it," he said, his callused hand smoothing back her hair. "You see, my mind was filled with a wood sprite who had claimed my heart on the eve of Beltane. But to satisfy my father, I journeyed to Maynooth to see the princess. She was beautiful beyond belief, and for the first time I felt as if an O'Flaherty chieftain had set his sights too high. But then we sat under the stars, and she told me of her part in that long-ago Beltane, and I knew that her father and mine were wise men after all. She was my destiny."

"I was the princess," said Nell.

"Aye." He rubbed his thumb over her lips. "You are my destiny. I knew it then, I know it now. Please marry me, Nell."

She pulled his head down to her mouth and whispered against his lips. "When you came to Maynooth and we met in the gloaming, I knew you weren't sure that you wanted me. But I wanted you, from the very beginning, just as I want you now."

Donal threw back his head and laughed. Then he kissed her open, smiling mouth and took the baby from her arms. "I'll leave you to prepare."

"For what?"

"The wedding, of course."

"Today?" Nell's mouth formed a perfect circle of surprise.

Donal cradled the infant in the crook of his arm. "The good father is anxious to leave for the abbey at first light. He is afraid that Maeve may expire before she is saved."

"Is that the only reason, my lord?"

His glance was wicked, and all at once she remembered how very young this man who would be her husband really was.

"I intend to spend tonight and every night in that bed with you, Nell. I imagine Father Michael knows that, too, which is why he wishes to see us properly wed."

The color rose in her cheeks, but she did not couch the words that came to her mind. "Make haste, then. This time I would have a true wedding night."

He met her glance from across the room. Suddenly, they were no longer sparring, and the air was charged and alive between them. "I promise you, Nell Fitzgerald," Donal said softly, "I will allow nothing to come between us on this night."

A gurgling sound broke his concentration. He looked down at the bundle in his arms and grinned. "With one exception."

Nell laughed. "An exception who demands food every hour."

"I foresee a most unusual wedding night."

"You don't really mind, do you, Donal?" she asked anxiously.

"I would have it no other way," he said, and Nell believed him, for anyone could see from the way he handled his wee lass that Donal was a man made complete by his children.

17

Belfast, Northern Ireland, 1979

From the guard towers, long fingers of light illuminated the silent grounds of Long Kesh prison, better known as the Maze. Slowly, the beams crawled across the empty yard, revealing rusted basketball hoops, a patch of grass, broken pavement, and chain-link fences bordered by three rows of barbed wire. It was very quiet, too quiet. The normal din from the IRA barracks where Irish politics was argued nightly had been reduced to an occasional oath or shout of laughter.

Two yards past the front guard entrance and seven feet below ground, Frankie Maguire turned off his flashlight and held his breath. He was down on all fours, crawling through an escape tunnel eight men had sweated for sixteen months to carve out of the rain-soaked earth. Failures, cave-ins, and close calls had postponed the escape for nearly six months beyond its scheduled date. Now that it was here, sheer stupidity would most likely bring the guards down on them.

"For fuck's sake, Frankie," whispered Liam O'Toole. "Don't stop now. There's sixty of us behind you, and we're nearly there."

Frankie held up his hand. "It's too quiet," he said after a minute. "Doesn't anyone have the brains t' make it look like an ordinary night?"

"What do y' expect when the average age in there is nineteen?"

He was right. There was nothing to do but continue. Frankie turned his flashlight back on and crawled as fast as he could nearly half a mile over the supports to the exit point. His knees were bloody by the time he pulled himself up out of the hole into the darkness of a summer night. Thirty men climbed out behind him before the shriek of sirens pierced the silence. Someone had sounded the alarm.

Like beetles under an unearthed stone, the men scattered in all directions, scrambling under fences, across roads, into ditches, some into the glaring headlights of Land Rovers operated by the RUC, some down through Dundalk and South Armagh across the border to safety in the Republic, some into safe houses stocked by nationalist supporters with food and provisions. More than half moved up into the hills and boglands of the breathtakingly beautiful county of Antrim, only to be rounded up and transported back to the Maze to serve the term of their sentences.

Frankie decided against crossing the border after spending an uncomfortable night in an abandoned famine house near the ocean. At first, every instinct told him to leave Ulster, to make a new life for himself in the welcoming, sympathetic, and Catholic Republic of Ireland. But something held him back, something he could neither understand nor explain. When his adrenaline rush slowed and rational thought returned, he knew in which direction to walk.

Before dawn, he made his way through the thickly forested glen to the back road. He followed it to the town of Carrickfergus. Judging by the loyalist colors painted on the curbs of the east side of town and the green, white, and orange painted on the curbs of the west side, it was a mixed community.

Frankie turned to the west. An RUC roadblock loomed before him. Fighting the survival instinct screaming in his head, he continued toward the barricade. A small boy, no more than three, ran out of the doorway of a nearby house. Thinking quickly, Frankie picked up the child. A woman opened the door.

"Where've y' been, Danny Browne?" she called out. "I've been waitin' on you for nearly two hours."

"Sorry, love." Frankie smiled engagingly. "Roadblocks held me up."

"I suppose it can't be helped," she said grudgingly. "Y're here now. Come in. There's somethin' on the stove for you."

Frankie forced himself to saunter casually up the walk and into the house. He set the boy on his feet, pulled out a chair, and sat down at the table. For a long time, the only sounds were the bubbling of oats, the hiss and whistle of the kettle.

"Thank you," he said at last. "I'm—"

She interrupted him. "It had better be Danny Browne for now. I'm Colette Sheehan. Pleased to make your acquaintance."

Frankie watched her dish healthy portions of oatmeal into two bowls. "How long have the barricades been up?"

"Since the prison break." She placed the bowls on the table, lifted the toddler to her lap, and picked up a spoon. "Are y' hungry, love?" she crooned, holding the food to the lad's mouth. The boy opened his mouth obediently. After half a dozen more bites, he pressed his lips together and shook his head. His mother laughed and released him. He ran into the sitting room and began to stack wooden blocks on top of each other. His mother turned her attention back to Frankie. "You've escaped, haven't you?"

"Aye." He saw no point in lying.

"Are you IRA?"

"Aye."

She stirred her oatmeal, and Frankie watched her. She was a pretty thing, near his own age, with black curly hair, rosy skin, and clear blue eyes. "You're not t' be worrying about it, Mrs. Sheehan," he assured her. "I'll be gone as soon as they clear out the roadblock."

"What were you in for?"

"Murder," he said bluntly.

Her cheeks whitened. He hurried to reassure her. "It was an accident. I didn't mean t' kill him. He slipped and fell. They put me away, and after that, when I was inside, I joined up."

She released her breath. "I'm sympathetic, mind you, but I don't want no killin'."

He nodded and resumed his meal.

"Y' don't have to go right away," she said suddenly. "Sometimes they keep the barricade up for more than a day."

"Your husband won't be wanting me in the way."

"Tommy was killed by a loyalist bomb durin' the last marchin' season. I'm alone with the boy. It would be a help to me if you stayed awhile."

"Who is Danny Browne?"

"He was my fiancé. We broke it off when he left for

London." She reached for his empty bowl and walked to the sink.

Frankie had spent four celibate years in prison, and Mrs. Sheehan was endowed with full curves in all the right places. He cleared his throat. "I don't mind staying for a bit if you'll have me."

She smiled over her shoulder. "I work at the café on the corner, but only until three. Tim, my boy, will sleep until noon. Do y' mind tendin' to him until I get home?"

Frankie looked up in surprise. He'd just confessed to escaping a prison sentence for manslaughter, and she was enlisting him to care for her son. Recovering, he nodded his head. He knew very little about children, but he couldn't refuse after she'd offered to take him in.

The hours he spent entertaining the lad passed quickly. Frankie was actually enjoying himself. Colette breezed in shortly after three and beamed to find her boy sticky with applesauce but apparently content. "I'll make tea," she said, moving to the stove.

Frankie downed three cheese sandwiches and a pint of Guinness before he realized that she was watching him. Suddenly self-conscious, he wiped his hands on a towel. "Is something wrong?"

She shook her head. "I'll put Timmy to bed. You can clean up if y' want."

He heard the sounds of water running, splashing, and the delighted shrieks of a happy baby. Grinning at the thought of chubby wee Tim in those fuzzy jumpers babies wore, Frankie rolled up his sleeves, forcing himself to stay in the kitchen and keep at the dishes.

"Danny," Colette called out from the back room. "Tim will be wantin' to say good night."

Frankie frowned. The name change would take some getting used to. Still, Danny was as good a name as any. He dried his hands and walked into the room Colette shared with her son. Timmy stood up in his crib, hair damp and cheeks rosy from scrubbing. His eyes crinkled at the corners, and he held out his arms. Frankie laughed and picked up the boy, lifting him high in the air. The baby smiled and kicked his legs, chuckling out loud when Frankie bussed first one cheek and then the other.

"He likes you," Colette said approvingly.

"He's a grand little lad, Mrs. Sheehan," said Frankie, laying the boy down in the crib.

"Colette."

"If you like," he said easily.

She followed him back into the kitchen and picked up a towel to dry the rinsed dishes he'd stacked efficiently on the counter. "How old are you, Danny?"

"Twenty."

She rubbed the plate and set it on the shelf. "Are y' married?"

"No."

Colette sighed. "Thank God for that."

All at once, he understood. "Colette, I can't—"

"Don't say it," she cut him off. "I'm not askin' for anythin' from you."

He rinsed the last dish and pulled the plug. The water made a sucking sound as it disappeared down the drain.

"I'm twenty-five," she said quietly.

Frankie leaned against the sink and crossed his arms. She really was appealing and incredibly vulnerable.

"I saw you comin' down the hill," she blurted out. She didn't have the words for the feeling inside her chest when she'd seen the lean, black-haired boy with the sun at his back walking toward her. "I don't care what y've done," she said instead. "I'm five years older than you. Is it all right?"

He reached for her then, pulling her into the v of his legs. "Aye, lass," he said gently. "It's all right with me."

Kildare Hall, 1986

Avery Graham accepted the glass of aged Irish whiskey that Jillian held out to him. He frowned when she walked to the tea tray and poured a cup. "Am I drinking alone today?" he asked.

"I don't drink during the day. Surely you know that by now, Avery," she replied.

He ignored the slight edge in her voice, rose to stand beside her, and sipped his whiskey. "Have you considered my proposal, Jillian?"

She looked at him, and his stomach clenched. Avery enjoyed beautiful things. Jillian Fitzgerald was twenty-four years old, a generation younger than any of his peers, wealthy, well bred, tall, slender, elegant, and so beautiful that it made his heart ache whenever he looked at her. "Surely you've reached a decision by now," he prodded her gently.

Jillian hesitated. "I've thought a great deal about it, Avery."

"Go on."

She set down her teacup. "Please forgive me for being presumptuous, and if I'm wrong, I do beg your pardon, but we are talking about marriage, are we not?"

"We are."

Again she appeared hesitant.

"For God's sake, Jillian, there is no reason on earth why you should be afraid of me."

"Of course not." Pink color flooded her cheeks, but she met his gaze steadily. "You see, Avery, for a very long time I've been under the impression that you prefer men to women. Therefore, I have never considered our relationship in terms of marriage."

"I see." He lowered his eyes to the amber liquid in his glass and kept them there. "May I ask you a question, Jillian?"

"Certainly."

"You've suffered my presence for some time now. There are those who might say you've encouraged me." He laughed raggedly. "Christ, I've even kissed you."

Jillian was in control once again. "Not very ardently, Avery. As for encouraging you, I like you. I consider you to be a very dear friend."

"But not a husband."

She tilted her head, and her eyes narrowed. "I'm not wrong about you, am I?"

"No."

"Why do you need a wife?"

He laughed, and the tension broke. "What I love most about you, my dear, is your intelligence."

She waited while he walked to the liquor cabinet to freshen his drink. He did not return to stand beside her but sat down on the couch.

Slowly, she made her way across the room and sat across from him, tucking her hands beneath her knees. "If you can't tell me, I will understand, but I will not be your wife."

He looked startled. "Do you mean to tell me that you are actually considering my proposal?"

"Yes, if you tell me the truth."

"I should like the same consideration from you, my dear."

Jillian nodded.

Avery looked around at the elegantly appointed room. It was an eclectic mixture of old and new, by far the

most charming sitting room in Ulster. Wood floors
gleamed under a crystal chandelier, antique candlesticks
wrought in the eleventh century for a woman named
Nest, ancient matriarch of the Fitzgeralds, Ireland's
own Helen of Troy and Jillian's direct ancestor, sat opposite each other on the mantel. A gilt-framed mirror
reflected Queen Anne tables, and a Louis XVI desk was
artistically arranged on the Persian rug. Family portraits
of the earls of Kildare lined the walls, and a Minton
tea service sat on a silver tray. "Surely it isn't the
money," he said dryly.

"No, Avery. I don't need money."

"I have a great deal, you know."

She folded her hands in her lap. "Congratulations.
So do I."

"Your mother will be pleased."

"My mother is not a fool."

He sighed. "Very well, Jillian. I'm under consideration for a very influential appointment. I've been asked
to serve as secretary to Northern Ireland with the stipu-
lation that I marry. If I do not, my political career ends
where it is now. Too many people, you see, have begun
to suspect what you already know. Marriage, to someone like yourself, will still the rumors."

Jillian marveled at the naïveté of a man in his middle
forties. Avery Graham was a brilliant politician. More
times than not, his had been the voice of reason in a
government on the verge of collapse. His politics were
conservative, as with all Irish Protestants, but he was
fair and one of the few who understood the benefits of
power sharing between the nationalists and the loyalists
of the Six Counties. From a professional but not aristocratic family, he had attended good schools, took his
seat as a member of Parliament on his twenty-seventh

birthday, and continued to be faithfully elected to the same seat ever since.

If Jillian had not spent so much time in his company, his sexual orientation might have escaped her. He was an attractive man, tall and very lean, his raillike thinness accentuated by loose-fitting, expensive clothing. Ash-blond hair was combed straight back over a high, sensitive forehead. His nose was long and straight, his lips thin, his chest narrow and slightly concave, a result of the asthma that kept him inside during Ireland's glorious springs. He had pale blue eyes, very fair skin, and the most beautiful hands she had ever seen.

She envied him those hands. Jillian suspected most women did. They were the hands of a pianist, long, slender, and exquisitely shaped. Avery was also extremely intelligent and unusually discriminating. Unfortunately, a number of his previous acquaintances had been indiscreet. He would not only have to marry, he would have to give up the lifestyle he preferred. "What would you expect of me, Avery?" she asked.

He swallowed the last of his whiskey and looked at her over the rim of the glass. "We would give the appearance of a happily married couple, live together, vacation together, appear at necessary functions. There would be a small amount of public speaking. That's all." He set his empty glass on the table, leaned forward, and spoke earnestly. "I know what I am asking of you is quite unfair, Jillian. You are a young and lovely woman. I was prepared to be your husband in every sense of the word. Now that you know about me, it isn't possible. If you marry me, you will be giving up a life of your own for as long as I am alive. What possible reason could you have for accepting my proposal?"

"Will you be giving up your life, Avery?"

He looked surprised. "Is that your requirement?"

"Yes."

"Why? Surely—"

She cut him off with a wave of her hand. "Please don't think that I have any misguided scheme to reform you. But you must understand that you will occupy an extremely public position. Each time you step outside your door, the media will be there. Your reputation must be spotless, Avery, or I cannot accept your offer."

"Why would you even consider such an offer, Jillian?"

She took a deep breath. "I want to adopt a child."

"I beg your pardon?"

"I want to adopt a child, and I can't unless I'm married."

Something flickered in his eyes and disappeared. "Will any child do, or is it someone particular you have in mind?"

Jillian laughed and relaxed. "You are also very intelligent, Avery. It is a particular child. Her name is Cassandra. You were straightforward with me, and I intend to be with you. Do you remember when my brother was killed?"

"It was a terrible tragedy."

"A boy on our estate was blamed for his death, but it was rather more complicated than that. His sister was involved with Terrence. That night, she told my brother she was carrying his child. After Terrence died, the girl disappeared. I tried to find her but never did. Five years ago, I did find the child. She had been raised in institutions. I've been sponsoring her. She's attending boarding school in Ireland."

"I'd envisioned a baby, not a half-grown child."

"Does it make a difference?"

"Of course it does." Avery's hands were shaking. He reached for his cigarettes, remembered he'd given them up, and cursed softly before recovering. "A child will disrupt our lives. She'll need to settle in, to accustom herself to our ways. It will be very difficult."

"Casey will be in school for most of the year, Avery. Surely you can bear to spend the holidays with a little girl who very much needs a family."

She had succeeded in shaming him. He was asking her to give up a normal life, children of her own. It was a small price to pay, after all, for a woman like Jillian. "Your brother must have been very dear to you."

Jillian's gaze never faltered. "Yes."

"You humble me, my dear," Avery said gently. "I apologize. If you do me the honor of becoming my wife, I shall welcome Casey into our home."

Jillian released her breath and smiled happily. "Thank you, Avery. You won't regret this. I promise you that."

Belfast, Northern Ireland

Frankie walked down the Falls Road next to the Peace Wall, crossed the street near Finley's Pub, picked up a copy of *The London Times* at the news agent, and pushed through the double gates of the Sinn Fein headquarters. Nodding to the man in charge, he climbed the stairs to his office.

"Danny, boy," Brian Dougherty called out to him from down the hall, "did y' hear the news? There's t' be a new minister for Northern Ireland. Avery Graham is under consideration."

Frankie pulled out a cigarette, swiped a match across the side of the desk, lit the tip, and inhaled. "Graham's a good man for a Brit," he said, blowing out a cloud of blue smoke. "We could do worse. But it'll never happen."

"Why not?"

"He's sweet."

Dougherty slid a copy of the *Belfast Telegram* into Frankie's field of vision and pointed to a front-page article. "It looks like he's taken care of that wee problem."

Frankie perfunctorily glanced at the paper. Then he took a second look. The headline at the bottom seemed to leap off the page, and for a full minute it felt as if his heart had shuddered to a stop. He read the headline again: "Fitzgerald heiress to wed candidate for minister to Northern Ireland." Frankie blew into his hands to stop their shaking, shrugged his shoulders, and leaned over his paperwork. "It doesn't concern us, so long as his politics are right."

Dougherty left the paper where it was. "We've got a solicitor on the internment cases. He should have a report by morning."

Frankie forced himself to pay attention. "Finucane's office?"

"Aye."

"I'll speak to him."

Brian frowned. "Are y' all right, Danny?"

Frankie threw back his head impatiently. "Have you nothing to do, Brian?"

Dougherty chuckled and left the room. Danny had been ill-tempered lately. Most likely, Colette had been pestering him again about a weddin' ring. Poor lass. She'd waited long enough.

Frankie waited a full five minutes after Brian had disappeared down the hall before picking up the paper. He stared at the pictures at the bottom of the page. They weren't formal engagement pictures, and they weren't taken together. Avery Graham's was a professional head shot. Hers was not.

She was dressed in a loose white shirt tucked into

jodhpurs and riding boots that emphasized long, shapely legs and slim hips. Her hair, neither light nor dark in the black-and-white photo, hung in a silky tangle to her shoulders. Eleven years certainly laid their mark on a woman. If it weren't for her eyes and that mouth that would make a celibate reconsider his vows, he would not have known her. Jillian Fitzgerald had grown into a beauty, just as he'd imagined she would.

Frankie never understood the flood of emotions that swept through him that day or what it was that made him decide it was time to marry Colette after eight years of sharing a flat and a bed. The day after they stood up together at St. Mary's Church, he made one last desperate appeal to Our Lady of Refuge, an orphanage for girls in County Fermanagh.

The nun in charge of records recognized his voice. Immediately, she connected him to the mother superior.

Mother Cecily Agnes had endless reserves of patience, but Frankie Maguire, alias Danny Browne, was beginning to concern her. The little girl's worries were nearly over if only this persistent young man would just go away. She made a quick decision. "I'm sorry, Mr. Browne," she improvised. "An application for the child's adoption has been accepted. Her file is sealed."

His voice was tight and bitter. "She's my niece. You had no right to give her away."

Her voice lowered. "I will not mention what you told me in confidence, Mr. Browne. But you are hardly in a position to take care of a little girl. How can you, in all decency, deny her the opportunity to be raised by a loving family?"

The silence on the other end of the phone relieved her and confirmed her first opinion of Danny Browne.

"The child's record has been sealed," she repeated.

"When she comes of age, she may choose to open it. I shall pray for you, Mr. Browne."

The amusement in his voice made her wince.

"You do that, sister. I'm sure it can't hurt," he said, and hung up.

Mother Cecily hung up the phone, crossed herself, and prayed to the Virgin for understanding and forgiveness. A lie of such magnitude had rarely escaped the lips of a mother superior.

18

Belfast, 1994

The explosion came from across the river. Danny Browne cursed, pushed himself away from the table where he was reading *The Irish Times*, and ran down the steps of the Linen Library, across Grosvenor Road to the lower Falls and the checkpoint.

The soldier manning the gates scanned his papers, searched him, and waved him past. Small groups of men clustered at the end of Divas Street on the border of the Protestant Shankill. The street was a shambles. Strewn with mangled bodies and their bloody parts, it looked like the front line of a war zone. The target, a mixed pub, was a smoking rubble. Charred beams lay in piles, wood sticks that were once stools and tables burned steadily on the macadam. Jagged shards of glass caught the reflections of a mockingly benevolent sun. Moans from the scalded throats of victims floated to the ears of the bystanders.

"Jesus Christ," Danny muttered, pushing his way

through. "Jesus fucking Christ. Someone call an ambulance."

John McCullough, chief of INLA, a splinter, more radical sector of the Irish Republican Army, saw Danny among the spectators. He took one look at his face and moved out of the shadows of the safe house, through the crowd, until he stood behind him. Clapping a heavy hand on his shoulder, he whispered in his ear. "Now, Danny, this has nothin' t' do with you. Mind your own business."

White-lipped, Danny shrugged off the man's hand. "I warned you, John. If you had anything to do with this, I swear on your son's grave that you'll pay."

"You're not that important, Danny boy. Not all of us recognize your authority."

Danny's eyes narrowed, and he turned so that his words would not be mistaken. "This time you will."

A rumbling sounded from the end of the road. He turned around in time to see three Saracens surging toward them at tremendous speeds. People dove for cover or ran screaming down the street in the path of the high-powered British tanks. Others stood, frozen in disbelief, as the guns swung back and forth, focusing on targets and spraying bullets into the fleeing crowd. Like wet sandbags, men, women, and children dropped soundlessly to the pavement.

A stream of curses spewed from Danny's mouth. Avoiding the tanks, he ran through the streets in the direction of Little India and the Kashmir Road. Bursting wildly through the door of the flat, he shouted his wife's name. "Colette! Are you here? For Christ sake, answer me."

Mrs. Flynn poked her head in from next door. "She's gone shoppin'. Tim called and said he'd be home tomorrow. Connor's with me."

Relief, so sweet that he swayed and nearly fell, swept through Danny. He braced himself against the wall. His son was safe. "Where is the lad?" he asked.

"Eating a bite of bread and jam. There's trouble at the barrier. Say hello to the boy before y' go lookin' for Colette."

Danny nodded and followed her into the kitchen of her flat. Four-year-old Connor grinned engagingly. "Hello, Da."

Love, complete and unconditional, washed through Danny. He picked up the boy, positioned him on his lap, and hugged him hard. Ignoring the stranglehold of his father's arms, Connor continued with his meal. "Mam's goin' t' buy ice cream," he said happily.

Tousling the boy's straight black hair, Danny laughed. "I hope y'll leave some for Tim this time. Your brother enjoys his ice cream as much as you do."

Connor drank down the last of his milk and wiped away the mustache above his lip. "Why are you home, Da?"

Danny buried his face in the warm, damp place between his son's chin and shoulder and inhaled the sweetness. "There's been a bit of trouble. I came t' see that you were behavin' yourself for Mrs. Flynn."

Fixing his blue eyes on his father's face, Connor nodded. "I'm good, Da. Mrs. Flynn says I may watch her telly." He appealed to the woman. "Isn't that right, Mrs. Flynn?"

"It is, darlin'."

Danny stood and set the boy on his feet. "I'll be goin' to pick up your mother now. Be a good lad, and y'll be havin' that ice cream before you know it."

Connor smiled happily and held out his hand to Mrs. Flynn.

"Don't bother yourself," Danny said to the woman. "I'll let myself out."

Out on the streets, the icy fear that gripped him when he first saw British tanks roll down the Springfield Road returned. He could only hope that Colette had found shelter with friends. He turned down the Falls Road and froze. Four bodies lay motionless in pools of blood. Two men were dragging the moaning and wounded into doorways. Burning lorries blocked the lanes, and the smell of gasoline and rubber polluted the air. There wasn't an ambulance in sight.

Rage blotted out Danny's fear. This was retaliation, not self-defense. These were families, unarmed, helpless, innocent, going about their business nearly a mile from the pub bombing, not IRA activists. A fist closed around his heart. Where was Colette? Making his way past the bullet-riddled walls of the wood and brick row houses to the barricade, Danny stopped everyone he knew. No one had seen her. At the gates, his identification card was refused.

"Sorry, mate," the guard said. "No one comes through."

Danny's hand clenched on the post. He gritted his teeth and forced himself to speak politely. "My wife is missing."

The guard pointed to the phone. "Call the hospital. Nearly forty people were taken to the Victoria. If she's there, come back. I'll see about a pass."

All lines were down. Grim-faced, Danny walked to the Divas Flats, ignored the elevator, and climbed to the seventh floor. It was empty. He sat down in a chair, his back to the door, lit a cigarette, and waited. Ten minutes passed. Footsteps sounded in the hall and stopped behind him. Still, he didn't turn.

A raspy voice broke the silence. "What can we do for y', Danny?"

"I need a favor, Paddy."

He taunted him. "The chief negotiator for Sinn Finn needs a favor. That's rich. It's been a long time since you've come t' us."

"Is what happened today any of your doing?"

"In a manner of speakin', although the Provos are not entirely responsible."

Danny's mouth twisted into a bitter smile. "There'll be hell t' pay for this one and months of negotiation down the drain."

"We've been there before."

Turning, Danny stared into the face of the man who'd been his mentor. It was an Irish face with a red complexion, light eyes, a square grizzled chin, and lightly veined skin. Padraic Fergus looked years older than he was. "Colette is missing," Danny said shortly. "I want the hospitals checked and a pass to get through the checkpoint."

Padraic nodded. "You'll have it, Danny. My prayers will be with you." He ignored the contemptuous look Danny threw at him. "Wait here. I'll be back."

Three hours later, Danny sat in a chair in the waiting room of the Royal Victoria Hospital. The frozen knot that was his heart refused to allow him the satisfaction of feeling. Even searing, unforgiving pain would be preferable to this emptiness.

The nurse touched him on the shoulder. "You can see her now."

Danny stumbled into the room where Colette lay staring at the ceiling. A sound came from his throat, and she turned. Tears filled her eyes. "I can't feel anything, Danny. It was a plastic bullet." She laughed hysterically. "The doctor said I was lucky it wasn't the real thing.

Then he told me I won't ever walk again. Oh, Danny, who'll take care of Connor and Tim when he comes home?"

He pulled up a chair, sat down, and took her hand. "Doctors don't know everything. We'll find a way, Colette. Somehow we will. Tim's a grown man, and Connor"—he swallowed—"Connor will be grand. You'll see."

"Poor wee lad," she said brokenly. "No one's watched him but me. You didn't want me t' work, Danny." There was feeling in her hands, and she clutched him desperately. "Remember how you told me that a wee lad needs his mother and that we would manage?"

"I do." He kissed her fingers. "Hush, lass. We'll sort it out. You'll be up and about in no time."

Belfast, 1997

"It's a waste of time," Colette argued angrily from the wheelchair where she spent all of her waking hours. "I don't want t' go back t' the hospital. Nothing's helped so far, and nothing ever will."

Danny closed the door gently behind him. Connor was due home soon, and he didn't want the boy to hear the argument that his parents kept alive between them. "It's a chance, Colette," Danny said reasonably. "Do you want t' stay in that chair forever?"

She turned on him. "If it bothers you so much, Danny Browne, y' know where the door is. I'm not askin' any favors from you."

Balling his hands inside his pockets, Danny walked to the window and stared outside. The view was a wall painted with orange, white, and green political slogans: "Sciorse," "Free the POW's," "No Conditions." Construction rubble littered the sidewalk, and boys playing at hurling climbed over it to fetch the ball. Unbidden, his mind called up an image, clean and pure, of green grass, dark woods, and golden dogs. Ruthlessly, he pushed it back. "I'm not goin' anywhere," he said gently. "You've never been selfish, Colette. Do it for the boys if not for yourself. Don't listen to me. Ask Connor and Tim if they want you t' take the chance." Forcing himself, he crossed the room to kiss her cheek and squeeze her shoulder.

Mrs. Flynn knocked at the door. "I'll fix supper for Colette and the boy a bit early tonight, Danny. Rumor has it we won't have power too much longer."

"Thank you, Mrs. Flynn," he said, zipping up his jacket. "Be sure to have a healthy portion yourself."

Kildare Hall, County Down

The final words of the Archbishop of Armagh filtered through Jillian's pain. "Let us lay Avery Graham, beloved husband and father, brother and friend, to his rest."

Lifting a shaking hand, Jillian stroked Casey's curly, mink-brown hair. Behind dark glasses, her eyes burned with the effort of holding back tears. How had they come to this? It happened so quickly, Avery's aggravated cough, his raspy voice, the whispered conversations, the fatigue, the bloodstained handkerchiefs he'd been unable to hide, and finally the diagnosis, cancer of the lung. He was dead in three months.

Casey felt Jillian squeeze her hand, but she was too miserable to acknowledge the comfort. She was twenty years old, and Grandmother Fitzgerald had drilled her in the importance of appearance at public functions. But this time something deep within her rose and refused to accommodate Lady Fitzgerald's sense of decorum. There wasn't a better man in the world than Avery Graham. Mourning had never seemed more appropriate. What would they do without him? Unchecked tears streamed down her cheeks.

In unison, the select group of invited friends and relatives chanted, "Ashes to ashes, dust to dust." Casey leaned her head on Jillian's shoulder and wept.

Across the flower-adorned casket, Jillian caught the eye of Thomas Putnam. He smiled bracingly. The young prime minister had flown in from London that morning to attend the service, a testimony to her husband's sensible and honest politics. Avery had been a Conservative. The Putnams were Labour.

Jillian sighed. She would miss Avery's wisdom. He alone had kept the lid on the simmering cauldron of Northern Irish discord. Both the loyalists and the nationalists trusted him. Even the skeptical Irish Republican Army occasionally listened when Avery spoke. Whom would Putnam appoint now? Who would keep the peace that Avery had maintained at Stormont despite the backbiting, the refusals to negotiate at the same table, the name-calling, and the occasional acts of violence by radical groups from both sides? So much unfinished business to sort through. Jillian didn't know of a single man in the entire United Kingdom who could step into Avery's shoes.

She never once suspected, not when the prime minister stayed at the reception longer than his obligatory thirty minutes, or when he singled her out and spoke of innocent inconsequential matters, not when he asked to speak to her alone and questioned her about the Drumcree problem, and certainly not when he remained after the guests had gone, explaining that he needed a personal favor. It wasn't until she was seated in the library, on the expensive Victorian settee where generations of Fitzgeralds had taken their after-dinner port, after he'd repeated the words for the second time, that she understood what it was that he asked of her.

Her face paled, and the famous Fitzgerald composure that her mother had worked so tirelessly to instill slipped momentarily, rendering Jillian speechless. When at last she found her voice, she politely declined.

He brushed aside her refusal. "The position is temporary, Jillian. I need someone of influence, someone who knew Avery's mind."

"It's impossible."

"Why?"

"I already have a position teaching at the university. Besides, I know nothing about negotiating with those people."

Putnam thrust his hands into his pockets and walked to the window. He was a commoner, born to a professional family with means. Good schools, a penchant for public speaking, and a nationwide frustration for the politics of Margaret Thatcher and her mouthpiece, John Major, had brought him the most influential position in England. He did not understand the minds of the aristocracy.

Jillian Fitzgerald was lovely, elegant, and, despite her husband's position, as remotely unapproachable as if it were the eighteenth century instead of the twentieth. But she was a Fitzgerald, and Irish memories were long. His advisers had assured him that she would be the most acceptable choice, a woman whose Protestant ancestors had fought for a united Ireland.

"I thought you'd taken a leave to be with Avery, and *those people* are your countrymen, Jillian. Who else will understand them better?"

"Any random person on the street," she replied

quickly. "You don't know your history, Mr. Putnam. The Fitzgeralds are hardly Irish. We came from Wales, and before that Italy. Somewhere around the eleventh century, the Fitzgeralds crossed the sea into Ireland, and then we became English, not Irish."

He smiled. Putnam was the quintessential politician. He knew when to retreat and when to push forward. It was time to give it his best. "You're leaving out a bit, aren't you, Jillian? Your ancestors lost everything, including their lives, for an independent Ireland. An entire house, a family, was wiped out at Tyburn, land and estates confiscated and burned, never fully recovered. The Fitzgeralds were kings of Ireland."

Strange images filtered through her mind, a blackened landscape, smoking ruins, a girl, thin and pale and desperately afraid. She pushed them away. "Perhaps the Fitzgeralds have contributed enough, or are you after more sacrifice, Mr. Putnam?"

"Without Avery, this entire peace process is in danger of falling apart. Never, since the partition in 1921, have Catholics and Protestants sat down together. The eyes of the world are upon us, Jillian. Everything is at stake." He crossed the room, took her hands, and pulled her to her feet. "There is no one else," he said bluntly. "You are the single person in all of Britain whom both sides will accept."

She wavered. "Have you asked them?"

He breathed a sigh of relief. "No. I'll make the announcement in the morning."

She laughed shakily and pulled her hands away. "Very well, Mr. Putnam. But if this turns into a fiasco and I fail miserably, it will be on your shoulders, not mine."

He stared, struck by the change in her appearance when she smiled. Jillian's noblesse oblige beauty softened. Her eyes spilled warmth and light, and her mouth— Putnam swallowed. History had been changed by women who looked like Jillian Fitzgerald. A thought occurred to him, and he grinned. Something told him that failure was as unfamiliar to her as it was to him.

Two days later, Jillian walked into the lobby of the Royal Victoria Hospital for her weekly visit to the wards. What had begun as an obligatory duty routinely performed in her role as a politician's wife had become as necessary to her life as afternoon tea, a tradition she refused to share with anyone other than her family.

The convalescent wing had long-term patients, regulars, whom Jillian saw every week. The children's ward, preoperative, and recovery were most rewarding and among her usual stops. Oncology and the terminally ill were more difficult for her and required mental preparation. The turnover on these floors was frequent and tragic. She forced herself to visit twice a month and left immediately after. Today was not one of those days.

Jillian was pleased to note the cheerful wallpaper and large windows in the children's wing, the result of her fund-raising efforts for the past two years. After passing through two sets of double doors to recovery and then up one floor on the lift to postop, she smiled, shook hands, and chatted with everyone who was awake, saving the small single room on the end for last. She looked at her watch. Two hours had passed since she'd walked into the lobby. She'd deliberately left the rest of her day free. The woman smiled when she walked into the room.

Jillian pulled up a chair and sat down. "Good morning, Mrs. Browne."

"Can you stay for a bit this time, Mrs. Graham?" the woman asked.

"I'll stay for as long as you like," replied Jillian, settling herself for a long visit. Colette Browne was a regular. Five different times she'd been operated on with minimal results. Her recovery had taken months, with most of her time spent in the hospital. She had two sons, one of whom could not remember his mother outside her wheelchair.

At first, Jillian stopped in out of pity. But with each visit she had grown to appreciate Colette's dry humor and her pragmatic wisdom, sometimes fatalistic, often hopeless, but always sensible, the line between right and wrong sharply divided. They had little in common, a crippled working-class woman with no education other than her own experience, and Jillian, born into a privileged family, who knew the names of every generation of her ancestors for a thousand years.

Without crossing the line into the forbidden territory of Christian names, both women exchanged confidences they normally would have kept to themselves. Because of Avery Graham's position, Colette intuitively understood that her relationship with Jillian could not progress beyond the walls of the Royal Victoria.

Jillian knew little of the life to which Colette belonged, but her innate sensitivity warned her away from broaching the subject of taking their friendship outside after Colette's periodic releases. Their conversations consisted of relationships with family and friends, dreams for the future, personal fears. Colette spoke of her husband, her children, and the hopelessness of life in West Belfast. Jillian shared her frustrations with her family, her difficulties with Casey, and finally, in a moment of reckless abandon and mutual rapport, the emotional toll of her ten-year-old agreement with a man who could never truly be a husband.

Colette, who had seen more than most women of

Jillian's class, was not particularly surprised by the younger woman's confession. Before Avery Graham's marriage, there had been a good deal of speculation about his sexual orientation. His marriage had done away with most of the talk. Colette believed the rumors to be false until she met Jillian. The woman was thirty-five years old, uncommonly attractive, and a mother, yet there was an untouched quality about her, as if she were waiting for something. Colette knew about Avery's illness even though it had not been publicly announced. She knew how it would affect Jillian, the public person. She wondered how it would affect Jillian, the woman.

After their usual exchange of pleasantries, Colette asked the question that Jillian had come to address. "How are you holding up, dear?"

Smiling bravely, Jillian began to recite the practiced commentary she had prepared for the media. Then she made the mistake of meeting the sympathetic gaze of the woman who had become her friend. Her lips trembled, and her voice broke. Widening her eyes to prevent the tears from welling over onto her cheeks, she tried to go on but couldn't. Finally, she gave up, leaned her forehead on the rail, and sobbed.

Colette muttered a brief "thank you" for the full use of her arms. She rested her hand on Jillian's expensively coiffed head and murmured words of comfort.

Minutes passed. The combination of soothing words and gentle hands worked their magic. Jillian's tears stopped. She lifted her head, smiled tremulously, and reached for the box of tissue on the side table. "Thank you, Colette," she said, and blew her nose.

Colette squeezed her hand. "You're very welcome, Jillian," she replied. Both women smiled at each other, grateful for the milestone they had passed.

Jillian's eyes were no longer puffy, but her nose was

still red when she heard the door to Colette's hospital room open behind her. At the sound of a masculine voice, she turned and smiled pleasantly. Her path had never before crossed with Colette's husband.

Danny Browne had learned to gauge the success of his visits by the way his wife responded to his initial greeting. Therefore, he waited for her reply before allowing his gaze to rest on the woman sitting beside her. When he did, he was sure the wild, uncontrollable lurching of his heart would send him crashing to the floor, a new patient of the Royal Victoria's cardiac care unit. Speechless, he stared at the girl who had promised to love him, the girl who had made him swear a sacred oath to come back for her.

19

Light from the hall silhouetted him, keeping his face and the details of his clothing steeped in shadow. Jillian's first impression of Colette's husband was that he was tall, with broad shoulders and defined muscles beneath his shirt and wool pullover. She wondered if he made his living out of doors.

It seemed as if he waited in the darkness for a long time before stepping forward. When he did, her eyes widened, and a jolt of awareness, like a current, passed through her. She felt anxious and uneasy as if every nerve were exposed. As she absorbed the details of his face, a thought, incredible in its enormity, formed in her mind. It couldn't possibly be, and yet— Logic discounted this man as a stranger. Intuition told her otherwise.

Colette was nearly ten years Jillian's senior, but her husband was not. He looked to be late thirties at most, with black hair, clean, sharp features, and eyes that went beyond description. They were dark gray in color, deeply set, and very clear, fringed with thick, feathery lashes.

Jillian was sure she had seen those eyes before, had dreamed of them, been haunted by them, but where? Why couldn't she remember?

Now, the message radiating from those eyes was unmistakable. He didn't like her. No, it was more subtle than that. He didn't approve of her.

There was something else there, too, a memory that was almost a connection, hazy and unformed in her mind. Jillian was too rattled by the man's regard to concentrate. His presence both frightened and energized her.

"Mrs. Graham." Colette's voice broke through her turmoil. "This is my husband, Danny Browne."

Jillian lost all ability to speak. *Danny Browne. Colette's husband was Danny Browne, chief negotiator for Sinn Fein. Impossible! The name was all wrong. It didn't suit him.*

Avery had spoken of Danny Browne often. He was Ian Paisley's nemesis. Paisley and Temple, leaders of separate factions of the Protestant Ulster Defense League, were no match for the articulate nationalist spokesman who relentlessly hammered at the loyalist position and looked good from every camera angle. Could this serious, silent man really be Danny Browne?

She needed to go home and think. Stammering like a schoolgirl, Jillian ignored Danny's outstretched hand and excused herself, saying that she'd stayed too long already.

Colette stared thoughtfully at the door through which Jillian had taken her hurried leave. Something had happened but she wasn't sure what it meant.

Danny's hand closed around a pair of beige leather gloves. "Your friend left these behind."

"She'll be back," Colette said, although the words sounded hollow to her own ears.

"How long have you known her?" Danny asked casually.

Colette shrugged. "Since the first surgery. She visits often."

"You've been visiting with Avery Graham's wife for over two years?" he asked incredulously. "Why didn't y' tell me?"

She frowned. "Why do I have t' tell you everything? She's my friend." She tapped her chest with her forefinger. "My friend. Do y' understand, Danny? This has nothing t' do with you. I didn't even tell her who y' are."

Danny sighed with relief. She hadn't recognized him after all. Jillian's shaken composure was the result of learning that Danny Browne, Sinn Fein negotiator, was Colette's husband, nothing more.

"That explains why she walked out of here lookin' shell-shocked. It was hardly fair, Colette."

"What do y' mean?"

Danny sat down on the chair Jillian had vacated. His shoulders sagged with weariness. "Right this minute, Mrs. Graham is tryin' to recall every word she ever said to you, on the small chance that she's divulged something that I shouldn't know. The price of such a friendship comes high, love."

"Meaning that she thinks I didn't tell her about you to gather information?"

"Aye."

Unexpected tears filled Colette's eyes. "I wouldn't do that. I know nothin' about y'r work. I thought she wouldn't come if she knew I was y'r wife."

Sympathy and something stronger than mere disappointment shone from his eyes. "It seems that you took the decision away from her."

Colette's voice trembled. "Do y' think she'll come back, Danny? I never had a friend like her before."

Reaching out he pulled her into his arms and rested his chin on her head. He stared bleakly out the small window. "I know, love," he whispered, "but I wouldn't worry. Jillian Fitzgerald knows something about loyalty."

Lost in her own misery, Colette didn't bother to ask him what he meant.

Jillian, dressed in sweatpants and an Aran sweater, a glass of sherry in one hand, a news clipping in the other, sat cross-legged on the floor of the library at Kildare. File folders with papers spilling haphazardly out of them surrounded her.

"Are you looking for something in particular?" Casey asked from the doorway.

Jillian shook her head, stuffed the clipping into the pocket of her Aran, and smiled nervously. "Come in. I can use the company."

Casey flopped down on the couch, groaned, stretched her arms, and tossed her head so that her curly hair fluffed around her face. "I've got to go back to school soon. If I don't, I'll never catch up."

Biting her lip, Jillian stood and added more turf to the fire. "I suppose it's best," she said slowly. "There's nothing more to do here."

Casey sighed. Her mum would never come out and say what she really wanted. "I could stay another week if you need me."

"You'll do nothing of the sort," Jillian replied bracingly. "I'll be fine. In fact, I'll be busy. You belong back at school."

Widening her gray-green eyes dramatically, Casey sat up and placed both palms against Jillian's cheeks. "I would like to stay until after the Stormont meeting," she said deliberately. "How do you feel about that?"

"As if you're the mother and I'm the daughter," replied Jillian sheepishly.

Casey grinned and leaned back on the couch pillows. "You're very retentive, Mum. But you already know that."

"How could I not be, with you reminding me every minute?"

"I suppose you didn't really have a chance growing up with Grandmother," Casey said thoughtfully.

"I suppose not," said Jillian, finally amused. Casey was part elfin loveliness, part practical sage, and by far the best thing that had ever happened to the Fitzgerald-Grahams.

From the moment they brought her home ten years ago, she'd charmed the entire household, a petite hazel-eyed minx with skinned knees, corkscrew curls tumbling in every direction, and a histrionic sense of drama that never failed to bring Avery to his knees. He'd adored her and she him. The unnatural, museum like pallor that settled over the household when she returned to school demoralized Avery and Jillian to such an extent that they drove down the next day to bring her home for good. She was enrolled in the local public school, and a tutor was hired to supplement her lessons. Casey, who'd spent her entire ten years in institutions, was only too happy to remain at home with a doting father and a mother young enough to be her sister.

With a child's intuition, she understood without being told that she was dearer to both Jillian and Avery than they were to each other. Her connection with Jillian was understandable. They were members of the same family, closely related by blood. Yet she'd felt it with Avery as well. From the moment they brought her home, she was the one who made their family complete, and she felt her responsibility deeply, coming home from university often and shortening holidays with friends. Leaving Jillian so soon after Avery's death was not to be thought of. Of course, there was always Grandmother Fitzgerald.

Casey repressed a shudder. Never had two women with the same gene pool turned out so differently than her mother and her maternal grandmother. Not that Lady Margaret was rude or unkind or even unpleasant. She was just so unfailingly proper, so frustratingly opinionated, that it was difficult to bear her company for more than twenty minutes.

Occasionally, when her grandmother drove up from London, and Casey looked up from the telly or the book she was reading, she would find the older woman's eyes on her with an expression in them that could only be described as calculating. Mum and Grandmother Fitzgerald had very little in common and rarely agreed on anything. The strain on Mum to stay polite during Grandmother's monthly visits took its toll on her. Fortunately, Grandmother had moved to a flat in London after she was widowed. No, Lady Fitzgerald could not be counted on for support when Casey left for school.

She nodded at the slip of paper working its way out of her mother's pocket. "What's that?"

Jillian's hand flew to her side, and she flushed guiltily. "It's nothing."

"May I see it?"

Slowly, Jillian pulled the photograph from her pocket and handed it to Casey.

"He's nice."

"Who?" Jillian asked casually.

"The man in the middle. It's Danny Browne, isn't it?"

The color drained from Jillian's cheeks. "Yes."

"I saw him speak once, in Belfast. Father knew him, didn't he?"

"Yes," Jillian said again.

"Why are you looking at his picture?"

"There are others in the picture," replied Jillian defensively.

Casey's straight black brows drew together, and she looked curiously at her mother. "Why are you looking at *this* picture?" she amended.

"Those men are part of the nationalist negotiating team," Jillian improvised. "I'll be speaking with them at Stormont."

Handing back the photo, Casey stood. "I'm going out to the stables. Ned says the new foal is due soon. Would you like to join me?"

Jillian shook her head. "Say hello to Ned for me. I'll see you in the morning."

Sipping the last of her sherry, Jillian turned her attention back to the man in the picture. It was all very clear now, the deep-set, rain-washed eyes, skin more olive than fair, his lean height and squared-off jaw. No one who'd known Frankie Maguire as she had could mistake the man he had become. Who would have thought that Frankie, alias Danny Browne, the loyalists' curse, would turn out to be Colette's husband? Something hard and hurting and completely unreasonable twisted inside her chest. He had promised to come back for her, and all this time he was married to Colette.

For most of the last two hours, Jillian had debated whether or not Colette had intentionally deceived her in order to gather information for her husband. In the end, she'd decided against it. Politics had never entered their conversations. There was an integrity about the handicapped woman that could not be manufactured. Colette valued Jillian's friendship too much to abuse it. The omission may have been deliberate, but Colette's reasons were pure. Jillian was sure of it. Now, the least she could do for the woman was to keep her husband's secret.

A strange lethargy had taken hold of her. She wanted nothing more than to curl up on the couch, pour herself another sherry, and pull an old Jane Austen novel from the bookshelves. Instead, she stuffed the papers back into their files and climbed the stairs to her bedroom.

After a lengthy bath, she turned off the lights and stared out the long windows. It was nearly ten and closing in on July, the longest days of the year. Dusk had settled over the pasture. The tall figure of the Kildare kennel keeper surrounded by six frisky, white-bibbed pups appeared over the ridge. Jillian caught her breath. Deep inside her, something old and forgotten woke, uncurled, and readied itself for an imminent and painful rebirth.

The trembling began in her legs and moved upward throughout her body and into her fingertips, until she could barely untie the sash of her robe. Still shaking, she climbed into bed and pulled the duvet up over her shoulders.

Stormont had been the seat of Northern Irish government until 1972, when the horror of Bloody Sunday flashed on television screens throughout the world, ending loyalist home rule, a power imbalance the Protestant majority had enjoyed and mercilessly abused since the plantation era of the seventeenth century.

Jillian, dressed in an attractive green suit that deepened her eye color to pine, walked through the front entry and looked around. The marble floors and Greek pillars of the impressive entry narrowed to long paneled halls with carved wooden doors. Behind a large desk, a young man in military guard's uniform stared at her curiously.

"May I be of service, miss?"

It was past time to be afraid. She lifted her chin. "I'm Jillian Graham," she said crisply. "I believe I'm expected."

Instantly, his demeanor changed. Leaping to his feet, he nearly climbed over the desk in his hurry to assist her. "Indeed you are. Please, allow me to show you the way, Mrs. Graham."

She smiled faintly. He was very young. "Thank you."

Jillian followed him down the long corridor to two elaborately carved double doors. The guard knocked firmly on the wood panels. Both doors swung open, and she stepped inside. Six pairs of masculine eyes stared at her curiously.

"Good morning, gentlemen," she said quietly. "I'm Jillian Graham, my husband's replacement but certainly not his equal. I'm afraid you'll have to put up with me until a more suitable candidate is found."

A collective sigh broke the silence. Danny Browne suppressed a grin. She was every bit the diplomat that her husband had been and far more attractive. Had she deliberated for months over her entrance, she could not have chosen one more suited to wither the objections of her opponents. Her humility had scored innumerable points with both sides of the negotiating table. That, coupled with her appearance, an aristocratic name that was featured throughout Irish history, and her step down the social ladder to marry a commoner, gave her instant validity among the men elected to determine the future of the Six Counties, the same men whose ancestors had mucked out the stables and toiled in the fields of the mighty Fitzgeralds of Kildare.

He wondered if she would recognize him and what would happen then. Pride wanted her to see him as he was, a man of position who'd come from nothing. Practically speaking, it would be a disaster. He was Francis Maguire, alias Danny Browne, an escaped felon wanted for murder. Reason told him she would have no choice but to report him to the authorities. But something else, a sixth sense perhaps and more than a hint of personal experience, reminded him that Jillian Fitzgerald had not always behaved predictably.

Once, long ago, she'd lied for him, braved her father's wrath to take his side and kiss his mouth. Could a person change so much in twenty years? Across the table, his eyes met the cool, level ones of Avery Graham's widow, and his chest tightened. She was beautiful and polite and nothing at all like the girl he remembered. Nodding briefly, he opened his notebook. "Shall we begin?" he asked.

They met much later, by accident, coming out of the facilities. Danny would have passed by with the barest of acknowledgments, but Jillian stopped him with her words.

"How is Colette?"

"Well, thank you."

"Is the surgery still scheduled for Thursday?"

Danny ran his fingers through his hair impatiently. Fancy her remembering that. "It is."

"Will you be there?"

"Of course, Mrs. Graham. She is my wife, after all." His scornful look was meant to wither, but she disregarded it completely.

Jillian kept her eyes on his face. He was making this harder by being difficult. She'd hoped, after this morning when she agreed with nearly every point of his position, that she would see something close to approval in his eyes. "I promised her I'd be there. Do you mind?"

"Why should I? It's Colette's surgery. She can invite the whole bloody world for all I care."

"Thank you," Jillian said formally, and moved away, more shaken than she appeared. Why hadn't he recognized her? Had she changed so much that there was nothing left of the Jilly Fitzgerald he'd known? Or perhaps it was something altogether different. Perhaps she had never meant as much to him as he had to her.

Driving home to Avery's town house on Lisburn Road that evening, she couldn't help wondering about the relationship between Frankie and Colette. They appeared to be an odd match, the woman old and used up before her time, Frankie fit, youthful, handsome enough for the cinema. How had they met, she wondered, and what was Colette like before the handicap had sapped her looks and energy?

She turned into the garage, gathered her briefcase, and fumbled for her keys in case Mrs. Wilson, her housekeeper, had stepped out. To her relief, the door opened before she turned the lock, and the smell of roasting meat wafted to her nose.

"Welcome home, Mrs. Graham." Jane Wilson relieved Jillian of her case and ushered her inside. "I've a good meal cooking," the woman said. "Would you care for tea or something stronger?"

"I've a long night ahead," answered Jillian. "Tea will be fine."

"I hope your day was a pleasant one."

Jillian walked wearily up the stairs. "It was certainly interesting. Has Casey arrived yet?"

"She called earlier. You're not to wait up. She may drive up in the morning rather than take a chance on the weather tonight."

Jillian's brow wrinkled. The sky was perfectly clear, and Casey had a reliable automobile. It wasn't like her to worry about the weather. "Did she say anything else?"

"No, Mrs. Graham, but she did sound a bit preoccupied. Very unlike Casey, if you know what I mean."

What could Casey be up to? Jillian considered the possibilities. Was she seeing someone? And if she was, why wouldn't she say so? More than likely, Avery was responsible. He had been a loving and proud father but not particularly receptive to any of the young men his daughter brought home. His attitude had given Jillian considerable worry. She was determined that Casey would live a normal life, which included, among other things, a husband and children.

Smoothing the lines from her forehead, she walked into the bathroom. Casey was twenty years old, nearly an adult. There was no reason she couldn't stay overnight in the country.

Slipping off her shoes, Jillian turned on the tap and watched the tub fill. After discarding her clothes in a heap on the floor, she poured bath salts under the flow, watched them foam, and stepped in, sinking down until the water reached her chin. The day had been informative but exhausting. There was so much she didn't know about politics. History was her specialty, Tudor history specifically. Except for what she read in the news, she had little knowledge of Irish politics after the sixteenth century.

Frankie Maguire certainly knew his history, as did David Temple. The two were well matched in intellect, although Temple was university-educated and Frankie was— She frowned. Frankie's background after he'd left Kilvara was another subject she knew little about. She would take care of that lapse tonight and tomorrow.

Out of consideration for Colette's surgery, and to bring herself up to date on the issues, Jillian had requested and been unanimously granted a recess until the following Monday.

Without looking in the mirror, Jillian pulled on leggings and a sweater before twisting her hair back into a knot at the back of her head. A knock sounded at the door. Jillian opened it and stepped back to allow Mrs. Wilson to bring in her dinner tray.

"Don't stay up too late, Mrs. Graham," the older woman cautioned her, taking in the delicate shadows beneath her eyes. "Nothing stays in a mind that isn't well rested."

Jillian smiled. Jane Wilson, a lifelong employee of the Fitzgeralds, had been admonishing her for years. "Are you telling me I'm not in my best looks, Mrs. Wilson?" she teased.

"Of course not," the woman protested. It would take a great deal more than lack of sleep to diminish Jillian's beauty. The severe styles she chose would have rendered a less classically lovely woman unfit to be seen outside the bedroom. The sleek do she preferred emphasized the purity of her jaw, the sharp, clean edge of her cheekbones, and the symmetry of her features. Not that she would have voiced her thoughts. Jillian had never been one to appreciate her own appearance or anyone else who made too much of it. "Ring if you need something," Mrs. Wilson said before exiting the room. "I'll be watching the telly in my suite."

After carrying her food to the table, Jillian arranged her papers, sat down on the couch in front of a crackling fire, and began to read. Four hours later, she stared into the glowing embers of the dying fire and cursed the Labour Party leader, Thomas Putnam, and the ignorance of a country whose educators and leaders believed that by leaving out the entire perspective of nearly fifty percent of the population, the "Catholic problem" would simply fade away.

There was no possible solution to the political nightmare in Northern Ireland that would appear reasonable to loyalists and equitable for nationalists. The horrific part of it was that she was now committed. Her face was on the front page of every newspaper in the western world, and the marching season, that orange-sashed, bowler-hatted, swaggering mentality that was no longer accepted anywhere in the United Kingdom outside Ulster, was a mere three weeks away. God help her. She alone had the power to order the marches stopped, if only someone would listen to her.

20

Frankie was in his wife's room, holding her hand, when Jillian arrived at the Royal Victoria the morning of Colette's surgery. Their heads were very close, and they were speaking softly to each other. The tenderness on Frankie's face and the unreserved love on Colette's raised a lump in Jillian's throat, and she turned away toward the waiting room, leaving them alone in their shared grief. Ashamed of her speculation about their relationship the night before, she wondered, not for the first time, if she hadn't thrown away something very precious in her arrangement with Avery.

The waiting room was empty except for a small dark-haired boy. From behind the station window, a nurse attempted to reason with him. "Your da will be back soon, and he'll take you. I can't leave my position."

Jillian sat down and reached for a magazine, flipping through the pages disinterestedly. The child became more and more restless as the minutes passed, squirming in his seat, walking back and forth from the nurse's station to the hall, where he would stare down the long corridor before coming back and leaning dejectedly against the chair.

She abandoned her magazine and summoned a smile. He couldn't be more than five. "Hello," she said softly.

He stared at her with round blue eyes. "Hello," he returned.

"My name is Jilly. What's yours?"

"Connor."

"Are you waiting for someone, Connor?"

"My da," the child confided. "He's with my mother. I'm not allowed to go in. But it's been a long time."

"I see." Jillian appeared to think. "I'm waiting for someone, too. Perhaps we can wait together."

The lad brightened and came closer. "I've got t' go to the loo," he said in a loud whisper, "but it's far away, and there's no one t' take me."

This she could do. Jillian stood and held out her hand. "I'll take you."

Gratefully, Connor slipped his hand into her larger one. A thought occurred to him. "I don't know where it is," he said.

Jillian swallowed a chuckle. "We'll find it."

Her confident manner appeased the child, and he followed her trustingly to the door.

The nurse stuck her head out the window. "What shall I tell his father when he comes back for him?"

Jillian brushed back a strand of hair that had fallen across her forehead. "Tell him that Jillian Graham took his son to the loo."

The nurse blinked in surprise. Mrs. Graham was a frequent visitor to the Royal Victoria, but she had never seen her in leggings and an oversized shirt with her hair scraped back from her face, secured with an elastic band.

Jillian waited outside the men's room for Connor. Within minutes, he came through the door, a look of relief on his face. "Did you wash your hands?" she asked.

Nodding, he held them up for her inspection. Jillian knelt down to examine them and smiled her approval. "There's a vending machine in the corner," she said. "Would you like some chocolate?"

"Aye, but it takes thirty pence, and I haven't any."

"I'll take care of that," Jillian said, reaching into her bag for her coin purse to remove two coins.

Connor was sipping the steaming chocolate and maintaining a steady flow of conversation when his father came back to claim him.

Frankie stopped short when he saw the woman beside his son. He'd forgotten all about Jillian's request to be present during Colette's surgery until they'd wheeled his wife through the double doors to the operating room. That she was actually there when he was sure he had discouraged her both surprised and annoyed him. "You're a bit late, aren't you? They've already taken her in."

Swift anger colored Jillian's cheeks, but she answered him coolly. "Actually, I'm not. I arrived earlier, but it looked as if I would be intruding." She tousled the hair on Connor's head. "Then I found him and decided I was needed here."

Frankie flushed at the implication he had neglected his son. "I asked the nurse to watch him," he said defensively.

"I didn't mean to criticize, Mr. Browne," replied Jillian. "When the woman couldn't leave her post, I stepped in." She hesitated.

"Go on."

"Perhaps it would have been better to leave him with someone at home."

Frankie ran his hand through his hair distractedly. "I told him he couldn't see her, but he insisted on coming."

"There's no harm done," said Jillian quickly. "We've managed quite well. How long will the surgery take?"

Shrugging, Frankie sat down and lifted his son to his lap, his arms naturally enfolding the small body. "Four hours, maybe five if there are complications." Absently, he kissed the top of Connor's head. "We've been through this before, haven't we, mate? It will all come about."

Solemnly, Connor nodded. "Will Mam walk this time?"

Jillian bit her lip and watched Frankie force a smile and attempt an answer. "Nothing's for certain, lad. You know that. Everyone's working hard to see that she does."

He nodded, yawned, and leaned his head back against his father's chest.

"Are you hungry, Connor?" Jillian asked. "You must be ready for a snack by now. Why don't we go and see if there's anything to eat in the café?"

Connor lifted his freckled face to his father's. "Can I, Da?"

"We'll all go," said Frankie, rising from his chair and holding his hand out to the small boy. "We'll call Tim when we're finished."

"Who's Tim?" Jillian asked when they were seated across from each other in the booth.

Frankie lifted an inquiring eyebrow. "Tim's our oldest son. Didn't Colette mention him?"

"Not by name."

"He's twenty years old," piped up Connor, "and I'm six."

Jillian blinked. The age difference wasn't possible. Frankie Maguire had escaped from Long Kesh prison shortly after his twentieth birthday. That was seventeen years ago. "Do you have other children?" she asked.

"No," said Frankie shortly, "just the two. Colette was widowed when we met. Tim is her son from her first marriage."

For some reason, it was important to him that she know their circumstances. To say that Frankie was confused and closing down on a bit of truth would be an understatement. Jillian Fitzgerald, sitting across from him in gray leggings and boots, with a shirt so large it looked as if it belonged to a man and her hair hanging in sunny wisps around her cosmetic-free face, was a far cry from the woman who'd entered the doors of Stormont on Monday before last. That woman had been intimidating in her elegance. He wouldn't have been able to talk to that woman, much less wait with her, sharing his anguished fears.

That woman would not have touched her napkin to her tongue and dabbed the pudding away from the sides of a small boy's mouth. She would not have reached out to squeeze his hand when the nurse came to tell him Colette's surgery had to be extended. That woman would not have interpreted the message on the surgeon's face, would not have scribbled her address and phone number on the back of an envelope or stuffed it into his shirt pocket. She would not have scooped Connor up in her arms and told him she was taking him home until his da could come for him.

That woman was Jillian Graham, acting minister for Northern Ireland. This was someone else entirely. This was Jilly Fitzgerald, the girl he'd trusted in the most defining moment of his youth, the woman who came to his rescue, now, at the lowest point in his life.

Jillian dispensed with formality and picked up a Walt Disney film on the way home. She asked Mrs. Wilson to change the menu and serve hamburgers and chips on trays in the sitting room.

Casey had arrived earlier that day. She raised her eyebrows but did not demur when her mother suggested a game of Monopoly. Finally, when Connor's eyes drooped, Jillian removed his clothing, buttoned him into one of Casey's flannel shirts, and, deciding against leaving him alone in one of the remote guest rooms, tucked him into a corner of the enormous couch. She looked down at him for a long time after he slept.

"Now will you tell me what's happening?" asked her daughter in a hushed voice.

Jillian took her arm and led her to a chair near the fire, across from her own. She sat forward, her hands clasped in her lap. "Do you remember the woman I told you about at the hospital?"

Casey nodded.

"I didn't know until last week, but Danny Browne is her husband, and this is their son."

The girl's mouth dropped open.

"I went to the hospital this morning," Jillian continued. "Her surgery didn't go well. Mr. Browne had the boy with him. There was no one else to take him, so I brought him home with me," she finished, rushing to end the story. It sounded preposterous, even to her own ears.

Casey stared at her mother. "You've got Danny Browne's son sleeping on our couch? Danny Browne, the nationalist negotiator? Mum, whatever were you thinking?"

Jillian drew back, offended. "Why are you looking at me like that?"

"What will happen when someone finds out? Isn't this a flagrant conflict of interests?"

For the first time since Casey had officially become her own, Jillian was appalled at her thinking. "I don't give a bloody damn what anyone thinks," she said, outraged. "This is a six-year-old child who had no one to care for him. If someone wishes to make something more of it, let him."

"I didn't say you've done anything wrong, Mum," Casey said. "I just think you should be prepared in case the press makes an issue of it. Think of what you'll say."

Jillian's anger evaporated, replaced by an amused exasperation. "Where was I when you surpassed me in maturity?"

"It comes from living with you," said Casey. "You're mature enough, Mum. Bringing home a needy little boy is far more typical of you than agreeing to assume Father's position. I can't imagine why Mr. Putnam insisted that you do this."

Jillian heard the edge beneath the words. "You're worried about me, aren't you?" she asked in astonishment.

"The media isn't very nice," replied Casey slowly. "I know you don't read the tabloids, but they ran some dreadful things about Father. I don't want that to happen to you."

"What things?" Jillian held her breath.

Casey shook her head, stood, and headed for the stairs. "I'm not in the mood. I'll see you in the morning."

"Casey."

"Yes?" She stood poised at the foot of the stairs.

"Is there anything you'd like to talk about?"

The girl's forehead wrinkled. "No. Why?"

"You seem troubled about something, and you're a day late."

Casey smiled and shook her head. "I can handle my life, Mum. If it gets to be too much, you'll be the first to know."

Jillian sighed and crossed the room to stand near the window. For a long time, she stared into the deepening dusk. The night would be cold. Already, frost had gripped the grass, silvering the rich green of the lawn. Where was Frankie, and why didn't he call? She crossed the room to look down on the sleeping boy and smiled. He looked very like Casey with his dark lashes and fair skin. She looked more closely. They really were similar. Perhaps it was nothing. Perhaps all children had that soft roundness of cheek, defined heavy eyelids, and squared-off, obstinate chin.

Jillian sighed and moved away. He should have called. The child stirred, searched for his thumb, and settled back contentedly. Her heart broke. No matter what had happened, he really should have called.

Somehow, between the surgeon's explanation of what went wrong and his condolences for Colette's passing, Frankie remembered that Jillian had taken Connor. He never knew how he found the elegant mansion on Lisburn Road. Somehow, the car he'd borrowed early that morning found its own direction, down Grosvenor and Donegall roads to Queen's University, below the fork where Lisburn and Malone split. On a hunch, he turned left toward the larger, more expensive houses and, before he became completely muddled, ended up on the street outside a number that matched the one on the envelope where Jillian had scribbled her address.

Headlights on, he sat in front of the ornate gate,

wondering how in bloody hell he was going to get through. As if in response to some signal, the gates opened. Frankie depressed the clutch, threw the stick into gear, and drove down the circular driveway.

Jillian stood in the open doorway, backlit by the warm glow of dimmed lights. Her hair was loose around her collar and very gold in the lamplight. Slowly, Frankie climbed the brick steps until he reached her. She tilted her head back to see his face, and, somehow, she knew. She touched his arm. His eyes darkened, and without a word between them, his pain flowed through her like a current.

She drew him inside, pushed his unresisting body down into an easy chair, and poured him a liberal glass of Irish whiskey. He drank it down in a single gulp. She poured him another and, when that was gone, waited for him to request a third. He didn't. Apparently, the grown-up Frankie Maguire was not prone to excesses. For some reason, it pleased her. The chair was oversized. She sat down, squeezing her frame into the space beside him.

"Will you tell me what happened?" she asked softly.

"Her blood pressure went down, and her heart stopped. They couldn't revive her." His voice was raspy and scraping, as if he hadn't used it in a long time. "I've never really been without her," he said helplessly. "I don't know where to begin. There's the funeral and Connor—"

"Connor can stay here for now," Jillian said quickly. "Tomorrow is soon enough to worry about the rest of it."

"Poor wee lad," he said brokenly, dropping his head into his hands. "How will I tell him?"

Jillian's heart ached for him. She slipped her arm around his shoulders and eased his head down, cradling it against her breast. "You'll find a way," she whispered, rocking him back and forth as if he were a child. "Children are stronger than you think. Don't worry, Danny. You'll be there to guide him through this. Tonight is your time to mourn."

Her words, soothing as balm to his bruised spirit, worked their magic. She had always been a clever little miss, naive in many ways but older than her years in others. He'd missed her during those prison years. God, how he'd missed her. His mind called up images of tanned legs and sun-streaked hair, of ocean-green eyes and a mouth made for far more than kissing.

The fire with its burning turf and the expensive liquor loosened his tongue and did strange things to his brain. "I waited for you," he mumbled against her shirt. "I waited until you married first. Then I stopped waiting."

Jillian frowned and continued to stroke his head, separating the fine black hair between her fingers. He was hallucinating, and it wasn't about Colette.

"It's too late now," he continued. "The day Colette was shot, I should have told her how much she meant to me. But I was afraid she'd think I said it out of pity. She thought there was someone else, someone I couldn't get out of my mind." He laughed raggedly and lifted his head. "Can you imagine it, Jilly? Ten years married, and the woman never heard the words *I love you* from her own husband. What kind of arrogant bastard wouldn't say three wee words to make her happy?"

Her childhood name on his lips undid her. Jillian pressed her face against his shoulder, allowing the tears to stream unchecked down her cheeks. "She knew you loved her," she murmured. "A woman doesn't need the words when a man comes home to her every evening, when he wakes every morning in the same bed and looks with pride on the children they made together. Colette knew you loved her, Danny. I saw it on her face. I saw it on both your faces this morning when I came to wish her well."

Jillian remembered the husband she had recently buried and the blandness of her own farce of a marriage. A fresh sob rose in her voice. She couldn't stop the words rushing from her lips. "Some women never know that kind of love. Because of what the two of you had together, Colette's life was sweeter than most."

Their roles had reversed. Now he was comforting her. She had slipped to the floor. He pressed her head against his chest. His free hand roamed across her back, up and down her arms, kneading the muscles, touching the pressure points at her shoulders and the back of her neck, all the while murmuring in Irish, soothing, one-syllable words that she didn't understand.

For Jillian, it was sheer heaven to be held in his arms, even when it was only comfort that he offered. She strained closer and lifted her face to find air space. Her nose touched the line of his jaw. Her lips were the merest fraction of an inch from his throat. He smelled of tobacco and the cold Belfast night, a man's smell. She inhaled. Something was missing. If only she could get closer. Instinctively, her lips parted. The tip of her tongue grazed the cord of his neck, sipping at a drop of perspiration, before retreating quickly.

Frankie froze. Was he losing his mind, or had he felt her tongue on his neck? Inside his chest, his heart thundered. Carefully, he pulled away and looked down into her face. Her eyes were closed, her face swollen with tears. He released his breath. Poor lass. Her own husband had died less than two weeks ago. She needed comforting as desperately as he did, and reassurance that life continued, that she was still young and alive and desirable.

He recognized the force leaping to life within him. Desire had become his front line. Since Colette's paralysis, he'd waged a constant and frustrating battle between the demands of his body and the strength of his character. This morning, in the operating room at the Royal Victoria Hospital, the battle was finally laid to rest.

If this woman were someone else, someone who had no hold on his heart or his past, he would have gladly and guiltlessly assuaged the ache of a two-year abstinence. He would have threaded his fingers through her hair, pulled her head back, and kissed her, sweetly at first and then hungrily, with all the repressed passion that years of denial had compounded. He would have tasted her skin, undressed her slowly, pressed her back against the cushions, sucked her breasts, exploring with his hands and mouth until she vibrated and opened beneath him. And then he would have taken her, fondling, urging, driving, until all the pain, the anguish, the regret, the mistakes, the false pride, and the pounding rage of an unfair, too early loss were swallowed up in his own release and in hers.

Then he would have wrapped up the son Colette had given him and disappeared with him down the streets of East Belfast, crossing the barricade to the west side of the city. The next time they met would be on opposite sides of a conference table, their eyes connecting coolly, never speaking or referring by manner or look to this night again, unless, by chance, they should have another wordless, emotionless, purely physical encounter.

For Frankie, whose formal education had been gleaned inside the walls of Long Kesh prison, class demarcations were as rigid as they had been a generation before. He had never known, within university walls, the easy intermingling of professionals with the educated sons and daughters of laborers. But neither was he uneducated.

Inside the cell blocks of Long Kesh, the Irish Republican Army rendered a stern disciplinary code. All prisoners were thoroughly immersed in the history, language, and political struggles of their country. Munitions experts were highly valued. An engineer could design an escape route, and a man who knew the periodic table could create a bomb. Mathematics, physics, and chemistry were cultivated, as were the humanities of poetry and journalism, the innately preferable disciplines of a race of storytellers.

Frankie Maguire knew his own abilities and had no difficulty debating the finest minds to be found in the United Kingdom. He was well aware that he was Jillian's equal in intellect, performance, and character. What he was not, or so he believed, was her social equal.

Because he would never sit beside her sharing the *craic* and listening to Irish music, or walk through Falls Park holding her hand, because they would never drink a pot of tea together in O'Doul's café or throw their laundry into the same washing machine, because the curbstones on her side of Belfast were painted red, white, and blue, and most of all, because she was the lord's daughter and he was the kennel keeper's son, he could never offer her what he would have offered a woman from his own class, whether it be friendship, sex, or something between or beyond the two, no matter how his body burned for a woman.

When her weeping had stopped, he set her away from him gently and leaned back against the cushions, closing his eyes. When he opened them again, she was kneeling by the fire, her face averted, throwing pieces of dried turf into the flames. Tactfully, he waited for her to speak first.

"It's cold outside. We've enough spare rooms to accommodate a houseful. Will you allow Connor to stay here for the night?"

He noticed that she didn't ask him to stay. "Connor has never been away from home before. He might be confused when he wakes and finds himself in strange surroundings."

He watched her take a deep breath as if to gather herself. Then she turned to look at him. "You're welcome to stay with him if you like."

Frankie hesitated. Normally, he would have refused, but he had never felt more miserable in his life. The thought of traveling the deserted streets of Belfast, fending off questions at the barricade, and walking into a cold, empty flat that would never again be warmed by Colette's presence was more than he could manage. "You are very kind," he said formally. "Thank you."

Jillian made up the bed herself, fluffing pillows, smoothing sheets, turning the electric blanket to warm while Frankie waited downstairs. When the room was ready, she leaned over the railing and called to him softly. She watched while he carried Connor, still sleeping, up the stairs and tucked him into the large bed. The child curled himself into a fetal position and wedged his thumb between his teeth. She bit her lip and blinked back another bout of tears.

"I'll stay here with him," she heard Frankie say.

Interpreting his words as her dismissal, she stammered a brief good night and left the room.

Later, after she'd bathed, changed into her nightgown, and pulled her own blankets around her, a tiny shard of envy warmed her cheeks and kept her awake. Her heart ached for Connor Browne and the pain he would face tomorrow. But tonight, his small body was curled up against his father's. He would feel the beat of a man's heart, the heat of his skin, the comfort of a human breath against his cheek.

Jillian, alone in her elegant four-poster, wondered what it would be like to share her bed with a man, to shape her body to the length of his, to feel hard muscle and rough hair, to fit her head beneath his chin and feel his hands slide beneath her gown, touching places no man had ever touched before.

Pressing her fist against her mouth, she abruptly sat up and reached for the bottle of pills her physician had prescribed after Avery's death. She swallowed one and leaned back against the pillows, ashamed of her thoughts. Frankie Maguire, the man, was too attractive. He was also the chief negotiator for Sinn Fein, her adversary. "Colette," she whispered into the darkness, "if only you had told me."

21

They came downstairs together, the black-haired man and his rosy-cheeked son. Jilly was in the kitchen pouring orange juice into glasses. She looked up to see them framed in the doorway. Her eyes met Frankie's, and she knew he hadn't told Connor of his mother's death.

"Good morning," she said.

"Good morning," the boy replied. "Is that breakfast?"

Jillian laughed. "Part of it." She nodded toward the woman at the stove. "Mrs. Wilson is making the rest. Say hello to her, and then I'll show you to the breakfast room. Casey will be down soon."

"Hello, Mrs. Wilson," said Connor dutifully.

The housekeeper flashed a broad smile at him. "Why, hello, Connor. Did y' sleep well?"

"Aye." He nodded solemnly. "I don't want to go home, but Da says we must."

"Well, then, I'll hurry and serve this breakfast. Run along now, so your da can bring you back again soon."

Connor lifted serious blue eyes to his father's face. "Can we come back, Da?"

Frankie hesitated. "We'll see," he said, no match for the hopeful look on his son's small face. "A pleasure to meet you, Mrs. Wilson," he said politely, before following Jillian out of the room.

Casey was already at the table eating a slice of buttered toast. She stopped chewing, and her eyes widened when she saw Frankie. "How do you do, sir?" she said after Jillian had completed the introductions.

"I've been better," said Frankie, shaking her hand and smiling warmly, "but thank you for asking. It's a pleasure to meet you."

"You, too, sir," Casey said eagerly. "I've heard a great deal about you."

Frankie grinned. "I hope you'll still sit down with me, lass."

Her eyes twinkled. "The nationalist cause is a popular one at Trinity."

"It's more popular at Queen's."

"My mother teaches there."

Frankie lifted his eyebrows. "I see."

Casey laughed. "Mum and I do well together, Mr. Browne. My father was a well-known face here in Belfast. He thought it would be easier for me if I weren't so conspicuous."

Frankie looked at her curiously. "Is it comfortable for a Protestant at Trinity?"

She considered his question. "I wouldn't know. There are very few Protestants at Trinity. Religion isn't all that important in Dublin. It's more so here in Belfast."

He settled Connor in a chair opposite Casey's before taking his own seat beside him. Something didn't make sense. His mind leaped to the obvious question, but he couldn't bring himself to ask it, not after Jillian's hospitality.

As if she read his mind, Jillian voiced what he couldn't ask. "Casey was raised in the Catholic faith. My husband and I adopted her shortly after we married."

Frankie frowned. Avery Graham's history was well documented. He was a Protestant, descended from Scots plantation immigrants imported by the Tudors to Ireland in the early seventeenth century. The Fitzgeralds had converted when Henry VIII threatened all who remained loyal to Rome with the executioner's ax. Why had two staunch Protestants allowed their daughter to remain Catholic?

Mrs. Wilson entered the room carrying two trays piled high with eggs, bacon, and sausage. She smiled at Connor. "Here we are, laddie. Food enough for a growing boy."

For Jillian, the meal was a surprisingly pleasant one. Frankie Maguire had beautiful manners and a way with words. He was also very comfortable with children. The teasing comments he exchanged with Casey, the way he managed to tousle Connor's hair or caress his cheek while passing the butter and winking across the table at Jillian, filled her with wonder. She had never seen a man so easy and so generous with his affection. The children blossomed and ate and laughed until she felt as if her heart would burst with contentment.

She caught herself staring at him, focusing on the way he formed his words, at the competent way he cleared his plate, sugared his tea, buttered his toast. Across the table, their eyes met and locked. Gray eyes, square chin, black hair. She swallowed and looked away.

He cleared his throat. "Thank you for your hospitality, Mrs. Graham. Connor and I will be going now."

Jillian nodded and stood. "Casey and I will see you out." Connor reached for her hand and held it as they crossed the lawn to the car. She knelt down to hug him before he climbed in beside Frankie.

"Please let me know when you've settled the arrangements. I would like to pay my respects," she said.

"It wouldn't be a good idea," Frankie said tersely. "You're too public a figure to be visitin' the west side."

"Nevertheless, I shall be there," said Jillian firmly. She squeezed Connor's hand.

Casey spoke from behind her. "Come back whenever you like, Connor. Mrs. Wilson always has cookies."

Connor looked at his father and then back at Jillian before nodding solemnly.

"I think he likes you, Mum," pronounced Casey as they walked back toward the house.

Jillian followed Casey through the door and closed it behind them. "He's so adorable with those blue eyes and rosy cheeks. I can't resist him."

Casey widened her eyes innocently. "I wasn't talking about Connor."

"Cassandra!" Jillian looked horrified. "How can you say such a thing? The man lost his wife yesterday."

Casey crossed her arms and leaned against the banister. "I understand that, and I'm sorry for him. But she was ill for a long time. I'm not suggesting that anything happened between you. I merely noticed that he enjoyed your company. There's nothing wrong with that." She did not add that any fool could see that Danny Browne hadn't been able to take his eyes off Jillian the entire morning.

"What are your plans for today?" Jillian asked.

"I'm taking a nap," said Casey, continuing up the stairs. "It's an indecent hour for people to be awake."

*   *   *

The funeral was an enormous one, even by West Belfast standards. Apparently, Colette had been well liked. Jillian, dressed in gray flannel with a scarf over her hair, stood in the back of the church, staring at Frankie's broad shoulders in the front row. Connor was in his arms, and a young, fair-haired man stood by his side.

She did not file past the open coffin with the rest of the congregation, nor did she wait in the long receiving line after mass to speak to Frankie. It was Connor who recognized her and darted through the crowd just as she was crossing the street to her car.

"Jilly!" he cried, running after her, his shrill, childish voice breaking through the controlled murmurs and hushed condolences of the mourners. "Jilly, stop. 'Tis Connor. Please, stop. I want to come with you."

She stopped immediately and waited for the little boy to reach her. He threw himself against her knees and clung.

Jillian knelt, gathered him into her arms, and hugged him fiercely. Casey had been just this size when Jillian had first seen her.

Frankie was shaking hands with Father Doyle when his son's voice pierced the quiet, crying out a name that had never failed to stop him in his tracks. *Jilly*. His eyes followed Connor's small figure as he dodged through the milling crowd and into the arms of a slim, elegant woman who most definitely did not belong in West Belfast.

Abruptly cutting off the priest's condolences with the barest of civilities, Frankie crossed the street to where Jilly waited with his son. Connor was crying with great hiccuping sobs. "Mam is gone, and I won't see her again. I don't want to stay with Mrs. Flynn. Can I come home with you?"

"Hush, love." Jillian's soothing voice brought back a flood of Frankie's forgotten memories. "Don't cry, my darling. It will be all right. I promise it will." A shadow blocked the sun. She looked up into Frankie Maguire's veiled gray eyes.

"You don't belong here, Jillian."

Jillian stood and smiled cheerfully. "Climb into the car while I talk to your da, Connor."

"Connor stays with me," Frankie said through tight lips.

Jillian's eyes blazed. "For heaven's sake, Mr. Browne. What's the harm in allowing him to ride with me? I'll follow you home."

She'd cried in his arms, and he was still Mr. Browne. Frankie lifted Connor against his chest. "Mrs. Flynn is waiting for us, lad."

"I want to go home with Jilly."

Frankie hesitated. "She can drive you home, but that's all," he said at last, setting the child on his feet.

He waited until the door was safely shut before gripping Jillian's arm. "Do y' have any idea how dangerous it is to be here? We've two weeks before the Orangemen march down Garvaghy Road, and you and your Protestant friends still haven't reached a decision. This isn't a tea party, Mrs. Graham," he said brutally. "Leave the Falls immediately. They'll lynch you given enough provocation, and I won't be able t' do anything t' protect you."

She stared at him, riveted by the accent that came back to him when he was angry. She wet her lips. "Stormont meets again on Thursday. I'll be at Kildare Hall until then. Let Connor come home with me."

"Connor stays with me. I want him safe."

"Belfast isn't safe," Jillian argued. "Kilvara has never been part of the troubles. He'll be safer with me."

"No."

"You're being completely unreasonable because you

dislike me," she said furiously. "Connor doesn't want to stay here. Kildare is beautiful. There are dogs and horses and forests and pastures." She was babbling, but she didn't care. "It's a wonderful place for a small boy. Colette would have agreed with me. You know she would."

Frankie stared at her. For an instant, he was reminded of the girl who once ran wild through the fertile pastureland of County Down. "I don't dislike you," he said slowly. "Where did you come up with an idea like that?"

She shrugged, suddenly close to tears.

He reached out, remembered where he was, and withdrew his hand. He was silent for a long time. Then he sighed and ran his hand through his hair. "If you can delay your journey, I'll bring him around tomorrow morning. It wouldn't look right for him to leave today."

Weak with relief, Jillian sagged against the car. "Shall I bring him home now?"

"Aye. Follow me. Drop him off in front of the house, and don't leave the car."

She slid behind the wheel and smiled shakily at Connor. "Tomorrow you'll come to the country with me. Would you like that?"

Connor nodded. "Will Da be comin' with us?"

"Perhaps," said Jillian, as though the thought had never occurred to her. "We'll invite him and see what he says."

Tim Sheehan slid into the passenger seat beside his stepfather. "Where's Connor?" he asked.

"A friend is driving him home. She's coming up behind us now."

Tim looked over his shoulder, his eyes widening in disbelief at the make and model of Jillian's automobile. "Who is she?"

"Jillian Graham," Frankie said shortly. "The Northern Irish minister's widow."

Tim stared at Frankie. "How do you know her?"

"She called on your mother in the hospital."

"Why was she at the funeral?"

Frankie shrugged. "Your mother and Mrs. Graham were friends."

Tim laughed bitterly. "Hardly."

"It's true. Colette told me herself."

Stroking his forehead, Tim stared out his window. The gray afternoon matched his mood. It wasn't enough that he had buried his mother. He had yet to tell the only father he had ever known that instead of returning to Trinity, he was now a recruit in the Belfast Brigade of the Irish Republican Army. Topping off his misery was the memory of a small heart-shaped face he would most likely never see again, and behind them, his brother was cozying up with a woman who would just as soon see him behind the walls of Long Kesh prison as speak to him.

Frankie glanced at his stepson. "Your mam was proud of you, Tim."

The boy shrugged.

Frankie continued. "She always said an education was a grand thing. You're a clever lad. I hope Connor—"

"Don't, Da," Tim interrupted him. "I'm not goin' back."

Frankie frowned. "What are you saying?"

"I'm not going back to university. I've joined up."

White knuckles showed through the brown of Frankie's hands. He forced himself to speak calmly. "Joined what?"

"The IRA."

Long minutes passed as Frankie negotiated a right

turn and waited for the light. "It's not a wise decision, lad."

"It's what you did."

"Which is why I can speak from experience and tell you it's not the way."

"I want the Brits out, Da. My mother's dead because of the bloody bastards."

"We're close, Tim. Both sides are tired of the killing. This time we'll reach an agreement. But even if we don't, a man doesn't join the IRA for revenge. Your mother wouldn't have wanted it for you. She hated it for me, and she'd hate it even more for you."

Tim stared moodily out the side window.

"Think about it," urged Frankie. "Don't do anything yet. Wait a month. See how you feel."

"I can't promise anything."

Frankie parked the car and watched the steady flow of mourners make their way into Mrs. Flynn's flat. The woman had been kind enough to prepare a proper wake for Colette, something he had completely forgotten about. "Save it for another day, Tim," Frankie advised the boy. "Today I want you to remember your mother the way she was."

Tim wiped the wet from the corners of both eyes and nodded. Suddenly, it was all too much, and the words he wanted to say had left him.

It was nearly nine the next morning when Frankie swung his car into the circular driveway of the town house on Lisburn Road. Jilly swallowed and glanced into the mirror in the entry before opening the door and stepping outside. Connor leaped out of the car and up the stairs while Frankie followed.

"I'm here, Jilly!" the small boy shouted gleefully. "Da says I'm to stay for three days."

Jillian laughed and reached for his hands. "That's right, love, and I'm very pleased to have you."

"Will Casey come, too?"

Jillian's eyes were on Frankie as he crossed the grass and walked slowly up the brick path with a small suitcase. "She'll drive down with us, but she won't stay. They're expecting her at school."

Connor released her and ran up the stairs. "Casey!" he shouted. "I'm here."

Frankie smiled ruefully. "I can't remember when he's taken to anyone like this. His manners need improving."

Jillian smiled. "Please don't apologize. It's wonderful to have a child in the house again. I wish I had a dozen of them."

She had only one and none born of her body. That was a question that burned to be asked. But, of course, he did not.

"You're welcome to come up with us, you know," she said lightly. "Kildare Hall has a wonderful library. You won't be disturbed unless you wish to be."

He stared at her curiously. He had always known what Jilly Fitzgerald was thinking. Jillian Graham was harder to sort out. "Thank you for the invitation. But I've a great deal of work to do. The Garvaghy Road Coalition meets this week, and they want answers." He dropped the small suitcase at her feet. "Perhaps you should think of some while you're vacationing at Kildare."

Jillian flinched, and her cheeks burned as if they'd been slapped. "Garvaghy Road was decided long before I came into the picture."

"But you don't disagree with the time-honored practice of allowing Orangemen to march through nationalist neighborhoods," he said sarcastically.

"The Orangemen have been marching on Drumcree for five hundred years. It's their tradition and their original parish church."

"It's in the middle of a Catholic area in Portadown."

"They'll march no matter what we say," she argued. "Your people will die."

A muscle jumped at the corner of his mouth. "It sounds as if the decision has already been made."

"It's not definite," said Jillian. "We're trying to persuade them not to march."

"I see. Again it's their decision."

Jillian's fists clenched. "Surely you can see the advantages of having them back down voluntarily?"

"What I see, Mrs. Graham, is that the British government negotiates with terrorists as long as they're Protestant."

She would have countered, but he turned to walk back down the path. "I'll come after Connor on Saturday," he said over his shoulder.

"He can drive back with me on Sunday."

Frankie opened the car door, slid into the driver's seat, and rolled down the window.

Jillian braced herself. But all the bracing in the world would not have prepared her for his blistering reply.

"Connor is my son, Mrs. Graham," he said brutally. "I suggest you have one of your own if your maternal urge needs satisfying." The moment the words were out, he wished them back, but the look on her face told him the damage was too great for mere apology.

Cursing himself, he floored the gas pedal and sped out of the driveway. Glancing into the rearview mirror, Frankie was suddenly smitten with shame. She stood on the steps, still as a statue, her face pale as eggshells, her eyes dark with pain. He was a cruel bastard. Drumcree wasn't her fault, and neither was Colette. Punishing her wasn't the answer. She didn't deserve his resentment. What had she done but befriend Colette, offer the hospitality of her home at the bleakest point of his life, and care for his son? Resolving to make it up to her, he turned into the lower Ormeau Road and crossed the barricade.

Connor took to Kildare Hall as if he had always run through the long corridors, climbed the wide staircase, filched sugared dough from the kitchen under the nose of a doting Mrs. Hyde, rolled in the stable hayloft, and watched in silent awe as Ned, the kennel keeper, tirelessly trained the newest batch of pups.

Jillian never tired of watching the small, black-haired boy run through the meadow, climb the low branches of the black oaks that lined the driveway, and tumble over squirming collies as they raced each other up the knolls. She loved the way he smiled benignly across the table from her at meals, working to manage his knife and fork and at the same time trying to keep his mouth closed when he chewed.

She loved the cowlick that turned back on itself over his well-scrubbed, freckled forehead, his cheerful conversation, and the exquisite sweetness of his sturdy body relaxing against hers when he fell asleep on the couch. Connor Browne, with his father's lazy grin, his mother's blue eyes, and his own adorable, six-year-old, matter-of-fact bravado, was well on his way to stealing her heart. She didn't want Saturday to come.

When Frankie's compact rolled down the winding lane and stopped in the car park, her heart sank. Bravely, she rose from her lawn chair and walked toward him.

He surprised her and held out his hand. "Good afternoon, Mrs. Graham."

She touched his hand briefly. "Mr. Browne."

"I hope Connor behaved himself."

"He was wonderful," she said sincerely.

Frankie grinned. "Come now, Mrs. Graham, be honest. Connor is six years old. He couldn't possibly have been wonderful for three entire days."

Disarmed completely, Jillian stared at him. Was this the man whose bitterness left her speechless only three days ago? "I assure you, Mr. Browne, he was," she stammered.

His eyes twinkled. "You are remarkably tolerant. Where is this paragon?"

"Please call me Jillian," she said impulsively. "Connor is with Ned in the kennel."

"Ned?"

"Our kennel keeper."

Something in his eyes leaped to life and just as quickly disappeared. "I see."

"Do you like dogs, Mr. Browne?"

"I thought we were on a Christian-name basis, *Jillian.*"

Color rose in her cheeks. He watched her stumble over his name. "Do you like dogs, Danny?"

"Very much," he said easily. "Shall we find my son?"

Matching his stride, she struggled for a comfortable topic of conversation. "How was the drive?"

"Fine, thank you."

"I'm sure you'll approve of Ned, Mr. Bro—" She caught herself, mentally cursing at the warmth rising once again in her cheeks. "I mean, he has three sons of his own."

He glanced at her out of the corner of his eye. Why was she so nervous? Jillian Fitzgerald was the type of woman a man noticed. At Stormont she wasn't at all self-conscious, even though she had been the only woman in a room full of men. He frowned. It was his fault, his and his damnable tongue. Who would have thought that a woman born into wealth and privilege, in the last half of the twentieth century, with the finest education money could buy, would measure her worth by the age-old standard of fertility?

Frankie had thought very carefully about the anguished look on Jillian's face after he'd left her house on Lisburn Road. That, and the fact that she'd adopted a child rather than have her own when she was obviously a woman who enjoyed children, led him to the obvious assumption. She was barren. An ugly word, *barren*. He'd looked up the definition. *Empty, lifeless, without issue*. No wonder she was afraid of him. He'd crushed her by exposing what she thought was her greatest failure.

"Jillian," he began, "I want to apologize—"

"Da." Connor ran across the clearing and threw himself into his father's arms.

"Connor, lad." Frankie lifted him high into the air and then back against his chest to engulf him in a breath-stealing embrace.

Any doubts Jillian might have had about Frankie's relationship with his son evaporated instantly. He was devoted to the boy. She smiled at the two dark heads so close together.

"Come in and see the puppies, Da. Ned said it was fine."

"He did, did he?" Frankie set Connor on his feet and took his hand. He looked at Jillian. "May I?"

"Of course," she said, flustered again. "Ned is in charge here."

Frankie remembered that it had always been so with the Fitzgerald kennel keepers. He smiled at Jillian. "After you."

Naturally, as if she had always done so, she reached for Connor's other hand. "Come along, Connor. We'll show your da the pride of Kildare."

"What does that mean?" the boy asked.

"It means that our collies are the very best of the breed. The Fitzgeralds have always had collies, and we take very good care of them. Here at Kildare, dogs are nearly as important to us as children. In fact, there was one dog we loved so dearly that I persuaded my mother to hold a funeral for her."

"Who was that?" asked Connor.

Jillian tilted her head, and Frankie, who had been listening closely to her story, noticed the long, lovely length of her neck and lost track of her words.

Connor brought him back. "What was her name?" he asked.

"Guinevere."

The name jolted him. *Guinevere.* The dog that first brought her to him, the one they'd nursed back to life. Pyers Fitzgerald's prize collie over whose emaciated body they had cemented their friendship.

Frankie stepped into the warm, doggy-smelling darkness of the Kildare kennel, and the memories came flooding back. Once again, he was a ragged boy with an aggravated stammer and an impossible dream. His throat closed. He turned away from Jillian's curious glance to collect his composure. Another lapse, and she might very well recognize him. He'd been a fool to come. But the temptation to lose himself in that time warp when all he'd cared about was passing his A levels and impressing a certain tawny-haired girl had been too great.

Connor pulled him by the hand. "Look, Da. This is Ned."

A rangy, dark-haired man, lean with corded muscle,

held out his hand. "Pleased to meet Connor's da," he said.

Frankie shook it, noticed that the kennel keeper was younger than he'd expected, and wondered why it bothered him.

Connor dropped to his knees near a stall and held out his arms. Two balls of gold-and-white fur leaped forward and knocked him into the straw. The boy laughed. "See, Da. They like me. Can we take one? Please, can we?"

Frankie knelt beside his son and lifted a puppy out of the straw. Expertly, he examined the narrow head, the silken fur, the graceful, drooping mouth. "We live in the city, Connor. A dog like this needs open spaces. She wouldn't be happy in Belfast. Perhaps Mrs. Graham will allow us to come back from time to time and see her."

He waited for Jillian to reply. When she didn't, he glanced up and saw her eyes, wide and startled, on his face. *She knew.* The blood drummed in his temples. He opened his mouth to explain, but the words wouldn't come.

She had watched him kneel in the hay. She had seen how he reached for the puppy, how his hand closed around the scruff of her neck, the way his fingers, long and careful, moved against the soft fur, soothing, exploring, caressing. Jillian's eyes moved from his hands to the line of his chin, the hollow of his cheek, the length of his lashes, the texture of his hair. He looked up.

She saw the color of his eyes, gun-metal gray bordered in black. Dear God! How could she go on pretending? Slowly, she lifted her hands to her throat and backed out of the kennel.

22

"Jillian."

Her name on his lips stopped her. She leaned against the wooden gate, buried her face in her arm, and drank in deep lungfuls of air.

His hand came down on her shoulder. "Jillian, please, let me—"

"I'm sorry," she gasped. "I don't know what came over me."

He frowned and dropped his hand, waiting for her to continue.

She lifted her head. The sun caught and deepened the golden lights radiating from the centers of her eyes. "I know what you're thinking, but I assure you, I'm not going mad, and it has nothing to do with this position of Avery's that I've inherited."

"Jillian—"

"You'll want to be on your way," she hurried on. "I'm sorry I didn't have Connor ready when you arrived. I'll bring his bag down for you."

He stood rooted to the ground as if his legs had lost the ability to move. Once, long ago, Jillian Fitzgerald had known him better than anyone. Those instincts were still strong within her, but she no longer trusted them. His breathing slowed. He had time, but soon, very soon, it would all be over. She would see through his polished manners, his added inches, his filled-out chest and shoulders, past the webbed lines fanning out from the corners of his eyes. She would look at him, and twenty years would disappear, and with them, Danny Browne and a lifetime of lies.

Six months ago, the prospect would have filled him with horror. He would have hidden himself as deeply and thoroughly as a man with a crippled wife, a six-year-old child, and an identifying Irish accent could hide. Now, he felt nothing more than an imminent sense of anticipation, as if for two decades his life had been on hold, waiting for this woman to unmask him.

Stormont Castle

Jillian stood between two marble pillars in the enormous drawing room at Stormont. In her hand was the most recent reply from the Garvaghy Road Coalition, currently housed in the castle's south tower rooms. In the north tower were David Temple and the Armagh Orange Lodge. A senior Northern Ireland official, serving as a liaison between the two, waited patiently at the door.

For three days, she had worked around the clock to find a reasonable solution to the Orangemen's annual Drumcree march, but neither side would concede an inch. Under the arrangements, the two sides would continue to occupy separate parts of the same building until the issue was resolved.

Jillian sighed. Damn Thomas Putnam. Under the guise of impartiality, he had assured both parties that the outcome, whatever it was, would be neither imposed nor predetermined. What rubbish. With the Catholics insisting the march should not be allowed without meeting the Orangemen directly, and the Orangemen refusing to meet anyone connected with Sinn Fein, the outcome could not be anything but imposed.

A woman dressed in tweed brought in a tray with tea and biscuits and set it on the table. Jillian added several cups and carried it down the hall and up the stairs to the north tower rooms. The Orangemen, Protestants from Armagh led by David Temple, rose in unison.

"Good afternoon, gentlemen," she said. "I've brought you some tea."

With the pouring finished and the men seated around the comfortable room, Jillian opened the discussion. "Gentlemen, I appeal to you. Be reasonable. This march hints at nothing but dominion. Why are grown men marching through streets where they are not wanted?"

Gary McMichael, a stout, stern-faced man, leader of the Ulster Democratic Party of South Armagh, spoke. "Drumcree is our original parish church. Our culture is at stake here. They have their music and their language and their games. We have our marches, and we'll not give them up."

Jillian's eyes flashed dangerously. "Our *culture*, gentlemen? To what culture are you referring? We are white Anglo-Saxon Protestants, born in the North of Ireland into a privileged class that believes that God allows Englishmen through the pearly gates ahead of all other ethnically inferior races. We can't have it all, Mr. McMichael. The price we pay for our privileged position is that language, music, tradition, in other words, true *culture*, is denied to us. This is Irish land. These people are the descendants of native Irish, and we, gentlemen, are the conquerors." Her voice gentled. "It would be a small but very significant act of compassion if you gave the order to stop the Garvaghy Road march. It would show the world that you truly want peace."

David Temple, the spokesman for Protestant Ulster, ran a hand through his wavy brown hair and spoke through clenched teeth. "The Catholics of Ballyoran and Churchill have no objections to a march without band music."

"Apparently, we don't move in the same circles, Mr. Temple."

Temple forced a laugh. "Come now, Mrs. Graham. There is no need for dramatics. I see no reason why things should not proceed peacefully as they have every year for two hundred years."

"Last year was not peaceful."

"An exception, I assure you."

"An exception that will surely be repeated should the Orangemen march along Garvaghy Road."

"Nevertheless, we will march. If we are prevented from doing so, people will die."

"How fortunate that you are not Robbie Wilson, Mr. Temple," Jillian said bitterly. "Those words coming from him would be interpreted as an act of terrorism. A warrant for his arrest would be issued immediately." She rose and smoothed her skirt with shaking hands. "But the Ulster Defense League and the Ulster Volunteer Force are not terrorists, are they, Mr. Temple? Only the IRA and Sinn Fein, who speak for twenty percent of our population, are acknowledged terrorists."

She waited for someone to speak, a slim, elegant woman blazing with temper, the mixed blood of the

Irish Sean Ghalls flowing through her veins. When the silence deepened and the men looked everywhere but at her, she threw them a last contemptuous glance, turned, and walked out through the double doors.

Near the long window with its pastoral view of the gardens, Frankie Maguire spoke softly to the tall, bearded man Jillian recognized as Robbie Wilson, representative for Sinn Fein and elected MP for West Belfast. Four representatives from the Garvaghy Road Coalition sat across from each other on low couches. A tea service and several half-filled cups cluttered the small tables.

The men had reacted to the Orange Lodge ultimatum as expected, with implacable expressions, low voices, and grave, clipped conversation. Not for a moment did Jillian believe they were as accommodating as they appeared. These were Irishmen, after all, although not a one drank anything stronger than tea. Neither did they use profanity, lose their tempers, or sink below the level of pure professionalism. So much for the English-generated myth of whiskey-drinking, hot-tempered brawlers. Jillian was inexperienced, but she was not unintelligent. The residents of Garvaghy Road were prepared for whatever came. They would have a contingency plan no matter what the Orangemen decided.

Frankie loosened his tie, unbuttoned the top button of his pale blue shirt, and leaned against the frame of the recessed window. He was having difficulty concentrating, and the reason for his lapse fanned the edges of his smoldering temper.

In a room done up in muted beiges and olive greens, its couches lined with men wearing gray and black, she stood under a glittering chandelier in a dress as soft and purely yellow as a Galway sunset. The sparkling crystals directly above her head lit her skin and framed her hair in a halo of light. She looked like the Virgin Mary, forever immortalized in the stained-glass panels of Saint John's Chapel.

He hated what this would mean to her. For Jillian, it would be a painful lesson in humility. The nationalists of Ulster had taken one look at her and decided that she, a Fitzgerald of Kildare Hall, would save them from Protestant triumphalism. When she failed to deliver, and she would fail, they would crucify her.

Stuffing his balled fists into his trouser pockets, Frankie stared out at the summer-green garden. She was not Avery Graham, a man who'd developed skin thick enough to take the disappointments of politics in stride. She would be hurt, bitterly hurt. He didn't think he could bear to see Jillian go through such a thing.

Glancing casually in her direction, he saw Robbie Wilson approach her. She smiled at the Sinn Fein representative, and Frankie's irritation increased. This was a political standoff, for Christ's sake. Why was she wearing a dress that belonged at a tea party? He saw Wilson shake his head and forced himself to concentrate. There wasn't a sound in the room when she answered him.

"Ten parades have already been rerouted away from the Garvaghy Road area. Drumcree is the only one left. It seems as if the Loyal Orders have made some concessions, Mr. Wilson."

"It won't hurt them to make more. Garvaghy Road is made up of Catholic families."

"I understand that it was originally mixed. Intimidation and ethnic cleansing forced almost all of the Protestant families to leave."

"We don't subscribe to ethnic cleansing, Mrs. Graham," Robbie Wilson said in his low, patient voice. "There are several Protestant families left in the Churchill area, and they are not crying intimidation."

Jillian clasped her hands together. She looked much younger than her thirty-five years and very vulnerable. "The Drumcree parade is an old and established one. In all the years since its inception, there has never been one act of provocation from the Orangemen. Bands play only hymn music, and for the ten minutes it takes to clear Garvaghy Road, they are completely silent." She pleaded with him. "Please, Mr. Wilson. Can't you ask your people to stay inside and wait for a mere ten minutes?"

The corners of Frankie's mouth twitched. Wilson was a man and no more a match for wide hazel eyes and a trembling mouth than any man present. It was a testimony to his great control that he did not stray from his original intent.

"No, I cannot ask it," he said gently, holding up his hand to prevent her from interrupting. "I am familiar with the statistics, Mrs. Graham. Fewer than ten houses actually have Garvaghy Road addresses. Seventy-five percent of the houses are between one hundred and six hundred meters away from the marching path. It is impossible for residents to see Garvaghy Road from the vast majority of homes along the street."

He sighed, removed his glasses, cleaned the lenses with the end of his tie, and put them on again. "The point is that the Drumcree march is as much about returning from a church service as the Nuremberg rally was about Bavarian folk dancing. The entire marching controversy is about territory. Garvaghy Road is an area where the symbols of the Irish state are in evidence everywhere, where the loyalty of the community is with Dublin rather than London. Marching through the heart of that community, preferably after locals have been given a good hiding by their buddies in the RUC, is the Portadown Orangemen's way of letting the natives know that they still rule the roost."

She was too pale. Frankie frowned and stepped forward. She turned her head to look at him, and the mute appeal in the hazel eyes was impossible to ignore. "You can't stop it, Jillian," he said tersely, dismissing the startled look on the face of the MP. Explanations would come later, when Wilson would demand to know in his calm, unintrusive way how he had come to be on a first-name basis with the minister to Northern Ireland. "They'll march, and the Catholics will riot. The RUC will bash in a few heads, shoot a few plastic bullets, and it will make all the papers. There is nothing you can do."

"There must be," she whispered. "We are all adults. Surely this isn't worth people's lives."

He was standing beside her now, and she tilted her head to look at him. "Save yourself," he said. "Call a press conference, and tell them what's happened here. Tell them that negotiations broke down, that the Orangemen will march against the better judgment of your office." Forgetting himself, he gripped her shoulders and shook her slightly. "If you say nothing and allow this to happen, your tenure will be over. No nationalist will take you seriously again."

The ticking of the wall clock and Frankie's harsh breathing were the only sounds in the still silence. Someone cleared his throat and broke the mood. Discreetly, Jillian extricated herself from Frankie's hold. The pink color staining her cheeks was the only indication that she was affected by what had just happened.

"Thank you, gentlemen," she said firmly, addressing the coalition. "You've given me a great deal to think about. I'm truly sorry about the turn of events, and I wish you luck. Now, I must notify the RUC of the Orange Order's decision to march."

In groups of two and three, the men left the room. Frankie felt a familiar hand clasp his shoulder. "Ride back to Belfast with me," Wilson said. "I'll drop you at home."

They had passed the roundabout and turned north on the M1 when he asked the inevitable question. "How well do you know Jillian Graham, Danny lad?"

Frankie stared out the window. Robbie Wilson was nothing if not thorough. He would figure it out sooner or later. "I know very little about Mrs. Graham," he began. "She visited Colette in hospital and came to the wake. She's been kind to Connor." He shrugged his shoulders. "That's all."

"Have you spent time with her?"

"A bit."

Wilson turned left onto the motorway and then moved right into the flow of traffic. "There's something else, isn't there, lad?"

Frankie remained silent.

"If it's something that can hurt our position, I want you t' pull out, Danny. There's still time."

"It's nothin' like that." Frankie hesitated. Wilson knew about the prison break. "She's Jillian Fitzgerald from Kilvara. I knew her long ago when I was Frankie Maguire."

Robbie Wilson cursed under his breath. "Does she know?"

Frankie shook his head. "Not yet."

"Will y' tell her?"

"Not unless there's a reason."

"I want you t' stay away from her, Danny. No more meetin's with her. We'll send someone else."

"I'm chief negotiator in the talks, Robbie. Who else is there t' send?"

Wilson's hands tightened on the wheel. "Sit tight. I'll sort it out."

They rode in silence until a conviction rose so strong in Frankie's chest he could no longer keep it inside. "She won't turn me in, Robbie. No matter what she knows, she won't go t' the law."

Wilson glanced at him speculatively. "I hope you're right, lad, for all our sakes."

The Belfast Telegram and *The Irish Times* both carried it on the front page: "Northern Ireland's Minister to Hold Press Conference." Frankie turned on the television and sat back in an easy chair, too preoccupied with the images flashing on the screen to admonish Connor for climbing onto his lap and dripping brown sauce on his shirt.

Jillian, her hair pulled back into a classic twist that emphasized the dramatic bones of her cheeks and the moss green of her eyes, stared at him from the tube. She appeared completely poised, but Frankie, who had memorized every nuance of her speech patterns, heard the husky timber of nervousness in her voice.

"Last summer," she began, "Northern Ireland witnessed a degree of public disorder which left a mark of shame. It damaged the image of this community in the eyes of the world. All of us, the people of Northern Ireland, have suffered. Since I was appointed secretary of state for Northern Ireland, I have made it clear that the problems associated with the marches have been my number one priority. I am sorry to say that my efforts, along with those of many others, have not borne fruit. I have no doubt that accommodation is the desired outcome of the vast majority of people in Northern Ireland." She drew a deep breath before continuing.

"Because an agreement could not be reached, and after a scrupulous weighing of factors and applying the law, the chief constable of the RUC has decided that the parade will continue under certain conditions. Mr. Flanagan has full authority. It is the rule of law. While I understand his position, a position that was taken because an accommodation could not be reached, I deeply regret this course of action." Her eyes were very bright and wide as she lifted a water glass to her lips.

"Let me be quite clear. I never wanted a position where there was a need for an imposed decision. Like the vast majority of people in this country, I wanted to see a local accommodation. I have done my absolute utmost to achieve that and will continue to do so. In the future, we will bring forward new legislation on parades. In shaping our proposals we will take into account the fears and sensitivities these issues arouse on all sides. To those who may be considering revisiting last year's tragedy on their friends and neighbors, let me say this:

"Think before you act. Think about the families whose lives you might threaten, whose hopes you will dash, whose chances of a decent job, a decent home, a decent future will diminish. No one is challenging the dignity and worth of the nationalist identity. Your voice is heard, and I will continue to listen—always. You have my word on that."

Frankie watched as she stepped back away from the microphones. He continued to watch as she extended her hand to members of the press corps and moved among them, weaving her way toward the door. He kept watching as clips of her speech were rerun. Only when Connor's head drooped against his shoulder and he realized they were sitting in total darkness did he stand, turn off the telly, and carry his son to bed.

He stayed in the shower for a long time. When the water cooled he toweled himself dry and slid between the sheets of the bed he'd once shared with Colette. Resting his arm on his forehead, he stared at the cracked ceiling.

Sleep eluded him. He glanced at the clock. It was after ten. Too late to call. Reaching for his wallet, he extricated the slip of paper from between the sheets of plastic and dialed anyway. She answered on the second ring.

"Jillian," he said after a moment of silence, "it's Danny Browne."

He heard her catch her breath.

"Hello, Danny," she said warily. "Is something wrong?"

"No. I just wanted to tell you that I saw you on television. You were very good and very convincing."

"Thank you." Her voice was warmer now. "How is Connor?"

"Poor little bloke. As well as can be expected."

He heard her silence and then the rushed words, nonchalantly offered as if fearing rejection. "He's welcome at Kildare anytime. You both are. Just let me know."

"That's very kind of you."

Silence, awkward and absolute, separated them.

"Well?" she asked at last.

"Well what?"

"Will you come?"

Again, there was silence.

"Danny?"

This time, he heard her voice behind the words, and his heart leaped in his chest. "Aye, lass," he said softly. "We'll be pleased t' come."

He never knew what triggered the rush of emotions that swept over him when he hung up the phone. Whatever it was, he couldn't stop it. His eyes ached, his shoulders shook, and the tension that he carried around within him every waking moment relaxed in a flood of tortured memory.

Turning his face into the pillow, he wept for the women in his life, the one he'd trusted with his secret, the one who'd taken him in and borne him a son, the one he'd lied to, cried with, burned for, and dreamed of, long before he'd learned a Catholic from Ulster had no right to dream.

23

⟡

Portadown, Northern Ireland

Jillian rubbed her arms, accepted the mug of milky tea from a woman with a sweet face and a tired smile, and walked to the end of Garvaghy Road, where the women's peace camp had been hastily constructed. Reporters were everywhere, swarming the small town with their equipment and unfamiliar faces.

Keeping her head down, she made her way through the milling crowd of cameramen, hoping to go unrecognized. Her slender build and straight shoulder-length hair gave her the appearance of a much younger woman. Denim trousers, canvas shoes, a backpack, and a light pullover aided her disguise. The women of Garvaghy Road knew who she was, however, and more than one thoughtful glance followed her as she walked, drank her tea, and stared down the road toward Drumcree Church.

Street artists were finishing several three-story murals on the walls of a large building. In huge white letters,

Jillian made out the words "Reroute Sectarian Marches." In the background, young girls were step-dancing on the road with the word *"Failte"* across the top of their banner and *"Bother garbh achaidh"* along the bottom. Another wall had two hands crossed at the wrist and tied with ropes of the Tricolour and the Orange Order, its message "Peace with justice." The atmosphere was one of nervous anticipation. Plans for a street festival the following day were in full swing.

At six o'clock in the evening, men and women lined up along the length of Garvaghy Road carrying signs calling for the rerouting of the parade. A car rigged with loudspeakers encouraged everyone to come out of their houses. Children were assigned to knock on doors prevailing upon everyone to participate. The air was charged with a tingling electrical excitement.

At eleven o'clock that night, Jillian stared at the armored vehicles rolling down the streets of Portadown. They were moving in to secure the area around Drumcree Church. Her nerves were stretched thin and humming with anticipation. Convinced that the march would be pushed through, she still naively hoped that at the final hour something would be done to stop it. "Please let them come to their senses," she said out loud.

"Don't count on it," said a voice from behind her.

Turning, she looked up into Frankie Maguire's handsome, unsmiling face. "I was wishing, that's all," she whispered.

"What are you doing here, Jillian?"

She winced. He did not sound at all pleased with her. Had she imagined his voice on the phone the other night? "I wanted to see what happened firsthand."

"The newspaper would have been a better source."

"You're here," she pointed out.

"Not by choice."

Jillian held her mug upside-down and poured out the remains of her cold tea. "Where else should I be?"

Frankie bit down hard on his tongue. She was as courteously polite as ever, and he was a rude bastard. "It isn't safe for you here," he said quietly. "Your sex won't protect you. The police are fully prepared to kick, throw, beat, and arrest anyone caught on the street."

"If I am kicked, thrown, beaten, and arrested, I can assure you someone will be very, very sorry."

"If you aren't killed or paralyzed by a plastic bullet."

She remembered Colette. "Oh, Frankie. I'm so sorry."

His eyes were the color of smoke. "This has nothing t' do with anyone but you. Go home."

"No."

His face went blank while his eyes moved over her, objectively noting the classic purity of her features, the worn trousers, the nubby pullover, and the sportpack hitched over one shoulder. Jillian Graham was more appealing and far more approachable in faded denims than she had been in a designer suit. She was also more obstinate, or had she always been this way and he hadn't noticed?

He remembered a freckle-faced firebrand leaping to his defense, reducing her mother to tears and her father to howls of irresponsible laughter. In those long-ago, careless, sunlit days, no one dared cross Jilly Fitzgerald of Kildare Hall. But this was different. She was in way over her head, and it was time someone did.

He reached for her hand, enclosing it in a viselike grip. "You're coming with me. We'll find a place t' sit this one out."

"Where are we going?"

"Keep quiet."

Jillian allowed him to lead her across the road, down a small side street, and into a modest home that had recently been occupied. A kettle still boiled on the stove, and the bathroom mirror was thick with steam as if someone had just showered. "Where's Connor?" she asked, leaning against the counter and rubbing the wrist he had just released.

"With Mrs. Flynn." He spooned tea leaves into a pot. "What do you hope to accomplish here, Jillian?"

She looked surprised. "Nothing, really. The rest isn't up to me." He handed her the cup. The heat warmed her hands. "I feel so removed from it all," she confessed. "Everything I know comes from what I've read. It isn't enough. I feel as if I were blind."

Frankie swallowed a mouthful of hot, sustaining tea. "We're not expectin' you to change what can't be changed. No one person can do that."

"What time is it?"

"Nearly midnight."

She looked around. "Where are we?"

"Sean Dunbar's home. He's the Sinn Fein representative in the area."

"Nothing is scheduled for hours yet. Do you think he'd mind if I napped on his couch?"

Frankie shook his head. "I'll wake you if anything happens."

Within minutes, she was asleep.

He watched her for a long time, her hand curling against her chin, the way her hair spilled across the cushion, her lashes resting like gold-tipped crescents against her cheeks, the even rise and fall of her chest when she breathed. She turned only once, sighing deeply, lashes fluttering, arms settling bonelessly into familiar places.

It hit without warning, instantly, irrevocably, like the

glancing blow of a boxer's punch. How long had it been? Two years? Three? A lifetime? Had he *ever* known that kind of desperate, hopeless desire, the kind that weakens the knees, strips clean the defenses, and exposes the longings hidden deep in one's soul?

He drew in his breath, walked unsteadily into the kitchen, turned off the light, and sank down into a straight-backed chair. The darkness settled him, bringing with it a semblance of sanity. Jillian was beautiful, and he was lonely. Colette's passing had stirred the embers of appetites he'd repressed since her accident. He was a man, for Christ's sake, and a bloody tolerant one. Three years was a long time. The platonic nature of his marriage had been Colette's choice, not his. It was only natural for a man, celibate against his will, to react when confronted with a lovely, compassionate woman who obviously adored his son.

It was impossible, of course. She was an aristocrat and a Protestant, not to mention his political adversary. The press would hang her for a conflict of interests that would make the Windsor scandals appear tame in comparison. He would end this cat-and-mouse game they played. After tonight, the only communication he would have with her would be across the bargaining table during peace talks.

The shrill blast of the community siren pierced the silence. Frankie leaped from his chair and headed for the sitting room. Jillian met him halfway, her eyes wide with terror.

"They've sounded the alarm," he said quietly. "It means British troops have secured the area around Drumcree Church."

"What shall we do?"

"Nothing."

"You didn't come here to wait in Sean Dunbar's house."

"No. But I didn't expect to find you, either."

Her eyes flashed. "I'm going outside, Frankie," she said deliberately. "Don't try to stop me."

He watched her sling the backpack over her shoulder, push open the screen, and walk through the door. Cursing, he flipped off the sitting-room light, zipped his jacket, and followed her. When he caught up with her and took her hand, she did not pull away. He found a spot on the corner with a good vantage point.

Peaceful protesters shouting encouragement lined the road. Above the joviality, Jillian heard the cadence of marching feet. Within minutes, the RUC, outfitted in black and wearing complete body armor, sealed off every route into the Garvaghy Road and encircled the protesting residents who began singing the strains of "We Shall Overcome." British Saxons and RUC armored Land Rovers moved into position.

It was nearly dawn. Fingers of morning light streaked the sky. Slowly, the police fanned out and approached the crowd. The protesters linked arms, tightened their circle, and began to pray. Jillian bit her lip. She wanted very much to look away, but Frankie's mocking glare kept her eyes stubbornly fixed on the nightmare unfolding before her.

Targeting the perimeters of the circle, the RUC began peeling away individuals, one and two at a time. Four policemen, swinging clubs, waded into the middle. They lifted the clubs above their heads and brought them down, full force on the heads, shoulders, backs, and arms of the protesters. Across the street on the sidewalk, another unit assumed the kneeling position, took aim, and fired. Bodies fell to the ground. Shouts, screams, and profanity sounded through the peaceful dawn.

Pressing the back of her hand against her mouth, Jillian watched as heads split open and nationalist blood spilled, once again, on the streets of Ireland. She did not protest when Frankie's arm came around her, his hand pressing her head into his shoulder, his voice murmuring a soothing mantra in a language she did not understand.

After three hours of physical brutality and military precision, the occupation and containment of the Garvaghy community was complete. The wait for the march began in earnest. Tensions were high.

Frankie pulled Jillian into the shadow of a building to avoid the inevitable confrontations among residents, the soldiers, and police. Hours passed. He no longer felt his feet. Jillian slept occasionally, her body a limp weight against his chest.

It was Sunday morning, and Saint John's Parish Church was surrounded with barbed wire. Surrounded by British tanks and soldiers in full riot gear, local priests carried tables to construct an altar for an open-air mass. Catholics assembled and knelt on the concrete while their priests prayed. Cameras flashed, and reporters spoke with hushed voices into their microphones.

At one o'clock in the afternoon, they came, a somber group of twelve hundred Orangemen, marching in rows through the ominous silence, backs straight, eyes forward, faces tight with fear, orange sashes bright beneath bowler hats.

An angry murmur surged through the crowd. "You call yourselves Christians!" a woman screamed.

"Rot in hell!" a man called out.

Within minutes, they were gone. But the rage of the community had increased. Nationalists spewed venomous insults at the RUC. Young men raised their fists and chanted to each other from the rooftops, "I-R-A, I-R-A, no ceasefire, no ceasefire."

Jillian watched in shocked silence as the citizens of Garvaghy Road were left to strip away the barricades, ropes, and barbed wire from the contained areas. "We can still sort it out," she said under her breath. "This is over. Next year will be different."

"Will it?" Frankie's mouth twisted bitterly. "When will you people recognize an ultimatum when you see one? The Catholics of Garvaghy Road are telling you that they want no part of Thomas Putnam's peace train so long as it has just two carriages, first class and Catholic."

Someone else might have assumed her unnatural pallor was the result of shock or pain. But Frankie, sensitive to her slightest nuance, knew that it was anger, white-hot and all-consuming.

"How dare you call me one of them." Her voice vibrated with rage. "How dare you sit across the negotiating table in the name of peace and deny that you're a terrorist when you've just admitted that you believe all power grows out of the barrel of a gun."

When he didn't answer, she smiled sadly. "I thought better of you, Danny Browne. I believed in the man who was Colette's husband. I hoped—" She took a deep breath. Her mouth trembled.

Words failed him. He reached out, but she backed away.

"Don't touch me." Her voice broke. "Please, don't touch me. I can't bear it." With a final anguished look, she turned and crossed the desolate street.

Bertie Ahern, the Irish Taoiseach, called the march a travesty. John Bruton, the Fine Gael leader, expressed regret over the course of events concerning Garvaghy Road. Eamon O'Cuiv, the new minister of state for the Republic of Ireland, criticized the heavy-handed approach of the RUC and the British troops. Thomas Putnam, prime minister of England, was furious.

Amnesty International had publicly denounced the actions of the British government and demanded that Mr. Putnam bring Britain's laws into line with international standards in relation to Northern Ireland and to set up a human rights commission. The group called for an inquiry into the significant numbers of deaths while in police custody.

Putnam's youthful forehead was furrowed as he walked back and forth across the wooden floor of his office at No. 10 Downing Street. His secretary's voice floated through the speaker phone. "Mrs. Graham is on the phone, sir."

He pushed the red light. "Jillian, are you there?"

"Yes."

"You've seen the papers?"

"Yes."

His voice rose. "What in bloody hell are we to do?"

"I beg your pardon?"

He could not miss the frost in her voice, and it grated on his already sensitive nerves. "I apologize," he said stiffly. "What is your opinion on the matter?"

"I would do exactly as they ask."

"That's preposterous."

"Why?"

"It makes us look like fools."

Was he imagining the edge to her words, or was Jillian Graham actually impatient with him?

"On the contrary," she said. "It will look as if you and the Labour Party are enlightened. Your government is still new enough to pull it off if you act quickly.

Institute parade legislation immediately, set up a human rights commission, investigate the Bloody Sunday murders, and enforce the rights of suspects to remain silent during police interrogation and trial."

"I'll call a press conference."

"That should help."

"When will the talks resume?"

"We expect trouble in Belfast," she said quietly. "When it's clear that the nationalists are appeased over Garvaghy Road, their leaders will come back to the table."

"I want to speak with Wilson and Browne first, before the press conference. Can you find them?"

The silence stretched out.

"Jillian, are you there?"

"Yes, Tom.

"Will you find them?"

"I'll try."

Jillian waited for the click at the other end of the line before replacing her receiver. West Belfast was a war zone and the last place she wanted to be. She could call Frankie at the Sinn Fein office, but the chances of finding him there were slim. He had given her his home number, but she shied away from using it. It was too personal and, after the way they last parted, too immodest. She would have to wait for him in front of his flat, and that meant crossing the barricades late in the day.

Perhaps she would see Connor. The thought lifted her spirits. He was such a dear little lad. She would bring something along to cheer him up. If small boys were anything like girls, they loved toys with moving parts. She would find something appropriate tomorrow.

The following morning, Jillian waited her turn in the queue of autos lined up to cross into West Belfast. Octagonal guard towers with automatic rifles pointed menacingly in the direction of West Belfast towered above the Peace Wall gate. Soldiers checked the papers of Catholics and Protestants wishing to cross over to opposite sides of the city.

A young man about Casey's age poked his head into her window. "Papers, please."

She passed them over, watched him scan her identification, and saw his eyes widen. "Begging your pardon, ma'am, the streets are a mess just now. I wouldn't go in for a few more days."

Jillian smiled politely. "Unfortunately, my business won't wait. Thank you for the warning. I'll be careful."

He nodded, handed back her papers, and waved her through.

She should have brought a driver or taken a black taxi, those notorious hearselike autos that operated in West Belfast under the direction of the Irish Republican Army. Driving her expensive sedan with its Ulster plates through smoke-filled streets was an invitation for trouble. She stared straight ahead, praying for lights to turn before she came to a full stop.

Ahead of her, a crowd of men, women, and children milled in front of the community center. On a hastily erected dais, a tall, dark-haired man with a full beard addressed the crowd through a loudspeaker. "I have demanded the rerouting of the parade scheduled for the Lower Ormeau Road," he said to the angry crowd. "All right-thinking people will agree with us."

A man shouted from below. "They said they couldn't hold the barricade against the Orangemen."

Robbie Wilson laughed, a short, sharp bark that held little humor. "Ask any nationalist how long he can hold a barricade on the Falls Road. He'll tell you forever.

The unionists behave the way they do because the British government lets them," he said. "If we—"

The low rumble of a tank engine drowned out his voice. Jillian pulled over to the curb and looked behind her. The color drained from her face. Three armored Land Rovers rolled slowly, steadily toward the assembly. A woman screamed. The crowd scattered in every direction, and the sharp crack of gunfire ripped through the chaos. Glass shattered, and the smell of chemicals filled the air.

From the end of the street, a small black-haired boy darted into the path of the oncoming tanks. Dear God! "Connor!" Jillian screamed. Horrified, she flung herself out of the car, praying that she would be in time. The dreadful crack of a sniper's rifle whistled past her ear. Petrol bombs and rocks crashed around her.

The boy's small body crumpled to the ground in a heap. The rat-a-tat-tat of gunfire came from all directions. Smoke filled her nose and burned her eyes. Jillian could no longer see. "Connor!" she cried out again. Falling to her knees, she began to crawl.

"They've shot a boy, the bastards!" The cry rang out from the street. "A wee lad is down!"

"Connor!" A man's agonized cry came from a shop on the corner.

Through streaming eyes, Jillian saw Frankie race into the street. A soldier in green camouflage lifted his gun and took aim. She opened her mouth to call out when a voice, calm and soothing, reached her ears. *Go back, Jilly. Go back now. I'll take care of this.*

Confused, Jillian stared at the scene in the street. Frankie had reached Connor and thrown his body over his son's still form. A woman stood over them, fearlessly facing the tanks. She spread her arms, encompassing the man and the boy in a circle of pale hair and wintry light. *Nell!* Petrol bombs exploded all around them, and bullets riddled building walls, car doors, lampposts, billboards, everywhere but inside the small nucleus of light.

Jillian looked back at the steadily approaching Land Rovers. Somewhere, through the chaos, she heard the voice. *Now, Jilly. Now they need you.*

Reacting instinctively, Jillian ran back to her car, turned the key with shaking hands, and careened wildly into the path of the oncoming tanks, stopping beside the two figures lying in the street. Frankie knelt on the pavement, holding the boy in his arms. "Get in!" she shouted at him, leaning across the seat to open the door.

He lifted a ravaged face to hers. "He's alive."

"We haven't much time." She forced herself to remain calm. "Get into the car. I'll take you to the Royal Victoria."

Somehow, she made him understand the urgency. Without another word, he climbed into the automobile.

Jillian never knew how long it took to drive through the angry streets of Belfast, but it seemed the longest journey of her life. She called ahead on the car phone and when she stopped at the emergency entrance to the hospital, a full retinue of doctors greeted them. Within minutes, Connor was stabilized and on his way to surgery.

Frankie was in shock. Even Jillian, inexperienced in medical science, knew what the blueness around his lips and the pallor of his complexion meant. Quickly, she called for help, slipped her arm around his waist, and led him to the waiting-room couch. A nurse and an orderly rolled in a gurney. Together they lifted him onto the clean white sheets and draped a blanket over his body. Then they wheeled him away.

Jillian looked at the cheerful picture-lined walls, at the stacks of colorful magazines arranged on the coffee table, at the coffee perking in its spot on the shelf. Then she sank down on the couch, rested her head in her hands, and wept.

24

Jillian's hand tightened on her cell phone. "I don't care where Mr. Flanagan is," she said tightly. "Either he returns my call within the hour, or I'll take steps to remove him from his position as chief of police."

The voice on the other end of the line was silent. "I'll relay your message," he said at last.

The doctor stepped into the waiting room. "The boy's injuries are not serious, Mrs. Graham. The bullet grazed his head, causing a concussion, nothing more. We'll watch him tonight and release him tomorrow morning."

Jillian closed her eyes. Then she opened them again, the picture of control. "How is Mr. Browne?"

"We've given him a sedative. He's sleeping."

"Does he know that Connor is out of danger?"

"Not yet."

"I'd like to tell him, if you don't mind."

"Of course. I'll show you to his room."

Jillian settled herself in a chair at the foot of Frankie's bed and prepared herself for a long wait. Frankie Maguire, sedated, his features relaxed in sleep, did not look at all like himself. He seemed younger, more vulnerable, the way he looked before he'd taken on the task of rescuing Northern Ireland from the British. What would he have been, she wondered, if circumstances had been different? He was well spoken and sensitive, an intelligent man, comfortable with animals and children. His manners were impeccable, and on occasion he had revealed a dry wit that surprised her. He was certainly adept at negotiating, reading between the lines, and isolating the pulse of an issue.

Everything else about his life was a mystery. She knew nothing about how he'd lived after he left Kilvara, the friendships he cultivated, the books he read, even the extent of his family besides Connor and Colette. He appeared athletic and knowledgeable about spectator sports, particularly boxing, but it wasn't an obsession with him. He drank his tea with milk and sugar, abstained from spirits, and, on occasion, smoked filtered cigarettes.

It was very little, really, the totality of a man and his parts. Certainly no reason for this all-consuming desire to ease his pain, to feel his glance from across the room, to connect beyond mere eyes and words, to sweep the hair back from his forehead, to feel the clean fineness of it slide between her fingers.

She drew a long, shuddering breath and deliberately focused her attention on the liquid dripping through the tube above his head. Clearly, for the first time in her life, she was besotted. After twenty-two uneventful years, she, Jillian Fitzgerald Graham, had found him again, the boy-turned-man whose smile shortened her breath and squeezed her heart into its present erratic rhythm. Ironically, he was the one man who despised everything she was. She laughed shortly, hysterically, remembered her place, laced her fingers tightly together, and brought her roiling emotions under control.

Mixed relationships were as common in other parts of the United Kingdom as they were in the rest of the world. Even Thomas Putnam's wife was Catholic. But in Northern Ireland, stepping outside one's faith for a mate was not encouraged. Only ten percent of the population married outside their religion. Frankie Maguire wasn't just a nationalist, he was a Sinn Fein nationalist, one of the chosen elite, elected to a council seat. His official position demanded that everyone having anything to do with the British occupation in Northern Ireland be consigned to the devil.

Jillian was not completely inexperienced. Because of her appearance, her wealth, and her family's position in society, she had been courted by a number of men before marrying Avery Graham. For the most part, they were charming, clever, and agreeable companions. But never once had she been inclined to do anything more than offer her lips in a chaste kiss before saying good night at her door.

There were times when she wondered if desire was something one was born with and if her requisite dosage had been misplaced or, worse, given to someone else. She knew that some women were cold. That explained the existence of the world's oldest profession. She'd read and heard enough to understand that many women did not enjoy sex to the same degree as their husbands did.

At times a restlessness claimed her, after a blatant invitation had been offered, when she'd admitted to a prurient curiosity and imagined what it would be like to take off her clothes and feel a man's body move over and inside her. But never had she wanted it enough to consider seriously acting on it, until tonight.

Her eyes flicked over Frankie's broad shoulders bordered by the hospital white of the sheets, lingering on his strong neck, his square chin, the slashing hollows below the bones of his cheeks, the black lashes resting on sun-dark skin. Jillian swallowed. She wanted Frankie Maguire, wanted him in ways she had never imagined wanting a man.

There was no hope for anything permanent. She understood enough of him to know he would reject that idea completely. However, he was a man, a man without a wife. And men had needs.

Jillian stood and walked to the side of the bed. Tentatively, she reached out to touch his cheek. The first signs of a new beard scratched her fingertips. She had needs as well. They were strong within her, especially one. It was madness really, even to think the thoughts working themselves into her head. She was a woman with no experience at all in seduction. But her time was running out. Nothing would be lost by asking. All he could say was no. Of course, she would have nothing left of pride or self-respect, and the tenuous friendship that had built up between them would be lost forever. "Nell," she whispered, "if ever I needed you, it's now. Please help me."

The tinny double ring of her cell phone interrupted her. She walked into the hall, pressed the receive button, and held it to her ear. "Jillian Graham," she said crisply.

"Ronnie Flanagan, here."

"Mr. Flanagan, I would like a full report on today's events in West Belfast, including the name of the person who authorized you to send Land Rovers into a peaceful assembly."

"Your information is incorrect, Mrs. Graham," the

police chief replied. "There were no tanks on the west side."

Rage drummed in her ears. "Listen carefully, Mr. Flanagan, and don't interrupt. I was there. Those bloody tanks were shooting at me. Now, either I receive an accurate report, faxed to my office within the hour, or I'll call the prime minister. Is that clear?"

"Aye," the clipped voice answered. "You'll have it."

Jillian switched off her phone and walked to the end of the hall to compose herself. When she reentered Frankie's room, he was awake.

Immediately, his eyes met hers. "How is Connor?"

"Recovering beautifully," she reassured him, moving to the side of the bed. "The bullet grazed his forehead, and he has a concussion. They want to keep him overnight and release him in the morning. He'll need a few days of quiet, but that's all." She wet her lips. "He was very lucky. You were both very lucky."

He nodded. His eyes were still on her face. "Thank you," he said. "I should have taken better care of him. If it hadn't been for you—"

She reached for his hand. His fingers closed around hers.

"Come home with me to Kildare," she said abruptly.

He stared at her, his expression unreadable.

"Connor needs rest. You've been working very hard. It's been a difficult time."

"No more than for you."

She looked down at her hands. "We could both use a holiday."

"Together?"

Color rose in her cheeks. "If you don't mind."

"Why are y' doing this, Jillian? Is it because of Colette?"

She was very aware of him. The question he posed

burned in his eyes. "It's not Colette," she whispered. "You said that you would come. Now seems like a good time."

Frankie knew it wasn't wise to see too much of her. Any fool would know better. But he was particularly vulnerable where she was concerned, and she knew all the right buttons to push. He was tired. He couldn't remember a time when he hadn't been tired. What would it be like to explore the rolling farm country of Kildare with Jillian again, where the stroll was more important than reaching a destination, where a woman's walk, like her conversation, had a languid, slow-moving grace? It was dangerous, but what wasn't? "Thank you," he said at last. "We'll be pleased t' come."

Frankie carried Connor up the wide staircase of Kildare Hall, through the door into a bedroom, and looked around. It was unlike any bedroom he had ever seen before. White clouds had been skillfully and realistically painted on robin's-egg blue walls. A white canopy stretched across a bed large enough for five children to sleep comfortably. Three mobiles with dancing cartoon figures hung from the ceiling. A box stuffed with toys, its lid left invitingly open, was pushed against the wall. Books, expensive hardbound copies of every children's story imaginable, lined the shelves. A rocking horse three feet high with real hair stood beside a life-size tin soldier, his arm raised protectively over a small table with dinosaur figures strategically placed across the top. A large television was mounted on the wall. Below it was a cabinet filled with tapes of animated children's videos. The colors red, white, and blue assaulted him from every angle.

He whistled a low, piercing note and set Connor on the bed. How could anyone sleep in such a room?

"It is a bit excessive, isn't it?" Jillian stood against the door, arms behind her back. "It was Casey's room a long time ago. We furnished it when she first came to us."

Frankie remained silent.

The color was high in her cheeks. "Perhaps it's too much."

Connor recovered first. His eyes sparkled. "Will this be my room?" he asked in a hushed whisper.

"Only if you like it," Jillian said quickly. "There are other rooms."

"I love it," replied the child reverently. "Please, Da. May I stay?"

Frankie looked down at the cherubic face leaning against his arm and relented. Poor little bloke. How could he ever give him this? Why not let him enjoy it while he had the chance? "Of course, you may stay," he said gently, "as long as Casey doesn't mind."

"She moved down the hall years ago," said Jillian. "I suppose I should have remodeled it, but there are other rooms, and I'd hoped—" She met Frankie's quizzical glance and faltered.

Mrs. Hyde poked her head through the door and smiled at Connor. "Welcome to Kildare, love. Shall I set everything to rights while Mrs. Graham shows your da to his room? I've two grandsons of my own," she assured Frankie.

Connor nodded. "Do you have chips today, Mrs. Hyde?"

"Connor," his father admonished him. "Whatever Mrs. Hyde is serving will be fine."

"It's all right, Mr. Browne. I've a basket of chips and a bite of fish all ready for the lad, if you don't mind. After all, it is almost tea time."

Frankie grinned. "So it is. Fish and chips sounds wonderful. Say thank you, Connor."

"Thank you."

Jillian crossed the room and leaned over the bed to kiss Connor on the cheek. Frankie could smell her perfume.

"Rest now, love," she said softly. "Your da will be back soon."

Frankie left his son to the redoubtable Mrs. Hyde and followed Jillian two doors down to a suite with a light, airy bedroom that looked down over the garden, a large modern bathroom, and a masculine sitting room furnished in muted colors and expensive period pieces.

"These were Avery's rooms," explained Jillian. "There are larger ones, but I thought you would want to be close to Connor."

They were separated by twelve feet, but never had the distance between them seemed greater. Frankie had never before stepped beyond the kitchen of Kildare Hall. Years ago, in the cozy glow of an old-fashioned cookstove, a woodburning oven, ice box, and pantry, all presided over by a woman from his own class, anything had seemed possible. He should have looked behind the swinging door to the long, glowing banquet table, the gleam of polished silver, the Persian carpets, the priceless paintings, and the rows of Fitzgerald ancestors peering down at him with their long English faces. He would have understood the limitations of his place long before and spared himself years of grief.

"Is it all right?" Jillian asked anxiously. "If not, I can—"

"The rooms are grand," he interrupted. "I'm sorry. If you'll give me a minute, I'll look in on Connor and meet you downstairs."

The hazel eyes lowered, hiding her thoughts. "Take as long as you like. There's no rush."

He'd offended her, or worse, hurt her feelings. "If

there's time," he said quickly before she closed the door, "I'd like to take a walk before tea."

"The paths are well marked. You won't get lost."

"Will you come with me?"

She looked startled, as if a man had never asked her such a thing before. He watched her gather herself and assume the Fitzgerald poise, expecting her to refuse him.

"I'd like that," she said. "I'll wait downstairs."

Frankie stared at the closed door for a long time. She'd agreed. Just like that. No coy glances through lowered lashes. No flirtatious smile or embarrassed stammer. Just a quiet acquiescence, an affirmation that she wanted his company as he wanted hers.

He ran his hand down his face and headed for the washroom. After a quick shave, he brushed his teeth and combed his hair. Rummaging through the cabinet, he found a bottle of expensive aftershave with the seal and price tag intact. Apparently, Avery Graham had discriminating tastes. He twisted off the lid, held the bottle to his nose, and applied it sparingly to his cheeks and chin. If she recognized the scent, he would tell the truth.

Connor was asleep. Frankie closed the door quietly and walked down the stairs. She waited for him in the drawing room, dressed in the same wide-legged beige slacks and white linen blouse she was wearing when he arrived. Her hair was twisted behind her head and held in place with something brown, the same brown that grew from her roots and lightened into varied streaks of toast and honey as it lengthened to her shoulders. Jillian had beautiful hair, the same hair she'd had as a child, thick and springy, milk chocolate in the shadows, dark blond where it caught the light.

"I checked on Connor," she said. "He's sleeping. Perhaps he'll be hungry later."

Frankie laughed. "He's always been a healthy eater. My food bills should be huge by the time he's twelve."

She slipped dark glasses on her head and came toward him. "Will he sleep through the night?"

He could see the poreless texture of her skin. English skin. "I don't know," he said slowly. "The medication tires him."

"Are you still in the mood for a walk?"

"Aye. Are you?"

She smiled. "Yes. Very much." He had sampled Avery's cologne, yet his smell was distinctively his own, a symphony that began loudly and slid into subtle tangling developments. The cologne had always been wasted on Avery, but then it was a scent designed to appeal to a woman, and, unlike Avery, Frankie had worn it for her. "Shall we go?"

They walked side by side. She was long-legged and used to hiking, but still, he shortened his stride to match hers. The hills posed no difficulty for him. His pace never changed, nor was he short of breath. Clearly, Frankie Maguire, the man, was comfortable out of doors, just as the boy had been. The Aran sweater and corduroy slacks he wore suited his lean, rangy frame, and his shoes were high at the ankle and thickly soled, ideal for hiking the roads of Ireland.

She led him through the hedgerow, single-file, to the path along the river. He stepped in front, climbed through first, and held out his hand to help her up the embankment. Jillian, who'd climbed the cliffs like a mountain goat from the time she could walk, reached up, placed her hand in his, and clung while he hoisted her through the shrubbery and up the hill. The path widened for a bit, and she was able to walk beside him again.

The silence had grown to the point where Jillian felt the need to speak, when he pulled her back against his chest and held his finger against her lips. "Shhh," he whispered, pointing to a thicket on the left. "Look."

Jillian stared into the darkest part of the thicket. At first, she couldn't see anything, but when her eyes adjusted to the dimness, she saw a silver fox with three kits, two red and one silver, still as statues, staring back at her. "Oh," she whispered, "I haven't seen the silver ones in years."

She felt his breath against her cheek when he spoke. "They're nearly extinct this far north. I haven't seen any since I was a child." He released her and once again moved to her side.

They'd climbed the bluff and looked down on the sun turning the river to liquid gold. Suddenly, it occurred to her that there might never be a better time to ask the question that had troubled her for weeks. Perhaps he would confide in her. She summoned her courage and spoke. "Why is it that no one seems to know anything about you, Danny? Have you always lived in Belfast?"

He pulled a strand of hair away from her mouth with his thumb. "A bit curious, are you?" he said lightly.

"More than a bit."

"May I ask why?"

She turned to face him. "Of course. As soon as you answer my question."

"And if I don't?"

Why didn't he recognize her? Jillian wasn't exactly a common name. "Are you hiding something, Danny?"

"Every man hides something from time to time."

"Not every man is so leery about answering a simple question."

The corner of his mouth turned up. "You can argue with the best of them, can't you, lass?"

She turned the full force of her meadow-green gaze on him. "Did you think I couldn't?"

He shook his head. "You're intelligent enough. But the spirit is bred out of you English girls, early on."

"You're changing the subject."

"Aye."

Did she dare ask him? Jillian took a deep breath. "I want to ask you a question. It's a favor, really. But unless you trust me, it won't work."

His heartbeat accelerated. "You want a favor from *me?*"

"Yes."

He was silent for several minutes. Her fists were clenched so hard that her nails dug painfully into her palms. When at last he spoke, her relief was so great she nearly collapsed.

"You befriended my wife when she needed you most. You saved Connor's life and mine. There isn't anything I wouldn't do for you, lass."

She waved her hand as if to brush aside his reasoning. "This isn't about Colette or Connor."

"What is it about?"

Jillian cleared her throat and mentally cursed the color that rose in her fair skin. It was now or never. "Do you fancy me, Danny?"

He froze. Something was happening, and he hadn't the slightest notion of how to prepare for it. Her question demanded an answer. "You're not hard on the eyes, if that's what y' mean," he said warily.

She nodded. "That's what I mean, part of it, anyway." She swallowed. "You don't find me repulsive or unfeminine or anything like that?"

"Lord, Jilly." He was trying to control his laughter.

"What a question, lass. Don't y' ever look in a mirror? There must be men right now asking themselves how soon would be the proper time to start queuing up at your door."

She looked up. "I know that I'm attractive. I need to know if *you* think so."

Every survival instinct immediately kicked in. He swallowed. "If that's what all this is about, yes, I find you attractive. Any man would. Even one who buried his wife not yet four weeks ago."

It was a warning. She heard it but chose to disregard it. Now came the hard part. There was nothing else to do but say it, now, before she lost her nerve. "I want to have a child."

His stomach twisted. "You have one."

She corrected herself. "I want to bear a child."

"What's stoppin' you, other than your political appointment, the state of our country, and the fact that you no longer have a husband? But maybe you've already chosen his successor."

Ignoring his sarcasm, she shook her head and forced out the words. "No. I need a man."

A muscle throbbed in his cheek. This couldn't be happening, not to him, not coming from her. "There are plenty to go around."

"I want—"

"Don't say it," he said savagely. His hands reached out, hard and hurting, on her shoulders. "Don't you dare say it."

"Danny," she said brokenly. "You know what I'm asking."

"Aye," he said, his face lit with rage. "I know what you're askin', and it's lucky you are that I don't have it in me to murder a woman." He shook her slightly, released her, and stepped back. "Do y' think because

I'm poor and Irish that you can use me? Do y' think I have no feelings for my own, that I can spill my seed, sire a child, and walk away? Did y' learn nothin' from Colette? Have y' not seen me with my son? I worship the bloody ground he walks on. Do y' think I could father a child and not have anything t' do with the raisin' of him?" His hands clenched. "Were y' born with a lump of ice instead of a heart, Jillian Graham, or did something happen to make y' the way you are?"

He didn't expect her to answer, but again she surprised him. "You're underestimating yourself. Perhaps it's you who doesn't look in the mirror." She pressed the back of her hand against her nose and sniffed. Then she laughed softly and shook her head. "You don't know very much about women, Danny, if you think I want you only for your semen." Her voice shook. She stopped, cleared her throat, and tried again. "Colette was my friend. She told me how it was between you since the shooting. I mean her no disrespect, but I didn't ask you as a last resort. I'm thirty-five years old. Men have told me they wanted me since before I understood what that meant. I've never been in love. I could fall in love with you, if only you would give me the chance."

He stared at her, stricken into speechlessness, despair warring with the bubble in his chest that he recognized as hope, delirious, impossible hope.

Jillian straightened to her full height and looked directly at him. "I'm going home, Danny. My room is on the second floor, the last one on the right. If you don't come, I'll understand."

His eyes watched the white blur that was her shirt until it disappeared over the rise.

"Jilly," he whispered. "Dear God, Jilly. What in the name of heaven am I goin' t' do with you?"

25

Jillian belted the sash of her robe around her waist and ran her fingers through her shower-damp hair. Avoiding the mirror, she turned off the light and walked into the darkened bedroom, relieved to see that only a small turf fire blazing in the hearth lit the room. She had humiliated herself beyond all limits and could not yet bear to look at her reflection. What had come over her? If her mother knew, she would have her committed. Not that she would ever know, of course, but if she did—

Jillian shuddered, threw herself onto the bed, and stared at the ceiling, her cheeks burning. She had wanted him to know her, to remember as she did. Dear God, how would she face him tomorrow? How would she face anyone?

A voice, familiar and amused, rose from the foot of the bed. *You're being absurd.*

"Nell," Jillian whispered. "Where are you?"

Here. A willowy feminine form materialized before

the armoire. Her hand reached out to touch the beveled glass mirror. *What a lovely thing. 'Tis so clear, like the calmest pool.*

"It's a mirror. You must have them."

Of course. But not like this. She leaned closer. *Is that really me?*

"I thought ghosts didn't have reflections."

Nell looked offended. *I'm not a ghost, and as far as I know, there is no protocol for ghosts.*

"What are you, then?"

Nell sniffed. *Certainly not a ghost.*

"I've done something dreadful," Jillian confessed.

I wouldn't call it dreadful.

"Were you there?"

Not really. Let us say that I am aware when you do something particularly unusual such as that fiasco in the street yesterday. Nell walked to the dressing table and sat down on the low stool to peer at herself in the mirror. She picked up a bottle of perfume and inspected it. Experimenting, she pushed down the lid, rearing back in surprise when the concentrated fragrance shot directly into her nasal passages. *My goodness.*

Against her will, Jillian laughed. "I know you have perfume."

Nell set down the bottle carefully. *Is that what it is?*

Jillian moaned, turned over, and buried her face in the pillow.

Listen to me, Jillian. Nell's voice was close to her ear. *To tell a man that you want him in your bed isn't such a terrible thing. Rather, it will make him take notice where he didn't before. Mark my words, he is thinking of you and what you offered this very moment. He would not be a man if he were not.*

Jillian rolled over. "Do you really think so?"

Open your eyes, love. I know what it is you want. You'll

find more than enough to surprise you. Nell smiled. *Take
a bit of that perfume, and dab it—* She leaned close to
whisper in Jillian's ear and laughed when she blushed.
Then she stood.

"Are you leaving?"

I'll only be in the way.

"Goodbye, Nell."

*There is something else, Jillian, something you don't un-
derstand. But it will wait, for now.*

Jillian blinked, struck with a wave of myopia. Nell's
figure blurred at the edges. Her features were no longer
clearly defined. For an instant, the fire leaped and spit
behind the grate, throwing arcs of light against the walls
before it died down again.

Frankie crossed his arms and leaned against the garden gate, his eyes on the figure silhouetted in the bedroom window. He knew the room was Jillian's. It was
the same one she had as a child.

He shouldn't have tempted fate. He should have
stayed away from Kildare Hall, but the idea of revisiting
the site where he had spent his happiest hours weakened
his resolve. That he would be near Jillian had nothing
to do with his irrational desire to step back into the
past, or at least it hadn't, he told himself, until she
mentioned her harebrained scheme to requisition his
gene pool for her own purposes.

Now that she had, he couldn't get past it. She was
smart enough to know how it would affect him. He was
a man who'd been too long without a woman. And
when a man knows that a woman looks at him that way,
he can't help but wonder what it would be like just
once to— His jaw clenched, and he bit down on the
soft inside of his cheek. "Damn you, Jillian," he mut-

tered under his breath. "I was willing to leave it alone. Now, look what you've done t' me."

It was late, after eleven. He'd stayed out for hours, haunting the roads he'd traveled as a boy, arguing with himself, reliving her words, imagining what it would be like to have her beneath him, her arms reaching out to pull him close, her lips and legs willingly parting for him. Now he was spent, his decision made, if only his body would cooperate.

His shoes made no sound as he climbed the stairs and looked in on his son. Pillowed against the soft down duvet, Connor's black head contrasted sharply with the white behind it. His arm curled under his sturdy body, and his chest rose and fell in the healthy rhythms of sleep. No help there. If Connor had his way, he would take up residence in the Kildare stables with Ned, the kennel keeper. Frankie's mouth twisted at the corners. He couldn't blame the lad for that. Love for the gentle golden dogs was in his blood.

Farther down the hall, his hands began to shake. Frankie leaned against the wall outside Jillian's room and struggled to control himself. How much was it possible to want a woman? It was as if all the years between had disappeared and he was a boy again, this time without the blindfolds. He would give Jillian Fitzgerald something of what she wanted, but only because he wanted it, too. And he would leave no part of himself behind to be raised as an English Protestant. Perhaps, when he told her, and he would tell her all of it, she would reconsider, erect that barrier of cool Fitzgerald pride, and refuse him.

He feared that less than the other possibility, the one where she was more woman than he'd ever hoped to have, where she would welcome him with loving words and worshiping hands no matter who he was or what he'd done, where she begged him to stay, offering her body and her heart and her home, unconditionally, the same little girl who'd said so long ago, "Then I'll be a Catholic, too."

It was past time to find out who waited for him in the darkened room, cozy with firelight. Heart hammering in his chest, he turned the knob and stepped inside.

She was sitting up in bed, facing the windows. Her arms were wrapped around her legs, her chin on her knees, and she wore something white and sleeveless.

Soft music from the stereo system muted the sound of his entrance. The door clicked softly when he closed and locked it. She didn't turn around. He settled back into the shadows to look at her, really look at her, for as long as he could stand it.

Her shoulders were slender and summer-tanned, the smooth muscles defined by her clasped hands. The delicate material of her nightgown covered generous breasts and long, shapely legs. She was tall. He preferred tall women. They were easier to dance with. He'd always fancied brunettes, but now he was sure there had never been anything as lovely as the way the light played on Jillian's hair, coloring the tousled strands whiskey gold, amber, and palest wheat.

Shining hair, slow-falling hair, bare shoulders, a naked back. Innocence, independence, seduction, had never been better combined. He noticed everything, his infatuation feeding insatiably on the sap rising within him. He needed this, all of it, her hair and skin, the freckles scattered across her nose and cheeks, the faintest scent of lilacs, the desire opening her face. If she would only look at him. Perhaps he would live after all.

She turned and looked directly into his eyes. He saw

the pink flood her cheeks and heard her words airy and breathless. "You came after all."

He nodded, making it easy for her. "Aye. How could I not?"

She watched him cross the room and sit beside her on the bed, her eyes wide and dark in the dim light. "I didn't think you would."

Inside him, the wanting roared, desperately, painfully, unleashed from its restraints. How could he have wanted so and pretended otherwise? Deliberately, he picked up her hand and pressed his mouth and then his tongue against her palm. He felt her tremble, saw her close her eyes and lean her head back against the pillows, saw her throat, long and lovely and exposed. He touched his lips to the smooth skin, heard the sharp intake of her breath, felt the softness of her breasts under his hands, and gave himself up to the power of his wanting.

Filling his hands with her hair, he breathed in her scent, opened her beautiful, sensual mouth with his tongue, tasting and exploring her lips, the hollow at her throat, the swells of her breasts, the dip of her waist, the curve of her hips, and the exciting, forbidden heat between her legs. He pulled away to look at her, to drink in eyes and legs and mouth and hair, the parts of her that had the power to send him over the edge.

"Kiss me again," she whispered, offering her mouth. "Kiss me now."

The kiss began as soft and searching, and then it wasn't soft at all. It was hard and dangerous and passionate, and when it was over, he leaned into her, his hands seeking out places where only a lover's hands may settle. "Now, this," he said softly, working at the buttons of her nightgown until they were undone and she lay naked and waiting and wanting while he looked and stroked and licked and sucked, all the while whispering words she'd never heard before.

"My God, Jilly," he said hoarsely against her throat. "I've no brain left t' speak of, and I'm thinking with the only part of me that has blood left in my body. Tell me you're ready for me, lass."

Her answer was to press against him, open her legs, and whisper into his ear, "I've always been ready for you."

He had no words left in him. Quickly, efficiently, he removed his clothes, dropped them by the bed, and knelt over her.

Jillian reached up to pull his head down, to trace his lips with her tongue. She felt the ridges expand on his shoulders and neck. He entered her all at once, filling her completely. For a timeless instant, she tensed and he stilled. Then she relaxed, and her tongue slipped inside his mouth.

With a low groan, he thrust deeply, matching her rhythm.

He heard her whisper softly in his ear and strained to hear her. "Please," the breathless voice pleaded with him. "I want you so much. Please, know me."

"I know you, lass," he murmured against her throat. "I never stopped knowin' you." The ache of withdrawal and the dizzying pleasure of her hot woman's flesh closing around him were too much, and for the first time in two years, he came, explosively, inside a woman.

"Jilly," he said, much later when it was finished and the soft body beneath his was beginning to arouse him again, "whatever am I going t' do with you?"

She didn't answer but looked up at him with wide, knowing eyes.

He couldn't help himself. "It was your first time, wasn't it?"

"Yes." It never occurred to her to lie. He was leaning on his elbow, and she was fascinated by the differences between them. How odd that women's bodies were immortalized when a man could look like this.

"My God, Jilly. Where have you been, a nineties woman like yourself?"

"I waited for you."

His face changed. Could she possibly mean it? Impossible. The hope rising in his chest flickered and died out. "Don't say that."

"All right," she said, keeping her eyes on his face. "I won't. What shall I say?"

He slid his hand possessively over her body and let it rest on the underside of her breast. "Say that you want me again."

She would say anything to feel him inside her again. Her voice was husky, alluring, impossible to resist. "I want you again."

The day dawned, warm and clear, the summer air spiced with the smells of growing things. Jillian stretched, felt the soreness between her legs, remembered, and reached out to touch him. He was gone. She opened her eyes and sat up. Through the long windows, she saw a figure moving across the downs, four collie pups leaping and wrestling, running to catch up with his long stride. She looked at the clock on the mantel. Ned wasn't due for another two hours. Besides, the kennel keeper had never moved like that, with a smooth, confident arrogance that ate up the ground.

She swung her legs over the bed. Barefoot, she tiptoed down the stairs and out the door, down the winding drive, through the organized garden paths, to the downs. Beneath her feet, the grass was wet with dew. She leaned against the trunk of a leafy black oak and watched Frankie Maguire throw sticks for the frolicking collies to bring back to him.

Behind her, deep in the shadows, Nell Fitzgerald waited and watched and remembered another time, another black-haired young man. Then she shook off the memory. It was their time, Frankie's and Jillian's, the two of them, time for their lives to come full circle. She would help if necessary, but experience told her not to underestimate the powers of love.

A breeze touched Jillian's face, touched her hair above her forehead. The day was already unusually hot. She watched the scene before her. It seemed to unfold in slow motion, a black-haired man, his sleeves rolled up, corduroy trousers loose and low on his hips. The pups jumped on him, and he laughed, his long, beautiful hands stroking their white bibs. She heard the laugh, saw the play of ropy muscles under his shirt and the deeply tanned skin on his arms, and her throat closed. Slowly, she moved into the sunlight.

He felt her eyes on him, turned, and watched her walk toward him, a honey-colored blonde in a sleeveless white nightgown, stained because of him and what they'd done together

He waited while she walked toward him.

"Hello, Jilly," he said softly.

She saw it there, in his eyes, and her heart burst. "Hello, Frankie."

"When did you know?"

"From the moment I saw you again in Colette's room at the hospital. When did you know?"

"I've always known," he said simply. "I've kept up with you over the years."

Jillian laughed shakily. "All this time, I thought— Why didn't you tell me?"

"I was afraid you would send me away."

Her mouth trembled, and she looked away. Had there ever been a case of such mixed messages? "When did you change your mind?"

He ached to touch her, to smooth her hair and taste her mouth and feel the delicious length of her against him again. "About what?"

"I asked you to give me a child," she reminded him.

"Oh, that." He reached down and scooped a pup into his arms, scratched its neck, and set it down again. She'd known who he was all the time, and still she'd asked him. "I haven't changed my mind."

Jillian's eyes widened. "You did nothing to stop it."

He grinned, and her heart melted. "I had good intentions, but I couldn't help myself." His smile faded. "I never expected you t' be untouched. Would you mind explainin' that one?"

She shrugged. "Avery didn't care for women."

He nodded. "I suspected that. But you were twenty-five when he married you. Why wasn't there anyone before him?"

Jillian lifted her chin. "That's none of your business, Frankie Maguire. Maybe no one wanted me."

Startled, he stared at her, a woman not afraid to show vulnerability and desire, who covered the ground like a dancer in slow motion, whose eyes and legs and mouth were carved indelibly on a man's brain until he was caught in her rhythms without understanding why. "You're insane," he said deliberately.

"Thank you."

His lips twitched. He threw back his head and laughed. It was good, so good, to hear his name again. That it should come from her was even better. Jillian Graham was still Jilly Fitzgerald, the smart-mouthed little miss who had once been her mother's cross to bear.

"What is so funny?"

He shook his head.

"Are you sorry?" she demanded, her hand a knuckled fist planted at her waist.

Frankie was no longer laughing. "No, lass. I'm not sorry."

"What if there's a child?"

A muscle jumped in his cheek. "Is the timing right?"

"Yes."

"Why me?"

Her eyes fixed on the top button of his shirt, where the pale blue fabric opened against the brown of his neck. She swallowed. "What do you mean?"

He crossed the distance between them and reached for her hand, feeling the delicate bones, a lady's hand. It had been only a matter of hours, and yet it seemed a lifetime since he'd touched her. "Unless I'm mistaken, it's not just a body to father a child you're askin' for."

"Yes," she said, "it is."

"How did you intend to go about it, Jilly?" he began conversationally. "Did you mean to take your clothes off and slide between the sheets with me the way we did, skin to skin, or did you mean to go about it clinically and expose just the body parts we'd be usin'?"

Her cheeks burned. "I hadn't thought that far."

"Sure you have, lass. You've enough imagination for that. If it's the way I think you mean, first there's a certain amount of familiarity and settlin' in. A man needs a bit of an invitation." He rubbed his thumb across her lips. "You have a beautiful mouth, Jilly, the kind of mouth that stops a man's eyes from leavin' your face. A mouth like yours is why we first painted on cave walls."

He touched that mouth with his lips, and somehow she was in his arms. His voice lowered, and his hands moved to the swells of her breasts. "These are pure fantasy," he murmured, lifting her gown to her waist, "and so is this." He touched her briefly between her legs.

She was hypnotized by his voice and the feel of his hands on her skin. He lowered her to the ground. The grass was cool on her back, and she felt him, urgent and hard, against her. Somehow she knew to stroke the length of him behind the soft corduroy, to slip the button out of its hole, to draw the zipper down, to push the fabric below his hips, to take him in her hand and squeeze gently.

He muttered an expletive in Irish, and she froze, terrified that she'd done something wrong. His breath stirred the hair on her temple. "Touch me, love. Don't stop. Sweet Jesus, Jilly. You're turnin' me inside out. Don't stop now."

"I want you, Frankie," she said, wrapping her hand around him, guiding him into her. "I want you inside me. I think I've waited my whole life for this."

Frankie closed his eyes, opened his mouth against hers, and drove into her over and over until everything he knew beyond this moment and this woman no longer mattered.

The sun warmed his back. Frankie stirred and looked down at Jillian wrapped securely in his arms. She looked back at him, a question in her eyes. He kissed her brow and the freckles on her nose. "You see, love," he said, "it's not just the passing of seed. You want something more intimate than that, and you want it with me. If you didn't, you'd go to some clinic and pick a test tube filled by an anonymous donor."

"What if there's a child? What then?"

"God help us both when we're found out. But I'm

not going away. If there's a child, I want you t' marry me."

"And if there isn't?"

His mouth tightened.

"Never mind," she said before he could answer. She pushed at his chest and he shifted to accommodate her.

"It isn't what you think," he said.

"What do I think?"

"That we were born to different situations, and I'm too proud to find a way around the differences between us."

"What is it, then?"

He hesitated, rolled over, and rested his head on the bend of his elbow.

She waited.

"Colette," he said at last, telling her only half the truth. "It's disrespectful to her memory."

"Colette is dead."

Frankie shook his head. "Not to me. Not yet."

Sitting up, Jillian fought against the hurting his words brought and pulled the nightgown down over her hips. He'd been hers first, long before Colette. "I want to know what happened to you. Why are you living under a different name?"

He sighed and hitched up his trousers. "It's a complicated story."

"We have a week, and I have a right to know."

He reached up and brushed her jaw with his thumb. "You, more than anyone, have a right to know. I'll not argue with that."

The tenderness in his voice nearly undid her. "Will you tell me?"

"Aye, lass. I'll tell you."

26

This changes things, you know," she said after he'd relayed the major events of the last twenty years of his life, beginning with his sentence to Long Kesh and ending with his appointment as chief negotiator for Sinn Fein.

Frankie's eyebrows rose. "How so?"

She looked at him, a graceful turning of her lovely neck. "You can't be part of a negotiated agreement. This isn't 1921, Frankie. All signatures will be verified. You aren't who you say you are. Any document that you sign won't be legally binding."

"It isn't impossible to assume a new identity. By necessity, many of us have become adept at it."

"They'll want school records, a certificate of baptism. If they find you, and they will, you'll go back to prison."

"You'll have to trust me with this one, Jillian."

She folded her hands and squeezed them tightly together. "I wish you would reconsider."

"I know."

Jillian bit her lip and looked away. They were in the garden, the wild, overgrown part where roses, huge and heavy with perfume, were never pruned but allowed to grow riotously, gloriously, with no particular plan or direction. Herbs climbed the trellises and through the weeds, wildflowers bloomed in rich, colorful profusion, and in the middle of the brilliant foliage, like minks in a den, the puppies slept, curled around one another in a patch of sunlight. "Did Kathleen ever try to reach you?"

"Aye." Frankie looked down at his hands. They were curled into fists. "She's dead now. The news didn't surprise me, not after the life she chose. She'd given up the baby, a girl. I found her for all the good it did me." The bitterness harshened his voice. "She was adopted. That's all I know."

Jillian could barely form the words. She should tell him, now, before it went any further. "Perhaps she's with a good family," she began.

"She is my flesh and blood," Frankie said tersely, "the only family I have left except for Connor and Tim. She probably thinks no one of her own wanted her."

Jillian's eyes flashed. "Perhaps she's not thinking that at all. Perhaps she's with people who do want her and who are giving her a better life than you could ever have."

He knew what he'd done the instant the words left his mouth. "Ah, Jilly. I've put my big Irish foot in it again, haven't I? Forgive me, lass. I'd forgotten that Casey is adopted."

She nodded, but her smile was wooden.

"After Da died and Kathleen disappeared, I promised myself that I'd find her, t' see if she's content."

Jillian could see the outline of his balled fist inside

his trouser pocket. She was beginning to understand. Frankie Maguire took care of his own. He was a nurturer, forced by circumstance into other roles but always true to the one that suited him best. First there had been Kathleen, later Colette and her son, and now Connor. She knew that if she, too, required the cloak of his care, Frankie would provide it. The only one unaccounted for was his niece and hers, Kathleen's daughter.

Jillian's hand rose to her throat and rested there. How would he feel when he learned that she had taken it upon herself to do what he could not?

She took a deep breath and released it. Amazingly, he laughed. "It's a serious turn we've taken, isn't it?" he teased her. "Enough true confessions. Why not let the rest of it go and enjoy the dogs and this rare sunshine?"

Jillian's heart flipped over. His smile was a weapon that he used to a dreadful advantage. "I have something to tell you, Frankie. I hope you'll be pleased—"

A sharp whistle interrupted her. The pups leaped to life, running toward the kennel. "It's Ned. I didn't realize it was so late. We should see about breakfast."

"Might I ask what y've been doing, that started up such an appetite, Mrs. Graham?" His eyes twinkled, and the Irish was thick as cream on his tongue.

She looked down at her body, very visible beneath the fine lawn of her nightgown, and blushed. "I think I'd better go inside. No," she said when he started to rise. "Let me go first. In case we see someone."

"Ashamed of me, Jilly?"

Her eyes met his, flared, and locked. "I was thinking of Connor. You're the one who said it was too soon."

His skin darkened beneath his tan. "My apologies, lass," he said softly. "I was thinkin' of other things."

Their glances held briefly. Then she nodded, and he

watched her walk away. Frankie looked at the sky, estimated that it would be at least fourteen hours until sundown, cursed softly, and followed her into the house.

A completely recovered Connor met him on the stairs. "Mrs. Hyde says Casey is comin' home tomorrow night," he confided to his father. "It's her birthday."

Frankie reached for his son, lifted him high into the air, and then brought him close to his chest. "Won't that be grand for all of us?"

Connor nodded. "Casey likes me. She said so."

"Of course she does," agreed Frankie. "Have you eaten, lad?"

"No." Connor shook his head. "I waited for you. Mrs. Hyde said you were down in the garden with Jilly."

Frankie winced. So much for discretion. "Perhaps you should call her Mrs. Graham."

Connor frowned. "I like Jilly. She told me it was her name."

Frankie sighed. "If it's already settled between you, I won't bother with it." He brushed the bandage on the boy's temple. "How's your head? Still a bit sore?"

"A wee bit, when I'm tired, but not now," he assured his father.

"Shall we wash for breakfast?"

Connor frowned. "Mrs. Hyde already tried t' wash me, but I told her I could do it myself."

Frankie stifled a grin. "Perhaps she's not accustomed to lads like yourself."

"Perhaps." He smiled impishly. "She does make wonderful biscuits, much better than Mrs. Flynn's. If I'm very good, she says I may have two."

"That's an incentive if I've ever heard one." Frankie

mussed the boy's shining hair. "Run along now, and let me wash."

Jillian stepped out of her door just as Frankie was about to walk into his room. His glance moved approvingly over her slim-fitting olive slacks and the creamy sleeveless blouse she wore tucked in. Tawny hair hung loose to her shoulders. "That didn't take long," he said softly.

Her mouth curved. "I'm a natural beauty, or haven't you noticed?"

She was flirting with him, as if they were two ordinary people and anything was possible. He couldn't resist her. "I've noticed," he said, his hand reaching out to close around her arm and pull her into his room, closing the door behind them. Gathering her close, he lowered his head to her mouth and kissed her, leisurely, the way he'd always wanted to, as if he had nothing more to do than explore the delicious feel of her mouth under his.

Jillian felt the privacy of the room surround her, and she relaxed, allowing her body to fit against him, filling his spaces. Soon she would tell him about Casey. But not now, not like this. Sliding her arms around his neck, she opened under his kiss.

Reluctantly, he lifted his head. "I need ten minutes."

She stared blankly.

"Breakfast."

"Of course." Reaching behind her, she turned the knob. "I'll entertain Connor."

The finger tracks in his hair were still wet from the shower when he sat down at the table. Jillian was listening with the appropriate amount of interest to Connor's rendition of a typical weekend in the streets of West Belfast.

"Jimmy and I play with the big boys near the cannery."

"Is Jimmy your friend?" Jillian asked.

"Aye, Jimmy Donovan." Connor licked a spot of jelly from the blade of his knife.

"Connor, mind your manners." his father cautioned him.

"We play at hurling," the boy continued, "except when Kevin wants the ball."

"Kevin?"

"Jimmy's brother. He's big," he said as if that explained everything.

Jillian nodded. "What do you do if Kevin wants the ball?"

Connor grinned. "We go into the hills and shoot birds."

"What?"

Frankie heard the panic in her voice and considered it an auspicious time to step in. "Tell Jilly how many birds you've bagged."

"None yet. We've only sling-shots, you see."

She did see. Quickly, she lifted her napkin to her mouth to hide her smile.

"Mrs. Flynn thinks I'm wicked t' do such a thing."

"Do you think it's wicked?" Jillian asked him.

Connor tilted his head to consider her question. Then he ran his tongue over his lips and rested it against the corner of his mouth. "Fox hunting is even more wicked."

"I suppose it is," she replied thoughtfully, remembering her father's pleasure in leading the first hunt of every season. Kildare was horse country, and every Fitzgerald could ride to the hounds. "Perhaps shooting at inanimate objects would be better."

Connor wrestled with the ham on his plate, gave up,

and picked up a sausage with his fingers. "What's that?"

Jillian leaned across the table and cut his ham into bite-size pieces. "Something that isn't alive and feels no pain."

"Those don't move," he said scornfully.

"Then you'll be able to hit them, won't you?"

Connor's eyebrows rose, an arrested expression on his face.

His father laughed. "She's caught you up neatly, lad. Think about it."

"Jilly, may I ride one of the ponies? Ned says I may if I ask you first."

"Your father is the one to ask, love."

"May I, Da?"

Frankie nodded. "Only if Ned stays with you and it isn't too much trouble. I wouldn't want that head of yours to open up again. After you rest a bit, maybe Jilly will take us fishin' down at the burn."

Connor's eyes widened with the kind of rapture Jillian remembered from her own childhood. "Will you, Jilly?"

Jillian laughed. "Of course, and after that, you can help Ned and your da with the dogs."

"You're very lucky," he said solemnly, the blue eyes very serious.

"Why is that?"

"To live in this grand place with horses and dogs."

Jillian's heart swelled. "We've chickens, too," she said when she'd collected her emotions. "If you wake up early enough, I'll show you how to feed them."

Connor grinned and ran through the door, the sound of his footsteps echoing on the wooden floors.

Suddenly self-conscious, Jillian concentrated on pouring exactly the right amount of milk into her cup before adding the tea.

"You should have had children," Frankie said softly. "A dozen of them."

She laughed. "Maybe not a dozen. A few would be nice."

"I'll try and oblige."

Embarrassment forgotten, she stared at him across the table. "Don't joke, Frankie, not about this."

"I wouldn't do that."

"Are you suggesting that we—" She stopped, wet her lips, and began again. "Avery died five weeks ago. It wouldn't be a tremendous leap for people to believe he left me pregnant."

His eyes were a cold gun-metal gray. "My child will never carry Avery Graham's name."

Jillian lifted her chin. "You told me that, for you, Colette was still alive."

"I also told you if there was a child, we would marry."

"Then we won't have one."

"It may be too late."

She balled the linen napkin in her fingers, threw it down on the table, and stood. "I married someone who didn't want me the way a man wants a woman. I won't do it again."

"Don't be daft." The muscle along his jaw throbbed. "You know perfectly well what y' do t' me. You've known it all along." He noted the trembling lips, the flutter in her throat, the clenched hands. His eyes narrowed. "In fact, I've a good mind to take y' back up those stairs with me and show you exactly what I mean." He rose from the table and slowly, predatorially, walked around to where she stood. She offered no resistance when his hands framed her face. And when his mouth covered hers, she slid her arms around his neck to deepen his kiss.

Jillian leaned back on her arms and lifted her face to the sun. Connor's head was pillowed in her lap, his chest rising and falling in the throes of sleep. Frankie stretched out beside her, eyes half closed, arms clasped behind his head. Below them in the clear depths of the stream, three trout were securely tied to a length of fishing line wound around a stake. The trickle of the current camouflaged most of the natural noises, but Frankie could hear the droning of bees, the call of a curlew, and the rustle of leaves as squirrels cavorted in their soft playground. Country sounds, light-years away from the roar of Belfast.

She spoke softly for fear of waking Connor. "Have you given up your dream of healing animals?"

"For the time being. If I'm not too decrepit by the time this mess is over, perhaps I'll go on to university and earn my degree."

"Why not do it now?"

"I'm no one, Jillian. I've no school records, no examination scores. The prisoners would have to be freed before I could begin to think of such a thing."

"Do you still want it?"

He was silent for a long time. She thought he'd fallen asleep. "Aye," he said at last. "I want it even more than I did yesterday."

Intrigued, she looked down at him. His eyes were closed, the dark sweep of lashes resting against his cheeks. "Why?"

"There's more at stake now," he answered. "It would mean I could be Frankie Maguire again. I could find my niece, give Connor his proper name." His eyes were open now, silver and very clear. "There wouldn't be so much between us."

She wet her lips. "That part shouldn't matter. After all, I know who you are."

"You always were a loyal little miss. But it doesn't work that way for people like you. Your family is an important one. Things will come out. It won't be easy, Jilly. There's the chance y' might have t' give all of this up. How would I feel ten years from now when you decide it isn't worth it?"

"And yet you're willing to risk all of it if there's a child. I don't understand."

"Children are all we've got. They're all that's important. It's how we go on. I won't have a child of mine not know who I am, what I am, or who came before him. That's why I can't give up my seed for Avery Graham t' claim the credit, no matter how fair and principled a man he was."

Jilly drew a deep breath. It was time to tell him about Casey. She opened her mouth to begin. Connor stirred on her lap, turned his head to the other side, and drifted off again. Jillian stroked his forehead. Perhaps it was better to wait a bit longer, when Connor was somewhere else. "He's a dear lad," Jilly said softly.

"Aye," agreed Frankie. "He is, indeed."

Casey saw the barricade through the trees and immediately applied the brakes as she rounded the curve. Throwing her arm across the back of the seat, she slid the lever into reverse. Before she could move, four men, their faces hidden behind black balaclavas, cut her off from behind. Three more came toward her on foot. Sighing, she released the wheel and waited for them to approach the car.

"Papers, please," the tall one with the light hair asked politely.

Casey reached into her purse and handed over her license. "What's happened?"

The man stared at her license, looking from the picture on the card to Casey's face and back again. She was a pretty thing. He wondered how long it would take her to recognize his voice. "Four Catholic murders by the UDF," he said gruffly. "We're not allowing anyone through unless we know who they are."

Her eyes widened. "Tim, is that you?" she asked incredulously.

"You're mistaken." He handed over her license and backed away. "Go ahead."

Instead, she opened the door and followed him. "Tim Sheehan, I know it's you. Come back here and explain yourself."

He broke into a run and melted into the trees. The men with him formed a single line blocking her view.

"I know that man," she appealed to them, a petite brunette with wild curls and gray-green eyes. "He's a friend of mine."

"If that's so, miss, you wouldn't want to be bringin' him any trouble, now, would you? Just get back into that fine automobile and be on your way."

"Tim!" Casey shouted into the trees. "Don't do this." Minutes passed. Defeated, Casey gave up, climbed back into her car, and drove slowly past the barricade. Why was Tim Sheehan, of all people, carrying an automatic rifle with a balaclava covering his face?

She would have known him anywhere. For the past six months, he had been her mathematics tutor. The abstracts of physics and computer science came much more easily to him than to her, and her exam results proved how effective he was. Casey had strongly resisted his suggestion that she no longer needed his services until he made her understand that there were other services he would much rather provide. That was two months ago. They had seen each other every day, until his mother's funeral. Tim had simply dropped off the face of the earth, leaving no forwarding address.

Seeing him here like this explained a great deal, but not everything. College students weren't ordinarily recruited by the Irish Republican Army. Perhaps she didn't know him after all.

The great iron gates of Kildare were open as usual. Casey negotiated the turn and drove slowly down the winding road to the house. In the front pasture, golden milk cows chewed on the rich summer grass, and in the back, sleek thoroughbreds whisked flies away with thick, shining tails. Where the sun dipped into the bosom of the downs, Connor Browne frolicked with the newest litter of collie puppies while his father and Jillian talked nearby. Casey smiled. She was home. Her mother looked happy, and there would be company for dinner. It was as good a time as any to share her news.

The spring lamb with mint was Mrs. Hyde's masterpiece. She served it with new potatoes, garden peas, and a fresh tomato salad. Chocolate cake, Casey's favorite, would be the grand finale.

Connor's mouth formed itself into the shape of a perfect circle when Mrs. Hyde brought in the cake ablaze with twenty-one candles. Casey glanced across the table at the longing in his blue eyes and held out her arms. "Come here," she said. "I need a bit of help with these. Will you blow them out with me?"

His face lit, and within seconds he was seated between Casey's knees, his eyes on the dancing teardrop flames before him.

"Make a wish," said Jillian. "Count to three and blow."

Connor closed his eyes and breathed in while Casey counted. On three, they blew together until every wavering flame was consigned to charred wick and dripping wax.

Jillian's eyes blurred. Casey was a lovely young woman, warm, compassionate, charming, and quite good at wielding a cake knife. She sliced five pieces from the enormous round, dished them up on plates, and announced that she, not Mrs. Hyde, would serve coffee in the library. There, surrounded with beautifully bound volumes collected by generations of Fitzgeralds, she made her announcement.

"Mum. You've been wonderful to me, and I don't want you to think that because I did this, it reflects negatively on you or my father."

"What are you talking about, Casey?"

"Let me finish."

Frankie looked on with polite curiosity.

Casey drew a deep breath. "Today I had my adoption records unsealed. I know my mother's name, and I don't understand why you didn't tell me in the first place."

Jillian froze. It was too late. Frankie would never know she'd intended to tell him.

Every instinct aroused, Frankie stared at Jillian. She was pale as death.

Casey continued. "Her name was Kathleen Maguire, and she was born right here in Kilvara."

27

Jillian's eyes met Frankie's, saw the banked rage in them, and turned back to her daughter, praying that no one would notice the tremor in her voice. "How long have you had this notion, Casey?"

"Forever, I think. I've always wanted to know."

"Why didn't you ask me?"

Casey's eyebrows rose. "When you told me about my father, I didn't realize you knew anything else."

Jillian was silent. Frankie lifted Connor into his arms. "It's time for bed." He nodded at Casey. "I've an interest in this conversation, lass, so, if you don't mind, I'd like you t' wait and finish it when I come back."

Casey's brow wrinkled. "I don't understand."

"Never mind, love," Jillian interrupted. "Just be agreeable and, for once, don't ask any questions. You'll have your answers soon enough."

Connor was exhausted. After a quick bath and a story,

he did not protest when his father pulled the covers over him and turned out the light.

Jillian stood by the fire feeding turf into the flames when Frankie returned to the library. Her color was back. Other than a slight tension through her shoulders, she did not appear as if her world had fallen down around her.

Perhaps it hadn't, Frankie thought grimly. Perhaps she already had all that she wanted. He leaned against the mantel, crossed his arms, and waited.

Casey started where she left off. "Mum? What does this have to do with Mr. Browne?"

Jillian turned, her eyes on the younger woman's face, her hands clenched at her sides. "Kathleen Maguire worked here at Kildare Hall. She had an affair with my brother. When she told him she was pregnant, he refused to help her in any way. There was a struggle at the hunting lodge. Terrence fell and hit his head. Kathleen left Kilvara. I was thirteen years old. Later, when I was older, I tried to find her. Instead, I found you. Adoption was out of the question until I married Avery."

Frankie breathed more easily. Even now, Jillian wouldn't betray him. Apparently, old habits died hard.

"But why did you tell me you didn't know who she was?" Casey's voice was thick with tears.

Jillian shook her head. "I don't know. It sounds ridiculous now, but at the time my mother was still sensitive about Terrence, and if I'd told you about Kathleen, the rest of it would have come out. It seemed such a private thing. I had no idea you were searching for your mother. I would have told you if you'd come out and asked." Her voice broke. "You are my niece, Casey, a Fitzgerald, my flesh and blood. I wanted you here at Kildare."

"What does Mr. Browne have to do with this?"

Jillian turned back to the fire. "Ask him," she said flatly.

Frankie sighed, crossed the room to sit beside Casey, and took her hands in his. "My name isn't Danny Browne. It's Francis Maguire. Kathleen was my older sister. She came to me for help when Terrence fell. At the time, my father was the kennel keeper here at Kildare. Jillian and I were"—he looked at Jillian's tense back and settled on the word "close"—"I asked her to say she was with Kathleen the entire night. Then I went to see if Terrence was really dead. The *ghillie* found me near the body, and I was accused of his murder. After four years in Long Kesh, I escaped and assumed another identity. I learned that Kathleen was dead. Given my circumstance, there wasn't a chance I could take you. Ten years ago, I found out that you were adopted." He stared at Jillian's unyielding back. "Until tonight, I had no idea who the family was."

"Was Terrence's death really an accident?" Casey asked.

"Yes." Frankie and Jillian spoke in unison.

Casey was incredulous. "Why would you take the blame for his murder?"

"It was a long time ago. Catholics had an even harder time of it than they do now. I was younger than Kathleen. I thought they'd go easier on me."

"Did they?"

"No."

"After all this time, you expect me to believe this was all coincidence, that you and Mum just happened to meet all over again?"

Jillian turned. "It's true. Frankie was sixteen years old when he left Kildare. I didn't meet him again until I knew Colette."

Casey pulled her hands from Frankie's. "How convenient."

"I'm sorry that you're upset, Casey," Jillian said softly. "But I don't know what I would have done differently. You never asked about your parents. I love you. I wanted you. There's nothing more I can say."

Frankie stood. "I'd like to know why you didn't tell me."

"I meant to, but I was otherwise occupied," Jillian said. "Surely you remember."

"Aye, I remember," he said bitterly. "I recall that you wanted something. The irony of it escaped me before, but now I realize why it was me you approached. Kathleen and I share a gene pool."

"Please." Jillian closed her eyes. "Not now."

Casey's brow wrinkled. She looked at Jillian's ravaged face and then back at Frankie's furious one. "What is going on?"

Her innocent question silenced Frankie. "Nothing, lass," he said gently. "None of it has t' do with you." He forced a smile. "It appears you have blood ties with a good number of people. Connor, for one, is your first cousin."

Casey's mouth turned up. "That's true. I've a whole new family to meet." She turned worried eyes on her mother. "Why are you so upset, Mum?"

Jillian's eyes brimmed with tears. She wiped them surreptitiously away. "I'm not, love. It's been a long day. Why don't the two of you become better acquainted while I go up to bed?"

"All right," Casey said dubiously.

Frankie stood. "Under the circumstances, perhaps it would be better if Connor and I left tomorrow."

"No," Casey burst out. "I just found you. You can't leave yet."

Jillian lifted her chin. "You're welcome to stay for as long as you like. I have some errands in the city tomorrow and will probably stay the night in Belfast. If you need anything, Casey will see to it." Keeping her eyes averted, she walked past the two of them, out the door, and up the stairs to her room. There she threw herself on the bed and buried her face in her arms.

She felt rather than heard the presence hovering over her. Nell's lilting voice attempted to soothe her. *It's not over, love. He's angry. That's all.*

Jillian's fingers squeezed the soft down pillow. "I'm not entirely to blame. He never told me he knew who I was, not even when we—" She stopped.

I know. Perhaps he was afraid.

"He said as much." She sat up. "He also told me that he wasn't going anywhere. Interesting, isn't it, how quickly he can reverse his emotions."

Nell sat down beside her. *I don't think it will be easy for him at all. Give him time, Jillian. He's a man.*

Jillian sniffed and reached for a tissue on the nightstand. "What does that have to do with it?"

Nell smiled wisely. *They see only one issue at a time. When he resolves in his mind what you've done and why, he'll come around.*

"And then what, Nell? What good will come of it? Frankie Maguire is an escaped felon. Danny Browne doesn't exist. Even if we could find our way beyond this Catholic-Protestant *thing*, what do we do then?"

Nell rose and walked over to the dressing table and peered into the mirror, once again fascinated by her own reflection. *You were a great help to me, Jilly. Do you recall any of it?*

Jillian frowned. "I believe it was the other way around."

Nell smiled and framed her face with her fingers. *I*

didn't think you would remember. She sighed. *The Fitzgeralds have always been a powerful family. You do remember our history?*

"Of course."

Gerald's lands were returned to him. My father's reputation was restored.

"Are you trying to tell me something?"

Nell turned, a straight, slim figure with glorious hair and eyes that spoke for her like sunlight on sea water. *Why do you suppose you were given your husband's position, Jillian?*

"Thomas Putnam said I was the only one whose presence both loyalists and nationalists would accept."

Has anything changed since then?

Jillian shook her head.

Apparently, Mr. Putnam requires your services as much as ever.

"I suppose so."

Are you accepting compensation, land, titles, gold?

"It isn't done that way anymore."

Isn't it? Nell smiled mysteriously. Her voice was fading quickly. *Think on it, Jilly. What could the prime minister of England do for you?*

Jillian panicked and scrambled off the bed, her eyes searching the room frantically. "Nell, wait. Don't go yet. I don't understand."

She was gone. Of course she was gone. Nell Fitzgerald didn't exist, at least not outside Jillian's imagination.

The night was warm, but goosebumps stood out on her arms. She shivered. Nell's apparition came more frequently when she was troubled, just as it had when Jillian was a child, before Frankie had become part of her life. What would a psychologist say to this invasion of an alter ego who had answers that Jillian did not? She was a grown woman, long past the need for an imaginary friend. Perhaps all this was too much for her. Perhaps she was losing her mind.

She walked over to the dressing table and sat down. The faintest scent of rose petals lingered in the air. With shaking fingers, Jillian traced the oval of her face in the mirror. What could the prime minister of England do for her?

Jillian stared in horror at the front page of *The Belfast Telegram*. Huge headlines, "UDP Responsible for Eight Catholic Deaths," dominated the front page. Groaning, she gulped down her tea, grabbed her satchel, and picked up her car keys on her way out the door.

George Mitchell, the American arbitrator for the peace talks, had called an emergency meeting. A Protestant paramilitary group linked to the Ulster Unionist Party had claimed responsibility for the murders. Violence was in violation of the Mitchell agreement. All parties were to vote on expelling the UDP from the peace talks.

David Temple's furious face was on every news station, claiming the murders were retribution for the murder of King Rat, Billy Wright, a rabid anti-Catholic paramilitary who had boasted of nationalist murders while serving his sentence in Long Kesh.

Jillian could feel the tension thickening the air of the conference room at Stormont Castle. She bypassed the room where Sinn Fein and the SDLP, the Social Democratic and Labour Party, argued behind closed doors and, without knocking, walked into the unionist meeting. Smoke filled the air. Jillian waved it aside, sat down at the long table, and waited. Slowly, one by one, the men joined her.

"Well, gentlemen," she said crisply, "it may appear that you have won, but you haven't."

A stunned silence greeted her pronouncement. Gary McMichael, president of the UDP, broke the silence. "I beg your pardon?"

Jillian's varnished nail tapped lightly on the gleaming tabletop. "Those of you who despised the very idea of negotiating with nationalists believe you have found the means to destroy the process."

McMichael cleared his throat. "I don't understand."

Jillian's face was a mask of icy calm. "Come now, Mr. McMichael. The man who drafted his party's objection to an all-Ireland council, breaking down the ramifications of unification according to international economic systems, employment, industry, wage structures, dispersion rates, income tax, currency, social charges on labor, and European integration, doesn't understand?"

McMichael cleared his throat but remained silent.

"Let me make it clear for you," Jillian said coldly. "It won't work, Mr. McMichael. I don't care if you've killed eight Catholics. I don't care if you kill ten thousand Catholics. Neither you nor your group of small-minded men will ruin what this government is attempting to do here." She leaned forward. "There will be an agreement, Mr. McMichael. You will not be expelled from the talks. You *will* participate, and when this is all over, your signature will be on a document that will serve as a manifesto to all political and paramilitary organizations in this country. Do I make myself clear?"

"What if we cannot agree?"

She stood and smiled sweetly. "We will. Until tomorrow, gentlemen."

Outside the room, Jillian leaned against the wall and took in deep, steadying breaths. One down, one to go. Bracing herself for the worse of two evils, she marched into the nationalist conference room, effectively terminating a half-dozen conversations.

Frankie Maguire straightened, his face expressionless, waiting for her to speak.

"Good morning, gentlemen," she said firmly. "Due to certain developments, we will not be able to meet today. However, we shall meet tomorrow as scheduled."

"All of us?" Seamus Mallon, the SDLP deputy leader, challenged her.

"All of us," Jillian repeated.

Frankie swore audibly. "If the IRA had broken the ceasefire, Sinn Fein would have been out yesterday."

Jillian's voice, low and clearly pitched, cut him off. "No one is leaving the talks until we have reached an all-parties agreement. These negotiations will not be dictated by terrorists." She lifted her chin. "I will not give the Irish Republican Army or the Protestant paramilitaries that kind of power. Good day, gentlemen."

Reluctant admiration softened the edges of Frankie's anger. Jillian Fitzgerald was no quitter. He had to give her that one. Now, if he could just get beyond the rest of it, the jumbled, warring parts of his brain that called up two different images, the one where she lay on the wet grass beneath him, her face flushed with sun and passion, and the one where she stared, stricken and guilty, caught in her own deception.

He'd lost his father, his sister, his wife. She knew it all, and still she hadn't told him about Cassandra, his niece, all that remained of his blood family except for Connor. If she'd planned it deliberately, she could have found no greater way to hurt him. She hadn't planned it, of course. She didn't have it in her to be cruel, and he wasn't so embittered that he'd lost all grip on reality. But he wasn't ready to forgive her, not yet, not when she still held all the cards.

*   *   *

Over the next two days, a drug dealer from Armagh and a loyalist paramilitary leader were shot. The IRA denied responsibility, but public opinion was against them. Jillian refused to discuss expelling Sinn Fein from the talks. Negotiations would continue. The deadline for an agreement was September, and she was determined that it would come from party negotiations, not Downing Street.

Frankie continued to treat her with the same professional courtesy that characterized their first meeting. Her heart ached. There was no other way to describe the sick, helpless feeling in her chest when he looked at her across the conference table as if there had never been anything more between them than the future of Northern Ireland.

She loved him. She always had. It came to her one night, all at once, without warning, as she sorted through old photographs. She found the one she wanted, a badly exposed black-and-white, its subject a dark-haired boy walking through long summer grass surrounded by collies.

Tears rose in her eyes. She blinked them back. She loved Frankie Maguire. There was no other way to explain her mad flight from all rational behavior. Her mother had been right, after all. For years, she'd lamented Jillian's preference for the difficult, the exotic, the road less traveled. Her casual disregard for the necessary restrictions of a woman of her class would bring her only heartbreak, Margaret had predicted, and so it had.

Jillian watched Frankie pore over yet another document, sleeves rolled to his elbows, hair falling over his forehead, mouth tight with sleepless strain, as he ruthlessly cut through unionist rhetoric, reshaping lengthy, unmanageable language into brilliantly clear, concise proposals, proposals the unionists would do little more than glance at because they were composed by a Catholic from West Belfast.

What can the prime minister of England do for you? Nell's words came back to her. This time, she knew the answer. Perhaps Frankie Maguire would never feel the same debilitating, stomach-tightening longing that she felt for him, but she could give him back his past.

Jillian pulled over to the side of the road and stepped out of the car to stretch her legs and admire the beauty of Lough Erne. County Fermanagh, the unspoiled lake country of Northern Ireland, was empty of crowds even in midsummer. Leaning against the car, she shaded her eyes and looked across the glassy water. Whooper swans dove for roach, perch, bream, and rudd. Dragonflies skimmed across the surface, and somewhere, high above the guano-stained limestone cliffs, a raven cawed, piercing the pristine stillness.

The town of Enniskillen in the heart of Fermanagh was the medieval seat of the Maguires, chieftains of Fermanagh who had policed the lough hundreds of years ago with their private navy of fifteen hundred boats. The origins of the island town were steeped in history in those long-ago days when the nexus was the main highway between Ulster and Connaught. It was also the site of Our Lady of Refuge, Catholic Orphanage for Girls.

Mother Cecily Agnes stood near the window of the richly paneled room that served as her office and watched the well-dressed young woman walk across the car park and up the stone steps. She hadn't seen Jillian Graham in ten years, but they had kept in touch. On the basis of their acquaintance, Mother Cecily had revised her opinion of Protestants.

She would not ordinarily have honored the woman's request, but there was a soft spot in her heart for the little girl with the fly-away curls and the embittered young man who had become a force in Irish politics. Mother Cecily was content with her role as abbess of Our Lady of Refuge. She had no priestly aspirations. Remorseful deathbed revelations did not have the same sanctity as those relayed within the confines of the confessional. She would tell what she knew and perhaps hold out a semblance of hope where before there was none.

Thomas Putnam greeted Jillian in the study of his residence at No. 10 Downing Street. It was a masculine room, dimly lit, dark with burgundy leather and mahogany furnishings. "Please, sit down, Jillian," he said, waving her to a wing-back chair. He noticed what he always did when Jillian Graham entered the room. She moved in an aura of natural elegance that came from generations of aristocratic breeding. She was immaculately coiffed, slim and elegant in a sage-colored linen dress, pearl earrings, and bone pumps. Eschewing the desk, he chose the Queen Anne reproduction across from her. "What can I do for you?"

"Thank you for seeing me," she began.

He folded his hands. "You've done a marvelous job with the negotiations. Refusing to allow terrorists to dictate your policies was a masterful stroke. Perhaps we'll see some progress now."

"Are you interested in a true assessment, Tom?"

"Of course."

She spoke directly, honestly, keeping her eyes on his face. "There will be a compromise. The unionists will keep their council majorities, the nationalists will insist on a north-south referendum, to which I believe we should agree. A type of quota system will be configured in order to promote civil rights for Catholics, and our courts will be filled with affirmative action lawsuits."

Putnam frowned. "In your opinion, is there a graceful way for England to remove itself from Northern Ireland entirely?"

"The unionists will never allow the North to become a sovereign nation, if that's what you mean. But eventually, the problem will take care of itself."

"How so?"

"Catholics are outbreeding Protestants at a rate of two to one. In twenty years, they will have the majority vote if we insist on keeping articles two and three of the Irish Constitution."

"So we wait?"

"Yes, Tom. We wait."

Thomas Putnam could read people. Jillian's white-knuckled hands and the delicate bruising under her eyes meant something. He leaned forward, his brown mop of unruly hair falling over his forehead. "Tell me why you're here, Jillian."

She wet her lips. "I need a favor."

Two hours and three phone calls later, a bewildered Thomas Putnam walked Jillian to the door, locked it behind her, and returned to his desk, where he sank down into the leather chair, leaned his head back against the warm grain, and closed his eyes. He needed a moment or two to internalize what he had just done. Jillian Graham was a force to be reckoned with. Good God. Had he really agreed to such a thing? How in bloody hell would he ever explain it?

28

Casey squinted at the fading numbers on the peeling door frame of the building that faced the street. The number was the same as the one she'd ferreted from the clerk in the housing office at Trinity. She swallowed, slung her bag over her shoulder, and climbed the stairs. Tim Sheehan was a hard man to track down, but she wasn't giving up.

An older woman with bright black eyes and pink cheeks answered the door. "No, love," she said when Casey asked for Tim. "He lives next door. But he's not home much since he went down to the Republic. His da should be home shortly. I'm Cora Flynn. Would y' care to wait here?"

"If it's no trouble," Casey said politely.

"No trouble at all," replied Mrs. Flynn. "I'll be happy t' have the company. Come in, love. Y' can help me with Connor."

"Connor?"

"Aye. Himself's wee brother. He's a dear lad but a bit of a handful for a woman my age."

Casey quelled the sudden surge of her heartbeat. There must be a thousand Connors in West Belfast. "When will he be home?"

"Anytime now. Sit down. I'll make a pot of tea. What did y' say your name was?"

"Casey Graham."

The door opened, and a child's cheerful voice called out, "I'm home, Mrs. Flynn. Is it time for tea?"

"Aye, laddie," she answered from the kitchen. "We've a visitor today, so wash y'r hands and mind y'r manners, in that order."

Connor's eyes had adjusted to the dimness of the room. He stared at Casey, and his blue eyes widened. "Casey?"

"Connor, is it you?" she stammered.

"Have you come to see Da?" he asked.

She improvised quickly. "Yes. When will he be home?"

"I don't know," said Connor matter-of-factly. "Sometimes he comes late. Mrs. Flynn knows."

"I see." Casey bit her lip. This was too much irony to take in at once. Tim, her Tim, must be Frankie Maguire's stepson. "What about your brother?" she asked Connor. "Will he be home today?"

Connor's forehead wrinkled, and he sat down beside her on the couch. "I don't think so."

Mrs. Flynn set the pot of tea on the table and arranged three place settings. "I've a tasty lamb stew on the stove," she called out from the kitchen. "There's plenty for all."

"Please don't go to any trouble, Mrs. Flynn," Casey protested.

" 'Tis no trouble, lass. Sit down now, and tell us how y' know our Tim."

Casey tucked a springy curl behind one ear and walked slowly to the kitchen table. "We met at Trinity," she said slowly. "He helped me with mathematics."

"Ah." Mrs. Flynn dished a healthy portion of stew into Casey's bowl. "Isn't an education a grand thing? Our Tim was always a bright lad, just like Connor here."

A firm knock sounded on the door, followed by a voice that made Casey's heart beat quickly again.

"Mrs. Flynn, I'm home. Is Connor here yet?"

"Aye, Danny," the old woman said. "Come in. We have a visitor."

Frankie stepped into the small kitchen, and for an instant, his smile of welcome froze on his lips. Almost immediately, it was replaced by a genuine grin of pleasure. "Casey," he said, holding out his hand. " 'Tis a pleasure to see you, lass."

Casey's face burned. Deception did not come easily to her. She gave him her hand. "Hello, Mr. Browne."

"She's come to see Tim," offered Mrs. Flynn.

Frankie's eyebrow lifted. "Tim?"

The delicious stew churned in Casey's stomach. "I met Tim Sheehan at Trinity," she explained. "He tutored me in mathematics. We became friendly. Until today, I didn't know he was related to you."

Frankie's mind leaped to a hundred different possibilities. "Is Tim expecting you, lass?"

"No," Casey confessed miserably. "He has no idea I even know where he lives. It's just that—" She looked down at her hands. "May I speak to you privately, Mr. Browne?"

"Of course." Frankie stood. "Save some of that stew for me, Mrs. Flynn."

"What is it, Casey?" he asked when they were settled on chairs in the living room of his flat.

Casey laced her fingers together to stop the trembling of her hands. "Do you remember the night of my birthday?" she asked.

Frankie nodded. It was a night he wasn't likely to forget.

"I was stopped at a barricade on the way home. The men wore balaclavas. They had guns. I recognized Tim's voice."

A thin white line appeared around Frankie's mouth. "Are you sure?"

Casey nodded. "Yes."

Frankie's eyes moved across her face, noting the delicate flush in her cheeks, the rapid breathing, the trembling mouth. "How well do you know Tim?" he asked carefully.

"I thought I knew him very well," she began, "but he didn't come back to school after his mother's funeral. Now I know why."

"Are you—?" He paused, uncertain about continuing.

"No," she said quickly. "It wasn't like that between us. We didn't have the opportunity."

"I see." Danny's mouth twitched. What a predicament. His stepson and his niece. "Does Jillian know?"

"No," Casey said quickly. "How could she? I didn't know myself."

Frankie was silent for a long time. The hard, grim-faced man seated across from her was nothing like the Frankie Maguire who had charmed her at Kildare. "Uncle Francis," she said softly, "is Tim involved with the IRA?"

A muscle throbbed in his neck, and for a moment she thought she'd angered him. But his voice, when he answered, was as courteous as ever. "I hope not, lass."

"That isn't an answer."

"I can give you no other."

"Don't you know?"

Frankie shook his head. "No. I don't."

Casey stood. "I want to see him."

"Why?"

"I must ask him."

"Is his answer that important t' you?"

Casey considered his question and answered honestly. "I think so."

"You know their story, lass." He quoted from the manifesto of the Irish Republican Army: "Out of the ashes rose the provisionals."

"I know it. I'm a Catholic, too, Uncle Francis."

Frankie stood and smoothed her curly hair with both hands. "But a very different sort of Catholic from the rest of us."

She lifted her chin. "I can't help that."

"No," he said gently. "I wasn't criticizing, and I wouldn't have it any other way."

Tears burned beneath her eyelids, but she refused to blink. "Will you tell him that I want to see him?"

Frankie nodded. "Aye. I'll tell him."

Casey bit her lip.

"Is something else troublin' you, lass?" Frankie asked gently.

She lifted green eyes to his face. Fitzgerald eyes. She was as much a Fitzgerald as she was a Maguire.

"It's Mum. You weren't nice to her when you and Connor stayed at Kildare."

Frankie sighed, quelled the urge to reach for a cigarette, and ran his fingers nervously through his hair instead. "No, I wasn't. I should probably apologize for that."

"She's different lately, Uncle Francis." Casey hesitated.

"Go on."

"I think it's because of you."

Frankie's mouth lifted at the corner. "Do you, now?"

"Yes."

He reached out and took her hands. "This isn't for you to worry about. Jillian and I will sort it out."

"Do you love her?"

"Casey, lass, if that's so, shouldn't Jillian be the first to hear me say it?"

Casey pulled her hands away, jumped up, and began to pace the room. Words, jumbled and wounding, poured from her lips. "Well, if you do, why don't you tell her so? I'm so tired of all this old baggage. She kept the lie you asked her to keep so that your sister wouldn't go to prison."

He noticed that she didn't acknowledge Kathleen as her mother.

She stopped in front of him. "All that's over now. Don't you see, Uncle Francis? It was meant to be. I don't think my birth parents were very good people. But you and Mum are. This can't all be a coincidence. First Mum finds your wife, and then I find Tim. I believe the two of you have been given a second chance."

"It isn't that easy," Frankie began.

"Why not?"

He laughed. "You're quite the romantic, aren't you?"

"Is there something wrong with that?"

Frankie shook his head. "You don't understand, Casey. Jillian is a Fitzgerald of Kildare Hall. Her people were kings of Ireland. She knows the prime minister by his first name. The queen mother drops in for tea with your grandmother, for Christ sake." He waved his arm to encompass the room. "Look around you, lass. This isn't exactly Kildare Hall. How would I fit into the life of a woman like that?"

Casey's lower lip trembled. "The same way I fit in,

Uncle Francis. In case you've forgotten, I'm a Fitzgerald and a Maguire. And I drove all the way from Dublin to see Tim Sheehan."

Frankie was ashamed of himself. When he left Kildare Hall, he was certain that Casey's loyalties lay with Jillian. He wasn't sure if she would ever seek him out. Now that she had, however inadvertently, he was behaving badly.

"I'm sorry, lass," he said gently. "I haven't forgotten who you are or why you're here. Go on back to Mrs. Flynn's and finish your tea. I'll find Tim for you."

Casey sat in her favorite corner in Bewley's Café on Grafton Street in Dublin, absentmindedly stirring her tea. An untouched maple pastry, Bewley's specialty, and a side salad with too many carrots and too little lettuce wilted before her. She had no appetite. She was worried about her mother. Jillian had lost weight that she couldn't afford, and the brittle, preoccupied look she'd worn throughout Avery's illness was back. Casey wanted to come home permanently, but Jillian wouldn't hear of it. It would all be over soon, her mother assured her. The deadline for an agreement was approaching, and with it would come the end of Jillian's tenure. She would resign her position and go back to the life she had planned for herself.

The problem was obvious. Casey could see it clearly, and she knew her mother could, too. Without their forced encounters at Stormont, Jillian and Frankie would no longer have a legitimate reason to see each other. She pulled at the corner of her pastry. There was nothing more she could do. The two of them would have to sort it out between them.

Sighing, she reached for her bag, pushed herself away

from the table, and stood. A tall blond man in his early twenties blocked her way.

"Hello, Casey," he said.

Her mouth dropped. "Tim Sheehan?"

"In the flesh."

"Where have you been?" she demanded, digging her fists into her waist.

He tucked her arm through his. "Shall we take a walk?" Without waiting for her answer, he led her out the door, past the street musicians and the shops, through the wrought-iron gates of Trinity College to the cobbled path. He adjusted his gait to hers. A cold breeze blew through the trees, and there was a promise of rain on the wind. Casually, as if he had the right, he turned up her collar and pulled her hand down into the warmth of his pocket.

"I know it was you at the barricade." Her words were sharp, accusing, an attempt to deflect the warmth that rose within her at the feel of his hands on her skin.

His fingers grazed her cheek. "How?"

Casey shook her head. "I know you, the sound of your voice, the way you're built." She shook her head. "It doesn't matter. It was you. That's all that's important."

"Why is it important?"

"Don't be ridiculous."

"Tell me, Casey." He stopped to face her. His voice was urgent, desperate, his eyes electric blue. "I drove like a maniac for three hours to ask you that question. I need an answer."

Tears choked her throat. She shook her head and looked away.

"Do you need me to say it first, lass? Is that it?"

Again, she shook her head. She, who was so good with words, could not force them past her lips.

He lifted her chin with one hand and tucked the flyaway hair behind her ears with the other. "Listen to me, Cassandra Graham of Kildare Hall. If you're foolish enough to care for a wayward lad like myself, I'll not throw it away."

She felt the warmth of his hand on her head and the soft pressure of his lips on her forehead. Then he pulled her against the leather of his jacket and hugged her hard. Closing her eyes, Casey wrapped her arms around his waist and burrowed her head against his chest. Her words were muffled. "I was so worried about you. Why didn't you call me?"

He smiled into her hair. "What would I say? I didn't know you wanted me for anythin' more than a mathematics tutor, although I was a bit suspicious at the end."

She wouldn't look at him. "Oh?"

"Aye." He set her away from him. "I wondered why a lass who passed her levels in the top two percent would need a tutor."

"How did you know?"

"The scores are posted."

Casey flushed. "It was the only way I could think of to make you notice me."

"All you had t' do was say it, lass." Reverently, he touched her cheeks, the bow of her lip, the short, straight nose. "There aren't many who would refuse you."

"I wasn't sure." She leaned against him. "You never appeared the least bit interested in anything other than books."

It was heavenly talking with her like this, holding the weight of her slight body against his. She shifted in his arms, turning to see his face.

"Tim," she murmured. "Aren't you going to kiss me?"

He swallowed. This wasn't a girl from the streets he held in his arms. It was Casey Graham, and she'd asked the question whether or not she knew the game. *Careful, lad*, he said to himself. *Go slowly*. "Are you in a hurry, lass?" he teased her.

"Yes," she said, surprising him. "I've imagined what it would be like for so long that I can't wait any longer."

Suddenly, he was nervous. She was too honest, too young, too good. "Shouldn't we talk a bit first?"

"No. Kiss me first. Then we'll talk."

No match for such a request, Tim lowered his head and tasted what he'd never dared imagine. When her small hands slid around his neck and locked and her mouth opened beneath his, he knew that he wouldn't walk away, no matter what it was that she asked.

Later, after they'd cleared up just when it was that each of them first noticed the other, Casey brought up the subject Tim hoped she wouldn't.

"How long have you been involved in the IRA?"

He met her eyes steadily. "Not long."

"Why did you do it?"

"You know the answer to that."

"You're a university student, Tim. Those people are from the streets. You have other options."

"Not all of us do."

"My mother and your stepfather are working very hard to see that they do."

Tim frowned. "If and when they succeed, I'll resign." He changed the subject. "Just how do you know my father?"

Casey opened her mouth and closed it again. Did Tim know that Danny Browne was really Frankie Maguire? "Didn't he tell you?" she hedged.

"He said that you tracked me down through a clerk in the housing office."

"That's right." She was grateful that she could be partially truthful. "I had no idea that Danny Browne was your stepfather."

Tim shrugged. "He didn't want it advertised."

Casey squeezed his hand. "I'm sorry about your mother."

Tim's jaw hardened. "She wasn't the same since the shootin'. That's the woman I'll miss, the one I remember from before."

"I met your brother."

Tim smiled. "Connor is a grand wee lad. I wish he had better memories of his mam."

"Were your parents happy, Tim?" she asked casually.

"Before the shootin' they were happy enough." Remembering his manners, he smiled. "Were yours?"

Casey chewed her lip before answering. "I thought they were, but now I'm not sure." She wondered if he could hear her heart pounding. "Did your father tell you that he brought Connor to Kildare Hall?"

"What are y' tryin' to tell me, Casey?"

She pushed back her hair and tried to sort out the confusing jumble. "A long time ago, my mother met yours in the hospital. They were friends."

Not by the flare of a nostril did Tim reveal his skepticism. Jillian Graham and his mother could never have shared a friendship.

"When my father died and my mother took his position, she met your father. Mum was at the hospital when your mother died. She took Connor home." Her brain moved quickly, discarding the dangerous subjects. "When Connor was hurt, he stayed with us. Your father stayed, too."

"So?"

Casey clasped both of her hands around Tim's large

one. "Would you mind terribly if they cared for each other?"

"Who?"

"Our parents."

Tim stared at her in disbelief. "My father and your mother?"

"Yes."

Tim threw back his head and laughed loudly. "That's rich. Danny Browne and Jillian Graham."

"Why is it so impossible?"

Tim searched for an answer. "Why? Because my stepfather is an ardent nationalist and your mother is an aristocrat."

"What if they get beyond that?"

He shook his head. "I don't know your mother, Casey, but I know Danny Browne. That will weigh with him more than anything."

"There's more."

Suddenly, Tim didn't feel like laughing anymore. "Go on."

Casey shook her head. "I can't."

"Why not?"

"Because it isn't my story to tell. You'll have to trust me."

He couldn't argue with her logic, not when there was so much he couldn't share with her. Threading his fingers through her hair, he pulled her head down to his shoulder. "I didn't drive all the way down here to talk about other people."

She laughed up at him. "What did you drive here for?"

"This," he said, lowering his head to cover her open mouth with his own.

29

Not by so much as the tightening of a jaw muscle did Frankie Maguire reveal the rage he felt at the cryptic message he held in his hand. Gary McMichael wouldn't even meet with him face-to-face, and yet he expected him to sign a settlement that would place the future of nationalist Ireland in the hands of loyalists.

He looked up. Jillian's eyes behind the enormous glasses she wore for reading were wary and speculative. They were alone in the nationalist conference room. "Did you actually believe this would be acceptable to us?"

"No."

Surprise flickered across his features. "Why did you bother?"

She sighed and removed her glasses. He noticed that her lips were slightly chapped as if she'd run her tongue over them again and again. "I'm obligated to show you every proposal, no matter how absurd. You can accept it or discard it, as you please."

"Is there anything else on the table?"

Jillian frowned. "Why would you ask me that?"

"I know Gary McMichael. His first offer is always outrageous. Gradually, he moves to something more palatable."

"But not close enough to accept?"

"Not yet."

"You won't get what you want, Frankie. To throw everything away because you refuse to compromise is foolish. The people of Northern Ireland, Catholic and Protestant, are tired of war."

"We can't accept an internal settlement. You know what happens on the elected councils. Sinn Fein isn't allowed a single representative position."

She leaned forward. "What will you accept?"

He could smell her perfume. His stomach clenched. "An all Ireland tribunal, dismantling the RUC, a bill of rights, housing, jobs for Catholics, all political prisoners released, and an end to British occupation in the Six Counties."

"Will the IRA agree?"

Frankie's eyes, gray as the Irish Sea, met hers without wavering. "I don't know."

"You must have an idea."

"If Sinn Fein agrees, the chances are good."

"What about the splinter groups?"

"I can't speak for the paramilitaries. Neither can McMichael."

"In other words, the killings will continue."

Frankie passed a hand in front of his eyes. "I imagine so, for a while, anyway. There is a small segment of our population, nationalist and loyalist, who have an interest in maintaining the status quo. When they realize they have no support, they'll go away. We'll be like every other country with an occasional crazy man for the press to go on about."

"Do you really believe that?"

"I have to, Jillian. If I don't, the last twenty years of my life will have been for nothing."

His intensity startled her. For the first time, she realized what it all meant to him, what he had given up to become a negotiator for a political party that had only just begun to be recognized as legitimate. Jillian wet her lips. "The deadline is very close, Frankie. I can't guarantee that my replacement will be as sympathetic as I am."

"I didn't realize you were."

"That's not fair." Hurt was all over her face.

He rose and walked to the window, fists balled deep in his pockets. "I apologize."

She followed him, stopping an arm's length from where he stood. "That's very big of you, but do you mean it?"

The muscles of his back were tight and bunched beneath his shirt. She wanted to reach out and touch him, to slide her arms around his waist and rest her head against his shoulder. But she knew better.

When he spoke, his words were filled with regret and a kind of bitter, wry humor. "I do mean it, lass. For some reason, my words don't come out properly when I'm with you, which is odd because there was a time when you were the only person they did come out with."

Jillian hadn't forgotten the boy with the aggravated stutter and how it miraculously disappeared in her presence. Hope rose in her chest. She was inexperienced with flirtation. This was the only man she had ever wanted. She moved close enough so that if he turned around, they would share the same breath. "Do I make you nervous, Frankie?"

Even though she hadn't touched him, she knew when his body tensed. "Aye," he said at last. "You make me very nervous."

Behind his back, she smiled. "Why?"

"Because you make me want things that are impossible."

"Nothing is impossible."

He turned around, and his hands closed around her upper arms. "Stop this, Jillian. I can't carry you up the stairs of that enormous house you live in, love you whenever the mood strikes, raise the children we could make together, and still be Danny Browne of West Belfast."

"What if you didn't have to be Danny Browne? What if you could be Francis Maguire of Kilvara? What if you could do all the things we talked about when we were children?" She searched his face, hoping for a sign, a weakening, a flicker of interest, any evidence at all to show that she'd moved him. For long moments, there was nothing.

Finally, he spoke. "This isn't a fairy tale, Jillian. It's Ireland, and we haven't had a happy ending in centuries."

Ridding herself of the last of her inhibitions, she did the only thing that made sense. Twining her arms around his neck, she pulled his head down and raised her lips to his. "Damn you, Frankie Maguire," she said against his mouth. "I'll not let you tell me in the same breath that you want me and that it's impossible. And I'll no longer allow you to use Colette as an excuse. She was more a friend to me than most, and I know she wouldn't want us to put this aside."

Her perfume and the softness of her lips were driving

him mad. He fought against it. "How could you possibly know what a woman like Colette would want?"

"Don't be an idiot."

He heard her words, soft and laced with laughter. Then he gave himself up to the demand of insistent hands, warm, willing lips, and the hot blood that rose inside him whenever his discipline slipped and his mind called up images of summer air and a stolen night that nothing could make him regret.

When his air had run out and he was half insane with the wanting of her, he lifted his head and breathed deeply, raggedly. "Jilly, lass," he rasped, "what do y' want with me?"

"Just be with me," she whispered.

"Are you—" he hesitated. "Are you all right, Jilly?"

She looked surprised. "Of course."

He slid his hand around to the back of her neck, threaded his fingers through her hair, and tugged her head down to his shoulder. "Y' look tired," he said, his lips moving against the curve of her neck. "Are y' sure there isn't something you want t' tell me?"

All at once, she understood. "No, Frankie. It's too soon."

"You will tell me, either way?"

She nodded.

"Why didn't y' tell me about Casey?"

"I would have, but Connor was there, and we kept getting interrupted. Then it was too late." She pulled away slightly to look up at him. "Why didn't you tell me you knew who I was?"

Framing her face with his hands, he ran his thumbs along the bones of her cheeks. "I didn't trust you."

Hurt swallowed her. "That's honest," she managed.

"Later," he continued, "when I did, I was afraid you would tell me t' go away. I needed more time."

"Why?"

She was relentless, exposing all that he felt, softening the razor-honed edges of his nerves until they were the soft mush of Irish oats. "Surely you don't need the answer to that one."

"That's exactly what I do need."

Jillian knew that Frankie Maguire wasn't a violent man. But his hands gripped her shoulders painfully, and he looked angry. For a moment, before he spoke, she was frightened of stirring the rage within him.

"You must know how I feel about you, lass."

Her eyes were steady and bright on his face. "But I don't."

His heart pounded in his throat. Why was it so difficult? He felt it. He even wanted to say it. Why, then, did his throat close around the words? The answer came to him. Once he gave voice to them, there would be no going back, and it scared the bloody hell out of him. "Is there a lock on the door?" he asked hoarsely.

Jillian was confused. "I don't know." She watched him stride across the room, bolt the door, and come back to her. He took her hand, led her to the couch, and sat down beside her so their knees touched.

Sliding his hands around her waist, he pulled her close. "It doesn't matter," he said fiercely, his eyes on her face. "None of what I say matters, because nothing can ever come of it. But I'll say the words if they please you. Do y' understand what I'm tellin' you, Jilly?"

She nodded. Understanding was not the same as accepting.

He drew a deep restorative breath. "Well, then, Jillian Fitzgerald, it's like this. I wanted more of what we had at Kildare. I think I've always wanted it. Even when we were children, I couldn't stop myself, thinking and hopin' what we told each other could really be. What

I couldn't believe was that you would feel the same. When you told me y' wanted a child, part of me was insane with jealousy. I wanted you t' want me, Frankie Maguire of Kilvara, not Danny Browne, Sinn Fein negotiator."

It wasn't what she'd hoped, but Jillian had long since reached the point of taking whatever it was he had to offer. If loving Frankie meant nothing more than stolen nights at Kildare, she would accept it gladly and be grateful. "I've never wanted anyone else but you," she whispered. "Somehow I knew, even when you were Danny Browne and Colette's husband."

She felt his lips on her throat. At the same time, his hands made their way up the silky smoothness of her hose-covered legs to the heated flesh above the line where the stocking ended and the softness of her skin began.

Leaning back against the firm pillows of the couch, she closed her eyes and forgot about Ireland, forgot about David Temple and Gary McMichael waiting in the other conference room, forgot that she was to bring an agreement to the table that would change the direction of Irish history, forgot everything but the feel of sure fingers unbuttoning her blouse and pushing it aside, slipping lacy straps from her shoulders, baring her breasts, a prelude to urgent lips sliding down the generous slope, opening over the exposed peak, licking, sucking, arousing, until her back arched and she felt him naked against her, the hard, swollen heat of him demanding entrance.

Her flesh closed around him, and it began, the delicious, mindless thrusting, the muffled words, the exploring hands, the gentle slapping of breast and belly, the explosion of desire that lifted her outside and beyond the ancient, forbidding walls of Stormont Castle and then back again.

"I love you, Frankie," she said when the drumming of her heart had slowed. "I know this is the worst possible time to tell you, but I do. I don't care if you don't love me back. Yes, I do," she amended, "but whether you do or not doesn't change anything for me."

He lifted his head and stared at her in wonder. "Have you heard nothin' I've said, lass?" At last, the words came freely. "I love you desperately. I'll go to the grave lovin' you."

"But you won't marry me."

"No. Not unless I have to. Danny Browne should not be marryin' anyone, not with a lie on my lips and in my heart. But I won't have you bear a child alone and give it Avery Graham's name."

"Has anyone ever told you that your pride is enormous?"

"Aye." He grinned and suddenly looked much younger.

Jillian's heart ached. She wanted to change the world for him, to bring that youthful abandon to his expression more often. Perhaps she already had. "We've increased the odds, you know," she said softly.

"I know, and part of me hopes it's so." He kissed her forehead, sat up, zipped his trousers, and tucked in his shirt. "This is insanity. I've lost all perspective. If someone had tried the door—"

"But they didn't." Jillian had buttoned up her blouse. "What happens now?"

He didn't pretend to misunderstand her. "Do y' want the lads t' know you've a Catholic lover, Mrs. Graham?" The Irish lilt at the end of his words was strong and teasing.

Her cheeks were pink, and her eyes glowed with the

warmth of a woman thoroughly satisfied. She smiled and took his dare. "I don't mind."

"Shall we flaunt it now or wait until you are no longer Northern Ireland's minister?"

"Perhaps we should wait."

He laughed. "A wise decision."

"I don't care for myself," she said. "I've never cared what anyone thought."

He knew it was true. But there was more to it. There were people depending on him, people he couldn't walk away from. Jillian Graham in her fancy town house off Lisburn Road knew nothing of the life he lived, the threats, the late-night searches, the harassment, the interrogations at Castlereagh, the bomb warnings, the shrill sing-song of police sirens, the fumes of tear gas, and the frightening, inevitable explosions that left what had once been a place of business or a gathering for friends a ruin of smoking, decimated rubble.

Jillian was not born into violence. Even if he were free to use his name again, he would not test her feelings by making her his wife, exposing her to danger by bringing her into war-torn West Belfast. A man was as weak as his weakest link. Fear of losing her would make him weak. He pushed aside the voice in his head reminding him that, even now, she could be carrying his child, and then all his arguments, the posturing, the excuses, the warnings, would crumble into dust like the faded, sepia-toned photos of the life he had given up the day he escaped from Long Kesh prison.

Thomas Putnam, the nationalists' hope for Northern Ireland, welcomed the Sinn Fein delegation into his rooms at Downing Street. Earlier, he had seen Gary McMichael, David Temple and the unionist attorneys. On his desk, he had a signed document bearing their

signatures, a document that outlined what Putnam believed would be the final position on the Northern Ireland peace initiative. Both sides had compromised and
come to an agreement on every issue except one, perhaps the most sensitive one of all, the disbanding of
Ulster's police force, a move that loyalist factions unilat-
erally opposed. Putnam was prepared to bargain heavily
in order to win nationalist support.

He knew that Robbie Wilson, Sinn Fein's chief representative, was sensible. He would not walk away without bringing home the hope of peace for his
constituents. Gerry Kelly was a firebrand, a retired
member of the Irish Republican Army who had served
multiple sentences in Long Kesh. In the end, he would
be ruled by Wilson. Browne was the only unknown.
The man had been a complete mystery until Jillian's
bombshell.

"Sit down, gentlemen." Putnam ushered them into
the mahogany-paneled room. "I believe we may have
an agreement."

A rare smile crossed Wilson's lips. "Shall we cut to
the chase, Mr. Putnam?"

Putnam frowned. "I don't understand."

Frankie interpreted. "Tell us what they can't
stomach."

Startled by his bluntness, Putnam stared across his
desk into eyes as cold and unrelieved a gray as the bleak
stones of Stormont Castle. Any hopes he had for a quick
settlement evaporated. "Very well," he said slowly.
"They won't agree to disbanding the RUC."

Frankie's eyes locked with Wilson's, and both men
leaned back in their chairs.

"Without that, Catholics have no hope of receiving
justice at the hands of law enforcement," Wilson said.

"They want a gradual attrition," explained Putnam, "a sort of affirmative action, if you will."

"How would it work?" Frankie asked.

"All new police officers will be hired from the Catholic population until the number reflects the percentage of the Catholic population."

Frankie shook his head. "We won't see Catholics on the force until the middle of the next century."

Putnam leaned forward in his chair. "What do you propose, Mr. Browne?"

"Twenty percent of the force to take early retirement immediately. New recruits, from the Catholic population, will replace them."

Putnam's forehead wrinkled. "What of the expense?"

"Benefits for retired police officers are significantly lower than salaries. The excess can go toward new recruits' salaries. It's a lot more than Catholics are makin' now. The way I see it, it's a wash."

It took the prime minister less than a minute to make his decision. "All right," he said. "Twenty percent to retire in order to make room for Catholic recruits. After that, a natural attrition with replacements pulled from the Catholic population until the requisite quota is met."

Wilson looked puzzled. "Just like that? Don't y' have to talk with someone?"

Putnam shook his head. "The unionist position specifies no disbanding of the RUC. I haven't disbanded it." Reaching for his pen, he made the necessary changes on the document and handed it, with a pen, to Robbie Wilson.

Wilson stood and took the pen, a lean, imposing man with thick, liberally salted dark hair. "Will you call a press conference?"

"I won't even wait until the ink is dry."

When the three Sinn Fein leaders had affixed their signatures, Putnam walked them to the door. "Mr. Browne," he said casually, "may I have a moment?"

Frankie's right eyebrow lifted. "Of course," he said slowly. "Go ahead, lads," he said to his party. "I'll catch up."

Robbie Wilson narrowed his eyes behind his metal-rimmed glasses. "We'll wait for you."

Frankie walked back to the mahogany-paneled office and settled himself in a leather chair. Putnam offered him a cigar. He declined.

"It appears that you have friends in high places, Mr. Browne, or should I say Mr. Maguire?"

Frankie stiffened. "I beg your pardon?"

Putnam seated himself and leaned forward, his hands forming a pyramid on the desktop. "I won't leave you hanging, Mr. Maguire. You have been issued a full pardon for the murder of Terrence Fitzgerald."

Frankie's head spun. Was he being set up? Every instinct told him to deny his name.

Wilson's next words were nearly as shocking. "Jillian Graham has requested that all charges against you be dropped." He reached into the top drawer of the desk and laid out the legal document. "You are a free man, Mr. Maguire, if that is what you want. Of course, you may elect to keep your identity. You've been Danny Browne for more years than you were Francis Maguire."

Frankie stared at him in disbelief. Only an Englishman would say such a thing. "Why?" he managed.

Thomas Putnam's dark eyes glinted. "You're a very lucky man to have Jillian Graham in your camp. We all are. There wasn't a chance in a lifetime of reaching an agreement like this without her. I'm most grateful."

He grinned. "Because of her, my approval ratings will soar. I'm only sorry it isn't time for reelection."

Frankie scooped up the paper and stood. "I suppose I should thank you."

"It would stick in your throat. Thank Jillian instead."

Frankie nodded. "I will."

"By the way," Putnam asked, "were you innocent?"

Frankie took his time answering, and for a moment Thomas Putnam thought that Jillian may have been wrong.

"Aye," he said at last. "Innocent of the killing but not of the hating. I hated Terrence Fitzgerald."

"Why didn't you fight the charges?"

Frankie's mouth twisted into a crooked smile. "You wouldn't understand."

Putnam sighed. "I suppose not. Do you think this will change anything?"

Frankie flashed his brilliant smile. "It must, Mr. Putnam. There is no other alternative for us."

The prime minister sat in his chair for a long time. Frankie Maguire had gone, and with him he'd taken what was left of the warmth and light. The man had nerves of steel and his own lethal brand of Irish charm. Putnam was enough of a politician to know that Maguire would be a formidable opponent if they were ever on opposite sides. Jillian had unleashed a tiger. He only hoped she knew how to keep him pacified.

30

Thomas Putnam's press conference stunned the world. No one really believed either side would compromise. An understandable reserve held the population of Ulster in a wary grip. Four hundred years of discord could not be settled by the mere stroke of a pen, or could it?

Jillian's telephone at Stormont hadn't stopped ringing. Finally, at seven o'clock the following evening, she left the building and drove home. Mrs. Wilson brought her a pot of tea and a sandwich, mercifully asked no questions, and left her alone in her sitting room on Lisburn Road.

Frankie and the Sinn Fein delegation would not yet have returned from London. Thomas Putnam had called earlier in the day to tell Jillian that Frankie's pardon had been issued. There was nothing in the prime minister's voice to indicate how he had reacted to her interference, and, desperate as she was to know if Frankie was pleased or angry, nothing would make her ask.

When the housekeeper tapped softly on the door, Jillian's heart began to race. She had told Mrs. Wilson that she was home to only two people.

"Come in," she called out.

Mrs. Wilson poked her head in. "It's Mr. Browne. Will you take it?"

"Yes. Thank you, Mrs. Wilson." Cradling the receiver against her ear with shaking hands, Jillian cleared her throat. "Frankie?"

"Hello, lass. I called as soon as I could."

His words flowed over her like warm honey, and her control shattered. She squeezed the receiver until her fingers ached. "Where are you?"

"At home." There was a brief silence. "Connor misses you."

She smiled into the phone. "Is it only Connor who misses me?"

"Perhaps I miss you a wee bit as well."

Jillian laughed. "Can we do something about that?"

"What do you suggest?"

"I could come there."

"Connor is here."

"Is there a reason I shouldn't visit Connor?"

His voice was low, husky, intimate. "Not tonight. Not for what I have in mind."

"Then come here."

"Now, why did I think you'd never ask?"

"What about Connor?"

"I'll wait until he's asleep. Mrs. Flynn will look out for him."

"Hurry," she whispered.

"Jilly?" Her name on his lips crackled and leaped through the telephone wire.

"Yes?"

"Thank you."

Smiling, she hung up the phone. Suddenly, she was no longer drained with fatigue. Humming to herself, she started up the stairs to her bedroom. A sound in the hall and Mrs. Wilson's welcoming voice stopped her. She turned around and walked down the hallway. Casey was leading a very tall, very blond young man into the sitting room.

"Mum," she said, her eyes lighting when she spied Jillian. "There is someone I'd like you to meet. This is Tim Sheehan."

Jillian smiled graciously, walked forward, and extended her hand. "Hello, Tim. How are you?"

"Well, thank you, Mrs. Graham," the boy answered politely, shaking her hand and releasing it as soon as possible. "Casey and I met at Trinity."

"I see." She looked at Casey. "Is there a holiday I missed?" Casey shook her head. "No, Mum. I brought Tim home to meet you because I love him and he loves me."

A great rushing sound filled Jillian's ears. "I'm not sure that I understand," she said slowly, "unless congratulations are in order. Is that what you're trying to tell me, Casey? Are you engaged?"

"No," Tim and Casey said in unison.

Tim Sheehan linked his hand with Casey's. "Not that we've ruled it out, you understand. It's just that we haven't known each other very long."

Jillian hoped her relief didn't show. Tim Sheehan looked like a perfectly respectable young man, but Casey was only twenty-one.

Casey was speaking again. "I brought Tim home with me because there is something you should know."

Jillian, her heart sinking, tried to appear cheerful. "Very well. Shall I sit down?"

Casey nodded. "Perhaps we all should." She waited

until they were seated across from each other, Jillian directly opposite the two of them.

"Mum, Tim is Danny Browne's stepson."

It took a moment to register. When it did, Jillian could no longer hide her relief. "That's it?" she asked. "That's all?"

"Danny Browne," Casey repeated, "the Sinn Fein negotiator."

"I'm not likely to forget who Danny Browne is, Casey," said her mother.

"Then you approve?" Tim asked incredulously.

"I knew your mother well. That alone would be enough. Besides, why wouldn't I approve of a young man from Trinity?"

"I'm a nationalist, Mrs. Graham."

Jillian leaned forward. "That's beside the point. We'll all have to work harder at accommodating each other from now on. As it so happens—"

A loud crack split the night sounds and crashed against the plate window. A wall of glass separated and shattered, hurling deadly, stilettolike shards in every direction.

Reacting instinctively, Tim reached for Casey, dragging her with him as he crossed the distance to where her mother sat, pushed the two of them to the floor, and dropped, covering as much of them as he could with his body.

"What is it?" Casey screamed.

His voice against her ear was deadly calm. "A bomb. Stay down. It hasn't gone off yet."

The wait was no more than three seconds. A deafening boom shook the foundations, ripping apart the front pillars, demolishing the porch, and completely gutting the wood-beamed entry.

Jillian closed her eyes, clutched Casey's hand, and prayed.

Eventually, the shaking stopped. "Do you have a fire extinguisher?" Tim asked calmly.

Jillian nodded and enfolded a sobbing Casey in her arms. "In the kitchen." she bit her lip. "Please, check on Mrs. Wilson."

Tim disappeared down the hall and came back with a pale-faced Mrs. Wilson and the fire extinguisher. Calmly, he broke the seal and proceeded to douse the flames.

Jillian stared at the remains of her porch. Then she laughed hysterically and pulled Casey and her housekeeper into a breath-stealing embrace.

"You're not hysterical, are you, love?" Mrs. Wilson asked nervously, extricating herself from Jillian's bear hug.

"No, Mrs. Wilson," Jillian assured her. "I'm just so grateful that we're all right."

"Are you hurt, Jillian?" a quavering voice called out.

Jillian hurried to the door and helped the elderly Mrs. Byrne from next door over the rubble. Sirens bleated from down the road, louder and louder, until they stopped in front of the house. Neighbors came out of their houses and converged on Jillian's lawn. Police in riot gear circled the house and slowly approached what was left of the entrance.

Frankie heard the news on the car radio just as he crossed the barricade into the city center. Throwing the stick into fourth gear, he increased his speed and careened wildly around the corner of Donegall Road toward the east side. The horror of the events blurting from the car speakers held him in a grip of pure terror. This was exactly what he had feared, what he had hoped to keep from Jillian. The trauma of a near-death experience and the threat of more had destroyed his marriage. He would not allow it to destroy what he now had, not even if it meant giving up Jillian.

His expression was grim. The war in Ulster was far from over. Her job was finished. His wasn't. A compromise had been reached, an agreement that fulfilled her part of the bargain. He was still mired deeply in it, caught like a lamb pulled down into the sucking terror of bog mud. Splinter paramilitary groups would continue to terrorize those who promoted peaceful coexistence. Sinn Fein and the Catholics of Ulster would need his services for quite some time.

Tightening his hands on the steering wheel, Frankie cursed out loud. How had he come to this from those long-ago days in Kilvara when his dreams had included a university degree, a small clinic, and a girl with hair the color of sunlight?

A line of police cars barricaded the entrance to Jillian's street. Dimming his headlights, he applied the brakes, turned down a side street, and killed his engine. He waited several minutes before leaving the car to jog down a back alley and vault over the brick wall of the house bordering Jillian's. Dropping to a crouch position, he waited for the police patrol to pass by. Then he crept across the grass and hid in the shrubbery.

An ambulance was parked in the gravel driveway. There was no sign of Jillian. Frankie's heart lurched painfully in his chest. Sweat beaded his forehead. If she was hurt— His jaw locked. Christ, had he found her only to lose her again? He wanted desperately to show himself and demand to see her. Fear of what he might find kept him silent.

Time slowed. Every sensation intensified a thousand times, the beetle crawling up his arm, the cramp in his leg, the painful, living rhythm of his heart, the smell of turned soil, the wet of dew-soaked leaves. Closing his eyes, he imagined her as he'd last seen her, moss-green eyes, hair streaked with summer sun, freckles peppering her nose, the faint sheen of heat on the bones of her cheeks, those absurd too-large glasses perched on the end of her nose, her mouth— Enough!

With a muffled curse, Frankie forged his way through the shrubbery, stomped the mud from his shoes, and walked through the side door into the house. He heard noises from the kitchen. Striding down the long hall, he followed the sounds, pausing in the doorway. For one startling, incredulous instant, he thought his mind had played a trick on him. He had expected to see a terrified and incoherent Jillian on the verge of shock, bolstered by Mrs. Wilson and the RUC.

Instead, seated on one side of the rectangular oak table were three elderly ladies in their bathrobes and slippers. Two had something that looked like pink sponges in their hair. On the other side, hands clasped, were Tim and Casey. All were sipping tea and helping themselves to a plate piled high with biscuits. Jillian and Mrs. Wilson moved back and forth between the stove and the table, refilling tea pots and offering comfort.

"It was nothing, really, Mrs. Brooks," he heard Jillian say. "Most of the damage was superficial and will be repaired by tomorrow evening."

"Those dreadful people." The old woman's voice quavered. "Why would anyone do such a thing?"

Jillian set the kettle down on the table, knelt by her side on the floor, and took the liver-spotted hands in her own. "There have always been those who need time to see the good in something new."

"Aren't you afraid for your family?"

Jillian tilted her head and thought before answering.

"Whoever did this didn't intend to murder anyone. There is no damage beyond the porch. Don't be frightened, Mrs. Brooks."

"I, for one, plan on staying right where I am," said the woman with pink curlers in her blue-tinted hair. "No one will chase me from my home."

Jillian stood. "I'm pleased to hear it. I have a phone call to make. Before I go, would anyone like more tea?"

A vicious poke from behind sent Frankie stumbling into the kitchen. "Who the hell are you?" demanded a man in the uniform of the Royal Ulster Constabulary.

Frankie found his balance at the same time as Jillian turned toward the door, saw him, and widened her eyes. "Frankie," she said, and then to the policeman, "It's all right. I asked him to come."

He waited until she stood directly before him. "You're all right," he said, conscious of the curious eyes upon them.

"Yes."

"I heard the news on the way over."

She nodded. "I'm sorry if you were worried."

A muscle jumped in his cheek. "Christ, Jilly, of course I was worried."

She lowered her voice. "Do you know who is responsible?"

He shook his head. "Probably someone who is unhappy with the progress we've made. There are hundreds of possibilities."

"Then we won't worry about it."

He was baffled. She said it as calmly as if her porch was blown to bits every evening. "You could have been killed."

"And so can everyone who walks the Ormeau Road every day. I imagine the danger is greater in London or New York or Los Angeles. None of that should stop us from living."

"Who were you going to call?"

"You."

"Not the prime minister?"

She looked surprised. "No. Why would I call him?"

"To resign, of course. You were the target because of your position. When that ends, so will the bombs."

"There has been only one bomb, Frankie, and my position will be over soon enough. I'll not leave before my time."

Suddenly, he felt lighter, as if a terrible weight had been lifted from his shoulders. For the first time in years, a scene flashed before him, a wild-eyed girl, all arms and legs and temper, throwing herself on the back of a bully. She had defended him against her brother that long-ago day in the Kildare stables, and he still remembered the rage it had called up within him. The woman standing before him was a Fitzgerald with a strain of fighting O'Flaherty blood. Perhaps she had more of that child in her than he knew.

"Da?" Tim's voice intruded upon his thoughts.

Reluctantly, Frankie tore his eyes away from Jillian and smiled at his stepson. "I see that Casey found you, after all."

"Aye." Tim looked from Frankie to Jillian. "She told me you two knew each other."

Frankie reached for Jillian's hand and drew her close to his side. "We do."

"She called you Frankie," Tim said. "Does she know?"

"Aye. She's always known."

Casey's eyes were round with surprise. "Does Tim know about me?"

Frankie shook his head. "Not specifically. He knows

why I changed my name and that I have a niece. That's the extent of it. Why don't you tell him?"

Tim frowned. "Tell me what?"

Casey smiled. "Frances Maguire is my uncle. His sister was my mother before Mum adopted me. I didn't know until my birthday, when I asked to see the records. It was a dreadful mixup, but it's sorted out now. I hope you don't mind," she said anxiously.

He thought for a minute. "We aren't actually related, are we?"

"Not by blood," replied Casey, who had already worked out the details.

He grinned. "Then I don't mind at all."

Frankie cleared his throat. "Tim, about your mother. I loved her very much. I hope y' know that."

The young man nodded. "I do know it, Da." His eyes rested on the possessive hold Frankie had on Jillian's hand. "Perhaps we should take over in here while you two sort out things."

Frankie looked at Jillian, really looked at her, and saw what he'd been too proud and too stubborn to recognize. He hadn't wanted to love an Englishwoman, even one whose veins ran with the blood of Irish royalty. But this was Jillian Fitzgerald. Despite her Sean Ghall roots, she was Ulster born, and somehow, the cool remoteness of the English conquerors with their pale eyes and their long faces and their thin-lipped humorless smiles had transformed itself into this woman with a spine of Irish steel, an infinite reserve of compassion, and a desperate courage that had brought her to the brink of a love that all but those bordering insanity would proclaim impossible.

Frankie no longer saw Jillian Graham, British aristocrat, English rose. He saw a woman whose eyes were as blue-green and as secret-filled as the churning Atlantic, whose mouth had softened and opened under his, whose lips had marked his skin in private places, a woman who wasn't afraid to say with words what was in her heart, a woman whose mind was razor-sharp, who covered the ground like the Kildare thoroughbred that she was, whose voice seduced and promised and caressed until he was mindless with wanting and waiting, until all reserves were spent, leaving him open and vulnerable, stretched out at her mercy, like a molting crab waiting for its shell to grow.

"You are going to get married, aren't you?" Casey dropped her bombshell as calmly as if she were asking for nothing more than buttered bread.

For the first time in her life, Jillian refused the bait. This was Frankie's cue. He was eyeing her warily. She met his glance without blinking.

"Have you thought it through, lass?" he asked, once again uncomfortably aware of their audience.

"What?" she asked sweetly.

"This marriage thing."

"No."

He glared at her. "Jillian—" Exasperated, he tightened his grip on her hand and led her out of the kitchen, down the hall, and into the firelit drawing room. There, he closed the door, locked it, and faced her. His expression in the flickering light was stark and angry. "What in bloody hell did you mean by that?"

"By what?"

"You know we've discussed marriage."

"Have we? My recollection is that I've mentioned it, and you wouldn't hear of it, unless, of course, you'd gotten me pregnant. Has anything changed?"

"I'm Francis Maguire again."

"Congratulations."

"I love you."

"You're Catholic."

"You said you'd convert."

She gasped. "I never did."

"You did, when you were ten years old."

She crossed her arms and remained silent.

"Will you?" he demanded.

"No."

"Why not?"

"Why should I have to?"

Across the room, hidden in the shadows of the netherworld, Nell frowned. This was not going well at all. These two people so made for each other were being unusually obstinate. If only she could show herself. Jillian always responded when Nell materialized. But she no longer had the power. She would have to rely on Frankie. He was pure Celt. His powers of perception would be stronger than Jillian's.

Nell closed her eyes and willed her thoughts to travel across time and take hold in Frankie's mind. *Tell her you can't live without her. Tell her the child has nothing to do with it. Tell her that you've always loved her.*

Frankie swayed and pressed his fingertips against his forehead. His head felt as if it were splitting apart.

"What's wrong?" Jillian asked.

"I've a headache, that's all."

Cool hands rested on his shoulders, urging him down on the couch. "Lie still," she said. "I'll fetch something."

Tell her that you need her, that your happiness depends on her.

"Jillian."

She stopped at the door. "Yes."

"Don't go."

She hesitated. "What about your head?"

"I don't need aspirin."

Fool, you know nothing of women. Tell her now.

Frankie groaned. He wasn't prone to headaches. What on earth was wrong with him?

Jillian knelt by his side and felt his head. He wasn't feverish. "I can call the chemist. Perhaps he'll recommend something."

I need you.

"I need you," Frankie whispered.

"What?" Could she possibly have heard him correctly?

"I've always needed you," he confessed, reaching up to touch her cheek. "I've loved you since I was fourteen years old. Don't abandon me now, lass. I want desperately to marry you, whether or not there's a child."

Better. Much better. You're doing very well on your own now.

"I'm not Catholic."

"I don't care what you are, so long as you'll have me."

Jillian closed her eyes and lifted a shaking hand to her lips. "You have no idea how long I've waited to hear you say that."

Miraculously, Frankie's headache cleared. "I won't have much t' offer you, not for a while. But I've plans, lass."

"Tell me."

He pulled her down so that her head rested on his shoulder. "What would y' say t' being the wife of a country veterinarian?"

"What about Sinn Fein?"

"I'll do my share," he said, drawing circles on her head with his fingers. "Twenty years is a long time. I've earned a bit of life for myself and my family."

"When did you change your mind?"

He smiled against her hair. "I always knew how I felt

about you, Jilly. But when I saw you servin' tea to the biddies as if nothing had happened, I knew I'd made a mistake. The signs were all there. There's nothing you can't do. You came to the hospital for Colette, and you showed up at the Garvaghy Road march. That day when Connor was shot and you drove in front of the tanks, I should have told you how I felt. I was too set in my thinkin' to see it, but you aren't an English lady, Jilly."

"What am I?"

"You're one of the *buannada*."

"What is that?"

"A warrior of ancient Ulster."

She laughed. "Are you telling me that I'm scrappy, Frankie Maguire?"

His words were gruff and low and filled with rare emotion. "I'm saying that you've taken me hostage, Jilly, and I'm more than willing."

Nell stood on the cliff of Inishmore where the ancient Celtic fort of Dun Aengus had partially collapsed into the sea. By her side was a large gray wolfhound, and on her lips was a satisfied smile. Her debt was repaid. There had been moments when she wondered if it would happen, but now there was no more doubt. Jillian had found her own happiness, with a bit of help, of course. And that was how it should be.

Just above the horizon, the sails of a ship had come into view. Nell waited patiently for another hour. The narrow wooden hull and its arc of sails were completely visible now. The ship was listing portside, and she could barely see the man on deck, but she knew. That black hair and upraised arm belonged to only one man, Donal O'Flaherty, and soon he would be home. Nell sighed. It was difficult to be alone so often, but her husband was an O'Flaherty. Legend said that the O'Flahertys were the descendants of men and mermaids. The sea was in their blood. But Donal was here now, and she would not shadow the time they had together by thinking of when he would leave again.

Turning, she followed the wagging tail of Donal's hound as he ran down the rocky trail to the hidden harbor where the boat would dock. She saw him clearly now, his face, sun-warmed and smiling, gray-eyed, with a gold pirate's ring in his ear. Later, when he caught her in his arms and she smelled the sea-salt smell of him, she knew that, difficult as he was, she would have no other.

Author's Note

On April 10, 1998, the eight political parties of Northern Ireland entered into a peace settlement that was twenty-two months in the making. A sense of relief tempered with caution was the mood at Stormont Castle. The unionists were better served by preserving the status quo, the nationalists by insisting on change. The result was a bit of both, with a Northern Ireland–Republic Council, a Bill of Rights, and the hope of Nationalists for a United Ireland some time in the next millennium when a majority of the people in the Six Counties vote themselves into one country.

On May 22, 1998, expatriated Irish and their descendants watched as seventy-one percent of the people of Northern Ireland, Protestants and Catholics, voted to end the violence in Northern Ireland and uphold the agreement reached by the eight parties.

Still up in the air are the fate of political prisoners, Catholic unemployment, whether British troops will, in fact, pull out of Northern Ireland, and the restructuring of the Royal Ulster Constabulary, Northern Ireland's police force.

Jillian Fitzgerald and Frankie Maguire are fictional characters. Robbie Wilson and Thomas Putnam are fictional names for contemporary English and Northern Irish leaders and members of Ireland's warring political parties. For the most part, their conversations within this novel are fiction, created for the purpose of moving the story forward.

Robbie Wilson's comparison of the Garvaghy Road march to Nuremberg in Chapter 22 was taken from an editorial written by Irish journalist Mairtin O'Muilleoir. Jillian's press conference speech was taken from Mo Mowlan, secretary to Northern Ireland, when she attempted to pacify the nationalist population on July 7, 1997, after the Garvaghy Road march.

The source of the Northern Irish conflict lies in the Geraldine conspiracy of the sixteenth century, when Henry Tudor executed every living Fitzgerald male at Tyburn with the exception of ten-year-old Gerald Fitzgerald.

Eleanor Fitzgerald was young Gerald's aunt, not his sister, and she married Donal McCarthy, not Donal O'Flaherty. For an entire year, she defied Henry Tudor and managed to keep her nephew safe until he could be spirited across the sea to France and safety.

The glory of the Fitzgeralds and their role in Irish history is well documented. From Italy, they settled in Wales, and from Wales, they married into Irish families, becoming more Irish than the natives and more beloved than the Celtic chieftains. Their holdings were vast, and they ruled Ireland, uncontested, for four hundred years, from their arrival with the Anglo-Norman conquerors to their destruction in the sixteenth century.

I have taken an occasional liberty with history in order to create a more evocative and timely story.

Please e-mail me at:
    jeanettebaker1@compuserve.com.

Visit my Web site:
    http://www.pertel.com/baker.htm.

Linda Lael Miller

SPRINGWATER SEASONS

Rachel

Savannah

Miranda

Jessica

The breathtaking new series....Discover the passion,
the pride, and the glory of a magnificent frontier town!

Coming soon from Pocket Books 2043

New York Times Bestselling Author

JULIE GARWOOD

RANSOM

Stepping back to the silver-shrouded Highlands of her classic tale *The Secret*, Garwood hails the return of two unforgettable heroes—Ramsey Sinclair and Brodick Buchanan—and follows a twisting labyrinth of deadly secrets and medieval splendor.

**Available now in Hardcover
from Pocket Books**

"Julie Garwood attracts readers like beautiful heroines attract dashing heroes."
—*USA Today*